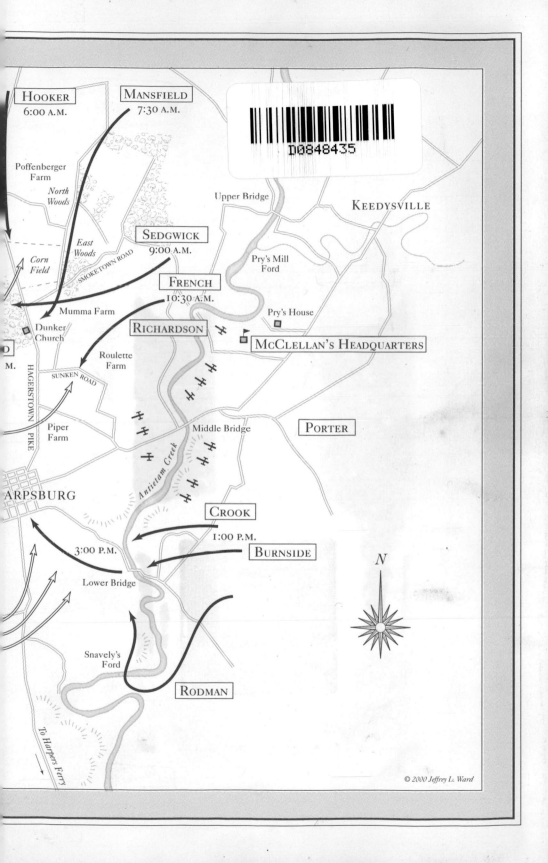

HOOKER
6:00 A.M.

MANSFIELD
7:30 A.M.

Poffenberger
Farm

*North
Woods*

KEEDYSVILLE

Upper Bridge

*East
Woods*

SEDGWICK
9:00 A.M.

*Corn
Field*

SMOKETOWN ROAD

Pry's Mill
Ford

FRENCH
10:30 A.M.

Mumma Farm

Pry's House

Dunker
Church

RICHARDSON

McCLELLAN'S HEADQUARTERS

HAGERSTOWN PIKE

Roulette
Farm

SUNKEN ROAD

Piper
Farm

Middle Bridge

PORTER

Antietam Creek

ARPSBURG

CROOK

1:00 P.M.

3:00 P.M.

BURNSIDE

Lower Bridge

N

Snavely's
Ford

RODMAN

To Harpers Ferry

© 2000 *Jeffrey L. Ward*

PROMISE OF GLORY

Forge Books by C. X. Moreau

Distant Valor
Promise of Glory

PROMISE OF GLORY

A Novel of Antietam

C. X. Moreau

A Tom Doherty Associates Book
New York

PROMISE OF GLORY

Copyright © 2000 by C. X. Moreau

All rights reserved, including the right to reproduce this book, or portions thereof, in any form. For more information regarding film and television rights, and other subsidiary rights not controlled by the publisher, please visit http://www. zackcompany.com.

This book is printed on acid-free paper.

Book design by Jane Adele Regina
Maps by Jeffrey L. Ward

Published by Tom Doherty Associates, LLC, by arrangement with the author's agent, The Zack Company, Inc.

A Forge Book
175 Fifth Avenue
New York, NY 10010

www.tor.com

Forge® is a registered trademark of Tom Doherty Associates, LLC.

Library of Congress Cataloging-in-Publication Data
Moreau, C. X.
    Promise of glory : a novel of Antietam / C. X. Moreau.—1st ed.
        p. cm.
    "A Tom Doherty Associates book."
    ISBN 0-312-87272-0 (alk. paper)
    1. United   States—History—Civil   War,   1861–1865—Fiction. 2. Antietam, Battle of, Md., 1862—Fiction.   I. Title.

PS3563.O7723 P76 2000
813'.54—dc21
                                                            00-031653

First Edition: September 2000

Printed in the United States of America

0 9 8 7 6 5 4 3 2 1

This book is dedicated to my grandparents.

And to James, who showed me the beauty of stolen bases, hanging curve balls, and line drives under the lights.

Acknowledgments

SPECIAL THANKS TO ANDY ZACK, MY LITERARY AGENT, AND THE ZACK COMPANY, INC. YOUR CONTINUING BELIEF IN ME AS A WRITER AND TIRELESS EFFORTS ON MY BEHALF WENT ABOVE AND BEYOND WHAT WAS EXPECTED AND YOU HAVE MY SINCERE APPRECIATION.

THANKS ALSO TO TOM DOHERTY, JAMES MINZ, AND ALL THE PEOPLE OF TOR/ FORGE PUBLISHING FOR THEIR CONTINUED ASSISTANCE AND SUPPORT.

SPECIAL THANKS ALSO TO BRIAN THOMSEN, MY EDITOR. HIS INSIGHTS, SUGGESTIONS, AND GUIDANCE PROVED INVALUABLE IN THE EDITING OF THIS MANUSCRIPT.

PROMISE OF GLORY

PROLOGUE

From a report written by Robert E. Lee and sent to Gen. Samuel Cooper, CSA, Adjutant and Inspector General, Richmond, Virginia, shortly after the battle of Sharpsburg.

CAPTURE OF HARPERS FERRY AND OPERATIONS IN MARYLAND

The enemy having retired to the protection of the fortifications around Washington and Alexandria, the army marched on the 3d September towards Leesburg.

The armies of Generals McClellan and Pope had now been brought back to the point from which they set out on the campaigns of the spring and summer. The objects of those campaigns had been frustrated and the designs of the enemy on the coast of North Carolina and in western Virginia thwarted by the withdrawal of the main body of his forces from those regions.

Northeastern Virginia was freed from the presence of Federal soldiers up to the entrenchments of Washington, and soon after the arrival of the army at Leesburg information was received that the troops which had occupied Winchester had retired to Harpers Ferry and Martinsburg.

The war was thus transferred from the interior to the frontier and the supplies of rich and productive districts made accessible to our army.

To prolong a state of affairs in every way desirable, and not to permit the season for active operations to pass without endeavoring to inflict further injury upon the enemy, the best course appeared to be the transfer of the army into Maryland.

Although not properly equipped for invasion, lacking much of the material of war, and feeble in transportation, the troops poorly provided with clothing, and thousands of them destitute of shoes, it was yet believed to be strong enough to detain the enemy upon the northern frontier until the approach of winter should render his advance into Virginia difficult, if not impracticable . . .

Influenced by these considerations, the army was put in motion, D. H. Hill's division which had joined us on the 2nd being in advance, and between the 4th and 7th of September crossed the Potomac at the fords near Leesburg, and encamped in the vicinity of Fredericktown. . . .

Respectfully submitted
R. E. Lee
General

From a telegraph message sent to Gen. George McClellan:

WAR DEPARTMENT
Washington, September 15, 1862–2:45p.m.

Major-General McCLELLAN:

Your dispatch of to-day received. God bless you and all with you. Destroy the rebel army if possible.

A. LINCOLN

CHAPTER 1

A STORM HAD COME UP THAT AFTERNOON, THE THUNDERHEAD rising black and ominous until the rains broke, leaving the roads and men sodden in its wake. The air had been thick with rain for an hour or more while the storm raged and lashed everything in its wake with hard, heavy drops and furious winds. He had watched from beneath his oilskin as a grove of small oaks bent and twisted beneath the sudden shower. The storm had passed quickly, but even now, sitting at the small desk he used in the field, Robert E. Lee was aware of the soft dripping of rain against the thin canvas of his tent.

He had been staring for some time at the map before him, searching the colorless lines for details of the roads he would use to move his army north. Lee rubbed his eyes, knew that he was too tired to make any further decisions.

He rose, rolled the map carefully, and slipped it into the small leather case. The air inside the tent was stifling, muggy with moisture from the rain and heavy with the smell of burnt oil from his lamp. He ran a hand over his face, felt the dull pain throbbing beneath his skin, knew that he could not work longer tonight. Better to lie down for a time. Even if he couldn't sleep, he would rest. He could rise early, work under the canvas awning in the cool morning air when his head would be clear.

He had spent the bulk of this day with his staff officers. Orders had been drawn up, forwarded to his generals in preparation for tomorrow's movement north. Arrangements made for supplies to be sent to points along his proposed route of march. All the small tasks necessary to the movement of the army had been undertaken. His staff officers were exhausted, in desperate need of a good night's rest and a hot meal.

He had sent them away an hour past to find whatever rest they could in their tents. He fumbled with the button on the front of his tunic, loosened it at last, knew that all that could be done today had been accomplished.

From his vest pocket he withdrew a small tintype of his wife, her image gazing back at him from beneath the amber surface of the paper. She was alone, in Richmond, waiting for him to return.

He closed the small locket with her image inside, the metal clasp snapping shut with a neat click. He sighed heavily, felt a heaviness deep in his chest. She had spent her entire adult life waiting for him to return to her; her youth, and her health, had slipped away while he pursued his career in the army.

It had all been for a purpose, or so it had seemed for the past thirty-odd years. A secure retirement. His army pension, and his savings, invested carefully over the years so that he and Mary could enjoy their old age.

He closed his eyes, knew that the things he had struggled for his entire life had been washed away with the first shots fired in South Carolina over a year ago. She had inherited farms and land from her father. All of it would have amounted to more than enough to provide for them. His sons had all been taken care of by their grandfather; his daughters would find suitable husbands.

The Rebellion. Everything had changed in the space of a few weeks, a lifetime of careful preparation destroyed in just moments in Charleston harbor.

A wave of remorse washed over him. Had he done wrong by her? In moments such as these, when no one was nearby, he was plagued by such thoughts. Mary was his truest friend, never questioning his judgment, steadfast through the worst of times. And now she was alone in Richmond, everything they had worked for gone, the Union army burying their dead in her lawn at Arlington House.

He sighed, tried to wipe away the fatigue. He had been given no choice. He was a gentleman and a Virginian, even before he was an army officer, and he had done the only thing he could under the circumstances.

He opened the locket, gazed at the silent image of his wife, the dark eyes staring back at him without reproach. Where had all the time gone? She had been, if not quite beautiful, very pretty in her youth. Her real charm had been a certain natural shyness and an ability to make him believe that she needed him. From the moment they first met he had felt that she needed him to guard her against all the dangers and troubles the world might present. He wondered now if she had only been flattering him by making him feel that way.

They had all gotten along splendidly without him while he was away with the army. Mary, the girls, even his sons. His time at home had always been warm, loving, but still he felt as though he was merely an appendage to their routine. Somehow he had never quite managed to feel that he was really an integral part of the household.

The thought struck him that maybe, during the early years of their marriage, when she was learning to be an army wife, she had truly needed him. Later, after he had forced her to become independent, she had needed him less. The children had always treated him as something of a visitor. The times he was home were one long celebration, he and Mary counting the weeks or days until his inevitable departure.

He slipped the image of her back into his vest pocket and stepped out of his tent. Above him a goose circled, the wind rustling through its feathers as it passed low overhead, its long neck extended with the effort of flight. Its call broke the stillness of the night, the sound clear, penetrating the darkness, forcing Lee to turn and stare after the bird.

He watched the goose disappear into the darkness, gazing into the vacant sky long after it faded from sight. Lee realized that the night had taken on a chill, the air crisp after the heat of the day and the sudden passage of the storm. It was not yet September and already he could detect a hint of winter in the evening breeze.

Autumn. It had always been a fine time of year. The weather would turn, the heat giving way to mild days and cool nights. Abundant harvests, farmers burdened with taking in the crops. It was a time of plenty in Virginia, his favorite time of year. Fall was a time of reflection, of quiet preparation; it had order and symmetry and the satisfaction of accomplishment. In Virginia, during the harvest, there had always been enough, even after the driest summers or the coolest springs.

All the years away, in all the remote postings in the old army, he had longed to return to Virginia. It had been a desire, a part of him, for as long as he had been in service to the old army. He had bided his time, patiently waiting for orders that would send him back to his home, back to his family.

He had come home, eventually. Not as he had intended, not ordered back to Virginia, but on a personal leave of absence. There had been problems, too numerous for an officer stationed a thousand miles from home to solve. The army had been generous with him, allowed him to remain in Virginia, see to his personal affairs while on an extended leave.

The secession of Virginia had found him at home, among his things in Arlington House, waiting for men in Richmond to make their decision. When news had come that Virginia was leaving the Union, he had resigned from the army, hung his uniforms in the big armoire in his room, and set off for Richmond to offer his services to his native state.

That had been almost two years past, and during the intervening months the war had done much to reduce Virginia's wealth. Occupying armies had levied heavily against the areas under their control. Virginia and her farmers were quickly becoming exhausted, unable to support their families, an invading army, and their own armies. The shortages this winter would be real.

Lee closed his eyes, thought of all the men who had died in the past weeks. The Federal army had been close, very close. They had forced their way up the Virginia Peninsula, driven to the very suburbs of Richmond.

He mentally played back scenes of his ragged infantry marching shoeless toward the sounds of battle. He was asking too much of them. The last campaigns had taken a fearful toll. Men, animals, and equipment were in desperate need of rest and refit. And yet, more was left to be done.

He glanced past the neat rows of tents around his headquarters, smelled the cook fires smoldering in the night, knew that his men were finding what rest they might wrapped in their blankets close to those fires.

Not long after he took command of the army he had issued a general order. That single piece of paper had given his army a proper name. The Army of Northern Virginia. Come what may, the task was theirs, and history would be their judge.

They had understood. Each of them, the thin, proud boys who had come to him from all over the South, and who now slept on the ground before him. He had given them more than a name; he had issued a challenge. Stand and fight, and perhaps die, but write your collective name in the pages of history as one of glory.

He smiled, glanced down at the ground, wondered if he had deceived them. These men were the best the South had to offer. Few of them understood the task they faced, the terrible reality of their situation.

The sight of them always stirred him, made him pause to consider if he were fit to lead them. The thin boys, standing in ragged formations, their eyes wide as he passed on the big gray warhorse. He felt a fierce swelling of pride, the emotion unexpected and yet familiar. He had felt that same pride before, in faraway places, in the old army. But this was somehow different.

The men who followed him now were anything but a regular army, but they were fine soldiers even if they lacked the trappings of an established army. Instead of fine uniforms and equipment, they were given foul rations and depended on clothing from home to cover themselves. They were unaccustomed to the discipline and regulations of the military, but they marched, and fought, with a determination that could only be envied by their foe.

Even their officers were unschooled in the arts of war. And yet most of them seemed to understand the peril of their situation. They understood that the loss of Richmond meant the loss of Virginia. And if Virginia should fall, the war, and any hope of a Southern nation, was forever gone. The creation of the independent South rested on their shoulders. It was the duty of the Army of Northern Virginia and of no other.

Duty. They must all do their duty. And duty meant an invasion of Northern territory. Draw the Federal army into the field, away from the fortifications of Washington, away from Virginia. And destroy it.

Lee took a few steps into the cool night air. A short walk would refresh him, then he would sleep. From near the fire he heard rustling, then, "General, can I be of some assistance?"

He saw his aide, Walter Taylor, through the darkness. A good boy, dark, handsome, from an old Virginia family. Uncomplaining even in the most trying circumstances. "You should be asleep, Mr. Taylor," he said quietly, thinking of his own sons. They, too, were soldiers in this army.

"General, is there something I can assist you with, sir?"

Lee slowly exhaled. Perhaps later there would be time for him to walk, be alone with his thoughts. "I would like to dictate some correspondence, Mr. Taylor, if you have nothing more pressing."

"No, sir," said Taylor, through his own fatigue. "It would be my pleasure."

"What news do we have from the Northern papers, Walter?" Lee asked.

"Some news, sir. It would seem certain that General McClellan has been placed in charge of the Federal forces around Washington since the defeat of General Pope at the old Manassas battlefield."

Lee nodded, "And what of General Halleck?"

Taylor paused, then answered, "He is to continue as the general in chief, if the papers are to be believed accurate." As if anticipating the next question, Taylor continued, "There is very little news of the sentiments of the people of Maryland for our cause, General. Baltimore continues to be under martial law, its citizens having expressed their dissatisfaction with the national government in the past. No real news of the western counties of Maryland, I'm afraid, other than the reports of our scouts and other sources that tell us the people there remain fixed upon the Union."

"Yes, very well." He had no real expectation of an uprising in Maryland, no reason to believe, other than their collective hopes, that the citizens of Maryland would rise against the national government. Lee paused, then asked, "Do you believe that Maryland will rise, Mr. Taylor?"

Taylor's face registered surprise, but he recovered his composure and answered, "One hopes so, General. Certainly with the suspension of civil authority in Baltimore one would think the people of Maryland might be sympathetic to our cause. There are other officers who might be a better source of inquiry, sir. Officers from Maryland, General."

Lee held up a bandaged hand, the broken finger encased in a splint. "I appreciate your assistance. It is a difficult question, and we are poorly informed of the situation in western Maryland."

Taylor's only answer was a slight pursing of his lips. For a moment he stood in silence, then asked, "Your hands, General, are they mending?"

Lee raised an eyebrow, shrugged noncommittally, knew that Taylor was deliberately changing the subject. "The doctor tells me it will be some time before they are healed."

The boy stared at him, his eyes showing fatigue, said nothing.

"Traveller," Lee said, smiling at the thought of the big charger he habitually rode when the army was engaged. The gray stallion was his favorite, a spirited animal, a fine mount that he had paid a small fortune for before the Rebellion. Mary had complained about the cost. It was an extravagance, and yet . . . he had always been proud of the big horse, never regretted the money spent, even for an instant.

"Traveller is ordinarily more respectful, sir, than to cause you injury," said Taylor, a smile crossing his features.

"He shied," said Lee, almost apologetically, embarrassed that his own mount had injured him. "Even our officers thought the cavalry was not our own."

"Yes, sir. These things happen," said Taylor. "It was an impressive victory, General. Even the Northern editors admit that now."

Lee nodded. A victory, yes. But there must be more, and quickly. The South could not long hold off the Northern armies waiting for them in their forts around Washington. Eventually they would overwhelm even the best armies the South could put into the field. Already he had pushed back two Northern armies that were each larger than his own. It could not be long before they would again move south, driving toward Richmond and the Confederate government.

He thought again of the rainy day after the battle at Manassas Junction when Traveller had shied. He had sat in an ambulance while the surgeon bandaged his broken hand, an orderly holding the stallion's reins. He had looked beyond the big horse and seen his victorious soldiers removing the shoes of the dead Federal infantrymen.

They were the best soldiers he had ever seen. Perhaps the best the world would ever know. But an army not properly equipped could not hope to win a prolonged struggle against a better armed and more numerous foe. General Longstreet had been blunt enough in pointing that out to him. Courage and gallantry, yes, but artillery also, he had said.

Longstreet. He was a fine officer. What he lacked in polish he made up for in ability. He had been among those who voiced their disagreement. Lee knew that the younger man would always speak his mind, forcefully, at times bluntly. He depended on him for that.

He had decided to organize the army into two corps. The first, and largest, would be led by General Longstreet. The second would be commanded by Gen. Thomas Jackson. Both generals were fine officers, well schooled in the arts of war, each capable of independent command.

Lee knew that he and Jackson were of similar minds. Perhaps too much so. They had the same instinct for battle, opportunity presented at an instant, exploiting every advantage without hesitation. He and Jackson preferred to operate on the offensive, probe the enemy, keep him on the defensive.

Longstreet was to be the counterbalance. He would have to be careful to weigh Longstreet's counsel, guard against being overly aggressive in pursuit of the enemy.

He had been right to move the army north. He must draw the Union army from its fortifications and destroy it. The Northern generals would make mistakes. He would wait for his opportunity, and then strike with all his might.

Taylor cleared his throat, brought him back from his reverie. He drew a deep breath. "Your young lady, Mr. Taylor. What news have you of her?"

"Betty?" asked Taylor, and Lee thought he saw the younger man color.

"Yes, Miss Saunders," he said. "Are you still fond of her?"

"Yes, General, I am," the young man said honestly.

"And does she give you hope, Mr. Taylor?" asked Lee.

Taylor glanced at his feet, "She is kind, sir, but tells me she thinks of me as a friend only."

Lee nodded. "And you are not encouraged by this?"

Taylor lifted his chin slightly. "I have not given up hope, General."

"That is well, Mr. Taylor," he said, remembering a girl he had danced with long ago on a soft Virginia evening. She was dark-eyed and pretty, and she had let him know with only a glance that impoverished young army officers, no matter how handsome, were not to be serious suitors. He turned away from Taylor for the briefest instant, felt the bittersweet sting of the memory. "Women are our greatest torment, Mr. Taylor. As well as our greatest delight. You might think of that in your present situation."

"I remain optimistic, General," said Taylor, smiling widely.

"Good," said Lee. "Perhaps my correspondence can wait until morning."

"Yes, sir. Of course. Is there some other way I might be of service?"

"No, Mr. Taylor. Go and get some rest," said Lee, smiling at the young man's dilemma. "Maybe a letter to your young lady, Walter, if you aren't too tired." He smiled at the young man, said, "If you still have hope, a line or two might be in order."

Taylor grinned, pleased. "Yes, sir, maybe that will be just the thing."

Lee lowered the wick in his lamp, watched it glow orange for a moment, then sat down to rest. It was bittersweet, no doubt, to be young, in love with a pretty, if difficult, girl, and away on the adventure of a lifetime.

THE DAY HAD DAWNED BRIGHT AND CLEAR WITHOUT A CLOUD in the sky. Stands of pine and oak cast long shadows over the roads that were still muddy from the previous day's rain. This part of Virginia was still heavily forested, the trees crowding the roads and bathing them in shadow. In places, where the pines were thickest and had crowded out the oak and hickory, a fine layer of needles covered the sandy roadbed. Men from both armies favored a bivouac in such a forest, the abundant needles being easily harvested in order to soften a night's sleep upon the ground.

The forest here was broken by farmland, small farms carved from the native timber and clinging to the roadside. The houses were some distance apart, usually small and constructed of brick. As the columns passed, soldiers would break from the ranks, shouldering the canteens of their comrades, and sprint for the well. Catcalls would follow them as they struggled to fill their canteens before their companies lurched too far ahead.

Thomas Jackson was a man in the prime of life, well acquainted with hard work and the Virginia countryside. He was often moody, soft-spoken, an eccentric with startling blue eyes set in a broad face. He read his Bible daily, found strength in the tales of the prophets. He was a man who believed that hard work and discipline were a form of worship, and he pushed his men and his animals nearly as hard as he pushed himself.

He had been given the nickname of "Stonewall" in the midst of a battle on the Manassas plain. The Richmond papers had picked it up and the name had stuck, but his men referred to him simply as "Old Jack."

Stonewall Jackson noticed that many of the meadows were dotted with single stalks of corn rising above the weeds, standing sentinel over the ever-growing johnsongrass and briars.

Here and there old men left behind to tend the fields stopped their work to stare after the long gray-and-brown columns that hurried past. By midmorning men and animals alike were laboring under the heat from the sun, sweating as they struggled to maintain the pace of the army through the rolling hills of northern Virginia.

A little after sunrise the long columns had resumed their march northward, toward the fords selected for the crossing. In their haste the Southern infantry marched without benefit of flankers or even skirmish companies.

The cavalry had ridden in advance of the columns and a steady stream of couriers were coming back with information about the activity of the Union army.

Stonewall Jackson watched as a regiment passed on the muddy road, the men joking and laughing in the ranks. From his pocket he withdrew a bit of cloth, now faded from exposure to the sun, and wet it with water from his canteen. He wiped his forehead, relishing the feel of the cool water against his skin, already feeling the heat that the day promised to bring. His uniform was clammy with sweat and covered with a fine layer of dust.

A fly buzzed lazily, lighting on his sleeve. He slapped at it and saw a small cloud of yellow powder rise from the sleeve of his tunic. Men in the ranks would be worse off than he, dirtier, more fatigued by the endless marching.

He closed his eyes tightly, squinting into the white light, and brought the canteen to his lips. The water was cool and mossy and tasted faintly of metal, and Jackson realized that this was the last Virginia water he would drink for a time. The Old Man meant to bring the fighting to the North, far beyond the Virginia border, away from the sacred soil of home.

He smiled slightly, relishing the thought of bringing the war to the enemy.

Jackson spurred his horse over a low rise and watched his men crossing the muddy water. Where it dipped into the river, the road was torn and rutted from the brigades that had crossed earlier, the water below the ford brown and dirty with the debris stirred by their passage. On the far side a regimental band struggled to play the men across the Potomac, the music faint and tuneless as it wafted over the brown water in discordant snatches.

Soldiers passing by took notice of him; a few waved or elbowed a messmate as they descended the road and entered the water. Periodically he heard a shout of "Stonewall," and he touched the brim of his hat in salute, never bothering to seek out the eyes of the man who had spoken.

Jackson urged his mount forward and let the horse drink its fill, sitting astride the animal in midstream. He glanced upstream, saw the tree-lined banks following the curve of the Potomac out of sight. Here and there an outcropping of rock rose above the flat surface of the river, otherwise nothing disturbed the placid water as it slipped past them on its way to Washington and the low country.

Before the Rebellion he had been an instructor at the Virginia Military Institute. The good people of Lexington had found him, if not exactly odd, then peculiar in an unflattering way. He had ignored them, as he ignored most people, and gone about the business of being an instructor and a husband.

His wife eased his rough edges, lessened the sting of comments made by small-town gossips. She was his strength, his friend, the one person who required no explanation of his habits.

Jackson knew that he loved her in a different way than he had loved Elinor Junkin. Ellie had been his first wife, a small girl with unreadable eyes and a smile that had made him flush from across a crowded room. She was dark and beautiful, and he had found that just to be in a room with her was almost more than he could bear. The thought of her brought about a stab of pain somewhere deep in him. He had been younger then, of course, and he had loved in the way that a young man loves, unsuspecting of the vagaries of life, the cruel nature of all things mortal.

His love for Ellie had been unrestrained, without reason or measure. She had captured a portion of his soul that he had not known existed, and he had surrendered it to her willingly, unabashedly.

Measured against the harshness of his upbringing, the long years at West Point, his love for her had been a bright, shining beacon that had overcome all sacrifice. For the first time he had understood why poets wrote endlessly of love or why music made grown men cry.

Those months with her had been the happiest of his life. He had found himself amazed by the smallest details of her existence. As though he had left her only yesterday, Jackson could recall the faint scent of her perfume after she passed through a room or the arch of her neck as she brushed her hair before bed. Even then it had all seemed extraordinary to him.

When she had announced that she was with child, he had discovered that what he had assumed was perfection on earth was to be improved upon. Secretly he had hoped for a girl, a child who would be a reflection of her mother. He had longed to watch the infant grow, to glimpse what Ellie must have been like as a young girl, to know a part of her that he had missed.

For months he had watched with an indescribable anticipation as his wife prepared for the birth of the baby. He had lain beside her at night, listening to her breathing, not daring to move lest he somehow upset the delicate miracle that was her body.

When at last the day had come, the house had been a flurry of activity. His wife's sisters flew about, his father-in-law paced nervously, a midwife was summoned. He had grimly smiled through the first few audible notices that his young wife was in pain, been reassured that all this was normal, no cause for alarm. After some time a doctor was called, a note of urgency detectable in the voice of the midwife. A pale man with wire-framed spectacles, delicate hands, and a leather bag full of instruments that clicked metallically had hurried up the steps to his wife's room, brushing past him. In more ordinary times they would have spoken; now the doctor barely glanced at him.

It had rained the day he buried Ellie and the small child, a slow, steady rain that had chilled the mourners who followed them to the cemetery. He had stood beside the open grave while a minister spoke woodenly about death, sacrifice, and God. Friends and family had been there; he had spoken with them, felt kind hands upon his shoulders, and a chilling, eviscerating numbness in his soul.

He had returned to his post at VMI within days, struggling to display no outward sign of his grief, of the death of his own spirit. He had taught himself to mask his anguish with polite acceptance of those wishing their condolences, to limit his outward display of mourning to only the small bit of black crepe on his uniform jacket.

But his grief, like his love, had known few limits. In his private self Thomas Jackson descended into the utter blankness of despair. With the death of Ellie and their small daughter, he had been denied any chance to prepare, to overcome by any mortal means the cruel fate that had been visited upon him.

His soul had become an abyss that harbored only the darkest, vilest images and emotions that his mind could create. The world moved about him endlessly, remorselessly, and each passing day was another day to be endured without her. A hundred times each day he glanced toward the hill above Lexington where she lay with their child in the ground and wondered what God had meant by the death of these two innocents.

He had hidden his thoughts and his emotions from the world behind a vacant expression and waited for the day when a cruel and unforgiving God would call him. He walked about Lexington content with the blackness of his soul and wary that insanity lurked just beyond the darkness of his innermost thoughts.

No words spoken by men could soothe the terrible anguish he felt or restore Ellie to him. He began to wonder why the Almighty had sought him, among all creatures on earth, to inflict this suffering upon. Jackson eventually felt his grief harden within him, if not to anger, then to something very much like it. His soul created a refined, exquisite fury of which he was the only master.

His vacant spirit was filled anew with this bitterness. He directed no emotions outwardly toward his fellows, nor did he take petty joy in punishing boys sent to the institute by their parents. Instead he grew ever more silent, brooding, unreachable.

He had gone about his days then, attended to his classes, felt nothing. He did not descend into drink, nor did he abandon services, although in his darker moments he felt as though God had abandoned him.

Eventually he recognized the first signs of healing within himself. It was nothing dramatic, barely noticeable, in fact, to even his closest companions. But it was there. He had begun again to enjoy the small pleasures of life. A conversation on the sidewalk on the way to a lecture, a letter from his sister, Laura. Time. It had been the only antidote for the poison that bred within his soul.

He had found Anna, after what seemed years of being alone, and they had been married. She was pious, devout, the daughter of a minister, just as Ellie had been. He had healed, in some sense, from the overwhelming grief he had known after the death of Ellie.

He loved Anna; she was a fine woman, a good wife. But it was a different love than he had known with Ellie. He could see that now. Perhaps it was that he had grown older, less passionate, more thoughtful. Perhaps the passage of time had eased his grief, allowed him to rationalize Ellie's death.

He did not pretend to understand these events, the emotions that had ruled him for so long. He was grateful that even in the depths of his greatest despair he had kept his own counsel, spoken of these matters to no one. He could not expect others to understand, to be compassionate toward him when he protested the will of the Almighty in his heart of hearts.

Jackson knew that he had, if not exactly made peace with the death of Ellie, he had forgiven God for taking her from him. The way back had been difficult, filled with self-doubt, anger, and contempt. He had been lost for long periods, given over to the worst emotions in his heart and soul. He had returned, but he was not the same man who had set out upon the journey. In him now was something fierce, something dark and ominous that had filled the void left by the death of Ellie and the small daughter he had never known.

Jackson did not understand it, nor did he attempt to. It was there, it was a source of strength for him, and he relied upon it in his darkest moments. In the heat of battle, when other men sensed their mortality, Jackson knew that he had forfeited his own long ago; and in that knowledge he found his strength.

Jackson sighed, turned his thoughts to the matters at hand. His eyes searched the distance, noting the blue haze covering the mountains. Somewhere to the north they would find one another, these two armies. Even McClellan would eventually catch on and move. Stuart's cavalry couldn't hide their movements forever. The Federal horsemen would find them, see the gray-and-brown columns from some overlooked or undefended mountain pass, and the reports would go back to Washington. McClellan would order his army from behind its fortifications and the pursuit would begin.

In his mind's eye he saw them, the vast Union formations with their artillery and wagon trains crowding the roads leading north. He narrowed his eyes, blinded by the light gleaming off the water, and saw not his own men but the Union army with its endless ranks of marching soldiers, waving guidons, and rows of shiny cannon.

The Union infantry columns would pack the roads, the air would be filled with dust from the passage of tens of thousands of feet, and couriers would gallop back and forth along the slow-moving columns. The blue cavalry would be far out in advance, riding ahead of the infantry, thundering down quiet country lanes, searching, probing for Jackson's own infantry.

The great Union army would move north, spread out over the fields and the roads the way a river swells and floods and crowds into a thousand small crevices when it rises beyond its banks in spring flood. They would move slowly, a bulging blue tide of men, wary of the heat and fatigue and the Rebel army waiting beyond the hazy mountains.

They would come. Slowly, as was McClellan's wont, but come they would. The cavalry would keep them back while the gray columns moved north. At some point Stuart's scouts would report to Lee that the Federals were strung out, vulnerable.

Then the gray columns would turn, converge upon some piece of ground that Lee favored, and the fight would be on. He had a rare ability to find them at their weakest, Jackson knew. Lee would be patient, strike in his moment, when McClellan was least likely to expect it.

The army had a faith in Lee that was truly rare. Jackson wondered that it was not improvident to place such faith in a mortal man. Surely Lee had been sent to them by Him. He sensed the man's greatness each time they met, and yet it was something more. He was more than any soldier, any general, whom Jackson had ever met. He had glimpsed it years before in Mexico. Lee had some rare, indefinable quality that ordinary men lacked.

The gelding stamped a foot, growing restless at the passing of the army. The horse needed to be let out, to be given a good run.

Jackson patted the animal's neck, pulling at a tuft of the coarse black hair, feeling the dust thick in the mane. He turned, looking over his shoulder toward the southeast, beyond the dark ridge of mountains where he knew Washington lay. He could sense the stirring in that now foreign city, the first beginnings of movement that meant the Union army was pursuing, the movement that would eventually lead to battle on some unknown plain, another general engagement, coming hard on the heels of the last.

So be it. Divine Providence had spoken, and mortal men must now serve His will. The gelding stirred restlessly as passing men greeted him with shouts of "Hello, Stonewall." He tipped his hat, the merest suggestion of a smile on his features, and acknowledged the salutes.

A rider approached, the dull sound of the horses's hooves thudding into the water. Jackson turned, saw the rider spurring his horse past the shallows. Jackson recognized the boy, Henry Kyd Douglas, even before he could see his features clearly. Douglas sat comfortably in the saddle, urging his horse into the water, moving steadily toward midstream. The army was marching in the direction of his home, the country becoming familiar to the young man. He would be useful in the coming campaign, a valuable addition to his small staff. He would have to remember that. Douglas would know the fords, the locations of the bridges, loyal families who could be depended on to give accurate information of Union movements.

The boy sidled his horse next to his own and saluted without ceremony. "Good morning, General."

Jackson nodded, tipped his hat. "Lieutenant," he said. Jackson noted his youth, as if for the first time realizing that Douglas was little more than a boy.

"The men seem in fine spirits, General."

Jackson nodded, "They do, Lieutenant," he said amicably. "It is always good to carry the fight to the enemy."

"Yes, sir, quite so," said Douglas. "Virginia has suffered at the hands of the Federal army, General. The men are anxious to take the war to the Yankees."

Jackson nodded, studying Douglas discreetly. He was a good-looking boy, young, very popular with the ladies. "Yes," he said absently, noticing that the last of the brigade had forded the Potomac and the baggage train was now beginning to enter the water. "There must be no looting," he said decisively, using his commander's tone. "Is that understood, Lieutenant? General Lee has been quite clear on that issue."

"Of course, sir. The men have their orders, General, and there has been no ill conduct to report. We are paying for the provisions we have acquired here, sir."

"There will be no depredations upon these people, Mr. Douglas. We must meet a higher standard," said Jackson.

"I believe that has been made clear, General."

Jackson nodded, noting that one of the mule teams had stopped midstream and was refusing to budge despite the earnest urging of its driver. Within seconds the entire baggage train had ceased its forward movement. The driver of the team glanced at the waiting line of wagons in obvious consternation.

"Sir, may I report?" asked Douglas.

"Go ahead," answered Jackson, only half listening as the mule driver began to work in earnest to get his team moving. Jackson dropped the reins and let the gelding drink as the teamster attempted to start the reluctant animals, stealing glances in the direction of the two officers. Jackson listened to Douglas as the quartermaster, Major Harmon, galloped along the line of stalled wagons. With a glance and salute in his direction, Harmon splashed into the Potomac and begin to curse the mules in earnest. The major hurled a stream of invective at the mules that brought activity to a halt. Even the young lieutenant stopped in midsentence as the major's cursing rolled over the broad expanse of water.

"General, I will go and advise the major that you are present, sir, and direct him to use more suitable language," said Douglas.

Jackson held up a hand to stop the young officer. He waited in silence as the major continued for some minutes. At last the mules drank their fill and the officer was able to get them moving again.

The team splashed off as the major rode over and saluted. "Morning, General. My apologies for the delay, sir."

"Major," said Jackson, offering a slight nod, "you seem to have gotten them started again."

"Yes, sir, I did that, General. But not without a little doing."

"My compliments to you on your vocabulary, Major. It is certainly one of the more expansive ones in the army, sir," said Jackson, the faintest hint of a smile on his round face.

The major grinned broadly. "Begging the general's pardon, sir, I'm a religious man myself." The officer paused, swiped at his forehead with the back of his sleeve. "But any mule driver can tell you that only colorful language will bring a mule out of cold water on a hot day."

Jackson smiled. "I will defer to your judgment and experience, Major, and the well-known propensity of army mules to lack the proper respect for authority."

Harmon saluted. "If it is any comfort to Mr. Douglas, sir, those are Union mules who have chosen to change their allegiance." The major smiled at Jackson, said in mock seriousness, "Of course, sir, that took the proper urging too."

"Quite so," said Jackson. "I trust you will continue to instruct those mules in army procedure, Major."

The major saluted and said, "You have my word on it, sir." Harmon took up the slack in his reins, grinned good-naturedly at Douglas, then said, "With the general's permission."

Jackson lifted his hand, smiled slightly, and the major splashed off. "Mr. Douglas, your report," he said.

"Yes, sir. The brigades are all up, sir. The wagon trains are moving well, and the cavalry reports light skirmishing with the Federals but no real attempts to cross the mountains."

"The garrison at Martinsburg? Has there been word of any movement there?"

Douglas gazed northward, as if he could find the answer in the haze hiding the mountains. "None, sir. Scouts report that the garrison has not left as of yesterday."

"Size?" asked Jackson softly.

"We believe that there are between two and three thousand men there, General. Infantry, mostly. Regulars and volunteers, sir."

Jackson ran a hand through his beard, his clear blue eyes gazing toward the approaching columns. He searched his memory for terrain features of the map he had studied the night before. Recalling details of it, he muttered, "The arsenal too."

"Sir?" inquired Douglas.

Jackson made no indication that he had heard Douglas or that he was even aware of the aide's presence. He continued to stare absently at the passing men. He noted their ragged condition, the threadbare uniforms, lack of shoes. They would find the going harder still when they entered Maryland; he held no illusions about that. He was a native of western Virginia, and he knew this country too. The small farms with their proud owners, who took their living from the land generation after generation. These people were fiercely independent, mountaineers who were not quick to form an allegiance and not apt to change it for any army such as this.

"Stragglers, Mr. Douglas?" he asked without warning. Jackson saw the younger man react physically to the question. He almost winced when he heard the words.

"There have been some men falling behind, General. They lack for shoes, sir. And the campaigning has been hard on them," said Douglas. "Many of the men are suffering from poor diet, sir. Green corn and apples have taken their toll. The Old Soldier's sickness is rampant," said Douglas tactfully. "We've come so far in so little time, General. The quartermasters haven't had time to supply the men as they've needed, and that combined with the heat has served them poorly."

Jackson raised a hand slightly, interrupting Douglas. "They'll not find that it will get any easier as we move north, Mr. Douglas," he said. "They shall have to stay up, and in good order, if we are to find success there. There can be no misunderstanding about this."

"No, sir, of course not," said Douglas uneasily.

"Every army will have stragglers, Mr. Douglas. It is your duty, and the duty of your fellow officers, to hold their numbers to a minimum." Jackson paused, "Our army cannot afford straggling. Our numbers are already reduced, and we shall need every man when we meet General McClellan's army."

"Of course, General."

Jackson glanced toward the far bank of the Potomac. Beyond it, in the canal, a boat had been overturned so as to form a bridge for the troops to cross over. Watermelon rinds littered the area around the boat, its owner having fled when the hungry Southerners confiscated his cargo.

"A detail of cavalry, Mr. Douglas."

"Sir?"

"For the stragglers. They should be rounded up and held on the Southern side of the river. Those who are too exhausted must be held here, in ranks, and with officers present, to direct them. Am I understood?" Jackson asked.

"Of course, sir. I'll see that a detail of cavalry rounds up the stragglers and forwards those who can rejoin the main body, General."

Jackson nodded. "The officer who is left for this detail must be dependable. And the detail should wait on the Virginia side of the Potomac. Any guns that have broken down should also be left for this detail, and the fords in this area patrolled with diligence."

Without waiting for a response Jackson splashed across the ford and into Maryland. The army was moving well, but not without losses from straggling. That could be a factor, and he made a mental note to again address the matter with his staff that evening.

His mind turned to the garrison at Harpers Ferry. It lay ahead, where the Potomac was joined by the Shenandoah River. The arsenal sat on a point of land between the two rivers, surrounded by rugged bluffs covered with trees. The Baltimore and Ohio Railroad crossed the river there, the trains making their way around the mountain and through the town. Before the war the trains had freighted the weapons made at the armory to waiting Union armies. Now the arsenal, and its garrison, sat squarely on the Confederate lines of communication as they advanced into Maryland.

The Federal soldiers in Harpers Ferry were there to protect the railroad, but they would not be frontline troops. Volunteers probably, with a smattering of regulars. He knew the small town, with its long rows of machine shops, orderly streets, and houses made from the local stone.

The commander at Harpers Ferry would know of the approach of the Southern army. The garrison would withdraw. It was the only sensible option. A defense of the town, situated as it was in the bottom of the valley, would be almost impossible if the attacking force placed artillery on the surrounding heights. He had seen the difficulty of defending the town firsthand, knew the ground, the country around the arsenal.

Lee would want the railroad destroyed; Stuart would need the horses. His soldiers would want the clothes and the provisions. The town, with or without the Federal garrison, would have to be taken. Lee would not leave it on their lines of communication while the army moved farther north.

If the garrison abandoned the arsenal, then Stuart's cavalry would take the town. If not, the infantry would close on it, then reduce the Union forces with artillery. Taking the heights were the key. It could be done in a day or two, he was confident of that. The most difficult part would be getting the guns up on the heights north of the town. A textbook enfilading fire would put the matter to rest.

Such a fire would call for separating his infantry divisions, placing them on opposite sides of the Potomac and Shenendoah Rivers. He recalled a lecture, long ago, at West Point. The officer giving the class had pointed out how a numerically superior army had divided in the face of the enemy, sending various subordinate units to encircle its smaller opponent. The opposing commander had sensed the plan of his enemy, determined that he had divided his forces, attacked aggressively, and beaten the separated elements of his superior foe. Jackson struggled to remember the name of the instructor who had given the lecture, details of the battle. Realizing that he could not recall the man's name, Jackson glanced again at the mountains, thinking of the Union commander in Harpers Ferry. He must know that he can't hold, he reasoned. He will abandon the town, burn the stores. That was the logical course. If not, Lee would order it taken.

A short battle. Few casualties. It would give them time to close up the long columns of infantry. Rest for the men, refit them with the captured Union equipment. Bring the stragglers up from the South. His men needed the respite; they had been campaigning hard for weeks. They were confident after their victories; spirits were high.

Winning was always good for morale. A quick victory, minimal losses. Lots of captured Northern equipment. It was a fine way to begin an invasion.

CHAPTER 2

THE DAY DAWNED BRIGHT AND CLEAR, THE MORNING CHILL quickly dissipating under a late-summer sun. Sunlight shimmered and danced above the road, the heat rising steadily, evenly, drawing the strength from men and animals as they marched over the slowly rolling hills.

The countryside spread before them, rising and falling with regularity, forest giving way to cultivated fields and small, neat farms. Livestock had been herded into the barns at the approach of the Rebel infantry, and farmers had abandoned their fields at the rumor of their approach. From behind curtains worried faces peered at the passing soldiers, and men spoke in whispers to their wives or crowded children into basements and springhouses. For long stretches the road rose and fell over rounded hills, dipping down to cross small streams, then rising again to reveal another empty stretch of brown road trailing off into the horizon.

The Southern soldiers pushed through the heat as men might walk through water. They wheezed and spat and cursed the foul yellow dust that hung over them in great clouds, and when they had the breath they damned Maryland and the heat or the army that had brought them north on roads laced with rock. For long stretches there would be silence, broken only by the soft sound of men breathing in great ragged breaths through cloths they had tied over their faces to shut out the dust.

The village of Frederick sits on a small plateau, the hills leveling off far above the valley of the Monocacy River. For the men in the ranks their first glimpse of the town was the spires of churches as they became visible, slender and white and rising majestically against the horizon. Then the smaller buildings came into view, and, at last, the town itself shimmering white and chalklike in the midday heat.

A patrol of gray-and-brown-clad cavalry entered Frederick ahead of the infantry, its lead squadron moving purposefully, the sound of the horses' hooves striking the brick streets and ringing through the otherwise quiet town. Without stopping to inspect the village, the lead squadron cantered out of town heading north, toward the hills beyond. Other troopers dismounted and climbed the steeples of the churches, turning their binoculars northward in search of enemy columns. There had been no sign of Federal cavalry during the previous days' reconnaissance, nor had there been any hint of the Federal army this morning. Behind them the Rebel columns marched steadily, smoky clouds of yellow dust rising above the roads, signaling their approach.

James Longstreet rode into the town, past streets with shuttered houses and empty yards. Longstreet, a large man with a full beard and steady eyes and the rank of major general in the Confederate army, peered out from beneath the shadow cast by the brim of his hat and wondered how much more the marching men could take. Friends who had known him for years called him "Pete," and understood that he was often moody and sometimes slow to move; but when he did move, he did so with speed and decisiveness. Longstreet was a careful soldier, a man whose quiet manner could deceive you, a man you had to be wary of in battle.

He glanced south, toward the Monocacy River, saw the road packed with marching soldiers, thought: *Heat will take more than a few of them today.*

Longstreet watched as the first brigade entered Frederick. There was little of the usual raucous behavior; men walked in bleary-eyed silence, stood wavering when the columns halted, too exhausted by the heat and the pace of the march to do more.

A sergeant shouted an order and the columns dissolved; soldiers filled canteens from wells or troughs that lined the streets or bartered with citizens for cold milk or fresh bread. From a neat brick house beside the road a pretty girl was leaning out of a second-story window, asking them what manner of men they were who would invade a peaceful town. The girl was nineteen or twenty, dark-eyed, small graceful hands perched on the window sill, a blue ribbon tied in her hair. A lovely sight, so far from home now. There was laughter from the soldiers in the street, a bawdy comment, the girl slammed the window shut; he saw her back as she disappeared into the house. More laughter, boys grinning under their hats, elbowing one another in the ribs.

Longstreet saw four or five men in formal coats and city shoes making their way down the street, casting sidelong glances at the soldiers. They collared an officer; Longstreet saw the man point vaguely in his direction, the civilians nodding appreciatively. He snorted, thought: *That will be the town's committee, come to welcome us or damn us.*

He clucked to the big mare, moved off, avoided the eyes of the men in the long coats. It was never good to talk to the civilians; there was nothing he could do for them and they were sure to put him in a foul mood no matter whose side they took. An aide could answer their questions; he had more pressing business.

He felt a familiar tightening in his chest, an apprehension, maybe, about what was to come in the following days. The army was moving north, into enemy territory, beyond the limits of their own country. There would be fighting up here, real fighting.

Best to get up in those mountains before the heat took too many more of them. It wasn't good to be strung out like this, away from your supporting columns, artillery all bunched up on the roads, or miles back tangled among the baggage train.

In the distance he could hear the sound of firing, a low rumble of distant thunder.

Only this wasn't thunder. He turned west, toward the mountains, saw only a hazy blue ridge, thought: *Can't be much. McClellan can't have gotten much up here, some cavalry patrols at best. Not infantry, not real infantry anyway. Maybe Stuart's cavalry has run into a patrol from the Union garrison at Harpers Ferry.*

He dismissed the thought, knew that the Federal cavalry was somewhere in those mountains, that they would know he was moving north, had entered Frederick City.

Not yet. They can't know yet which way we mean to move when we leave here. They'll be worried we're after Baltimore or Philadelphia.

He continued working his way up the column, pushing north, searching for Lee's staff. He would speak to the Old Man about those guns. Maybe Stuart had sent word back.

The anger rose in him suddenly, uncontrollably, like a fever sweeps over you, rages through your brain, clouds your reasoning. Lee had decided to move north, draw the Federal army out of its fortifications, force a battle north of the Potomac River. He had argued that they should find a spot between Washington and Richmond and sit for a time. Try to refit the army as far as was possible.

But the Old Man had been set on the invasion. His mind had been made up, and there was no way to dissuade him. But the army wasn't ready; the men and animals were exhausted. Men had dropped out of the march with every mile they moved north, and now they were in enemy territory and their movements would be known; and even McClellan could see they were vulnerable.

Longstreet spotted Lee's staff moving along, behind the general's ambulance, a ribbon of horsemen following the wagon where Lee rode. He touched the horse's flanks, urged the animal into a trot. Longstreet reminded himself to ask after Lee's health. Be a gentleman. That was important to General Lee. Good form. It mattered in this army, not so much in the old army, not out West. Other things mattered more there.

Longstreet spurred past Lee's aides without speaking, pulled his mount up alongside the ambulance, nodded. Lee smiled back, and Longstreet was suddenly aware that Lee was no longer a young man. He appeared the same neat, courtly Lee, but beneath it all Longstreet could see the strain in his features, the small lines around the dark eyes.

"Mornin', General," he said easily, his eyes moving warily across the horizon.

"Good morning, General Longstreet," Lee said politely. "I find myself under escort this morning, I'm afraid," said Lee, holding up his bandaged hands.

Longstreet paused, knew he wouldn't ask after Lee's health. Something in him . . . wouldn't let him give the Old Man that. Petty, like a child, but he couldn't bring himself to it. Too damn prissy, the whole lot of them at times.

"Ah, well," said Lee, a tone of resignation in his voice. "In time . . ." he started to speak, then paused, a new roll of firing welling up in the distance. The sound died away and Lee continued, "I've been listening to those guns, General."

Longstreet nodded, "Any word?" he asked. He kept his eyes low, shaded in the brim of his hat, wondering if the Old Man could feel his anger.

Lee gestured for the driver to pull off to the side of the road, smiled brightly at Longstreet. The teamster pulled the wagon off the road, and Longstreet dismounted, the horse dropping its head and cropping the grass as soon as he let go of the reins. An orderly helped Lee down from the wagon and Lee nodded for Longstreet to follow. They walked into a meadow, the grass brittle and dry, wilted with summer heat. Longstreet walked west, toward the rolling hills and the mountains beyond. He said nothing, knowing that Lee would come to it in his own time. He glanced back, watched the column of men moving along.

"I am told that the Federal army has not abandoned Harpers Ferry," said Lee calmly, the dark eyes showing nothing.

Longstreet nodded. "The garrison at Martinsburg?" he asked.

Lee shook his head, Longstreet noting his fine features, the simplicity of his uniform. Around him, everywhere, men were dirty, ragged, unkempt, the hard marching showing in a thousand different ways. Lee was simply dressed, a long gray frock coat, polished boots, a broad brimmed hat, the white beard neatly trimmed.

He had heard stories, of Lee the cadet at West Point, impeccable, never a demerit. The Old Man stood before him now, showing no sign of the heat, calm, dignified. Men passing nearby pointed, elbowed their fellows, pointed in Lee's direction. *He's born to it*, thought Longstreet. The army sensed it, even the lowliest among them. Men will follow Lee simply because he is Lee.

He could see that Lee was thinking, a plan forming. He must wait now. A few more steps. Lee stood beneath a tree for long moments, his back to the road.

"Do you know General Miles?" Lee asked suddenly.

Longstreet searched his memory. "Dixon Miles," he said slowly, thinking. "A bit. Stayed loyal to the old Union. I'm told he's in charge at Harpers Ferry."

"Yes," agreed Lee. "I expected the garrison to have been abandoned by now."

Longstreet nodded. Something had the Old Man worried. "Would have been the smarter thing," he offered.

"General McClellan would not make such a mistake," said Lee, the dark eyes clouded, guarded.

"No, don't suppose he would," replied Longstreet. He followed Lee's gaze west. The mountains rose, solid and green, shimmering in the September heat. Longstreet thought of his men, worn from the summer's campaigns, climbing those mountains.

Lee said evenly, "The garrison at Harpers Ferry must be reduced. I cannot leave it on my line of communications."

Longstreet nodded, waiting, said nothing. Thought: *He'll come to it now. McClellan's not reacting like he's planned and now he's going to change his own direction, force McClellan's next move.*

"You don't agree?" asked Lee, turning to face him, the eyes steady, searching.

Longstreet drew a slow breath, cleared his throat, searched for the right words.

"Speak freely, General Longstreet," said Lee.

The Old Man was flushed, his face red. Longstreet couldn't resist a slight smile, knew Lee had been waiting for just this conversation.

"The guns and other supplies will be useful, and if you're bound on movin' beyond Maryland, we'll have to run 'em out of there," he said slowly.

Lee paused, his features unreadable, his face drawn, controlled. "Go on, General," he said, "I must know your thoughts."

Longstreet hesitated, lifted his eyes against the bright light to the mountains beyond. "We're a long way from home already," he said at last. "If we can draw McClellan out, make him come at us on our terms . . ." He stopped, gazed at Lee, wondered what he was after. Longstreet drew a breath. "This war won't be about occupying cities," he said slowly.

Lee nodded, watching, waiting for him to finish.

He ran a hand through his beard. "This one won't be fought like the last one. We're not Europeans," he said, a trace of apprehension in his voice. "We've got to destroy their army, not take command of their cities for a few days, or even for a few months."

Lee nodded as Longstreet continued, "Even if we took Baltimore, or Philadelphia, we couldn't hold it." Longstreet stopped, knowing that Lee would finish it for him. His mind is made up, Longstreet knew. He wants a fight, but he's already got an idea of where and how it should be done.

Longstreet scraped the toe of his boot across the grass, said, "I believe that you have a plan, General. It's my duty to carry it out."

Lee said quietly, "I came north to give battle, that much you are aware of. But this army must do more than give battle. There are other considerations, and we must remain mindful of them."

"Europe, you mean?" asked Longstreet. "The British?"

Lee nodded. "The president believes that a victory would enable them to recognize us formally."

Longstreet shook his head from side to side. "We'll get no help from them." He paused, studied Lee from the corner of his eye. "Nor the French."

Lee turned to him, quickly, his face masked, unreadable. "You seem certain."

"This is our fight. They'll sit this one out until we've won or lost it on our own." Longstreet hesitated, wondered what was on the Old Man's mind. At last he said, "They're not that short of cotton. And they know if we win we'll sell them whatever we've got for the as-kin'."

Lee smiled back, "Of course you are right," he said quietly. "They cannot enter the war for reasons other than cotton." Both men stood in silence for a moment before Lee continued, "I have several operations in mind, but we must secure our communications through the Shenandoah Valley in order to ensure our success. Then decide which course is the most favorable for our purposes."

Longstreet nodded, knew Lee would come to it now. Knew the Old Man was planning something big, a drive far into the North. End the war with one bold stroke. "Harpers Ferry?"

"It is on my line of communication. I cannot advance upon my intended line of march so long as the garrison remains."

"Uh-huh," said Longstreet, knowing now that Lee planned on moving well beyond Maryland, beyond the mountains, into Pennsylvania.

"A detachment will leave the main body, proceed to Harpers Ferry, and descend upon the garrison from three directions. The route of the largest division will be constructed so as to force the abandonment of Martinsburg."

"And after the garrison is taken?" asked Longstreet.

"Its capture will open the northern Shenandoah to our Quartermaster Corps. The main body will move west, rejoin with the others at Harpers Ferry, then move north, assuming a new line of march."

Longstreet stared again at the mountains to the west, avoided Lee's gaze. He understood now, Lee meant to move north, drive into the heartland, let McClellan and the others think they were headed for Philadelphia or even Ohio, then wheel on their army and force them into a big fight well away from any fortifications.

Longstreet's hand went into his pocket and he withdrew a small knife he used to trim his cigars. Absently, he turned the small knife over in his hand, touched the metal, smooth and worn from years of use, repeating the gesture for some minutes.

It was too much. *Someone has to tell him*, thought Longstreet. *Jackson won't, and that leaves me.* At last he asked, "My thoughts, General Lee?"

"Of course," said the older man.

"I'm against this," he said flatly, his voice brittle.

"Go on," said Lee.

"The Union army has suffered a series of defeats; no doubt they're feelin' it over there." He jerked his head south toward Washington. "But so long as we're up here, they've got to come after us, and they'll have some advantages." Longstreet paused, searching for the right words, then continued, "A soldier fights differently when he fights on his own ground." He waited, pulled a cigar from his pocket, knew that Lee was waiting for him to finish. At last he said, "Seems to me we're already a long way from home."

Lee nodded, seemed to agree. "Some of our men have resisted coming north. It would seem that they object to an invasion of the United States, preferring to defend their own country."

"Yep," said Longstreet, thinking of the Carolina regiments that had refused to cross the Potomac. "But that doesn't change our immediate problem. We are here, an invading army; they've got to come after us. Let's get a few days ahead of them, pick a spot, rest the men up, and let 'em come at us." Longstreet stopped, looked at Lee, knew the Old Man's mind was set. At last he said, "They will obey you, General, no matter the course."

"But you see it differently?" Lee asked.

"We're in their country; people will tell 'em where we've passed. We'll lose men with every mile we move north, and they'll make use of the railroads to move their men in from Pennsylvania and Ohio and up from Washington."

There was a long pause, Lee studying the mountains, saying nothing. "You are correct, of course," said Lee "But we are here, and I intend to move north, and Harpers Ferry must be taken before we can move farther."

"You mean to invade Pennsylvania then?"

Lee nodded, "I mean to continue our march northward. Virginia must be spared further hardship." Lee's voice took on the tones of command as he said, "We must disrupt the North's ability to wage this war. Simply defeating their armies is not enough. We should already have resolved the issue if it were."

Longstreet knew that Lee was right. They had beaten every army the Northern government had put into the field, and still they came on. "We can't outlast them, no doubt about that."

"We must carry the fight to them," said Lee. "But I will not have this army terrorize the"—Lee paused, searching for the right words— "citizenry," he said at last. "We must meet a higher standard."

Longstreet glanced at Lee, saying nothing, wondering if Lee had been about to refer to the Northerners as countrymen. *He's a rare mix*, thought Longstreet. *An aristocrat, a gentleman*. But there was something else to Lee, something that escaped most men, something harder, less obvious. Something that most soldiers, and more than a few generals, lacked. Longstreet could not put a name to the quality, could not define it, but he knew that Lee possessed it in abundance. He had glimpsed it on the Virginia Peninsula and again on the plains at Manassas.

In the final analysis, when it counted most, Lee was a fighter. Behind the courtly manners, the aristocratic composure, Robert E. Lee harbored a fierceness that defied understanding.

Lee was a career officer, one of the army's best. He had been superintendent of West Point, the officers who were now fighting who had not been his classmates had been his students. Now he led an army against them, against his own country.

There was no way around that. They had broken the faith. Lee, Jackson, all of them. He turned toward Lee, studied the quiet man for a moment, thought: *No way back now.*

Late at night, around their campfires, with a bottle going around, his officers spoke of it in hushed voices. Their friends on the other side, the old army, postings on the frontier, all the old times. Longstreet realized that Lee could never be a part of such a discussion, never show any remorse for the course taken. He was the commander of an army, his men unfailingly loyal, but he was a prisoner of sorts. And this camp, these men, were his keepers. Lee must always be Lee, above it all, alone. "No choice," he said absently, softly.

Lee turned, a puzzled look on his features. "Hmm?" he asked.

Longstreet shrugged, "We had no choice, I guess. About leavin' the old Union. Even comin' north. If we're to win we've got to bring the war to them, sooner or later."

"Yes," said Lee.

"No way to just sit it out," offered Longstreet.

"No," said Lee, his voice waiting, expectant.

Longstreet shook the thoughts from his mind, knew now was not the time. He turned his mind to the capture of Harpers Ferry. "What are your plans for the capture of the arsenal?" he asked.

Lee smiled, slightly, the corners of his mouth turning up beneath the white beard, the great dark eyes soft. "I would like it taken as soon as is practicable. You would move by the quickest route with your corps from Frederick for the encirclement. Your movement would be screened by General Stuart's cavalry, and you would have such of the reserve artillery as you find necessary."

"General Jackson's corps?" asked Longstreet, "How would it be used?"

"As a blocking force, to prevent a movement northward from Washington by General McClellan."

Longstreet turned, fought back a reply. The army separated, mountains between his command and Jackson. They would be operating deep in the enemy's own country. Lee's plan was risky, disastrous if the Federals caught them in the open, unable to concentrate.

"You do not agree, General?" Lee asked.

"I don't care for the idea of us splitting up this far north." He looked away, not wanting to meet Lee's gaze, said, "We're already weak from all the straggling, and its going to get worse the farther we push them north."

"The men are not keeping up with their units, I am aware of that," said Lee. "I have ordered the cavalry and the provost marshals to bring them forward. A day or two at Frederick City will enable them to return to us."

Longstreet took a deep breath. "It is more than a matter of straggling," he continued. "The men are exhausted. Our animals are spent. They've been campaigning for weeks,"

Lee held up a hand. "The men will do their duty," he said quietly. "We shall find fresh mounts and provender in Maryland. The arsenal will provide us with other supplies, munitions, shoes for the men."

Longstreet said nothing. No point in arguing it further. "Well," he said after a time, his breath rushing out of him with the word.

"Well," said Lee slowly.

Lee placed a hand on his sleeve. "I shall think about your advice," he said. "Thank you."

Longstreet knew that Lee had made his decision, understood that this was his cue to leave. "I'll get back to my men then," he said. He walked across the meadow, the column of soldiers moving steadily in front of him.

The mountains to the west weighed in his thoughts with a physical presence, pressed themselves against him like a weight. They should find a piece of ground, settle down, let McClellan come to them. Stuart could harass their movements, demonstrate against Washington. That would serve to make McClellan more cautious than was even his habit. Tie his men up behind their fortifications, reduce the numbers that would march against them.

An orderly handed him the reins to his mount. He put one foot into the stirrup, steadied himself, then swung into the saddle, the leather creaking with his weight. He glanced back across the meadow, saw the solitary figure beneath the tree, gazing west. *He'll come to it,* thought Longstreet. *The army must remain together this far in enemy territory.*

He had said he would think about it. From Lee, that was enough.

SOMEONE HAD PUT A PLATE OF PEACHES ON THE TABLE IN HIS tent and Longstreet stared at the fruit for some minutes, trying to remember the last time he had eaten a peach. The evening air was filled with the sounds of troops settling in for the night; someone was picking a banjo, the notes coming slow, men singing a familiar tune. He rose from the tent and walked toward a stand of hickorys, saw a solitary figure among the trees, recognized Sam Hood, the compact, fiery, red-bearded commander of one of his divisions.

He walked slowly toward Hood, nodded in recognition. "Sam," he said.

"Evenin', Pete," said Hood.

Longstreet withdrew the peach from his pocket, held it toward Hood. "Hungry?" he asked.

Hood smiled, white teeth gleaming through the red beard. "Nope. Had my fill of Yankee peaches," answered Hood.

There was a long silence, neither man speaking. They had been friends a long time, a very long time. But now he was in charge and Hood was a proud man and there had been trouble over some ambulances captured near Manassas and Hood was under arrest. Removed from his command, riding at the rear of his own infantry.

"I hear we're headed for Harpers Ferry," offered Hood at last.

Longstreet cocked an eyebrow, shook his head in amazement. "Word does get around fast," he said.

"S'pose so," said Hood. "Still, that's what they're sayin'."

"Mmm," said Longstreet, splitting the peach with his knife, inhaling the fragrance of the ripe fruit. "You sure?" he asked Hood, again holding the fruit out in offering.

Hood shook his head, barely glancing in his direction.

Longstreet shrugged, "Don't mind if I eat in front of you then?"

Hood stared ahead, said, "Not a'tall. You go ahead, Pete."

"Thanks," said Longstreet.

"I hear Jackson's corps is going to take the Ferry. That right?" asked Hood.

"Yep," said Longstreet, through bites of peach.

"You turn the Old Man down?"

"Yep," said Longstreet, thinking: *Now he'll come to it.*

Hood shook his head, refused to meet his gaze. "I'll be damned," he said after a moment.

Longstreet smiled into the dark, said, "He means to move north. Beyond Maryland."

"Figured as much," said Hood. "You got any idea on how far?"

"Nope," said Longstreet slowly. "Didn't ask."

"Old Man's got his dander up, I suppose," said Hood. "All that business down in Virginia with John Pope, him wantin' to arrest civilians for treason and such."

"That's part of it," agreed Longstreet.

"We headed any place in particular, Pete? There's talk goin' around about Philadelphia, or Harrisburg."

Longstreet breathed in the night air; a cicada began its drumming in the branches somewhere overhead.

After a long moment he said, "Probably not." From beyond the trees the sound of laughter drifted toward them. *This is the good part of it,* he thought, *standing here in the dark, the campfires and the laughing and the talk of home and girls and dances long past.* "Lee is after their army. He wants to draw them away from Washington, bring 'em to battle in the open far enough away from the capital that he can run 'em to ground after it's over, finish it with one big battle up here. Harpers Ferry is just a sideshow."

Hood turned to him, the pale blue eyes shining through the dark. "No place for McClellan to hide up here. The Old Man knows that, Pete."

"Suppose so," said Longstreet quietly.

"Coup de grâce," said Hood smiling. "Ain't that what the French call it? Give 'em one last good punch and call it quits?"

Longstreet smiled, felt his mood lightening, grateful for Hood's company. "Is it?" he asked. "Sounds awful pretty when you say it like that."

Hood shook his head, pulled at the long, red beard with a practiced motion. "It'll be a lot of things, but it won't be pretty."

"Nope."

"Jackson's boys gonna take the Ferry, then? That's settled on?" he asked.

"It's settled."

"My boys would've liked a turn at them supplies, Pete."

"Can't blame 'em for that," he said.

Longstreet could feel the tension fading away, knew that some part of it would be better now. Hood was proud, too proud to come out and ask for his division back, but there was time yet. They would settle it soon enough.

"Won't be much left by the time we get there," said Hood gloomily.

"We're not headed there," said Longstreet evenly.

Hood glanced at him, his eyes suddenly bright, and Longstreet could see he was as ready as the others to have one more big battle, no matter the risks. "What's General Lee got in mind for us?"

Longstreet shrugged. "We'll move up toward Hagerstown, wait for Jackson to clear out Harpers Ferry, then join up somewhere north of the Potomac."

"Huh," said Hood, and Longstreet could see that he had hoped for something more. Hood grinned mischievously, asked, "Got any of them peaches left?"

"Missed your chance, Sam. That was the last one."

"Well," said Hood, "I suppose I'll go and see what some of the boys are up to this evenin'."

Longstreet smiled, began to say something, then thought better of it. Let him come to it in his own time. There were days yet before any fighting. Hood would be back before the army engaged, there would be time, they could settle it then.

"Be seein' you, Sam," he said as Hood walked away.

Hood waved. "Peter, I'll be around," he said easily.

He stood there for long minutes, the cicada drumming noisily into the night, listening as the army settled in around him. Overhead, stars shone through a clear sky, promising heat tomorrow. Longstreet started slowly for his tent, wondered if sleep would come.

He brushed past his staff, waved them away, lay down on the cot to rest. He closed his eyes, thought again that this was the best of it, all of them here, together, like boys skipping school. It was almost like it had been before, except now the enemy wasn't quite the enemy and there was the suspicion that somehow the whole damned thing was twisted and sideways and couldn't feel right no matter what and somehow you had no business being here.

He tried to shake the thought from his mind, push it away, and then he remembered the epidemic that past winter in Richmond and the faces of his children slick and shining with fever and the helplessness swept over him again.

For a moment he was in the rented house in Richmond, his wife crying and George Pickett with his arm around him, telling him that it was God's will and that mortal men weren't meant to understand the deaths of children, and inside he was coming apart, and he knew that nothing could ever be good again, not really.

Longstreet rose, sat bolt upright on the cot, wiped a hand over his face in the darkness, suddenly grateful that he was a commander and therefore alone and no one could see him. He fought to gain control of his emotions, push it all out of his mind. Better to work, study a map, occupy himself in some way.

He sat at his desk, grateful for the darkness, wondering when McClellan and the others would come after them. Soon, it would have to be soon. Already they would know that Lee had moved the army north. A day, maybe two, and they'll figure out we're going after the arsenal, they'll know we've split up.

The Old Man was right about McClellan. He had all the trappings of a fine officer, but he was bookish, a dandy, a pretty boy who lacked the stomach for a real fight. Something missing there that you couldn't quite put your finger on, but Lee had sensed it, was moving on it. He shook his head, almost smiled in the dark. Trust the Old Man to know it, take the chance. Still, he couldn't have brought himself to split the army this far north.

Lee must have nerves of steel.

Longstreet loosened his tunic and lay back on his cot. He closed his eyes, a horse whinnied far away, reminding him of home and the smell of leather and a mare he had ridden long ago on a summer day. He would sleep for an hour or two, then the camps would be quiet and he could rise and do some work in peace.

Longstreet smiled at the thought that McClellan was studying the maps, trying to piece it out, anticipate Lee's next move.

Longstreet slept, fitfully, dreaming of the faces of his children and friends he had known out West, and silent deer in a winter forest, and through it all, in the back of his mind, there was one thought: *God help us if McClellan catches wind of our plans.*

CHAPTER 3

MAJ. GEN. GEORGE BRINTON MCCLELLAN STOOD BEFORE THE long mirror in his bedroom, his soldier's eye noting every detail of his appearance. With a practiced motion the commanding officer of the Army of the Potomac pulled the long uniform jacket taut beneath the sash that marked him as a general in the army of the United States of America. Soldiers, he knew, judged an officer by his appearance, and he had every intention of making the best impression upon his soldiers.

He inhaled deeply, noting with satisfaction his martial appearance, brushed a bit of lint off his sleeve, then turned and left the room. The fate of the nation rested on his judgment and the abilities of an army he had organized and trained. If he failed, if they fought and lost, the Union was dissolved.

His enemies had almost cost him the command of his army. In fact, they had removed him from command. Lincoln, with his meddling and interferences, had ordered him off the Peninsula at the moment when he was poised to renew his drive on Richmond. Total victory had been within his grasp when they had ordered him back to Washington, removed him from command.

Appointed old Halleck over him, general in chief, they had named him.

He was relegated to life in the rear, stripped of command of his beloved Army of the Potomac, men he had trained had been detailed to serve under other officers less able than himself.

He was forced to stand by while unit after unit was removed from his command. They had ordered them all to General Pope, for the defense of Washington; that is what they had told him. His grand army had been taken from him just when he was poised to move again.

While Pope frittered away the opportunity, he had been humiliated. Ignored by the president and Halleck, his soldiers were absorbed into Pope's army. Fighting units that he had trained from raw recruits and built into a military organization had been fed piecemeal into Pope's disastrous campaign.

His army had been frittered away.

He had tried to warn them. He had risked everything to do so. Sent one telegraph after another advising them that Jackson would trap Pope's army between his own and Lee's. They had not listened, and disaster had been the result. Even with his boys in the fray, the Rebel numbers had been too much. Pope's blundering had nearly brought them all to disaster. Thomas Jackson might not be a gentleman, but he was a soldier, and good Union boys had died in order that Pope, Halleck, and the others might learn that lesson.

For his warnings he had been repaid by angry rebukes from the president, a president who thought he could learn the art of war by reading a smattering of textbooks, a man with so little understanding of soldiers and things military that he thought it possible to change commanders of an army as one might change shirts, and with equally as little effect.

They had come to him in time, and he had decided to accept their humiliating offer for the good of the country. Within days General Halleck, commander in chief of the armies, had been back, the president in tow. Both of them appeared at his door, without any word of their coming. They simply knocked in the middle of the day and asked him to take command of the army, or at least what was left of it.

He had accepted, of course, and he had done so with grace, for he was, after all, an officer as well as a gentleman.

He took one last look in the mirror, assuring himself that his uniform was properly adjusted, and then descended the steps to his breakfast. Fitz John Porter was waiting for him, a sheaf of papers in hand. McClellan smiled. "Good morning, John," he said brightly.

"Sir," said Porter, "I've got the morning's returns."

"John, we'll be moving the army today," he said, relishing the words, knowing that his men were waiting for him in their camps around Washington. Everything seemed different somehow this morning. There was tension in the air, the promise of excitement, action. It would be days yet before they found the Rebel army, closed with it somewhere north of Baltimore, maybe, but already he could feel it as though it were a living, breathing being.

Porter cocked an eyebrow, said, "There are some reconnaissance reports here also. Some of them are confusing at best. The overnights particularly. Lots of movement around Frederick. A big column appears to be headed west."

"What are you thinking then?" asked McClellan.

Porter began to speak; McClellan held up a hand to stop him. "Join me for a ride, will you? I've a mind to have a look at some of our men as they start off. Good for morale, you know, let the boys see that I'm back in charge."

"Of course," said Porter, smiling.

In the yard his staff was waiting, a small squad of cavalrymen nearby, the troopers gawking, straining to catch a glimpse of him.

McClellan smiled, turned to Porter as they walked across the porch, "Stay close by, John, I've a few ideas I would like to run past you. Some things I'm considering for this campaign."

"Of course," said Porter.

He swung into the saddle, waited a moment for Porter to find his horse, knew that it was important for them to be seen together. Porter was under a cloud of suspicion after the last battle at Manassas. There had been accusations, charges that he had deliberately delayed moving his men into battle so as to compromise General Pope's operations. Ungentlemanly things had been said, and now there was an official inquiry and the papers had gotten hold of it, and a fine officer like Porter had been damaged by the suspicions and whispers of lesser men.

They swung into the street, the big horse sensing the excitement, sidestepping, prancing. McClellan smiled, glad to be moving the army away from Washington, back into the field. "We'll be going after them today, John," he began. "Their main body is reported to be near Frederick, Maryland."

"You have something in mind then?" asked Porter.

McClellan nodded, indicated a direction. "Let's take a look over there," he said, "see whose brigade that is."

Suddenly they were riding past ranks of men and then he was recognized and the soldiers were cheering and pointing at him and the movement of the brigade had been halted while he cantered past. The big stallion sensed the moment and began to toss his head, blowing hard, and McClellan rose in the stirrups and waved his hat toward the ranks of smiling boys.

He turned toward Porter, said gaily, "It's grand, isn't it?"

Porter nodded, smiled tightly, said, "The men seem anxious to be off."

"Yes," he said. McClellan pulled up on a small rise, waited on the big horse as another brigade swung smartly out onto the street and began marching past. Porter reined in beside him, his staff and the cavalry escort remaining a respectful distance behind.

"I've spoken with the president," McClellan began, "and I'll be moving the army north in pursuit of the Rebels." He paused, then, "I've decided to divide the army into three wings, in order to take advantage of the road network and avoid having everyone in column for miles on end."

"Yes," said Porter.

"I'm told that Robert Lee remains in command."

Porter glanced at him, said, "There are rumors that Lee will stay, even after Joe Johnson has recovered from his wounds."

McClellan smiled. "That will serve us well," he said.

"Really?" asked Porter. "You prefer Lee then?"

"Somewhat. I know his reputation as an engineer. There was some work he did out West, Saint Louis, I believe. Dams and things on the Mississippi River, long before the rebellion. Very successful, I'm told." McClellan wrapped the reins lightly around the saddle horn. "Lee is a good man, very old family, you know."

Porter said nothing, watched the passing columns of blue infantry. There was loud cheering as each new unit recognized the familiar figure astride the black horse. At last he said, "Any guess as to what kind of soldier Lee is?"

"A bit," said McClellan, withdrawing a cigar from a small leather case in his jacket pocket. He offered the case to Porter, who refused. "I faced him once before, early in the Rebellion."

Porter turned, the surprise obvious on his face. "You mean on the Peninsula, of course?"

McClellan raised a hand, took the salute of passing officers. "No, earlier, during the very early months, out West."

"I wasn't aware," he said after a moment.

McClellan could not resist a grin. "Don't be so shocked, John. There are other battlefields than those between us and Richmond."

Porter laughed, said, "I suppose so, but the papers give them damn little attention."

McClellan smiled. "You're right about that; this is the big show, and the war will be decided by us, here." He paused, then continued, "It was in the western part of Virginia, near the border with Ohio." He trimmed the end of the cigar. "A nasty affair, all in all. It was a winter campaign, small operations really, lots of cold rain. The men were new, volunteers, for the most part. We had only a very few officers who were Academy men."

"How did you find General Lee?"

McClellan shrugged. "Competent, as you would expect. He's West

Point, you know, a bit before you and I. But still, he's an Academy man."

"Yes," said Porter.

"In the end we were able to get around his flank, drive him off the mountain where he had taken up his main line of resistance."

"What kind of a commanding general do you find him?"

McClellan paused, thought for a moment. At last he said, "He fought well before Richmond, on the defensive. Quite steady, I would say." McClellan stroked the muscular neck of the big horse, felt the coiled muscle beneath the shining coat. "It will be a different game now. Lee will have to face us in the open, away from parapets and with extended supply lines." He turned toward Porter, fixed him with his commander's gaze, "We shall need every man who can be spared. Lee's greatest asset is his superior numbers."

Another brigade was marching past, guidons snapping in the breeze. McClellan smiled widely, saluted them, felt a swelling of pride in his chest. He had trained these men, prepared them for battle, and now he was to lead them again, despite the best efforts of the Washington politicians. Porter's horse stamped restlessly, and McClellan turned toward him again. "Lee is a fair commander, but he lacks experience in the field and a certain something." McClellan paused, wondered what word he was looking for, what quality it was about Lee he could not place.

"Well," said Porter, "no matter now. The men are in a fine fettle."

"Yes," he answered. "We shall advance on a broad front in order to anticipate any movement by Lee toward the likely objectives."

"You believe they are driving on Philadelphia?"

"Perhaps," he answered. "In any event I must be prepared to counter any move they make. I shall have to structure my advance so that I can protect both Washington and my baggage trains."

Now came the difficult part, he would have to explain to Porter that he would be left behind. The Fifth Corps, and its commander, would remain to guard Washington for the time being.

"John," he began, "I find it difficult to say, but under the present circumstances I will be leaving the Fifth Corps here, at Washington."

There was a long silence, Porter staring straight ahead, his eyes locked on some distant point. The words "present circumstances" hanging in the air between, palpable, distasteful.

At last he said, "I understand."

"Difficult times," said McClellan. "We have all had to swallow a bit of our pride in order to deal with the current administration." He hesitated, wondered what one said to a fine officer like Porter, whose reputation had been questioned by men who had never heard a shot fired in anger. He glanced at Porter, saw the dark features locked in an unreadable mask. "Did you know they offered command of the army to Burnside?" he asked at last.

"I had heard as much."

McClellan turned toward Porter. "He turned them down, of course. Told Lincoln that he wasn't fit so long as I was available."

"Yes," said Porter.

"We've been friends a long time. Burn and I were Academy classmates." Then, "Did you know Powell Hill?"

"Somewhat," said Porter, "he went south, I believe, early on."

"No shame in that, you know. They are doing what they believe right, all of them." There was a long silence, the road empty of troops for the first time. In the distance bugles were blowing, drums rolling steadily. He recognized the "assembly" being blown by what could only have been a very inexperienced bugler.

The atmosphere was charged with excitement despite the early hour.

"Before the war, at West Point, Powell Hill and Burnside and I were all very good friends."

"I had heard as much," offered Porter.

"There was the usual fun, away from the Academy," said McClellan, thinking of the long hours in the one tavern that welcomed young cadets and didn't inform the West Point authorities. There had been lots of drinking in smoke-filled rooms, loud laughter, and talk about girls you had known, or wanted to know, and home. Promises to visit after graduation, talk of soldiering and gallant deaths, and every now and then an honest moment when one of them wondered aloud if he lacked the courage for the fight. "Those were good times," said McClellan, smiling.

Porter stroked the neck of his horse, said, "Hill is a division commander if our reports are correct."

"Yes, I believe you are right. He should be. He's a damn fine officer, a good man." He paused. "He almost married my Ellen."

Porter turned, surprise registering on his features. "I hadn't been aware."

McClellan chuckled, enjoying the humor. "Her father objected to her marrying an army officer."

"Old Colonel Marcy?"

McClellan laughed, feeling relieved, knowing that Porter's amusement was genuine. "Yes," he said smiling, "imagine the irony of it. When she married me I was railroading, in Chicago, an occupation her father found imminently satisfying, and now here I am, commander of our principal army."

Porter grinned, obviously amused. "She's quite a beauty, as I remember her, George, if you don't mind my saying so."

"You aren't the only man to notice," he said, pleased at the compliment. Ellen was a beauty, and more than one suitor had noticed. Their romance had been a drama acted out over years, not months. He had been certain of his affection for her from the first moment, but she had refused him. She had not been coy in her refusal, only honest. The memory of that rejection brought a twinge of pain even now.

"She and Powell Hill were engaged at one point."

Porter turned, obviously surprised.

"A few years ago," he continued. "Colonel Marcy was out West, and Powell was stationed near the Marcy home." McClellan almost laughed aloud. "He's a fine man. Ellen might have done much worse."

"Suppose she might have," said Porter, appearing perplexed.

"The engagement was broken off after Colonel Marcy protested." He stopped for a moment, remembered the terrible sadness Ellen's rejection had caused him. He had gone to Europe for the army, a year spent observing foreign armies, and all the while he had thought of her and only her. Powell Hill must have been devastated. "Eventually Powell found someone, married a girl from Kentucky. Lovely woman," finished McClellan.

Long minutes passed, more troops marching by, a steady procession of men who shook the bricks underfoot with their footsteps. Citizens had come out from their houses, were cheering the passing blue columns, throwing flowers into the passing ranks from second-story windows. There was a shout of orders and a color sergeant uncased the colors and then the flag was waving magnificently in the summer breeze at the head of the long column of shining faces.

"Superb," said Porter, the pride in his voice obvious.

"He was there, you know," said McClellan absently.

"Sir?" asked Porter.

McClellan turned, knew he had not been paying attention. "Powell Hill. When Ellen and I married. Powell Hill traveled halfway across the country to be there. Give us his best and his blessing."

Porter understood. Said simply, "Right thing to do. Good of him."

"When this is over," said McClellan, "We shall all be together again." He turned toward Porter, "All of us from the Academy. We've got our differences, but they are honorable differences. No reason gentlemen can't resume their friendships when this business is over."

"No," said Porter, "I suppose not."

McClellan turned toward him, said very deliberately, "The fighting will end, John, and either they'll come back to us or they won't; but we are all gentlemen and we must conduct ourselves as such." For a moment neither of them said anything, McClellan remembering the days before the war, Chicago and the house he had shared with Ellen, long before talk of disunion and rebellion. After a moment he said, "Our job is to preserve the Union, prevent them from capturing the capital, destroying the army and the national government."

"Of course," answered Porter.

"Simple enough, really," said McClellan. "The difficult part will be after the fighting has stopped, putting it all back together, restoring the proper men to government."

"Yes," said Porter.

He turned toward Porter, "It is never premature to think of one's future, John."

"You mean political office? Something of that nature?"

"Yes," said McClellan, "I have already been approached by influential men, asking me to consider a run at the presidency when all of this is over."

"I had heard something of that nature," said Porter. "I supposed that you would consider it."

McClellan smiled, slapped Porter's sleeve in good humor. "Think of it, John! To be in charge, Congress filled with good men who hold similar positions as our own. Think what we could do."

"Right now I'm more worried about preserving my name, seeing this inquiry through," Porter said gloomily.

"Ah, John, that's temporary. They will have to exonerate you in the end."

"Maybe," said Porter darkly.

"Well," said McClellan, "we'll part company now, for the time being. But give some thought to what I've said. No war lasts forever, and they're reasonable men over there. This will end in time."

"Of course," said Porter unhappily. "Of course you are right."

McClellan reached out, touched Porter's sleeve. "In a few days,

John, once the army has moved beyond Washington, I'll send for you. Have your corps ready to move on short notice."

Porter nodded, said nothing.

McClellan took the slack out of the reins, felt the big horse tense, said, "A few days, John, no more."

McClellan glanced at his friend, then turned the big charger down the street and trotted away, his staff trailing behind, the troops gawking and cheering as they passed.

THE TWENTY-SEVENTH INDIANA HAD BEEN HERDED OFF THE road by sergeants and officers; men exhausted from the heat and the previous day's marching had simply slumped to the ground where they stood. The soldiers who made up the regiment were all veterans, having fought their way through most of the summer's battles, even though they had been held in reserve on more than one occasion, only hearing the firing from a distance.

Cpl. Bart Mitchell loosened the leather bindings of his pack and dropped it to the ground, his hands immediately going to the raw spots on his shoulders where the straps had bitten into the skin with every step. He laid the heavy, rifled musket down, carefully, across his pack, admiring the weapon for the thousandth time. He had never seen anything like it before joining the army. They had left Indiana with a variety of smoothbore muskets, but once the regiment had been mustered into Federal service those guns had been replaced with the newer rifled muskets they now carried. The best gun he had seen back home was an English-made double-barreled fowling piece owned by an uncle and far too valuable for him to ever consider owning. His rifle was every bit the equal of that gun, and every man in the regiment had one.

Around him men were taking off their shoes, complaining about the heat and the hard marching and a hundred other things, but most were just lying down in the long grass, shading their eyes from the sun, trying to steal whatever rest they could. Mitchell took a long pull from his canteen, the water warm and tasting of metal. He spotted John Bloss, one of the company sergeants, and walked in his direction.

"Hey, Johnny," he said amicably. "Any word on where we're headed?" he asked.

Bloss smiled in greeting, his face showing a day's growth of whiskers under a fine coating of grimy yellow dust. "Nope," answered Bloss, "the generals ain't seen fit to inform me yet."

Mitchell smiled, enjoyed the joke. "They'll probably send word any minute. You just wait."

Bloss grinned, a big toothy smile amid whiskers and dust. "I 'spec they will," he said easily.

"Hot one today," offered Mitchell, glancing at the cloudless sky.

"Yep," said Bloss, "but at least we're out of damn Virginia."

"Yeah," agreed Mitchell. "This is a sight better, even if it is a mite hot."

"Reckon it's true, about McClellan being back in charge?"

"Maybe," said Bloss, "least that's what everybody is sayin'. "

Mitchell glanced past the big sergeant, across the meadow where the regiment lay sprawled. In all directions, as far as he could see, other units were being ordered off the road, given the command to fall out. Men were carrying away fence rails, walking toward a long line of trees in search of wood, a scattering of blue jackets headed for the trees. Here and there a feathery wisp of smoke drifted skyward in the heat, the first sign of the cook fires having been started. "Well," said Mitchell, "if anybody can whip them Johnnies, ole' Mac can."

"Mebbe," answered Bloss.

Mitchell turned toward Bloss, asked, "What's got into you?"

Bloss shrugged, said, "I'm sick of the whole damn business, Bart. These here Johnnies want to leave the country, I say let 'em. Just let 'em go, and let's be rid of them. I got no fight with them anyway I can see, and I'm damned tired of stompin' all over hell's half acre lookin' for 'em. First it's McClellan, then it's Pope, now it's McClellan again." Bloss stopped, started to say something else, then said simply, "The hell with all of 'em, from McClellan on down."

"Aw, you're just sore from all the marchin' and stuff; you ain't serious."

Bloss shook his head, his sunburned face red with anger. "No, sir, that ain't it. Not at all. I'm just sick of chasin' after 'em, and every time we get 'em in a corner and go for 'em our generals get it all wrong and we take a lickin'."

For a moment neither of them said anything; then Mitchell spoke. "Want to go take a look over toward them woods? See what we can scare up? Might be a farm on the other side of them trees; maybe we can make a trade for some fresh eggs or a jug of cider."

"Nah," said Bloss, "what's the chance of that? The Rebs passed here a day or two back and they've cleaned the place out."

Mitchell smiled, tried to lighten his friend's mood, said, "Wish I was back home now. I'd be eatin' apple butter and white bread. Nothin' beats that."

Bloss glanced at him. "These army rations sure don't beat it. Worst excuse for food I've ever heard of."

"Yeah," said Mitchell, thinking of the small house by the creek in Indiana. The well there was clean and deep and never ran dry. He and his brothers had helped their father dig it in the rich soil of Indiana. They had lined the walls of the well with stones taken from a nearby creek, and the water was always cool, even on the hottest days. Beside the well a small springhouse squatted, its roof barely rising above the grass, the stone walls covered by lichen and moss. He had gone there as a boy, on hot days, and sat for hours in the cool shade of the springhouse. In winter he had helped his father cut blocks of ice from the pond and haul them to the spinghouse on wooden sleds. They covered each block with a layer of sawdust, and even on the hottest summer days the big chunks of ice lay cool and damp amid the jars of milk and butter.

"Damn hot," said Bloss, and the small farm in Indiana was lost as Mitchell's thoughts jerked back to Maryland and the Rebels and the hard marching of recent days. He swiped at a fly that buzzed insistently around his ears, said, "Yeah," absently. He had noticed that boys he had known all his life, from good families, boys who'd attended service every Sunday back home, cursed like the devil's own once they were away in the army. He and Bloss were no exceptions, although at times, mostly late at night, when the others were asleep, he had felt no end of shame about some of the things they had done.

"You ever think about it, Bloss?" he asked.

The sergeant cocked an eye toward him, squinting into the brilliant sunshine. "What's that?" he asked suspiciously.

"Ah, you know. 'Bout all the stuff we're doin' here in the army?" Bart Mitchell paused, knew that Bloss didn't want to open this old discussion. Mitchell suspected Bloss felt as guilty as he did about the stealing. The army called it "foraging," but no matter what word you hung on it, when you went to another man's farm and took what was his without paying or even asking, it was stealing. No way around that, and they had all done it. Even the ones who had said they would only do it down South. They had foraged in the camps around Washington, and in Maryland in the last day or two. The regiment would go into camp for the night, the guard details would be set, men ordered to find wood for fires, and others sent off to find what they could to eat in order to break the endless monotony of army rations.

He glanced at Bloss, saw the familiar blond head, said stubbornly, "Don't seem right, the lot of it. Even if the officers say it's all right, it don't make it so."

"You ain't goin' to start with me about all that again, are you?" asked Bloss, the irritation plain in his voice.

Mitchell shrugged. "Maybe," he said. They had different officers now, some of them sent out by the army to replace the others who had fallen sick or been shot up; but it made no difference who they were, they had no right to tell them to steal. No right at all.

"Well," said Bloss, "if that's the case then, I would just as soon go and hunt up something to eat. If you don't want to come along, you don't have to; I'll eat your share."

Mitchell smiled, started to get up from the grass with his friend. "Guess I'll come along in that case," he said. "A body could use a break from these army biscuits."

"Yep," said Bloss, "let's just us take a walk over yonder through them trees and see what's to be seen."

The two walked for some minutes, the regiment at their back, the sun climbing high overhead in a cloudless sky, a warm breeze occasionally blowing through the grass, bringing no relief from the heat. They entered a wood, walking uphill through dappled shade, all the while seeing little sign of habitation. At last they caught a glimpse of sunlight through the trees, a clearing ahead. Bloss pointed, saying nothing, and Mitchell drew the haversack closer to him. Inside he had coffee, a little bag of sugar, and another of the coarse army salt that was issued to them. With any luck the farmer's wife would trade some bread for it, or maybe a pie.

They left the cool shade of the woods and entered into a broad orchard. Apple trees stood in neat rows as far they could see, the branches nearly empty of fruit. He glanced up one neat aisle of trees, saw that only one or two apples hung from each branch. "Wonder what happened to the apples?" he asked absently. "You'd think these trees would be full this time of year."

Bloss stared at him for a long second, the blue eyes shining. The sergeant grinned at last, shook his head. "Damn Rebels ate our apples, that's what happened."

Mitchell laughed, felt foolish, wondered how he could be so blind at times. Depend on Bloss to reason it out ahead of him. Small wonder they had seen fit to make him a sergeant. "Well," he said, "I guess we can still take the few that're left."

Without a word he and Bloss began to fill their haversacks. The two worked in silence until the haversacks were full; then both of them sat beneath a tree and began to eat.

At last Bloss said, "Reckon we should head back?"

Mitchell shrugged. "Maybe," he said. "I don't see any farmhouse."

Bloss looked around, said, "Apples would be hard to explain anyway, less we left 'em here, came back later for 'em."

"Suppose so," said Mitchell.

"You still worried about takin' stuff without askin' for it?" asked Bloss.

Mitchell shrugged. "It ain't right, no way around that."

"Well," said Bloss, "way I got it figured, better this farmer gives us a few apples than he does like we done and joins the army. Cheaper all the way around for him to give up a few apples."

"Yeah," said Mitchell, "you're probably right." He was thinking of the small clapboard church that he had helped to build with his brothers and father, and the quiet man who preached there every Sunday. "Maybe," he said, shading his eyes with his arm, knowing that it wasn't right, that no matter what Bloss said it was stealing, and that was against a higher law than the army could teach you. He wondered what they would say about it back home. But Bloss was right, this wasn't back home and there were those at home who should be here and weren't, and others he had seen standing in the shade of their porches while the regiment marched past to defend their state.

"Besides," said Bloss, "we could just as soon be dead in a day or two. How would that sit with the folks back home? Think anybody's gonna worry about a few apples then?" he asked.

"Probably not," agreed Mitchell.

Bloss stood, slapped the dust from his trousers, said, "Let's start headin' back then, see what the other fellers managed to find."

"Chicken would be nice," said Mitchell.

"Soup," said Bloss, "that's what I'm after, if any of the boys gets us a chicken. I'd like to have some soup, or maybe a stew. With big chunks of potatoes, and maybe some carrots in it and the meat just fallin' off the bones."

Mitchell laughed. "Not much chance of that, Johnny."

"Nope," agreed Bloss, "not if the Rebs been around here."

"Probably not a chicken for miles, unless I miss my guess."

They fell silent as they descended the big hill and entered the wood again. They walked among the big oaks and chestnuts for some minutes, Mitchell glancing skyward, through the leaves and shafts of sunlight, thinking of the swing his father had made and hung from the limb of a walnut tree in their yard, and the time he had kissed a girl under a lovely autumn moon. That had only been a few months ago, but a letter from home had informed him that the girl was promised to someone he didn't know; and he was in the army, and they had been marching for miles, and George McClellan was back in command, and that was better even if it was only for the time being.

Bloss stopped suddenly, and Mitchell almost ran into him, so concentrated had he been on his own thoughts. "What are you doing?" he asked.

"Look," said Bloss, pointing through the line of trees.

Mitchell followed his gaze, saw only the forest, trees rising from the leafy ground, stretching skyward. "What?" asked Mitchell. "I don't see anything."

"Past the trees," said Bloss, indicating a spot in the clearing. "Must've been the Rebs who left it."

Bloss walked on, Mitchell following, and they left the forest and entered the bright sunshine. Mitchell shaded his eyes, squinting, trying to see what his friend had been pointing at, unable to see at all in the overwhelming light. "What?" he asked again.

A lone tree stood in the clearing, amid the ashes of a dozen old campfires. From one of its branches a coat hung. It was gray and had braid on the sleeves, and Mitchell reasoned that someone had hung it there to dry after washing.

"Must have been some of 'em camped here," said Bloss, "away from the others."

"So," said Mitchell, "we been passing their old camps for a couple of days now; ain't nothin' special about this place."

Bloss smiled, said, "Maybe," in that way he had that let you know he knew something you didn't. "Let's look around a bit, see what we can find."

"What for?" asked Mitchell. "The Rebs ain't left much of nothing for us."

"Maybe," said Bloss, "but there are all sorts of fresh fish in the new regiments and they'd be happy to trade anything they have for a genuine souvenir of the Rebel army."

Mitchell smiled, knew that Bloss was right, that the volunteer regiments that had recently joined the army were full of boys eager to trade anything for a memento to send back home, impress their friends. He began to walk slowly through the long grass, searching for something, anything that he could use for trade. After half an hour he had only the broken half of a brass compass tossed aside by some officer, and several miscast bullets. He found Bloss on the other side of the meadow, asked, "Find anything?"

Bloss shook his head. "Just a busted-up canteen and that ole' coat some johnny tossed off." Bloss held out his hand. "I cut his buttons off it, figured some rookie might trade for 'em."

"Maybe," said Mitchell, "better'n nothin' anyway."

"Yep," said Bloss, sitting down in the long grass. "You have any luck?"

"Nope," said Mitchell, sitting down also, stretching out in the dry grass.

"Oh, well," said Bloss, "it was worth the try anyhow."

Mitchell lay back in the grass, the sun warming him along the length of his body, instantly drifting toward sleep. Hard marching the last few days; not like them to move this quick. It was McClellan's hand at work, he was sure. There had been much speculation among the boys in his regiment; now that Mac was back in charge they expected big things. He settled into the grass, felt something pressing into the small of his back, ran a hand beneath his coat to pull out the offending lump. He found it, pulled it free of the clinging grass, held it up for inspection.

"What's that?" asked Bloss.

Mitchell shrugged, said, "Don't know." In his hand he held a paper wrapper, the side that had been pressed into the earth damp. He began to unwrap it, saw with a start that it was tobacco, some cigars. "Hey, now, some Reb dropped his cigars!"

Bloss leaned toward him, said, "Let's see what you got."

Mitchell tossed the wrapper aside, held the cigars out for Bloss to examine. "They're a little wet," he said.

"So," said Bloss, "we can just lay 'em in the grass; sun'll dry 'em out in no time." Bloss took one from him, inhaled the aroma, shrugged. "Never smoked myself, but we can trade these for something I bet."

Mitchell laid the others on a bed of grass, exposed the wet underside to the sun. "Few minutes they'll be good as new."

Bloss lay back on the grass, shaded eyes from the sun, said, "Save the wrapper they were in, sometimes they wrap cigars in tobacco leaf. Maybe we can cut it up and sell it off as chaw."

Mitchell laughed, slapped his friend's arm. "Even the rookies aren't that stupid, Bloss," he said.

Bloss smiled, said, "Save it anyway. Souvenir of the Rebel army."

Mitchell smiled, knew Bloss would make a trade for it. He picked the paper up, noticed the neat script on the paper. Probably some Reb had been sent the cigars from home and a relative had written a letter to him on the wrapper. Folks did that, paper being hard to come by, and expensive. He rolled onto his side, smoothed out the creased paper, had a moment of doubt about reading someone else's mail, remembered the kindly man who preached every Sunday in the small church. It wasn't right, what the army did to you, made you forget your upbringing, do things you would never do back home where folks knew you, held you accountable for what you did. He started to put the paper down, knew that Bloss would laugh at him, and that he would certainly read the letter anyway.

At the top of the page he read the words: *Headquarters, Army of Northern Virginia Special Orders, No. 191*. He felt a surge of excitement as he skimmed down the page, read the names of Rebel generals he had heard countless times, read about in the newspapers. All of the names were there; Lee, Jackson, Longstreet. His excitement grew to a point where he could no longer focus on what he was reading. There were the names of places that were unfamiliar to him, roads and other things he knew nothing about, but his eyes kept returning to the heading, the words that explained it all. *Headquarters, Army of Northern Virginia, Special Orders, No. 191*.

He kicked Bloss, said, "I got something here, Johnny. We got to git back, let the captain know. The colonel even. We got to tell 'em about this, show 'em this letter."

Bloss lifted his arm very slightly off his eyes, said sleepily, "What's so important about a cigar wrapper?"

"This ain't no cigar wrapper," he said nervously. "It's orders for some Reb generals. The big fellers too. Lee and Jackson, and Longstreet." He held the paper out to Bloss, who took it, staring at him.

After a minute Bloss said, "Damn! It does look real, don't it?"

Mitchell was standing up, his legs quivering with excitement. "We got to tell the captain," he said. "And we got to get movin' now, Johnny." He grabbed the letter from Bloss's hand, folded it into a neat square, said, "Let's go, Johnny!" Before Bloss could get to his feet, Mitchell was trotting across the meadow, headed back toward the regiment, his heart racing.

He turned, saw that Bloss had started to follow, then gone back to where they had been lying in the grass. He yelled, "C'mon!"

Bloss jogged steadily toward the spot in the grass where they had been lying, picked up the two haversacks with the apples, then bent and picked up the cigars he had forgotten in the grass. Bloss held them aloft, smiled, began running in his direction.

GEORGE MCCLELLAN STOOD IN A CIRCLE OF OFFICERS, THE crumpled paper with the neat script on it moving slowly around the circle, being passed from hand to hand by his staff officers. He inhaled the smoke from the cigar, realized that it tasted bitter and hot in his throat.

Just nerves. This damn letter could be a ruse. Lee might have planted it just to draw me in.

He moved his gaze slowly around the circle of officers, studied each face, wondered how the order could have been left lying where his men would find it. The possibilities seemed endless; the chance of it being real seemed equally as unlikely.

He noticed that one officer seemed particularly anxious to speak, the man fairly trembled with excitement. He gazed at him, couldn't recall the name. He was regular army, but not familiar. McClellan raised an eyebrow, asked, "Colonel, what can you tell me about this paper?"

The man smiled, said, "General, its just that, well . . ." The colonel glanced nervously about the circle of officers.

"Go on," said McClellan, "if you know something about its contents, let's have it. I'll decide what weight to give it."

The man nodded, swallowed hard, said, "It's just that I served with Colonel Chilton before the Rebellion, before he went South. I know his signature, General, and I'm confident that's his signature on the bottom of that document."

McClellan puffed on the cigar, waited for the stinging smoke to clear, said, "Fine. Very well, Colonel."

The colonel realized he was being dismissed, saluted, turned to go. McClellan asked, "Anything else, Colonel?"

"No, sir. I can't vouch for what's in the document, sir. I've no way of knowing it's accurate, but I'm confident of the signature."

Someone handed the paper back to McClellan and he read it for perhaps the tenth time in as many minutes. At last it began to make sense. The reports from his cavalry that had come in outlining Rebel troop movements without any discernible pattern. Civilian reports of marching columns of Southern soldiers where none should have been seen.

Now McClellan could see the pattern, divine Lee's intent. He knew now why Jackson's columns had recrossed the Potomac back into Virginia. He had mistakenly believed it was a raid, a foray onto Northern soil, followed by a quick retreat back into Virginia. At worst a feint designed to draw his army away from the Washington fortifications, then drive on the capital when he was out of position.

He knew now that he had been wrong. Lee had no intention of attacking Washington. Nor did he mean to engage the Union army in Maryland. The papers in his hands made that plain. Lee intended to invade the North, drive into Pennsylvania, all the way to the Susquehanna River. Capture Harrisburg. Perhaps Philadelphia.

Old Halleck with his foolish insistence that the garrison at Harpers Ferry must not abandon the old arsenal had upset the Rebel commander's plans. Lee had been forced to turn from his main line of march and engage the garrison at Harpers Ferry in order to secure his lines of supply and communication with Richmond. In order to do so, he had divided his army into smaller commands and surrounded the arsenal. Even now his army was divided, separated by mountains and rivers.

McClellan raised his gaze westward toward the mountains. Some of the Rebels were now on the other side of those mountains, separated from their comrades by miles of difficult terrain. All he had to do was cross those mountains and fall on them with his entire force. Lee might have the larger army, but he had lost his advantage in numbers by dividing his army into smaller, independent commands. It was a classic mistake, and he would apply a textbook solution.

McClellan was light-headed, euphoric. He had the Confederate commander's operation order in his hands. It was a magnificent opportunity. He must issue orders, get the men moving. Cross South Mountain west of Frederick City and fall on the scattered Rebel commands. It could be over in a few days, the Rebellion crushed, the Union saved. It was up to him now.

He glanced again at the papers in his hand, read the heading, "*Headquarters, Army of Northern Virginia, Special Orders, No. 191.*" He had no doubt of the document's authenticity. He glanced at his staff officers, shook the papers in his hand. "Now I know what to do," he said excitedly.

CHAPTER 4

Gen. Daniel Harvey Hill, CSA, fastened the top button of his tunic and walked toward his staff, who had gathered around a small fire. He nodded stiffly as an aide handed him a steaming cup of coffee. He thanked the man, cradling the cup, feeling its warmth against his hands. Dawn had not yet come to the mountains as Hill quickly ate breakfast and prepared to make a reconnaissance of the terrain upon which his brigades had been posted.

He had awoken that morning, stiff and sore from the pain that he habitually felt in his back, thinking of his home in North Carolina and cursing the chill that creeps into a man's joints when he sleeps on the ground. The endless marching through the worst type of hot, muggy days, had been followed by cool nights that brought a chill to their camps that was not warded off by their thin, army-issue blankets. His back had been worse of late, the pain radiating along his spine in white-hot rays that shortened his breath and tested his self-control.

Hill took a sip of the steaming liquid that passed for coffee in the Rebel army. It was bitter and watery, his only comfort being that it was hot. He looked at an aide, a Major Ratchford, who had handed him the cup, and asked sarcastically, "Sugar?"

Ratchford shook his head. "I've heard of it, sir, but I don't believe that I've ever known any person in this army who has actually tasted the stuff."

"Coffee?" asked Hill, holding his cup aloft, continuing the game. He had known Ratchford before the war, when the young man had been a student at the college in North Carolina where he taught. Ratchford had been a serious student of divinity, dull and dry, and Hill had thought he possessed little wit. He had volunteered for the army from a sense of duty, never having spent a day in uniform prior to the Rebellion. Army life had changed him; the camaraderie of camp life had brought out other aspects of his personality. Among Hill's staff he was known for his jocularity.

The major shook his head, said dryly, "Waste of good beans is against standing orders, sir. No coffee bean in the Army of Northern Virginia shall undergo the humiliation of grinding and boiling, General. The division quartermaster has ordered us to cook 'em. Rumor

has it that they can be boiled with mow grass and hayseed in order
to make a fine stew."

Hill smiled in appreciation of Ratchford's humor, wondering if all
the joking compensated for a lack of military knowledge. "Well," he
said, "my compliments to the chicory root then."

The young major smiled. "You may also want to thank the sassafras
tree, too, General."

Hill took another sip of the bitter fluid, grimaced. "Maybe not,"
he said, smiling at the officers around the campfire. Men were grinning, laughing in the darkness, appreciative of the rare moments of
good humor he shared with them.

Ratchford took a long sip from his coffee, smacked his lips in apparent satisfaction. "Perhaps you could help us settle a wager, General."

Hill cocked an eyebrow, said, "Maybe."

"Well," began the major, "we have been discussing the merits of
Confederate lice versus Union lice."

"Go on," said Hill, feigning interest.

"Now, the general opinion of most of the officers in this division
is that Southern lice are, by far, a superior breed to Northern lice."

Hill looked at the man, said, "And you desire my opinion, Mr.
Ratchford?"

"Yes, sir. We have agreed to abide by your decision, General."
Ratchford cleared his throat, said in an exaggerated stage whisper, "I
regret to inform you, General, that there are officers in this command
who believe Northern lice superior to our homegrown stock. They
have advanced a theory, sir, that the colder climate found in northern
regions imparts a certain hardiness to the critters native to that country."

Hill paused, studied the group of amused faces around the campfire. "What position do you favor, Major?" he asked.

"I am of the opinion that the Southern lice are exceptional, sir, and
without peer in the lice world," said the major proudly.

Hill smiled, resisted the impulse to laugh. "Major," he began,
"would you understand if I begged to delay giving my opinion on
this matter until further study?

Ratchford bowed in mock gravity, said, "Certainly, sir. Although I
am shocked and disappointed that an officer of your stature would
not render an immediate opinion on the matter."

Hill chuckled, marveled at Ratchford's ability to play the camp

jester at this early hour. "Yes," he said, "I suppose that is understand-
able."

"I shall attribute this to your lack of a proper cup of coffee, General,
and hope that it does not indicate a more serious character flaw."

Harvey Hill smiled. "Thank you, Major."

Hill took another tentative sip from the cup. "After the war is over
I suppose we shall all have a difficult time readjusting to polite society
and its small pleasures." Hill looked at the young major, said point-
edly, "Major Ratchford, you in particular may find the adjustment to
polite society difficult."

Men chuckled into the darkness, murmured their assent. Ratchford
smiled, bowed slightly.

Hill took another sip of the ersatz coffee, said dryly, "Becoming
reacquainted with the taste of real coffee will not be one of those
difficulties." More laughter, men smiling, standing close to the fire,
hands outstretched, warming themselves in the chill air. Hill nodded
to Ratchford, moved away from the group of smiling men. "What
news do we have from General Stuart and the cavalry?" he asked.

Ratchford shrugged. "About the same as yesterday, sir," he answered. "Our scouts report Federal cavalry moving up fast along the
east slope of the mountains, a brigade or maybe two of infantry in
trail."

Hill took a deep breath, wondered how far ahead Longstreet and
the others were. Lee had sent word back that he was to hold the
roads, stop the Federal infantry from crossing the mountains. The
Old Man had not bothered to add the phrase "hold at all costs," but
Harvey Hill had understood well enough.

He thought for a long minute, wondered how he was to do it.
There was never enough information . . . or men . . . or cannon. And
now he was alone on top of this damn mountain with a brigade or
two of infantry and he was being told to hold against God only knew
what.

"Any word of where the Union main body might be?" he asked
Ratchford, knowing the answer.

Ratchford shook his head, said gloomily, "General Stuart has pulled
his cavalry back south in order to defend some of the other passes."
Ratchford shrugged, added, "He doesn't feel that more than a brigade
or two is in front of us at present."

There was a pause, Ratchford swallowing hard, then saying, "The
cavalry has reported that the Federals are not uncovering their posi-

tions, sir. They have had trouble determining just where the Yankee army is at present."

Hill felt his anger rise, fought to control his emotions. Stuart was guessing. "That's his damn job, Major, to uncover their damn army, expose their position and line of march. Why the hell else do we have cavalry?"

He silently cursed Stuart and his cavalry for the thousandth time. *Guessing* about what was out there. He was being left to defend the army's rear with one damned division, and Stuart could only guess at what he might be up against.

"What about Longstreet?" asked Hill. "Has he got his people turned around yet? Are they headed back our way?"

"We've sent dispatches back, General. But there's not been any word yet."

"Where'd he go into camp last night, Major? Do we know?"

"Boonsboro, sir. About another twelve or thirteen miles north of here."

Hill glanced beyond Ratchford, saw that the troops were up, cook fires being stoked, tents coming down in the early gray light, the great white sheets of canvas disappearing into neat rolls.

The Old Man knew they were in trouble. That meant Longstreet would know. And Hood. They would come, fast as they might, but they were hours away at best.

Takes time to turn an army back on itself. The infantry would become snarled with the wagon trains if they weren't careful; there would be delays, no way around that. Even Sam Hood and Pete Longstreet would be able to move them only so fast.

That meant he was on his own, at least for the next several hours. Whatever was out there, beyond the mist, he had to deal with it with the men at hand. He glanced at Ratchford, said, "I want every man pushed into the lines. Cooks, teamsters, orderlies. Everyone is to be on the line. Send the wagons and other equipment back down toward Boonsboro with instructions that they are to get the hell off the road as soon as they see Hood's infantry coming our way."

Ratchford nodded, waited for him to continue.

At least they had the good ground. The Yankees would have to come up the mountain, look right down into their guns.

Ratchford cleared his throat, said nervously, "There's another matter, sir."

"What now?" snapped Hill.

"Some of the brigades are reporting that there are several roads that approach the main passes through these mountains."

Hill stared at Ratchford in stunned silence, despaired at what Ratchford might say next, felt a bitter, sinking sensation deep inside. "And?" he asked.

"They are waiting for your orders, sir. The brigade commanders are reporting that they don't have enough men to properly cover all the approaches, and they want to know which ones you want them to defend."

Hill let out a long breath, resisted the temptation to scream at the man. Wouldn't do any good, he knew. He swallowed the last of his coffee, said, "Major Ratchford, perhaps you and I had better go and have a look around before the damn Yankees get any farther up our mountain."

"Yes, sir," said Ratchford.

"We'd better have a look at those roads you've heard about."

Ratchford nodded. "Should I send for your escort, sir?"

Hill shook his head. "Won't be necessary," he said. "We'll only be gone a few minutes, and I don't expect to find them up to any mischief this early in the morning."

"Yes, sir," said Ratchford, gulping down the last of his coffee and swinging into the saddle.

Hill mounted his horse and rode to the east, watching the sky lighten with the rising of the sun. If McClellan's army was close behind, sunrise would show them in the valley. Hill and Ratchford rode slowly, noting the terrain, the thickets lining the road. Occasionally Hill made note of a desirable piece of ground, Ratchford jotting down notes in response to Hill's terse comments.

Within minutes they came upon a small farm, the house rough-hewn from logs, mud chinked between the wood. The smell of woodsmoke mixed with manure hit him as they entered the yard, and Hill thought: *Hard life up here, tough people.* The farmer appeared, a small, wiry man, lean face, with a shock of black hair beneath his hat. Hill smiled, said, "Good morning, sir."

"Good morning to you," said the mountaineer.

Hill noted the condition of the man's clothing, the silent children at his feet, staring at him and Ratchford, liked the way the man stared back at him, held his eyes. "I was wondering if you might be able to provide me with some information?" asked Hill.

"Yes, sir," said the man amiably. "I reckoned some of you soldier fellers would be by, asking after them Rebels that passed here a day or two ago."

Hill smiled, knew the farmer had mistaken him for a Union officer. There was a twinge of guilt, something from his catechism came to him, the thought not quite complete, but there. Wrong to deceive him, not a lie really, but just as wrong. "They came by here, did they?" he asked innocently.

"Yes, sir," said the farmer. "Herds of 'em moving up the mountain. They was a mighty sorry-looking lot too. Most of em only wearing rags, their hats and shoes all busted up, what of 'em *had* shoes."

"That so," said Hill, smiling to the major. "Still, they have a reputation for being stand-up fighters."

The man nodded, "Reckon that's true enough. Ain't much for looks though."

"Did they give you any trouble?" asked Hill.

"No, sir. Not so that you could say. They drank most of the water from my well, and they did some big talkin' about what they was going to do up Pennsylvania way, but they didn't give me nor mine any trouble."

Hill smiled again at Ratchford, looked about, noting the small cabin, the fields cut from the woods on the side of the mountain. "You must know the roads about here well."

"Born and raised on this mountain," said the man proudly.

Hill nodded, "What are the best roads over the mountain?" he asked, "supposing I want to move a great many men and wagons over them."

"Well," said the man, pausing while he considered the question. "Suppose that depends," he said slowly. "Where might you fellers be headed?"

"Boonsboro," offered Hill.

"Reckon you might want to go through up at Turner's Gap, just a mite to the north."

Hill nodded, "And if we were headed to Sharpsburg?"

"Well, Fox's Gap is a bit to the south; you could take that one."

"And do both passes have only one road leading to them?"

The farmer shook his head, "Nope. They's a few ways of gettin' there."

Hill and Ratchford exchanged an alarmed glance. "Other than the main road, what other roads lead to the passes?" asked Hill.

"Now, I don't know that them roads have names," said the man.

"For the most part they are just farm lanes that folks use to get to the gaps."

Hill nodded. "And do these lanes join with the main roads?"

The man scratched his head. "Some do, others don't. Some just follow the ridges to the gaps, others run from farms to the gaps, and back the other way to the big roads. Cain't say for sure 'less you got one in mind."

"Have you seen many cannon?" asked Hill.

"Well, I suppose I have. But they are mostly yours, and from what I have seen of them they are on the valley road by the church."

Hill exchanged another glance with the major. The man had just indicated that Union batteries were on South Mountain. Cannon never came forward without proper infantry support. That could only mean that the Federals were nearby and in some force.

Hill began to speak to the man but was cut short by the scream of a shell. His horse tensed at the sound, and the children of the mountaineer began to cry. Hill dismounted, took the halter of his mount in one hand and tried to soothe the animal. He noticed one child, alone, crying, while her father gathered the others and headed for his house. Hill approached the girl and stroked her hair, "You should not be so upset, my dear," he said.

The girl looked at him, continuing to cry. Hill took her hand and began walking with her toward the cabin. He thought of his own children, heard their voices, their laughter. Today was Sunday. His wife would be taking his girls to services this morning. He thought about the familiar routines of the Sabbath before the war had interrupted all their lives. The fine meals, the droning of the minister in service, the singing of the choir. In his mind's eye Hill could see plainly the walnut railing around their box in the church, hear the bell calling his family to Sunday service, feel the starched stiffness of the white shirt he habitually wore to church.

He felt the warmth of the tiny hand in his, breaking his reverie, and said again to the girl, "You have nothing to fear, child." He searched for the right words, something that would put the small girl at ease.

The girl sniffed, wiped her eyes with the back of a hand.

Children had always been a mystery to him. Their world was the world of their mothers, inhabited by women with soothing voices and strong hands, a foreign place that he had never really understood. A mother's silent touch was more valuable to a small child than every word ever spoken by a father. The mystery, and the wonder of it, had been ever more apparent to him since the birth of his own girls.

Harvey Hill knew that he loved his children as much as any father, but they inhabited a society in which he must always be something of a visitor. He glanced again at the small girl, looked about the farmyard for some sign of her mother. "Where is your mother, child?" he asked.

The girl extended one small arm, pointed toward the roughly built house.

"Ah," said Hill. "She's probably waiting for you inside."

The girl smiled, said, "Yep. She stays to the house when folks come callin'."

Hill nodded approvingly. "Of course she does," said Hill, smiling down at the girl. "Do you know I have a girl just about your age at my house?" he asked innocently.

"Really?" said the girl.

"It's so," said Hill. "But she doesn't live on the top of a fine mountain like this.

"Not many folks live here," said the child matter-of-factly.

When they were a few steps from the cabin, Hill released the girl's hand and watched as she walked into the cabin. The major handed him the reins as another shell screamed nearby. Hill swung into the saddle, looking back over his shoulder at the cabin. The girl peeked out of the doorway, waving shyly. Hill tipped his hat to her, then rode out of the small yard and back onto the pike.

"Look's like the Yankees are getting an early start, General," said Ratchford.

Hill nodded, pushing his horse to a trot and heading for a vantage point where he could observe the movements of the Union forces in the valley below. Great stands of oaks and pine crowded the road, the leaves shimmering and green through the early-morning mist, the trunks disappearing into the gray haze. The narrow road slanted past deep ravines, the slopes thick with mountain laurel and briars, wild, impenetrable vegetation that clung to every precipice, wrapped itself around the great trunks, closed off the light from above.

They were coming on hard. Harder than he had known them to in the past. Something had changed. The Federals were marching hard, pushing their infantry to the limit.

Harvey Hill pushed ahead, seeking a spot where he could get a view of the valley below, his mind filled with apprehension, almost certain of what he would see. Longstreet would send help, but if he didn't, or if they didn't get here in time . . .

A branch whipped across his face, the bark stinging him, a dozen unseen thorns raking his skin, cutting into the flesh. He swiped a hand across his cheek, saw the red on his glove, tasted the salty blood. He cursed once, Ratchford's horse plunging ahead, more branches whipping back at him as the animal broke trail.

Hill silently prayed that Stuart was right, that beyond the trees and the mist in the valley below was no more than a strong reconnaissance force sent forward by McClellan. His boys could handle that, take them coming up the hills, shift regiments and batteries, hold them off while Longstreet and Hood got into position. The ground was good. He could take advantage of that, compensate for his lack of men. He glanced skyward, searching for the sun, wondered how far along the day was, thought: *Too soon, too soon. They're a long way off yet, and they'll be no help for hours, and what's to be done has to be done by me and mine.*

Ratchford pointed to a clearing up ahead, sunlight pouring through a break in the forest. He nodded, indicating he wished to take a closer look, the major coaxing his horse down a steep ravine, the animal white-eyed amid a small avalanche of rock and dirt, picking its way gingerly toward the light shining through the tangle of branches and vines. Hill bowed low in the saddle, dodging branches pushed aside by the major, sweeping others aside with one hand, then leaning far back against the saddle, his horse straining, sliding down the mountain, his weight thrown against his legs and the stirrups and the creaking leather. Before he could look up, he heard Ratchford say suddenly, "My God!"

Hill squinted into the bright sunlight as he came into the small clearing; looking over the side of the mountain, he saw before him the entire valley floor and the eastern slope of the mountain. Ribbons of road swung through the valley and up the mountain toward him and Ratchford. Dust rose from the roads, and for as far as he could see, Harvey Hill saw marching soldiers.

Great long columns of blue soldiers streaked the green of the valley amid the neat fields, then ducked out of view amid forest, only to reemerge unbroken, marching steadily in the bright forest light, moving slowly, fearlessly, inexorably toward him. Columns of Union troops covered every road. The marching men were near enough for Hill to make out officers on horseback and regimental colors flying at their

front. The training in Hill overcame his awe at the spectacle, and he
began silently counting the flags and guidons. When he had counted
enough regimental colors to convince himself that he was watching
two full corps of the Army of the Potomac he stopped. Hill whispered,
"Now I understand what Gideon must have meant."

Ratchford paused, appearing to be mesmerized by the scene below
them. At last he asked, "Gideon, sir?"

"The Old Testament," Hill answered absently, whispering as
though he were in church. "Gideon," said Hill slowly, not breaking
his gaze on the approaching columns. "As fearsome as an army with
its banners flying."

There was a long pause, Hill continuing to stare at the Union army
in the valley below. "Now I understand what Gideon must have felt
when he saw the Roman army, its banners unfurled, marching through
a hostile land without fear." He turned toward Ratchford, knew that
the young major would know that they could not hope to hold back
such a large force for more than a few hours, if that.

The two officers sat in silence for some moments, gazing at the
spectacle before them. In the valley, everywhere, there was movement, as though an army of blue soldiers had sprung from the earth
beyond the mountains during the night and was marching ceaselessly
toward him.

Hill could see the screen of cavalry in advance of the infantry as
they moved up the side of the mountain. For the first time in his life
Harvey Hill experienced a consuming feeling of loneliness. Astride
his horse, gazing at the enormous force arrayed against him, he felt,
if only for an instant, overwhelmed.

Harvey Hill gazed at the rising sun, trying to judge the hour. No
later than eight o'clock. They would run into his skirmishers soon
enough; that would force them to break ranks, get off the road, spread
out. Then they would probe his lines, search for a spot they liked,
throw a brigade or two at him. His boys could handle that; there
would be some time. He glanced again at the sight before him, knew
that they were not fools, that good men marched in those ranks, men
who would know what to do once they ran into his brigades. Those
officers would come after him for real, stack units one behind the
other until they had overwhelming superiority, and then they would
push over him like a wave breaking over a rock. Hill realized that he
feared that moment, not because of the possibility of death, but because of the certainty of failure.

Lee and Longstreet and Hood and all the others would be left open, uncovered. The Yankees would pour down the mountain and there would be nothing to stop them; and then the race would be on to get back across the Potomac with whatever was left.

Hill took a last long look at all that lay before him. Wondered at the sight of it, knew that one purpose had brought all those souls together on this day, awed by the single will manifested in the valley below him.

Without speaking he wheeled his horse around, started back up the mountain to find his men.

CHAPTER 5

THE FIRING HAD WELLED UP SUDDENLY, BEFORE THE LIGHT WAS even up over the trees, tumbling down the mountain in long rolls that meant someone's infantry had gone in and run up against the Rebels. He had heard it a little after dawn and he had known then that everything he had been told by McClellan's staff was probably wrong and that the situation up front would be confused and men would be cursing McClellan and Burnside and him and wondering why the damned army could never get it right, not even once.

Maj. Gen. Jesse Lee Reno, United States Army, West Point class of 1846, brushed past his aides and mounted his horse, determined to ride up the mountain until he found someone who did know what was going on. He cursed McClellan's staff silently, wondering why they could never, not even once, know what the damned Confederates were up to. He moved the big horse steadily uphill, weaving through infantry and wagons and artillery struggling to climb the slope. He sensed that the morning was already going badly. Beyond the usual tangle of men, wagons, and equipment that clogged the roads and made movement next to impossible, he could sense the confusion. Some units were struggling up the mountain, while others were off to the side of the road, lighting fires, brewing coffee. No one seemed to know what to do or when to do it.

He urged the horse forward, determined to move ahead, up the mountain, see for himself what was going on. There had been a dustup this morning, some skirmishing as they jockeyed for position on the mountain with the Rebels. Nothing unusual about that when two armies were close to one another, like two big men circling each other, each throwing a punch now and then to test the other man's skill. Then someone had lunged in, and they had settled down to the real fighting.

But he had been told by McClellan and the peacocks around army headquarters that the Rebels were miles away, somewhere west of the mountains. There had been rumors that McClellan had captured Lee's operational orders, talk of a spy, nothing solid—the usual speculation that swirls around headquarters tents.

They had come on them almost blind, blundered into them in the morning darkness. A few scrapes with the cavalry, the infantry sent forward, and then here they were, dug into the side of the mountain, daring you to come after them. Infantry. Not dismounted cavalry, but infantry. Pleasonton and his damn cavalry hadn't known about that. He had been told all the Rebels had on the mountain were a few squadrons of dismounted cavalry. The first shots of artillery had dispelled that myth. No cavalry travels with guns like those.

He had been thinking about that all morning, wondering why the Rebels had chosen here to make a fight of it. Lee's army was supposed to be beyond the South Mountain passes now, somewhere west of Boonsboro, if their own cavalry reports could be believed. But here they were, in force, putting up a fight.

It didn't add up. Why fight here when the bulk of your army was miles away? Lee was too good a general to make a mistake like that. Same for Longstreet and Jackson and the others. That meant something had gone wrong with their plan; they had slowed down for some reason. Not like them, not like them at all. And now here he was run up against their infantry, and it was more than a rear guard, and none of it made sense to him, not really.

He sighed, thought: *Good a place as any. They've got the ground; we'll have to come at them uphill.* No mistakes, he told himself. They won't make any; neither can I.

Ahead there was a fluttering of flags amid the trees, and he instinctively headed for it. See who was running the show up here, determine what was going on. Under the fly of a tent was Sam Sturgis. Good man, steady, made his name out West, in the saddle, fighting Indians. An old friend, from West Point, long ago it seemed now. He pulled up, dismounted, handed the reins to an orderly. "Morning, Sam."

Sturgis smiled in recognition, dark eyes, a barrel chest under the blue tunic, a powerful man with thick hands that gripped his in a quick motion, then, "Jesse, how are things?"

Reno shrugged. "Came to ask you that same thing, Sam."

Sturgis laughed, that tense laugh that comes too quick, has an unnatural sound of it. Reno shuddered, thought: *Oh, God, not again, not now. We need this one. We need to win, show them it can be done.*

Sturgis withdrew a cloth from his pocket, wiped the sweat from his forehead. "Tough goin' up ahead," he said.

"Yes," said Reno, "I expected as much from the sounds of the firing."

"They mean to make a fight of it." Sturgis nodded toward the summit. "Ground favors them, that's for certain."

"Suppose so," said Reno. He glanced up the narrow road; there were men filing past, leaning forward, climbing in the morning heat, sweating. Deep defiles on either side of the road, steep rocky country covered in thickets and brambles and laurel that clawed and tore at marching men. Brush so thick that infantry couldn't move through it even on level ground. "Tough country for a fight," he said. Then, "How are the maps?"

Sturgis laughed again, not like before, genuine, smiling, the corners of his mouth creased with good humor, and Reno felt instantly better. "Same as always, Jesse. Useless."

Reno smiled, remembered Sturgis as a cadet at the Academy, always the slight air of disrespect, never taking the army more seriously than he had to. Reno chuckled, suddenly grateful that Sturgis was here, said, "We'll have to push 'em off this mountain, Sam. McClellan is already sending to me, asking how long it's gonna be."

Sturgis turned, glanced up the mountain, said slowly, "I can't figure it, Jesse. I was told that there would only be light resistance up there, some cavalry at most. Now I got at least a couple of brigades in front of me, maybe a whole division."

"Gonna have to move 'em off, Sam. We're committed. Whole army is comin' up behind us."

Sturgis shook his head, said slowly, "Well, I'll be damned."

Reno glanced at his friend, said, "You're gonna have to go back in, Sam. Stay with it, push 'em off this road. I'll send you whatever I've got handy, but it's gonna be up to you."

Sturgis smiled, said, "Aw, it ain't that. We'll move 'em off, or maybe we won't. What I can't figure is this. What kind of bug got up McClellan's butt? Never known him to move like this before, especially when the other fellow looks to make a fight of it."

Reno nodded, had thought as much himself. "It is a bit out of character for him, isn't it?"

Sturgis cocked an eyebrow, said, "Out of character?" He shook his head. "Not having a fresh polish on his boots is out of character, but this . . ." Sturgis paused, grinned wildly at Reno, said, "I'll be damned if I can figure it, Jesse."

Reno laughed, enjoying the joke, thought: *Old Sam, none better.* "You know who's up there?" he asked, jerking his head toward the crest.

"Harvey Hill is what I've heard. We've got a few prisoners. That's what they're tellin' us anyway."

"Harvey Hill, huh?"

"Yep."

"He'll be tough," said Reno. "Be a scrap."

"That's the way it's shaping up." A pause, then, "McClellan really planning on bringing the whole army through here?"

"That's what I'm told," said Reno. "Right over these mountains."

From the road they heard cursing, a team of mules was struggling against their harness, laboring to bring a cannon up the mountain, the driver yelling and snapping his whip over them, the big gun creaking forward by inches. "Not much of a place for artillery," said Sturgis.

"Suppose not," said Reno, "but we'll move what we can into position. Your infantry will have to do the rest."

Sturgis ran a practiced eye over the struggling team, said, "I'm still probing, trying to find their flanks." There was a long pause, then, "I think they're thin, Jesse. Can't say why, but I do. Something about this one is different."

Reno nodded, waited. Sturgis was an old soldier, a man you could depend on in a fight. Not much of a talker, maybe too many years out West, where the country was so big you could wander for days without seeing another being, where one mistake could mean death. In a country like that talk wasn't as important. Reno understood that, understood that Sturgis had been changed by the time spent on the limitless plains. You had to give him time, let the thoughts form, wait for him to bring them out. "How do you see it, Sam?" he asked.

Sturgis shook his head. "It's thick up there, rough country. Tough place to try and maneuver, for us or them. That means Harvey Hill will be defendin' the roads, the crest of the mountain. He'll be in position, wait for us to come to him. Whatever he's got on the top of that mountain, he's had time to move into position, prepare his defenses."

"Probably so," said Reno, knowing that Sturgis had reasoned it out already.

"Can you give me a few hours, Jesse? A little time, move some of my men around up there, try and feel for his flanks, get around him if I can?"

Reno took a deep breath of muggy air, blew it out in a long stream that emptied his lungs. Time. No man had it to give. Already he could feel the tension building behind him, the units assembling at the base of the mountains, feel the impatience of McClellan and his damned staff officers. Like water behind a dam, and he and Sturgis were caught between it all. They would want to know what the delay was,

why the army was being held up. "Give you as much as I can, Sam."
He looked into the dark eyes, knew that Sturgis had been watching
him. "No promises. Word comes up from headquarters, and you'll
have to go in with whatever you've got in place."

Sturgis put his hat on, said, "Figured as much. Do what you can
though. I'd be grateful."

Reno reached out, shook the leathery hand, felt the other man's
strength, said, "Sam."

There was a long moment when neither man spoke, the light fine
and white, and Reno could see every detail as though for the first
time; and all the years between the Academy and now slipped away
and he and Sturgis and all the others were sharing a joke on the frozen
parade ground, the Hudson slipping by below in the mist, and the
enemy was someone you would never know. Then he withdrew his
hand and Sturgis was walking back to his headquarters without looking back and he wondered if they would ever talk again.

SMOKE COVERED THE MOUNTAINSIDE, DRIFTING LAZILY DOWN
toward the Union men behind trees and stones that rose from the ground
in a thousand places. Here and there men were firing at movement in
the trees below, single shots, aimed at flashes of blue below them, shadows moving among the oaks and juniper, and that clung to the slopes.
The occasional breeze would lift the smoke, tear a ragged hole in the
otherwise impenetrable curtain, and blue soldiers would appear. A flurry
of firing from both sides would be followed by the ripping of bullets
through leaves or thudding heavily into trees.

Harvey Hill had lost track of the time, only knew that the sun was far
overhead and that none of the couriers he had sent back to urge on
Longstreet and Hood had returned to him. He had managed to hold his
ground, fend the Union soldiers off as they fought their way up the
mountainside, shift his guns to meet each new advance.

Someone approached, handed him a steaming cup of coffee and a
biscuit, thick with ham and a bit of cheese, and he bit into it hungrily,
savoring the smoky taste of the meat. He sat on a rock, eating the food,
relishing the taste of it, peering into the dense foliage below, wondering
where they would try his lines next.

He began to rise, felt the pain knifing along his spine, his breath coming in gasps. He settled back onto the rock, waited for it to pass, to release
its hold on him, allow him to move. He cursed, once, beneath his breath,
damning the unseen nerves that never quite released him from the con-

stant aching, the sudden spasms that forced him to his knees. He glanced about, prayed that none of the men or his staff officers had noticed. *Not today,* he thought, *of all days. Today I need to be able to move, to ride. It's no damn good to sit here on this rock like a statue.*

In the valley below, through the midday haze, he could see the Federal army gathering, pushing onto the slopes, crowding the base of the mountain. The roads below were a smoking, coiled mass of men and guns, and all of them were headed his way.

There was a shout from somewhere to the left. The Yankees were coming again, dodging between trees and rocks, creeping steadily forward, searching, probing, trying his lines in a dozen places. No gallant charges of massed formations in this country, too rough, the ground broken and unreliable. A popping of single shots rippled down the line, his boys taking their time, firing at them carefully. The deliberate firing meant only one thing: his men were short of ammunition. Someone over there, behind the outcroppings of rock, someone who had been in a fight before, would figure it out before much longer, push his men forward in earnest.

A puff of white smoke billowed white against the trees, rolled out toward him, turning instantly black, angry. They had gotten a cannon into position, were trying to elevate the tube enough to take him under fire. The shell ripped into the empty ground between the lines, careened wildly off a bit of rock, skidded to a stop in the brush. There was jeering laughter from some of his men, catcalls, taunting the men farther down the slope.

An aide galloped up, pulled his horse up short, the animal white-eyed with fear. The boy ran toward him, a young lieutenant from somewhere in the Carolina low country and whose name he could not recall at this instant. A fair-haired boy with bright eyes and a serious nature, whose father was a minister who was acquainted with his wife and who expressed the opinion that the South must win because their cause was just and that God would not let other men prevail.

Harvey Hill swallowed the last of the biscuit and returned the salute of the young lieutenant. "You've got word from General Longstreet?" he asked.

The boy drew himself up, said, "Yes, sir. General Longstreet's compliments, sir."

Hill listened, stared past the boy at the valley below, knew what Longstreet must say, the only thing he could say, that he was marching hard and that if all went well he would be here by dark, but not before; and in the meanwhile he must hold or the entire army, not just the operation but the army itself, was in peril. And that if McClellan had sent his cavalry through another pass and they got between his men and Longstreet, then all was lost and the men who would die today would die for nothing. And that, in the end, he would fail and the justness of their cause mattered precious little.

He held up a hand, stopped the lieutenant from talking further, mumbled his thanks. From the right there was more firing beyond the trees, just beyond his sight, among the boulders and the vines and a thousand green leafy things that he couldn't put a name to. Through the dappled sunlight he could see long, slender streaks of flame, thick smoke drifting down, clinging to the ground, sliding away from them. From below there was cheering, the beating of a drum, steady, strong. A regiment moving into place, taking its position on the line, extending the Union position.

They were coming, moving up, spreading out in front of him, sending out patrols, trying to find the limits of his lines. He could feel their gathering strength, beyond the thick tangles of mountain laurel and fragrant juniper and the coiling smoke they were building up, stacking units along the roads, entire regiments sliding into position, an ever-widening line that was spreading out, expanding, attempting to engulf his own.

Sooner or later whoever was in charge down there would know, a patrol would come back, report that they had not been able to establish contact with the enemy. Then they would swing around, move in behind him while the others kept up a steady fire on his front. Matter of time, really; even the most junior officer could figure it out. Just keep pushing along his lines, keep sending patrols forward, probing, until you come up empty, push your men into . . . nothing.

Timing would be critical. He couldn't afford to hold his boys in place too long. There would be a struggle, but eventually it would be every man for himself if he held his boys too long, beyond what his numbers and the ground would allow. They would fall back, slip off the mountain as best they could, try to find Hood and Longstreet and the others, get back to the main body. In this country it would be difficult, trying to keep them all together, move down over broken country. He had to try and hold on, at least until dark. If he could hold that long, then maybe they could break off, disengage, march through the night to rejoin Longstreet and the others. Once the sun set he would be all right. Damn difficult thing to move units to the attack in the dark; not likely in this ground either. Save his boys if he could hold on till then.

A shell ripped through the air overhead. Men ducked instinctively, the big missile sending a spray of black dirt over them, the ground shattered and smoking where it had struck. A horse screamed, ran past trailing its livery, its sides slick with blood, until someone stepped from the ranks

and sent a bullet into its brain and it spun to the ground, twisting, screaming, biting at the air. An officer was yelling, conserve ammunition, and
the Yankees were coming again and the firing picked up and men were
shouting with hoarse, wild voices amid the overwhelming thunder of a
thousand rifles.

Above the roar someone was shouting to him, a young captain he did
not recognize. An officer was down, Garland. Fine man, an able officer,
trusted by his men. The captain was talking, his face streaked with fear.
Garland's brigade had begun to give way, shaken by his loss. That happened, often. He had seen it before. Soldiers grew to believe that so long
as one man, one officer, was unhurt, then they too were unbreakable. But
let that man go down and panic would sweep through them like a breeze
moves high among the trees, rippling the leaves, sending them into flight.
Odd, unexplainable, and yet he had seen it many times, among even the
most battle-tested regiments. He signaled to a staff officer; the man nodded, understood, galloped away.

The firing was falling off now, single shots, pop, long pause, another
pop. More catcalls, come on back, his men, taunting the Yankees. Angry
faces below, turned back toward them, a slow melting away, faces toward
the enemy, men disappearing into the brush, a slow, simmering anger. *No
fear there*, he thought. *Not long now, they'll be back, try us for real.*

The blue uniforms were falling back all along his lines, out of sight,
beyond the curtain of branches, into the shadows, among the rocks, hud-
dling out of sight, regrouping. They would come again, he knew, in a bit,
when the wagons had brought up more ammunition and fresh men had
been herded into their line. No shortages over there, plenty to go around,
just a matter of bringing it all up, moving it into place.

His boys were holding on, men ambling back during the lull, filling
canteens and cartridge boxes from the wagons. There was laughter, small
groups of men behind bits of stone wall, trees felled across the road, the
tops cut and thrown in a tangle of branches. *No fear here either.*

In the distance a rumble, slow to come, welling up out of the valley
to the west. Hesitant, gradual, then building, a long, low rumble from far
away, beyond the trees and the valley, unseen, creeping steadily toward
him through the muggy air. He turned, searched through the branches
for a sign of a storm, saw only blue sky winking back at him through the
leaves.

Another rumble. A lovely distant sound of heavy cannon firing. He felt
his breath coming in quick gasps, tried to fight down the notion that
nothing was going according to the schedule laid out by Lee, but he
couldn't escape the sense that something was terribly wrong, things had

gone awry and now Jackson was firing on Harpers Ferry or maybe Long-street had run up against Yankee cavalry in the valley west of them and wouldn't be here after all.

Harvey Hill thought: *Jackson. Got his guns in place and now he's giving the Yankees a pounding at Harpers Ferry.* He turned back toward the east, wondered how many hours he could hold them, keep the blue soldiers below at bay.

It was going to be a close thing, a very close thing. No matter whose guns were firing, it was going to be entirely too close; and he was here with a few thousand men and not enough ammunition for them or his guns and the whole damn Yankee army was down below and marching toward him.

Harvey Hill looked up at the sky for the hundredth time, saw the sun high overhead, light pouring down through the leaves and the branches, a steady stream of light falling in silent shafts to the forest floor, thought: *If we can just hold until dark, it will all be fine.*

LONGSTREET RODE BESIDE THE COLUMN, MOVING THROUGH THE midday heat, trying not to breathe the hot air that was filled with dust. Soldiers who had fallen out of the march, given in to the sun and the heat and their own fatigue, lay sprawled in the grass or were stumbling along the outside of the column, trying to catch up to their commands. Men were marching, heads down, through the heat and the dust, lurching forward with every step, straining against the sun and their own thirst and the clouds of dust that boiled up from the road and settled on their clothing, fought its way beneath their caps, parched their mouths and throats and lungs.

There had been no rain in this part of Maryland for days and the dirt of the roadbed had been pounded into a fine powder by the passage of his own columns only the day before. Now his men were retracing their steps, heading back for South Mountain and the passes that the Old Man had ordered Harvey Hill to defend. The wells along their route had, for the most part, been emptied by the troops ahead, adding to the misery of the men marching in the rear of the column.

The country here was flat, a high grassy plain with few streams that spread itself between South Mountain to the east and a series of ridges that marked the course of the Potomac River farther west. South Mountain rose above it all, a long tree-covered spine of rock that separated them from the Federal army. The ridge shimmered in the distance, blue and green against the sky, promising a hint of cool air at its summit, which

Longstreet and the others knew was only a deception they allowed themselves.

There had been little word from Harvey Hill since midmorning. Just
a courier or two with the terse message that what appeared to be the
entire Union army was on the eastern slope of South Mountain and would
they please hurry the hell up as he had only one slim division with which
to defend the passes over the mountain. He had ordered Hood's division
to be on the road before daylight, countermarching, heading for South
Mountain.

Ahead Longstreet caught a glimpse of mounted men, Hood's staff,
wheeled his horse around the marching infantry, conscious of the dust he
was stirring, wondering sometimes how they kept going. He glanced
down at them from atop the big horse, red faces swollen with the heat,
wild-eyed, moving steadily through air so thick it seemed to cling to you,
hold you back with every step. Wet, clammy air, with no hint of a breeze.
He glanced at the sky, searching for clouds. If only it might rain and
break the heat, even for just an hour or two.

Longstreet rode into the circle of officers, nodded to those he knew.
"Hello, Sam," he said easily.

Hood looked up, said with that wonderful, slow, musical voice, "Pete,
how are you today?"

Longstreet nodded, smiling at the sight of Hood. "Sam," he said amiably, "I've been better."

Hood nodded. "Been better myself, Pete. Can you spare a minute to
talk to an old soldier?"

Longstreet grinned, felt his mood improving, looked into the pale blue
eyes, saw the confidence, wondered at the likes of men like Sam Hood,
felt instantly better somehow. "Sure, Sam."

"Pete?"

Longstreet looked at Hood, his reverie broken. "Yep," he said easily.

"Pete, why don't we ride together a bit."

"Which way?" asked Longstreet, smiling.

Hood grinned, slowly, held his gaze. "Probably ought to head for the
sound of them guns. Harvey Hill may be having a bit of trouble by now."

They moved off, their horses walking easily beside the marching columns. "You get over that fuss about them ambulances yet?" asked Longstreet.

Hood looked straight head, said nothing. Longstreet saw his features
change, almost imperceptibly, and understood that Hood had taken a
stand. *Hard man to move*, he knew, *once he's dug in. None better in a stand-
up fight.*

They rode for some moments, Longstreet at last speaking, breaking the awkward silence. "Still a mite sore about that one, are you?" he asked after a pause.

Hood turned to him, his face a portrait of determination. "Did what I had to do, Pete. My boys took them wagons, and they was ours by rights." Hood smiled, suddenly, unexpectedly, his teeth showing white against his dusty beard, and Longstreet was thinking he wants this to end; and then Hood said, "The boys would've expected me to raise the issue."

Longstreet nodded. Honor was always an issue in this army. Hood had been prepared to fight a duel over a few captured wagons. Would still have the duel. He smiled at the irony of it, a duel, in the middle of the war. Hell of an army.

"How're the Texans?" he asked, knowing that Hood's brigades were loyal beyond all reason, that sometimes men fight more for each other than they do for a flag or a country and that Sam Hood understood that, knew that he had been given the highest honor a man could be given by his soldiers. Sam Hood, a Kentuckian, an outsider, a man not born and raised on the frontier, had been welcomed into that strange and savage fraternity.

Longstreet thought suddenly: *A blood bond. Can't ask Sam to go against that. He can't. Won't.*

He exhaled a lungful of muggy air, wondered silently how the army stayed together at all. Knew that in some measure it was Lee who made it possible, that no one else could, that without Lee they were all smaller somehow. "You heard anything from Harvey Hill?" he asked, changing the subject.

"He's pressed, if the couriers have it right. Stuart pulled out this morning, or maybe yesterday. Took his cavalry south, trying to cover the passes down that way." Hood removed his hat, fanned himself with it, said flatly, "He's in a tight spot, Pete."

"We're all in a tight spot," said Longstreet grimly.

Hood laughed. "Still the prophet of doom and destruction, I see."

Longstreet fought the urge to laugh, felt suddenly very foolish. Riding beside Sam Hood, on his way to fight over a spot of ground no one would ever care about except today. He shook his head, wondered just for a moment at the insanity of it all.

Longstreet became acutely aware of Hood staring at him. He held up a hand to forestall any question. "Sam," he said, after a moment, "last night General Lee got word that McClellan has a copy of our orders for the campaign. Captured them a day or two past, near Frederick City."

Hood let out a low whistle, "Well, that explains a good bit. Not the least of which is why McClellan finally gathered his skirts and looks to make a fight of it." Hood patted his horse's neck. "Anybody bother to tell Harvey Hill that yet?" he asked, looking ahead to the mountains.

Longstreet smiled, said, "My guess is Harvey Hill is looking at the bulk of the Yankee army from the top of that mountain. He knows all he needs to know."

"Yep, you're probably right," said Hood. "Gonna be one hell of a fight for them passes."

Minutes passed in silence before Hood continued. "What's the Old Man say about all this? You been talking to him?"

"General Lee," said Longstreet slowly, "is in favor of staying with the plan to take Harpers Ferry. After Jackson takes it, we'll concentrate the army, probably near Sharpsburg, draw up behind Antietam Creek." Longstreet paused. "He sent some cavalry over that way, have a look at the ground."

Hood smiled widely. "Got to give that man credit. General Lee ain't one to stray from his purpose." Hood shook his head from side to side. "God help George McClellan," he said, laughing. "He'll be looking for a job before this one is over with."

Longstreet raised an eyebrow, glanced at him. "I'll be damned if I can see the sense in it, Sam. McClellan knows what we're about. He's got the bigger army, he's better equipped, and he may be a damn fool, but even he can see that he's got one hell of an opportunity here." Longstreet paused. "I just can't see the advantage to it. We should pick our spot, make them come to us." Longstreet paused, then said, "Or just plain get the hell out of here and back south of the Potomac while we can."

Moments passed, the horses plodding along, their hooves slapping the dust, raising small clouds of yellow powder with each step. At last Hood said, "Pete, you're my superior officer, and lately we ain't been on such good terms; but we been friends a long time, so I'm gonna' explain this to you as a friend."

Longstreet looked at Hood, repressed the urge to say what he was thinking, that they were all mad. All of them, from the privates up to the generals in this army, all of them who believed in their own invincibility and killing men over a few wagons or something he had said or a game of cards. Instead he said, "Go ahead. God knows I don't understand it."

Hood reached across and slapped Longstreet on the arm in a good-natured gesture. "Hell, if you don't understand General Lee, what chance do you think George McClellan has of divining his purpose?" Hood shook his head, laughing. "C'mon, Pete, think about this. McClellan has our plans, knows just what we're up to here in Maryland. So what does he do? He moves out of Frederick City in typical McClellan style. That means he'll be moving at about half the speed anybody else would, and he'll be towing four times as much gear as any other general who ever marched on God's green earth. He's read all the papers, so he credits us with having twice the number of men, animals, and cannons that we've ever seen. The farther he gets into his pursuit, the more he'll worry about all the things that can go wrong.

"He'll expect General Lee to do just what you're saying. Find a good piece of ground and sit tight. Let McClellan come to him, then fight it out. 'Cause that's what he'd do. Hell, that's what I'd do, for that matter. But he won't think that Lee is in a position to defend the passes over South Mountain; and since his army can't march more than a few miles each day, he won't expect us to countermarch from Hagerstown and make a fight of it at South Mountain."

Hood paused, brought his horse to a halt, pointed at the mountains. "He'll run into Harvey Hill up there, and Hill will fight like a mad dog because, well, because he's Harvey Hill. McClellan will be confused. It's not going according to his plan, not even according to our plan. He'll call a halt, hold a council of war, ask his generals what's going on. They'll have a powwow, and some of them will be for pressing the fight; others will say something different. And all the while McClellan will begin to doubt himself. He'll start to question everything he's done in the last few days, wonder what we're really up to. And in the meantime Jackson will take Harpers Ferry, and we'll give Harvey Hill a hand up there." Hood nodded to indicate the mountains. "And then we'll disengage and form up together on the Antietam or some other spot General Lee likes." Hood paused, watching Longstreet's reaction. "You're still gonna' have your fight, Pete, just we're gonna' have this scrap first."

Longstreet started his horse forward again. "Wish I had your confidence, Sam."

"Aw, c'mon, Pete. It's just like poker. The player who wins is the one who knows the other feller's way of thinking, not the one who holds the best cards."

Longstreet nodded. "Guess I don't much care for the cards we're holding at present," he offered.

Hood grinned, wildly, the light fierce and feverish in his eyes, said, "It ain't the cards, Pete. Its the nature of the man playing the game. All we have to do is carry out the Old Man's orders."

Hood looked at his men, marching steadily in the bright sunshine. "This is a rare army, Pete. Rare. Never seen anything like it." He paused for a long moment, drew a deep breath, asked, "You?"

"No," said Longstreet honestly, knowing it was true, "never before. Not in Mexico, not anywhere."

"They're fighters, Pete. No mistakin' it. And they got faith in Robert Lee, and our time is now, here, on this field, and not anywhere else. In the end, that'll make the difference."

"I hope you're right, Sam," said Longstreet. He glanced at the younger man quickly, aware that he should release Hood from arrest. He was a soldier, and his Texans would follow him like they would follow no one else. Longstreet knew he couldn't do it, not yet. Later this evening maybe, before they got in among the Yankees and Harvey Hill's brigades up on the mountain.

"Aw, sure I'm right," said Hood. "When was the last time you remember me being wrong?" he asked sarcastically.

Longstreet smiled, shook his head. "Poker," he said.

"Yep, just think of it as poker, Pete."

"Well," said Longstreet.

Hood chuckled, wiped the sweat away from his dirty face. "I could go for a drink just about now."

Longstreet held out a canteen. Hood took it, tipped it back, pulled at the water. "I was hopin' for something more substantial."

Longstreet grinned, caught Hood's eye, saw the old Hood shine through, knew the ambulances had been forgotten. "Yep," he said, "might be able to rustle up somethin' later." He glanced at Hood. "Find me in an hour or two, if you've a mind to," he said. Longstreet spurred his horse. "Sam, I'll be seeing you. Stay out of trouble."

Hood tipped his hat and waved good-bye.

RENO LOOKED UP FROM HIS MAPS AND THE SCATTERED DIS-patches, saw shadows lengthening across the little clearing that had become his headquarters. He noted that the sun was going down, dipping beneath the ridges above him, the light failing, slowly, surely, glowing in the tops of trees, the valley below already dim, bathed in shadow. He pulled his watch from his vest pocket, glanced at the face, knew that time was without meaning, that what mattered was how far they could push them, move them off the crest of the mountain before darkness covered everything and the fighting stopped.

He could feel that they were breaking, giving way, slowly. If he could just get another regiment, maybe a brigade into line, one more good push. He was close, very close.

He mounted his horse, determined to ride to the front. Sort things out. It had been difficult, his commanders unable to direct the battle properly. Tough ground to attack over, thick woods, impenetrable brush, all the while his regiments trying to move uphill, maintain their formations among the ravines and boulders. They had fought splendidly.

He would make a reconnaissance of the lines, get a picture of how things were taking shape. He swung the horse out onto the road, moving past the line of broken men limping down the mountain, eyes downcast, spiritless. Shots rang out, scattered volleys, nothing steady. They were losing contact. The Rebels were trying to disengage, break off the fighting for the day.

He rounded a turn, the pines closing in on the road, leaning over the small track, fighting for the sunlight. At once prisoners under guard filled the road to his front. He drew the reins in, the horse sidestepped, snorting, wary of these intruders. Long lines of gaunt soldiers walked past, heads up, defiant. He noted the lack of uniforms, the homespun cloth, a fair sprinkling of what had once been U.S. Army–issue clothing. One man in particular drew his attention. "You, sir," he said loudly, "a word."

The prisoner stopped, broke from the ranks of his fellows, stood silently before him. From somewhere in the marching ranks he heard a catcall. Encouragement. Give 'em hell. The prisoner met his gaze, stared back evenly.

"Your name, sir," he said.

"Samuel," drawled the man, "Samuel Pickens."

"Mr. Pickens," he said, still using his commander's voice, "I'm General Reno, commander of the Ninth Corps."

The prisoner nodded. "Figured you was somebody important," said the man. "That's a fine animal, General."

Reno patted the horse's neck. "I brought this fellow with me from the frontier. A soldier can't afford to let a good mount slip away. They're far too hard to come by."

Pickens nodded, his face thin, brown from the sun, a lean face, hard eyes. "Reckon good horseflesh is good horseflesh, no matter who a man sides with in a fight."

Reno permitted himself a smile. "You're a Texan, sir, are you not?"

The prisoner nodded. "I am," he said proudly.

"General Hood's command?" he asked.

The soldier nodded again, stared at him, steadily, easily. "Yes, sir. Sam Hood's Texas Brigade. Where might you be from?"

Reno paused, wondered at the man's brazenness. "Virginia," he said evenly.

"Don't surprise me none that a Virginia man would know quality in a horse," Pickens said.

Reno smiled, enjoying the exchange. "How is General Hood?" he asked.

"Full of fight," the soldier answered quickly, "same as ever."

Reno laughed. "I'll bet he is," he said. "And how are you fellows in the ranks faring?"

The prisoner smiled. "We're a bit stretched," he said, "but we got plenty of fight left too." The man glanced at his comrades, marching down the mountain. "Reckon we're a long way from callin' it quits."

Reno nodded. "Suppose you are at that." He looked at the sullen prisoners being herded by, saw the angry faces turned his way, the hard stares, knew with an awful certainty that it mattered little if they pushed the Rebels off the mountain today. *There would be more fighting, much more, before this could end and we can all go home.* "Well, Mr. Pickens," he said, "you'll be looked after by my men, treated fairly."

The Texan nodded. "We took a few of you fellers up there," he said, nodding to the crest of the mountain. "Mebbe' I can get exchanged."

"It's entirely possible," offered Reno.

The prisoner nodded. "Reckon there's some fightin' left yet 'fore that can happen."

"Yes," said Reno. "Good luck to you."

Pickens nodded. "Good luck yore-sef, General," he drawled.

Reno raised his hand, touched the brim of his hat in salute. "Thank you," he said, pressing a heel to his horse's flanks. He saw his surgeon nearby, waved him over, a small neat man, compassionate, not used to the vagaries of war, life in the field. Reno thought him bookish, even for a medical man, wondered if it were just the spectacles the doctor wore. He smiled, said, "Well, Dr. Cutter, it would seem we are having quite a day."

Cutter smiled, said, "Yes, I suppose so."

From ahead he could hear firing. Single shots, not the steady roll of massed fire. "They're breaking off, Doctor."

"Yes, General, it's been a long day for our men."

Reno guided his horse around a column of men, saw the regimental flag, new men, green troops. Massachusetts men, volunteers. From the woods on either side he could hear shouted commands. Officers looking for men in the gathering dark, trying to organize scattered companies and herd them into a line. "Damn," he said, to no one in particular.

"Pardon?" said Cutter.

Reno shook his head. "We're losing our advantage, Doctor. We've pushed them all day, but now they will use the darkness to break contact with our men. By morning there'll be enough of them up here to hold these passes for as long as they want." He rode into an open field, saw men moving, emerging from the woods. Green troops, separated from their command, hunting for their regiments before darkness closed in on them. "Harvey Hill and Sam Hood won't lose a minute," he said.

Cutter grinned, seemed uncertain of what to say. "They will fight," he said.

Reno sighed. "Damn funny war," he said, "all of us fighting each other. You would think we were strangers, the way we go at killing one another." Reno remembered something the prisoner had said; the man had wished him luck. No hint of animosity. Damn funny war.

"Should I try and find the officers in charge of these men, General?" asked the doctor.

Reno paused, "No," he said, looking about the field. "In the dark, with unseasoned volunteers, it will be all they can do to find their men and establish some sort of line for the night." Behind him, two orderlies guided their horse into the field a discreet distance behind. From ahead he heard excited voices and men yelling.

Reno saw the flash, felt the bullet strike him. An enormous solid force in his chest, the air rushing out of him, a tightness in his chest where a second before there had been nothing. One of his orderlies was screaming, telling them to stop firing. More shots, from the west, probably some of Hood's men.

The pain hit him first, then the sudden wave of nausea. He ran a hand over his chest, felt the warm blood, waited for another rush of pain. None came, and for an instant he believed it would be all right.

Cutter was saying something, asking him if he was hurt. He dismounted, unsteady, almost falling from the saddle. He lost his grip on the pommel, started to fall, then felt Cutter and an orderly brace him, lower him to the ground. His horse glanced backward at him, ambled off, grazing on the short grass in the meadow.

"Don't worry, General," he heard Cutter say from what seemed a long way off, "it doesn't appear serious."

They rolled him onto a blanket, four or five soldiers carrying him off the field, and he felt suddenly foolish, lying there helplessly, his boots hanging out over the end of the blanket. He felt something in his chest, not pain exactly, just a strange sensation of liquid warmth. He knew then that Cutter was wrong.

An officer leaned over him, and he recognized Sam Sturgis, with the strong hands and the quick laugh and suddenly he felt better knowing that Sam was nearby and would see to things.

"Hello, Sam," he said evenly, "I'm dead." He was surprised at the strength in his own voice, felt a faint glimmer of hope.

Sturgis smiled down at him, laughed once, a real laugh, the old Sam. "Hope it's not as bad as all that," he said.

Reno tried to smile. In the distance he heard a volley, then the Rebel yell. Hood. He had his men up; the fight would be on, Hood and Harvey Hill and all the others. They would give nothing away, make no mistakes.

"Gonna be close, Sam," he said.

Sturgis looked down at him, said, "Probably so."

The thought struck him that all of his own men on the mountain were green, new to the army, untried in combat. Somehow it didn't seem a fair fight; there had been no time to get them ready, make them understand, teach them.

Hood would take full advantage of that. Push them right back down the mountain if they weren't careful. They were good boys, but it was all new to them. It was all happening too fast; the army wasn't able to maintain the pace, train them properly, before committing them to battle. There should have been more time, months of drill, time to learn . . .

Reno felt a terrible sadness overtake him. He could feel it all slipping away. Everything they had all worked for, all the years, all slipping away, all of it for nothing, in the end. Odd, that after all the years it had come to this. He had always thought it would be the British. Not the boys he had been at West Point with all those summers past. *Not like this; it shouldn't end like this*, he thought. It would be lost now, no matter who won. It would never be the same; he understood that now. Can't put it back together, not like before. They had all lost something, all those young faces standing to attention under the old flag. Something more than men die in a war, but he had never understood it before. Not in Mexico, not on the western frontier. Now he understood, and it was too late.

Men were bending over him. Cutter, others. His boys were too green. Harvey Hill and Hood and the others had known that, counted on it, knew that they had the good ground here too. He grabbed someone's sleeve, pulled the man close, the face hazy, out of focus through the pain. It was Sturgis. Good old Sam, depend on him. He would write the letters, tell them back home what had happened, see to that for him. "Sam," he said, "my boys."

"Don't worry about it; I'll see to 'em."

"Tell them that I am with them in spirit, if not in body."

Sturgis was nodding, promising to do it.

He looked at Sturgis. "I'm dead." He paused. Sturgis, Sam Hood, Harvey Hill. All of them, good men, brothers, come to this in the end. It didn't seem fair, wasn't right; they all should have known better, refused to do it, just refused to fight one another. That would have been the better thing; now he saw it clearly, saw past his own anger and outrage, and yet . . . They couldn't do that, at least not refuse and be true to themselves. Duty and honor and a lot of things that had seemed important but weren't, not really. Damn funny war this.

He looked at Sturgis, saw the calm, steady eyes, knew that it would be all right somehow, felt a great flood of affection for the man, for all of them. "Good-bye," he said to Sturgis.

The orderlies laid him under a big chestnut, the black sky woven through its branches. Men were bending over him, Sam Sturgis was talking, issuing orders in that great deep voice, close by, afraid to leave him, there to the last. Reno gazed at the stars moving through the crooked branches, knew that night had fallen, saw the great velvety darkness sweep over them, knew that it was dark on the mountain and the fighting was done for the day and Hill and Hood and the others would be waiting for them up there in the morning and more of them would die tomorrow.

Beyond the voices he heard birdsong, far away, a single bird, lovely clear notes cascading, drifting down the mountain from a long way off. A mockingbird he knew. His mother had told him once, long ago, that only the mockingbird's mate would answer its call, a rare thing, a song of beauty and devotion, a thing to be cherished. Reno closed his eyes, waited long moments, listened for the answering call, heard only silence.

LONGSTREET TOOK THE CUP OF COFFEE OFFERED BY HIS AIDE, the metal hot, stinging his hand. He gulped the coffee, grateful for its warmth, wondering where someone had found the sugar and the coffee, then said, "We'll move back off the mountain later tonight. Leave some of Stuart's cavalry behind, protect our retreat."

Harvey Hill nodded, threw the remainder of his cup of coffee into the fire. "It was a close thing, Pete."

Longstreet nodded. "Yep," he said. He paused, saw that Hill was angry. Knew he was right to be, waited for him to speak. Harvey Hill had been asked to do the impossible, very nearly done it, and now some in the army would blame him for not having done more.

He looked into the lean face of Harvey Hill, said, "General Lee has ordered us off the mountain. We're to march for Sharpsburg as soon as possible."

Hill nodded, moved away from the fire. Longstreet watched him disappear into the dark. He sighed. "Well," he said.

Hood smiled across the fire, his face lit by the flames. "Not going to worry me about McClellan's pursuit, are you, Pete?"

Longstreet sighed. "How many men did you lose today, Sam?"

"A few," said Hood. "Boys pitched into them; it was a bit of a scrape."

"They're getting better, Sam. Learning the trade," said Longstreet.

"Had to happen," said Hood. "Everybody learns a little something if they stay with it long enough."

Longstreet rolled a log closer to the fire, sat down, warmed his hands. "General Lee give you your command back?" he asked.

Hood smiled. "He did."

"I thought he might," said Longstreet easily. "Saves me the trouble of having you court-martialed."

Hood laughed. "Somebody has to lead my boys. They won't follow just anybody, you know."

"They're fine soldiers," said Longstreet. "Texans," he mumbled. "Saw a bit of the West in the old army." He stared into the flames, searched for something to say to Hood, knew that there was nothing to say.

"Old Man won't consider making a fight of it here, Pete? On top of the mountain? Damn good ground. We could hold McClellan off up here while Jackson and the others take Harpers Ferry and rejoin us."

Longstreet shook his head, said, "It won't work. We're too spread out, and McClellan knows it. We've got to disengage, concentrate the army, pick it up someplace else close by."

Hood murmured his agreement, sat beside Longstreet. "Pete," he began, "I've never been able to speak too easily about certain things. Guess I'm not the most genteel fellow."

Longstreet held up a hand to stop his friend. "It's not necessary, Sam." The memory rushed up at him, unexpected, shrouded in grief, a memory of his children, the house in Richmond draped in black crepe, his wife sitting alone in the front room, late into the night.

Hood nodded, gazed steadily into the flames. "Felt I ought to say something, Pete."

Longstreet nodded, looked into the flames. "Consider it done, Sam." He tried to shut out the the memory, had the haunting sensation that it would never go away, that it would never be better. Only his boy left.

Hood rose, threw his coffee into the flames. "Have a drink, Pete?" he asked.

Longstreet looked at Hood, took the small flask from him. "Where'd you find this?"

"Liberated from one of the good citizens of Maryland." Hood smiled, his beard orange in the firelight. "It's nothing your mama ever set the table with, but it ain't bad in its own way."

Longstreet chuckled, took a long pull, the whiskey warm and smooth, burning down his throat. "Not bad," he said.

"Nope," said Hood. "Good for what ails you."

Longstreet nodded, wondered if Hood had meant something by his last remark, dismissed the thought.

"Well," began Hood, "reckon I'll go and see about my boys."

"Yes," said Longstreet, "they'll be the last off the mountain. Get 'em moving by midnight, Sam. And keep 'em quiet if you can."

Hood stood, slapped the dust from his trousers. "Pete," Hood said slowly, "don't worry so much. These boys would march to hell and back for Robert Lee. And they'd fight Lucifer when they got there if Lee gave so much as a nod in that direction."

Longstreet glanced up, saw Hood standing in the light from the fire, staring down at him. He knew that Hood was right, that the men in this army would follow Lee and Hood and the others anywhere, no matter the cost. Longstreet closed his eyes for an instant, had a vision of bodies lying in the rain, of great empty fields of dead soldiers. "Yes," he said slowly, trying not to let his voice betray his thoughts. But none of them understood, not really. It wasn't about who was bravest, or even who was right. It was far simpler than that. It was about rifled cannon and repeating carbines and horses worn to the point of exhaustion, and a thousand other things that had nothing to do with courage or bravery or glory.

Sam Hood would never understand that, and if he did, it wouldn't matter. Life wasn't so precious to Hood that he would sacrifice his honor to keep it. He held the halter of Hood's horse, felt the great silent strength of the animal, waited while Hood swung into the saddle, hoped that somehow Hood wouldn't leave, that he would stay a few more minutes, but there were no words to tell another man that, no right way to say it. In the morning they would be off again, all of them laughing and joking, convinced of their own invincibility, looking for a good spot to make their stand.

One last grand fight, with music and charging horses and cavalry sabers. Fields of glory. They all spoke of it, Hood, and Stuart, and the others, dreamed of fields of glory, talked about it, and honor, and duty. The nobility of dying for your country, writing your name on the rolls of honor, the sort of thing that he could never understand, not really.

In his heart he knew Hood was right. They would march anywhere for Robert Lee. And if there had been no Lee they would have marched anyway, not just for the South, but for a promise of glory. The whole damn lot of them, march and fight until not a single man was left, and everything would be lost except their notion of honor, and what was that in the end?

Hood smiled down at him, a slight smile, the blue eyes pale, shading the fierceness, the determination, tightened his reins, nudged the big horse away. Longstreet was silently glad that his friend didn't know his thoughts. He knew he was fighting something inside, something none of the others wanted to acknowledge, none of them had any interest in: Hood and Jackson and Stuart and the others with their talk of cavalry charges and glory and the whole damn notion that somehow your beliefs mattered more than your tactics. He watched Hood disappearing in the dark, the night closing in around him, had the vision again, a smoky field, rows of soldiers. For a moment it all seemed clear, and then it slipped away, like a gray mist above still water, and the thought was gone and he couldn't call it back. He shook his head, knew that Louise would call it a premonition, told himself not to think more on it, let it go.

Longstreet stood, started to ask Hood to stay another minute, maybe have another taste of that whiskey. Instead he said "Be seeing' you, Sam."

Hood smiled, a smile tinged with sadness, tipped his hat, said a quiet good night.

Longstreet raised a hand, knew that Hood had been thinking of his children too, and something welled up in his throat, and he knew he should say something to Hood but he didn't trust himself to speak; and then Hood was gone, beyond the light, and a wave of unspeakable sadness swept over him. He sat in the glow of the campfire for a time, undisturbed, waiting for it to pass, knowing that it would, that it always did. There would be more fighting, and soon, and men would die and boys he had known for what seemed forever would be gone and it was best not to think too long on it.

Longstreet stirred the fire for long minutes, staring into the coals, his mind racing with a thousand disparate thoughts. A day, maybe two before McClellan would force a general engagement. They would have to concentrate the army, tomorrow maybe, another day of hard marching. He could rejoin Jackson, draw up behind the Potomac, force McClellan to come to them or deny battle.

Longstreet mounted, rode through the night toward Lee, anxious to see the Old Man, feel his strength, his confidence, draw his own strength from that.

Men were moving off the mountain, long files of dirty soldiers walking silently beside him in the night. In the ranks of the marching soldiers there was not much talking. Men spoke in hushed tones, huddled together in small groups, making their way down the narrow road.

Another day. Two at the most.

CHAPTER 6

AMBROSE BURNSIDE SAT HEAVILY IN THE SADDLE, A BIG MAN, with enormous whiskers that stopped just short of being a full beard, he was plainspoken and unassuming, somewhat shy, a man aware of his own limitations, unaccustomed to soldiers cheering at his approach. That sort of thing was better left to men like George McClellan.

The soldiers lining the road now, staring, taking their caps off as he passed, made him feel even more conspicuous than he normally did riding the big gelding.

Burnside smiled, waved at the soldiers as he rode by, felt enormously relieved when he spotted Jacob Cox ahead, grateful that their attention would be diverted from him, that the stares and the cheering would fall away, that he would have someone to talk with shortly.

He swung off the road, headed for Cox, a small, neat man from Ohio. Volunteered for the army when the fighting had started. Burnside seemed to recall a past in politics, but an able man, nonetheless. He moved past lines of men kneeling by cook fires, rows of tents, a burial detail being formed, shovels over their shoulders like rifles, filing off toward a low stone wall where the fighting had taken place the day before. Beyond the soldiers, at the base of the wall, he saw the shapeless waxy mounds that had been men. He had a momentary impression of piles of wash, but then he saw the arms and boots and he understood, beyond any doubt, and a wave of unexpected sadness passed through him like the shadow of a bird that floats past on a summer day.

"Good morning, General," said Cox.

Burnside smiled. "General Cox, how are you this morning?" he asked.

"Fine, sir." Cox waved a hand, pointed toward the crest of the mountain. "The mountain is ours, General. Not a Rebel in sight, with the exception of those we have made prisoners," he said.

Burnside nodded. "They won't have gone far, General Cox."

Cox smiled. "No, sir. But they've gone and it's our men who have forced them."

"Fair enough, sir," said Burnside, "fair enough." He paused, looked about him at the field. "They've given us reason to be proud of them." The meadow where Cox had pitched his headquarters tents was small, a mountain meadow, shrouded in early-morning mist, lined on all sides by oak, and hickory, and straight, tall pines that fought for light and substance in the rocky ground. His eyes strayed back to the wall, toward the soft mounds of bodies that had been living, breathing men only a few hours before.

Someone was speaking, angrily, the words fast, clipped, the tone plain. Burnside turned, saw the man, a lean man who looked as though he had never had enough to eat, simply dressed, his hat rolled into a knot in his hands.

"His home has been damaged in the fighting?" he asked.

Cox hesitated. "Ah," he started, "no, General."

Burnside cocked an eyebrow, "What is the nature of his problem?"

"He feels that his well has been ruined by our men, General," said Cox.

"Ruined?" asked Burnside. "Has it gone dry?"

"No, sir," answered Cox, "some of the burial details have been throwing dead Rebels down his well."

Burnside looked at Cox. "I see," he said. He nudged his horse forward. The officer speaking to the farmer turned, saw him, saluted. Burnside returned the salute, then looked to the man. "Good day, sir. I am General Ambrose Burnside, United States Army."

The man nodded. "Daniel Wise, General. Pleased to make your acquaintance," he said.

"The pleasure is mine, Mr. Wise," said Burnside, feeling suddenly pompous, looking down at the man from astride the horse. He dismounted, extended his hand. Wise looked at him, clear eyes set close together in a lean, sunburned face, but it was the hands that caught his attention. Wise had the hands of a farmer, red and chapped, with great swollen knuckles that closed on his own like a vise. "I understand your well has been used to bury Rebel soldiers," he asked.

"Yes, sir. That it has. And now it's no good to me or anyone else." Wise looked toward the well, added, "It's ruined, sure enough."

"And my men are responsible for this, sir?" asked Burnside.

"They shore are," said the man, "them fellers yonder."

Burnside watched as the man pointed to a group of soldiers. He watched them for a moment, leering, smiling faces above dirty uniforms. "Major," he said, addressing the officer from Cox's staff, "are those our men?"

"Yes, sir, they are," began the major, "but I can assure the general . . ."

Burnside held up a hand to stop the man. "I need no assurance, Major," he said. "If those men are ours and they have ruined Mr. Wise's well, then it is our duty to make right this situation." Burnside looked again at the farmer, noted the simple clothing, saw that Wise was watching him, waiting. "How long would it take for you to dig another well, sir?" he asked.

The farmer turned, looked at his well, ran a hand through his hair. "Don't know, right off," he said slowly. "Mebbe' a few days, mebbe' a week." Wise cupped his chin in one hand, "Mebbe' longer, General," he said. "This here ground is mighty rocky."

Burnside smiled through his thick whiskers, enjoying the exchange. "I see," he said slowly, "and yet wells do go dry, sir, do they not?" he asked.

"True enough," said the man evenly. "But we don't use another man's well for a common grave," offered the farmer. "Least not in these parts."

Burnside nodded, knew that Wise was right. Beyond any defense the army might offer, beyond any reason they might have, the farmer was right. "Your point is well taken, Mr. Wise. My men have transgressed."

For a long moment no one spoke, and then Burnside realized he would have to say something, do something to set the matter right. At last he asked, "How do you propose we remedy the situation, sir?"

"Well," said the farmer, " 'peers to me you got plenty enough fellers here who could lend a hand in diggin' another well."

Burnside repressed a grin. The man's logic was simple but honest. "We have an abundant supply of men, that is so," he said. He looked about Wise's field, saw the small, rough house.

His soldiers had been marching and fighting for the better part of a full day, with little respite. The Rebels were retreating. He glanced at the sun; the hour was early yet. General McClellan would order them forward within the hour unless he missed his guess. His men would be lucky to have enough time to prepare breakfast. "I am afraid that we will have to find a different solution to our problem, Mr. Wise," he said. "My men will be off this morning; and although there are many of them, I cannot spare any to dig another well."

The farmer nodded. "I figured you fellers would want to be off soldierin' before too much longer." Wise turned, glanced in the direction of his ruined well. "Still, that well yonder ain't no more use to me, and I cain't do without water up here, whether you fellers stay or not."

He wondered how the man would get on now, with soldiers buried in his yard, in his well, bodies turning to mold beneath the thin mountain soil. What to tell his children? His wife? And yet he was not a rich man. For Wise there was no leaving this place; he was tied to it, scratching out a living on the top of the mountain, in the thin air, and the poor soil, and the bright light.

Burnside turned to the officer. "What is the army paying for burials of late?" he asked.

The major spat a long stream of tobacco juice into the dust, grinned conspiratorially. "About fifty cents per burial, General," he said.

He stared at the officer in disbelief, the anger rising.

He, too, had dealt with the government. Before the war, he had left the army, invested in a repeating rifle design. There had been talk at the War Department of buying quantities. He had sunk all his savings into it, everything he had, all on a promise made by a government official.

The contract had never materialized. He had been ruined, destitute. He had borrowed money, sought a job, all from old friends, boys he had known at West Point who had done well for themselves. Powell Hill had loaned him enough money to get by, more than that even. Powell had been generous, very generous. George McClellan had found him a job, railroading, out West. He had scraped by, saved himself and his family, with their help.

He had come through it all, but only because of their help. He looked at the major, then back to Wise. Daniel Wise was not a man of means; for him there were no friends from the military academy who might be generous, who might loan him enough money to move on, start new someplace else. For him there was only this farm, and children who needed to be fed, and dead soldiers in his well.

"Major," he began slowly, "I believe that we are responsible for ruining this man's property. I want you to pay him a dollar for each body that has been thrown down his well. Am I understood?" he asked sternly.

"Yes, sir, I understand," said the officer, "but I'm not sure we know how many seccesh got thrown down the well, General."

Burnside flushed, stifled an impulse to scream at the man, struggled to control his emotions. The officer had stood by while his men threw dead soldiers down a well, and now he had the impertinence to try and cheat the owner of the property. "If you can't determine how many men are in the well, then we shall let Mr. Wise give us a fair estimate." He paused, glaring at the major. "A dollar per burial, Major, not a cent less."

The officer nodded. "Yes, sir," he said.

Burnside mounted, touched his horse with his spurs, began to ride off, then stopped. Soldiers and officers in the area turned, waited for him to speak. He turned again, faced the officer. "I'll hear no more about dead soldiers, Rebels or otherwise, being thrown down wells, sir. Is that clear?" he said, loud enough so that all the officers in the area heard him.

The major looked at him, narrow-eyed, the resentment plain on his face. "It's clear, sir," he answered.

Burnside brought his reins across the neck of the horse, moved off toward the summit of the mountain. He forgot about the surly officer, farmer Wise, the dead soldiers in the well. A breeze was blowing down the mountain, cool morning air laced with the scent of honeysuckle and goldenrod. A fair sky overhead, a pallid sky, a late-summer sky with a pale moon that Burnside knew held the promise of heat, real heat, and that the marching men would wilt like so many flowers under the summer sun as the day wore on.

He pushed his horse past a marching column, rode around the men as they struggled up the side of the mountain, past stands of poplar, the leaves fading pale green to yellow, anticipating autumn. A breeze rustled the trees high among the branches, moving them gently, a shower of dry leaves falling in its wake.

He gained the summit at last, a spare, rocky place that had been cleaved by great forces in unseen times, where stunted trees grew bent by a steady wind from the west. Beyond him, stretching away toward the northwest, was a narrow, flat valley. The day was hazy, another sign of the heat to come, and he removed his binoculars and searched the roads below for signs of the Rebel army.

He saw little beyond a few farms, the neat barns rising from green pastures, a dark line of trees following the course of a creek. He inhaled deeply, tasted the morning air, wondered that he was out ahead of the entire army, nothing but a few cavalry patrols between him and the Rebel army.

In the distance, beyond the smoky haze, there was a sudden rumble, a low, angry murmuring that started slowly and built steadily. Trees blocked his line of sight, impenetrable oaks and briars that grew thickly over the slopes, but Burnside knew what lay ahead. A few miles, at most, Jackson and half the Rebel army were shelling the arsenal at Harpers Ferry. The other half of Lee's army lay up the narrow valley, near Hagerstown; just beyond the haze and the pastures and another line of rocky blue ridges was Longstreet. And he had two entire corps between them, poised to strike.

McClellan had been right, Lee had overplayed his hand, sent his army in two directions. Now his men were between the two halves of Lee's army. An easy march over South Mountain, and then turn in either direction and they would have half the Rebel army separated from the other, the trap sprung.

Mac would be ecstatic. Leave it to McClellan in the end. He had always been the best among them from the very first. All of them had seen it, the other cadets at West Point, the army instructors, all of them had known. George McClellan had all the qualities that spelled success, guaranteed you that there was something unique and enviable about the man, that he was destined for greatness.

Burnside knew then that he had been right to turn down command of the army. It was more than a matter of being a gentleman. There was that, of course. The president could be forgiven for not understanding it, that other men, lesser men than George McClellan, had seen to it that he was removed from command of of the Army of the Potomac, that others less able than he had been brought to the fore, considered for command.

But in the pinch, it had to be George McClellan; no one else could have done it. Moved the army north after its defeats in Virginia, chased the Rebel army down, gotten between them in short order.

Now George would bring them to battle. Lee, Jackson, Longstreet, and all the others would be beaten.

The war could be over in a matter of days.

And all because George McClellan was in command.

GEORGE MCCLELLAN ROSE FROM HIS DESK, AWARE THAT RIDERS were approaching, anxious to see who they might be. He had established a temporary headquarters at the base of South Mountain. They had pitched his headquarters tents nearby, a long, neat row of white canvas that stretched across a small meadow some distance from the dust and noise of the road where troops were moving even at this early hour.

His desk had been placed outside, beneath a large oak, and he had worked beneath its canopy in the fresh air, smoking endlessly, the thought nagging him that his wife would complain of the frequent cigars and the lack of proper meals.

Across the meadow he saw the riders dismount, recognized the familiar figure of John Porter, began walking toward him. His eyes were gritty and tired with fatigue, but his spirits were soaring.

He stopped, watched as Porter approached, genuinely glad to see his friend. He smiled warmly. "Good day, General," he said pleasantly.

Porter smiled, extended his hand, said, "George, congratulations on your magnificent victory. My officers tell me that the Rebels are retreating all along our front."

"Yes," said McClellan, feeling the pride surge in his chest. "We have beaten them badly, if I am correctly informed."

Porter laughed, a bass masculine sound that made him feel instantly better. Around them men were smiling, talking of the great victory of yesterday. Porter grinned, said, "Quite a return awaits you in Washington, you know. The papers are full of your advance, the fighting here. Lee retreating, that sort of thing." Porter winked, said conspiratorially, "The ladies are anxious for your arrival."

McClellan laughed, felt the tension melt away. "I hope that I do not disappoint them." He took Porter by the elbow, guiding him away from the gathering of staff officers and couriers who stood nearby. "We have much to discuss, you and I, General," he said.

Porter nodded. "Yes," he said, "things seem to be going very well, George. You've made quite a stir in Washington already."

McClellan took a deep breath, enjoying the moment, hoping the campaign would last a few more days, that Lee and Jackson wouldn't slip back across the Potomac before he got at least one more chance at them. He smiled at Porter. "Lee is in full retreat," he said.

Porter nodded. "Moving back across the Potomac?" he asked.

McClellan nodded. "His army is making for the fords near Sharpsburg."

"And our forces are pursuing?" asked Porter.

He grimaced, wondered how even Porter could expect him to form a pursuit with the army back under his command for only a few days. He attempted a smile, said tightly, "These men are exhausted. I must allow them time to rest." There was a lull in the conversation; the two men walked in silence for some moments.

Porter cleared his throat, began, "George," he said, uneasily.

McClellan caught the hesitant tone in Porter's voice, knew that Porter had some issue to discuss. He was fresh from Washington, would know the rumors, what was being said at the War Department. "Speak freely," he said, "I depend on your friendship, as well as your advice."

Porter took a deep breath. "You know, George, that there are those who do not wish you . . . " He paused.

McClellan raised an eyebrow, glanced at Porter. "Success?" he asked.

Porter stopped walking, looked directly at him, the dark eyes cloudy, unreadable. "Yes," he said firmly. "That's the matter precisely."

McClellan smiled broadly. "After our victory yesterday, the president's cabinet will not be in a position to criticize me in private, more the less in public," he said confidently. McClellan felt a flush of anger, remembering the disgrace of being removed from command. He looked at his friend, saw that Porter did not share his confidence. "You disagree, John?" he asked.

Porter paused, then said, "I do."

For a brief moment McClellan looked into Porter's face, saw the concern, felt it all crashing down around him. They were plotting against him again, officers in Washington who were jealous of his success. Petty men who cared little for the Union, who cared mostly for their own schemes, men who wanted him removed from his command no matter the harm to the army or the country.

He felt the flush of anger, fought back an impulse to find his horse, ride back to Washington, and rage at them, contemptible fools who plotted war from their comfortable desks and believed themselves more capable than he.

Instead, he drew in a deep breath of morning air, looked at Porter, felt enormously weary in an instant, asked, "Will I ever be rid of them, John?"

Porter stared at the ground, shook his head. "I'm not sure," he said at last, his voice tinged with resignation.

"What is it this time? What have they accused me of now?"

Porter knitted his brows, then said, "As always, they wait for you to fail. Some small mistake they can seize upon, defame you to the president." Porter paused. "They talk of replacing you, appointing another officer to command the Army of the Potomac."

"Who?" asked McClellan. "General Pope?" The thought flashed across his mind that they would recall Pope. There would be days of bumbling; Lee would threaten Washington again with his horde. He shook his head, said, "No, they can't recall General Pope. The public would never stand for it. He failed miserably last time, and he would fail again."

He glanced toward Porter, sensed the other man's discomfort, a tension. He asked, "You have heard a name, I take it." There was another long pause. He glanced at Porter, saw the answer flash across his face, thought:

He has heard someone's name, knows that they're waiting to relieve me. At last he said, "We've been friends a long time, John."

Porter looked down, apparently embarrassed, a stricken look on his fine features, said darkly, "General Burnside's success in the Carolinas has not gone unnoticed, George."

"General Burnside is a fine officer," McClellan said automatically, "and he is a friend." For a moment he said nothing, ingesting the news. There had been this sort of talk before; there were always rumors, speculation.

Before the army had marched from Washington, Burnside had come to him, told him that the president had offered him command of the army. Without so much as a by-your-leave they had offered command of his army to Burnside.

Burnside had been noble, refused the command. It was the right thing to do, the act of a gentleman, beyond the understanding of those who would remove him.

"Am I to believe," began McClellan, "that the president and General Halleck are *again* speaking of offering command of my army to General Burnside?"

Porter shrugged, "There has been talk. No names have been mentioned, but the rumors circulate."

"As always, the politicians in Washington expect the impossible of me and of this army," he said bitterly, angrily. He shut his eyes, fought to control his emotions, warned himself against making an angry outburst, saying something he would regret.

"I am afraid you are right," answered Porter.

He wondered silently if it was always to be this way, the eternal questioning by men who lacked his skills, his military experience. He shook his head in disgust, knew that he was fighting two battles, two enemies, both bent on his destruction. He sighed, felt the familiar tightness in his shoulders, the tension that seemed to live there, to plague him with the slow, nagging pain that never really eased. After a moment he looked at Porter, tried to smile, asked, "What do you advise, John? Surely they cannot have expected more of me than I have done this past day."

McClellan swung an arm out toward the pasture, indicating the field where the battle had been fought the day before. "My men have won a brilliant victory. The Rebels are in full retreat; they will move back into Virginia in a day. Two at most. We have regained Maryland," he said. "We have fought a foe of superior numbers, on ground of his choosing, favorable to the defense, and we have beaten him severely."

He shook his head, wondered at their great endless stupidity, envisioned them studying their maps and charts in some smoky room at the

War Department far from the sound of gunfire, said angrily, "What more might they ask of me?"

Porter looked straight ahead, at last answering. "They will claim that you did no more than drive the Rebel army back into Virginia. That next spring, after the roads dry, we will again be forced to fight an invading army."

McClellan stiffened, sensed that what Porter was saying was true, that the newspapers would claim that he had not done enough. None of them understood, truly understood, what was required to organize an untrained mass of boys and make them an army.

He took a cigar from the case in his pocket, remembered the complaints Ellen had made of his constant smoking, wondered what she must be thinking now, what she would think when the stories came out in the papers. He looked at Porter, felt suddenly grateful for his presence, his candor, knew that what Porter was saying was true, that other men were conspiring to remove him.

"I have saved the Union from a marauding enemy army," he said bitterly. "Will that not satisfy them?"

Porter nodded. "They will say that you have only driven the Rebels from Maryland, George," he said.

McClellan looked angrily at Porter. "You agree with them? You think that our victory is not complete?" he asked, the words coming fast, edgy.

Porter held up a hand. "Our victory here, on this field"—he nodded at the stone walls, the broken equipment strewn about the meadows—"is a sound one."

"But," said McClellan, "you believe I might have done more."

Porter shook his head. "No. Not yesterday. You could not have done more, or even better."

"Go on," said McClellan, wondering what was on Porter's mind, what he knew. What was going unspoken.

"The president has made it plain that he desires the Rebel army be destroyed, that General Lee be forced to capitulate." Porter hesitated. "But now we must not rest; we must drive on the Rebels. No matter the condition of our troops, we must pursue General Lee."

McClellan was silent, his hand inadvertently going to his pocket, touching the telegram there. It was from Washington, the president. *Destroy the rebel army if possible,* the president had written. "Yes," he said absently, "you are correct."

Porter looked about, saw the men cooking their breakfasts, waiting for orders. "These men, George, to whom do they belong?"

"General Burnside's wing of the army, the Ninth Corps, with the First

Corps in reserve," said McClellan. "They performed splendidly yester-day," he said proudly. "General Burnside directed the battle personally. I have spoken with him this morning, and he feels that his men would benefit by rest today." McClellan ran a hand across his hat, brushed the dust from the nap, remembered that Burnside had done a fine job of handling his wing of the army during the fighting.

"Perhaps . . ." Porter began, then stopped.

He turned, expectant, waiting, saw that Porter was thinking. "You were saying, General?" he asked.

Porter raised a hand, shifted uncomfortably. "Ah, it is of small conse-quence," he said, "and not my place at that."

"Go on, John," said McClellan. "I must have the advice of my officers."

"Well," began Porter, "if General Burnside feels that his men are fa-tigued from battle, then can we not bring my corps up? My men are fresh, George, and they are regular army, not volunteers."

"You're thinking of the pursuit? Chase Lee to the Potomac."

Porter nodded. "General Lee is retreating, but he must recross the Potomac. If he is making for the fords at Sharpsburg, then my men can, at the very least, harry his retreat."

The thought struck McClellan that it wasn't right somehow, that Burn-side should have the honor of pursuing Lee's retreating army. By rights the pursuit of a fleeing foe belonged to the portion of the army that had defeated it in battle. It was a time-honored tradition. Burnside was a friend, a brother officer.

"Sir?" asked Porter.

McClellan's reverie was broken. "Yes?" he asked.

"Shall I order my men forward?"

McClellan held up a hand, signaling that Porter should wait. He put his hands behind his back, paced a few steps. Porter's men were regular army. Accustomed to hard marching, disciplined. Lee would be moving his columns along rapidly. He would gain the fords by noon, late in the afternoon at worst. He would leave a small rear guard on the northern bank, a few batteries to guard the ford from the southern side, oppose any crossing by pursuing federal units. Porter would be chasing a ghost. Lee would not offer battle again north of the Potomac.

To send Porter after the Rebel army now would do no harm. The cavalry was already out, harrying the retreating Confederates. Infantry support from Porter's men would bolster their pursuit. He would have to be careful, not overextend Porter, offer Lee a tempting target, unsup-ported by friendly units.

His decision made, he nodded. "Yes, bring your columns up through

General Burnside's corps," he said. There was a sudden sharp stab of conscience as he said it, the thought that he was betraying an old friend for a new one.

He shook his head, dismissed the thought. Burn would understand, know that he had only done what any commander would do. Exigent circumstances, fortunes of war, pursuit of the enemy. Burnside would know; he would understand.

Porter smiled. "I shall order them forward at once."

"Yes," said McClellan, "move them up at once."

"A general must use all the resources of his army," said Porter, as if reading his mind.

McClellan nodded, smiled, felt suddenly better. "Precisely so," he answered.

CHAPTER 7

THE SHENANDOAH RIVER DESCENDS IN A SERIES OF WINDING curves from the Blue Ridge Mountains toward Harpers Ferry, the clear water slipping past shallows rippled by limestone and around boulders worn smooth by the passage of the river. Upstream from Harpers Ferry the river widens, the steep banks lined with hickory and oak and broad stands of chestnut, impassable to armies, difficult even for cavalry, except at a few fords.

The Shenandoah turns from its northerly course to skirt the spit of rock where the arsenal at Harpers Ferry had been built, moving past the small town, joined there by the Potomac, the waters of both rivers merging silkily, gliding west, the Blue Ridge towering above their rocky beds all the while.

Stonewall Jackson was familiar with Harpers Ferry, knew its strengths, its weaknesses, the country surrounding it. He had commanded there the previous year when the Confederate army had captured the arsenal, and as he peered into his binoculars he knew the particular difficulties of defending the small town as well as any man.

A thick fog had rolled in during the night, cool night air condensing above the warm water; and now the fog lay in the valley, hovering above the two rivers, gray and torn, shifting with the slightest breeze of early morning, obscuring everything, the voices of the Federal soldiers in the town rising from below floating toward him from beneath the mist in disembodied snatches of sound.

To the east he was able to see the huddled mass of Maryland Heights, its steep slopes covered in foliage, the trees clinging to the sides of the mountain, vague and indistinct in the gray light. Beyond the summit, concealed beneath the shimmering green canopy of oak and hemlock, the division of Lafayette McLaws was waiting, if all had gone according to plan.

He motioned to an aide and the signal gun was fired. Orders were shouted, strong voices calling in the gray light, and the batteries began to find their rhythm, the heavy brass cannon leaping with each recoil, the crews soon sweating and straining to work the pieces, muscling the heavy cannon back into place after each shot. From the direction of the town a single cannon fired in response to his guns, the shell

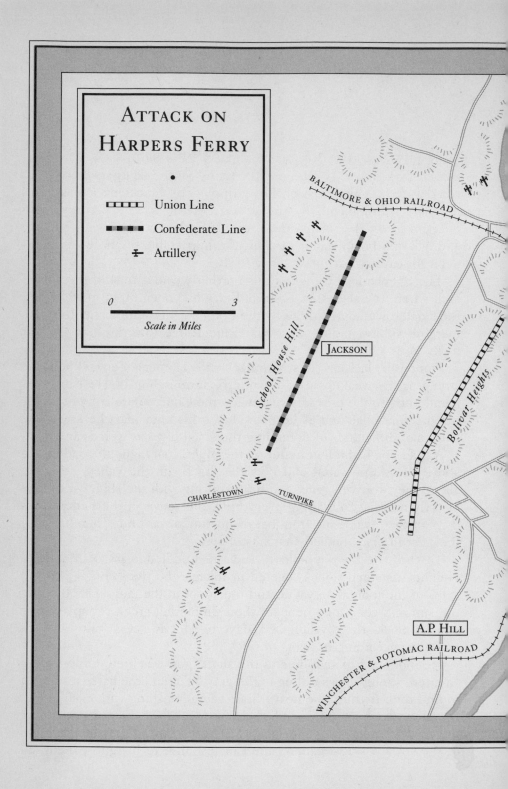

ATTACK ON
HARPERS FERRY

•

▭▭▭ Union Line

▬▬▬ Confederate Line

╪ Artillery

0 ▬▬▬▬ 3

Scale in Miles

BALTIMORE & OHIO RAILROAD

School House Hill

JACKSON

Bolivar Heights

CHARLESTOWN TURNPIKE

A.P. HILL

WINCHESTER & POTOMAC RAILROAD

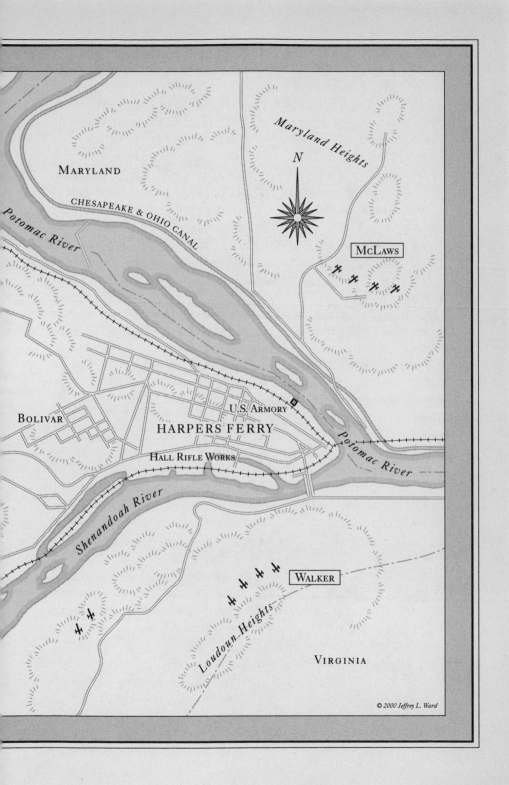

falling well short of his works, a black geyser of smoke and dirt rising between the lines.

He smiled grimly, wondered again why the Union commander had tried to hold on, why he had not simply abandoned the town, fired the military stores, saved his men. Across the river there was a bright flash of orange, and he knew then that McLaws had taken the heights, that his guns were responding to his own firing.

It was no accident that Lee had assigned the taking of the heights to McLaws. He was a competent officer, slow, plodding, methodical. Jackson knew him from the old army, a man of great physical strength, an officer who would never be brilliant but who could follow orders, a man who accomplished what he set out to do if the mission was clear and if nothing extraordinary took place. Legendary strength, determination of a bull; a man you could depend on so long as nothing went far from wrong.

He glanced again at the heights, knew that if sweat and muscle could move cannon up those heights, then McLaws would have done it. No finesse, nothing fancy, but that wasn't what was needed here.

Relief washed over him at the sound of the firing from the distant bluff, and he silently thanked the Almighty that McLaws had taken the heights, managed to get at least a gun or two up the mountain. Had he not . . .

He shook off the thought, wondered again at the reports that the Federals were moving well, closing in on them from the east. The thought flashed across his mind for the thousandth time that if McClellan got across South Mountain, McLaws would be left uncovered, helpless, unable to turn and get off the mountain before McClellan took him in reverse.

Unlikely. It all seemed improbable, despite the reports from the cavalry and the firing that he had heard late the day before. Not like them to move that fast, not like McClellan to move at all.

Kyd Douglas approached, smiling, a boy playing soldier, enjoying it all, the uniforms and the excitement, even the hardships. "Morning, General," he said brightly, happily, anxious to lend some assistance.

Jackson nodded. "Mr. Douglas."

"The infantry are almost in position, sir."

He turned, saw the line of men standing in ranks, expectant, waiting, knew that for them there was no joy in what was about to take place, only grim determination. From the town there was the sound of a loud explosion, the noise rushing up from below, reverberating, bouncing off the rocky cliffs, rolling away, fading in the distance. A shell had found an ammunition locker, the powder exploding with a great crashing that sent wood and bricks flying somewhere below, in the town, out of sight. Beneath the mist, he knew, men were dying.

There were nervous glances from the soldiers in the ranks. He could feel them watching, waiting for him to give the signal, move them forward. Not long now. He would order the guns to stop firing, conserve their ammunition, move the infantry forward.

Across the top of the rise he could see the Union works, a log barricade, men walking about, shadows caught in halting, half-seen motion behind their fortifications. In front of their line they had felled trees; the tops had been thrown together, twisted into a tangle that would slow his men, give the Federal cannon a chance to fire on them. The infantry over there would be waiting too. It would be decided close in, if it came to that.

He waved Douglas over, said, "Order our batteries forward; I want them to cover the advance of our infantry."

The boy nodded, made ready to leave, hesitated, said uneasily, "Yes, sir."

He turned to Douglas, his mind clear, focused, seeing it all, knowing what would happen, what must happen. Knowing that if he delayed another hour, another day, then Lee and Longstreet and all who followed them would be trapped north of the river, forced to fight with their backs to the Potomac, his men unable to support them.

"You have a question, Mr. Douglas?" he asked coldly, sternly, staring straight ahead, concentrating on the enemy behind the logs, waiting for his infantry.

"How close should our guns be run up, General?" There was a long pause, Douglas's voice unsure, reluctant.

He choked down his frustration, cautioned himself not to snap a reply at the boy as he was wont to do. None of them understood, not really. It was simple, if you thought about it simply, but none of them seemed to grasp it. Warfare was a matter of finding the enemy, bringing him to battle, fighting him to the death.

Too many of his officers were like Douglas. They saw it all as a great adventure, a matter of honor, or principle, or a thousand other things that mattered not at all in the final analysis when two armies faced each other across some field.

Better not to think, to grow too close to men who might die tomorrow, or even today. Better still not to remember the old army, think of the men on the other side as comrades, friends. They had been that and more, but now they were the enemy and he could not think of them any longer as comrades. It mattered little now that they had all been together once, friends.

Lee would not agree, would not allow himself to think of them as the enemy. Lee could not bring himself to it, could not speak ill of them. To Lee it was all a matter of duty, something that had to be done and so you did it, and you tried not to remember all that had passed before; and hopefully, when it was over, they might all be friends again. Lee retained his compassion, harbored no ill will toward the men beyond the barricade.

But he was not Lee, could not hope to be Lee, even for a moment. A man like Lee you watched, you learned from him, you followed orders and hoped that you didn't disappoint him; and when it was all said and done, maybe you had been of some service.

Lee was admired, revered even. His reputation grew daily, and when men spoke of him they spoke in the hushed tones you used in the back of church before service, as though he were something more than a man and you didn't want to offend him by interrupting when he might speak.

Lee had that effect on men, made them better than they were, even if it only lasted a short while; and when he was gone, it was as if the light had gone from the room and everything was dimmer and less clear than before and you no longer felt as though you could live up to something better than yourself. But he was not Lee, and so he removed himself from his compassion, and his memories, and he thought of the men beyond the barricades as the enemy, not as men even, and that made it all easier somehow.

It all seemed clearer, in some ill-defined way, if he did not remember all the old times, the campaigns gone by, when they were together, and they shared everything, or sometimes nothing, but they were together, and that made it seem all right. And so he chose not to remember, not to think of what had been, what had passed between them in other times. Other men might call it cowardice, but that was his way and he knew no other, and it was his strength, and he drew on it when he faced them, and he offered an explanation to no man.

There was a brief moment, a year past, when it might have been settled without blood; but that moment had passed and blows had been struck, and no man was capable of changing that.

Too much had passed. Too many battles, too many deaths, for things to ever be the same. Now it was only the fighting that mattered, and even that paled in comparison to what really mattered, and that was victory, never giving them a moment when they might feel triumphant, never allowing them to sense that somehow they might prevail, put it all back the way it had been before. But it could never be like that again, it wasn't possible; and all of them, the men around him now and the men in the valley below, knew it.

In his heart he understood that even if he were to survive the war, to live beyond the marching and the fighting and the killing, that he could never be at peace with them again. It was far simpler than that. They had become the enemy, not an ill-defined enemy that you despised from a great way off, but a flesh-and-blood enemy that bled when you fired on him, whose guns killed and maimed those around you, and whom you had sworn to destroy in the very depths of your soul.

And so now it was different, they were different, and it was as if he had never known them, never shared a meal or a drink or even hardship with them. Men who had been friends, companions, were now his enemy, and nothing was simpler or clearer than that. And the enemy was someone you went after, you cornered, you fought to the last; and they were waiting for his soldiers beyond the mist and the tangle of fallen trees, and they had rifles and cannon that tore flesh and destroyed formations and made it all more clear in one instant than any textbook he had ever studied.

In the end it mattered little that young officers like Kyd Douglas, who were not really officers at all but merely boys off playing soldier, did not understand him. What mattered was that they had confidence in him, obeyed him when he gave an order, feared him. That mattered, and precious little beyond that, and so he turned toward Douglas and he thought, not of the men who would die, or the endless casualty lists in the Richmond papers, and not of the families back home who would wait for a letter that would never come, and he said, "Order the batteries run far enough forward that they might load with double-shotted canister and instruct them to fire on those barricades as our infantry advances."

He raised a hand, stopped Douglas from saying anything, stared straight ahead, beyond the Federal lines. After a moment he said, "See to it, Mr. Douglas, and be clear about my instructions to the battery commanders."

The boy saluted and wheeled off on his horse. Jackson glanced at the sun rising steadily over the mountains to the east, calculated that his guns had been firing for close to an hour. That meant a caisson or more of ammunition for each piece had been expended. The ar-

tillerist in him calculated the expenditure of ammunition, the number
of wagons in his train carrying ammunition for the cannon.

He would have to stop the bombardment and soon. He would need
his ammunition to cover Lee's movement back across the Potomac,
or to throw against an attack by McClellan if it came to that.

He glanced again at the sun, wondered that the day was slipping
by, worried again that he was behind schedule. The thought that he
was falling behind, that Lee was waiting for him, that he and the rest
of the Confederate army were separated and vulnerable and rivers
and mountains and miles of road lay between them, nagged at him,
festered in the back of his mind, pressed upon him like a weight.
Each moment that passed bore into him, brought him closer to failure,
McClellan closer to victory.

The arsenal should have been taken by now, reduced by artillery,
captured by his infantry. The army should have been concentrated,
moved beyond Harrisburg, beyond reach of the advancing Federal
columns. Lee and Longstreet were waiting for him, holding McClellan
at bay with whatever they had, buying more time with lives, perhaps even the life of the army.

But now he was out of time and so his infantry must advance
whether or not he had properly prepared the enemy works with artillery, and he could not afford to expend much more ammunition in
any event. He rested both hands on the pommel of his saddle, stared
at the ground for a long moment, wondered at the cruelty of it all,
knew that there was never enough of anything, but certainly there
was never enough time or ammunition.

He motioned for a courier. The man spurred his mount, drew close,
saluted hastily. "Go to General Ewell," said Jackson without pream-
ble. "Advise him that now is the time for his guns to cease firing."
The courier galloped off through the early-morning mist. Ewell's batteries were the signal guns. Walker and McLaws, if they followed his
instructions, would know that his infantry was making their attack
now, would follow his lead, cease firing with their cannon.

He turned to glance at his staff, saw the expectant faces, knew that
they were becoming accustomed to winning, driving the Federals before them. Douglas was trotting toward them on his horse, sitting the
animal perfectly, calmly, as if he had been a soldier his entire life.
Jackson signaled him over, waited.

"Sir," said the aide expectantly.

Jackson held up a hand, "Not yet, Mr. Douglas," he said. The
infantry brigades were forming for their attack. Gray-and-brown lines

of men stood quietly, shoulder to shoulder, rifles at right shoulder arms, bayonets held aloft, a gleaming metal forest hovering over their heads, moving ceaselessly as the men shifted, the flags hanging limply in the heavy morning air. Units were shuffled into place, below a slight rise, unobserved by the enemy, a long line of silent men that extended into the gray mist, blended with it, melted out of sight beyond his vision.

From across the field a cheer rose, he lifted his head, saw the reason. A battery of artillery was advancing to a position between the lines. He watched as the guns were wheeled into line, mud and turf flying from the heavy wheels in symmetrical arcs, the artillerymen moving quickly into action. One of the crews unlimbered a gun and fired a shot, the heavy iron ball skittering along the ground, slamming into the Union breastwork with a dull thud, bounding recklessly over the logs. There was another cheer from the Confederate infantry, men laughing, nervous laughter that had the smell of fear about it, men in the ranks turning to one another, speaking softly as the laughter died away.

A rattle of musketry rose from the Federal lines, smoke rolled out from between the logs, drifted lazily over the field, merged with the fog and mist that hovered everywhere. Behind his brigades there was the splat of lead hitting branches and the trunks of trees, leaves drifting lazily to earth, cut by unseen bullets. The Federals were aiming high, shooting over the heads of his men.

A horse whinnied in pain, a long, screeching gasp that raced along the grass and scythed through the ranks, an inhuman sound that unnerved men. Soldiers standing in the ranks were turning, looking toward the battery where the animal had gone down. The gelding was struggling to rise, swinging its head with the effort, unable to get to its feet, its eyes savage and wild with fright.

Douglas rode up, drew in just short of Jackson and the others. "Major Pegram sends his compliments, General," the boy said above the din. "He has assured me he will engage the Yankees as our men go in, sir."

"Very well, Mr. Douglas," said Jackson, not lifting his gaze from the field, wondering when someone would have the presence of mind to shoot the downed horse. "Keep yourself available to me; I may have further need of you." There was another high-pitched scream from the horse; men were shouting for someone to shoot it. A single shot, clear, distinct above the other sounds, and the animal settled to the earth with a sickening final gasp.

From the left Jackson heard the steady throb of drums, a brigade assembling, preparing to advance, moving into the line on the double-quick. A roar of musketry followed, crashed down over him, rolled away. Ewell was beginning his attack; someone had gotten close enough to order a volley. There was a long, high-pitched shriek of massed men, a savage yowl that rose above everything, pierced the heavier bass sounds of battle.

Moments now before the attack would begin in earnest. The firing from the town had slackened, almost nothing from beyond the barricade to their front. He knew that the Union gunners would be saving their ammunition, loading a single powder charge, ramming home two charges of deadly canister, waiting for his infantry to come within range.

Beyond the town and the river, high on the bluff, more cannon were firing. Slowly, a measured steady fire, the shells arcing down, falling in neat semicircles, plunging into the mist that hung over the town, exploding with sharp thuds beneath the gray curtain. McLaws was conserving his ammunition, each shot distinct, careful. Jackson glanced again toward the towering bluffs, knew that McLaws would have limited ammunition available to him. Better to get the infantry under way before he was forced to quit his bombardment, give away their weakness.

To his right there was a swelling of sound; men were screaming, yelling. Not a battle cry, not like before when they were making ready to advance; this was different, less primal, the sound mixed with laughter, excitement.

Another cheer from the Rebel brigades beyond his vision. A staff officer shouted, the man's words indistinct beneath the noise of cannon. Other officers behind him were smiling, pointing toward the Federal works.

Riders had bounded over the Federal barricades, a dirty white cloth trailed behind one of the men. A flag of truce.

Along the lines to his front the barrage slowed, then stopped, almost abruptly. There was a sudden ringing in his ears, smoke drifting in huge mottled swaths of black and gray, obscuring men and horses, filling his nostrils with the bitter smell of powder.

A single horseman broke from the group of riders, cantered toward them, appeared unsure of just where to go, his face a mask, unreadable, emotionless. He nodded to Kyd Douglas, motioned him forward with a slight wave of his hand, and the boy was bounding off amid flying hooves and small bits of sod kicked up by his horse, galloping toward the Union officer.

Jackson waited, resting his hands on the horn of his saddle while Douglas spoke with the Union officer. From beyond the town, high above, cannon continued to fire. Single shots, breaking the silence, ringing down the stark, rocky walls of the canyon, rolling away over the water.

A second Southern officer appeared, trotted his horse lazily toward Douglas and the Federal officer. Jackson recognized Powell Hill, one of his division commanders. A man as small in stature as McLaws was large. Powell Hill was a fine officer in the fight, but temperamental, jealous of his reputation, his position in the army. A difficult man to command.

A week past Powell Hill had failed to have his division assembled and on the march at the appointed hour. He had ridden along the delinquent column, herded regiments and brigades onto the road, gotten them moving without Hill. There had been an angry exchange between them later that morning, accusations had been made. Hill furious, sputtering, offering his sword, refusing to serve without satisfaction.

Jackson had ordered Powell Hill under arrest, confined him to the rear of his column, Jackson blind with his own anger, at the failure to obey orders. Hill had attended West Point. There was no excuse; he was a professional. You obeyed orders, you accomplished the mission, you did not make excuses to superiors. It was as simple as that and Powell Hill knew it, and he would have his men on the road when ordered or he would leave.

His instructions had been clear, precise; he had left no margin for error or misunderstanding. Hill had failed to abide by them, had cost him precious time, disobeyed an order.

That had only been days ago, a week at the most. He had restored Powell Hill to the command of his division only yesterday, when Kyd Douglas had spoken on his behalf. It was the prudent thing to do; there was a battle to be fought and Powell Hill was a fine division commander. There would be plenty of time after the campaign to court-martial him; right now he needed Hill in command of his men so long as there was fighting to be done. Other matters could wait.

He urged his horse forward, walked the animal toward Hill and Douglas and the Federal officer. He was met by Douglas, his face restrained, excited. "The Federals wish to surrender, sir," he said. "They are asking the conditions of your terms, General."

Jackson nodded to the young aide, trotting his horse toward Powell

Hill and the Union officer. He said, "You will introduce us, Lieutenant Douglas."

Douglas nodded. "General Thomas Jackson, allow me to present Brigadier General Julius White, United States Army."

Jackson bowed stiffly to the officer, noted the clean uniform, the polished buttons gleaming against the blue cloth. "My compliments to you, sir," said Jackson formally. Powell Hill sat his horse, said nothing, his face a mask, his pale eyes cloudy, unreadable.

The Union officer bowed. "General Jackson," he began stiffly, "I am here to ask you the conditions under which I might surrender my men, sir."

"You must surrender your command unconditionally, General White," said Jackson. "We are prepared to treat you honorably, but I cannot give you terms other than these."

There was a long pause, White's face ashen, bloodless. At last he said, "I understand, sir. I would request that my officers be allowed to retain their sidearms as well as their mounts."

Jackson nodded. "Yes," he said, "of course. General Hill will see to the specifics of your surrender and will draw up the documents for your signature. Your men will be well treated."

"Thank you, General."

Jackson touched the bill of his cap, glanced at Powell Hill, reined his mount back toward his own lines. He called over his shoulder, "Ride with me, Mr. Douglas."

The boy drew alongside, smiling. "We've had a fine day, sir. All the brigades are reporting very few casualties."

Jackson nodded, mumbled a reply. "We must prepare the men for a movement north, Mr. Douglas."

"Yes, sir," smiled the boy. "We'll be joining up with General Longstreet's command then?"

Jackson ignored the question. There was no need to tell Douglas what his plans were; he would know soon enough. "Order the regimental commanders to have their men cook two days' rations. I want them ready to march as soon as possible. We will be moving by day's end."

"Yes, sir," said Douglas. "I shall have the orders drawn up and passed to the regimental commanders."

Jackson walked his mount to a grassy knoll. Already Union soldiers were appearing above their breastworks, shouting to his men, bartering. He glanced at the sky, saw the sun, a clear circle of light beyond the gray air. It was early yet. Plenty of time for the men to make the most of the captured Federal stores, cook their rations, exchange their rags for captured Northern uniforms. They would rest during the afternoon heat, resume their march late in the day.

What news he had indicated that McClellan was moving rapidly, pressing toward South Mountain, threatening to drive his army between the two wings of the Southern army.

Stuart and his horsemen would have to delay them. It shouldn't be overly difficult. It was a matter of deploying a light gun or two, blocking a road with a few dismounted cavalrymen, force the Yankees to break their column of march, assume a battle formation. A few shots in their direction and then the cavalry could remount and ride out of harm's way, repeat the procedure at the next likely spot. That would slow the Federal columns, particularly if it were done in the mountains. Stuart and his men were expert at it; it should give Jackson the balance of a day to rejoin Lee and Longstreet, concentrate the army.

Lee would pick a good piece of ground, force the Yankees into a battle on terrain of his liking. Time. Now it was a matter of time. And distance. His men were accustomed to hard marching, and they would be ready to move in a few hours. He silently thanked the Almighty and the Union officer who had not been quick enough to fire the arsenal. His troops would eat well today.

He glanced about, saw Douglas waiting, watching him. "Mr. Douglas," Jackson began, "are you familiar with the fords of the Potomac River north of here, near Sharpsburg?"

"Somewhat, sir," said the young lieutenant.

"What would their condition be at this time of year, sir?" asked Jackson.

Douglas hesitated. "The closest ford between us and General Lee is Boteler's Ford, near Shepherdstown, General. It is passable this time of year."

Jackson waited, saw the younger man was thinking. Jackson remembered the boy lived close to Shepherdstown; he would know the country. "Passable for an army, Mr. Douglas?" he asked.

"The ford will be rocky, sir. And it can be deep, but it is passable for men and animals."

Jackson nodded. "That is very well, Lieutenant, but we also have a fair number of cannon and our baggage train with us. We must be able to move them across this ford."

Douglas hesitated, then continued. "We will be able to move cannon across, General. The river is not too deep at Boteler's Ford, and the ford is a fairly wide one, sir." The younger man hesitated, then asked, "Will the army be moving north of the Potomac, sir? To rejoin General Lee in Maryland?"

Jackson placed both hands on the pommel of his saddle, leaned forward, looking toward Harpers Ferry. He ignored the younger officer's question, thinking instead of General McClellan. He would know soon that Harpers Ferry had fallen. If he were to advance rapidly to the northwest, he could move enough men to Sharpsburg by the end of the day to force Longstreet and Lee into a battle they had no hope of winning. Lee would have the Potomac at his back, the one ford his only line of retreat. The Rebel force at hand would be outnumbered by at least two to one, possibly far worse. It was imperative that his men start northward as soon as possible to rejoin Lee and Longstreet.

"This army will move north to the ford at Shepherdstown at the first possible moment, Mr. Douglas," he said absently.

"Yes, sir," said the aide.

"I desire that it be made clear to my officers that we must reach Sharpsburg and the Potomac fords with all haste."

"Yes, sir," said Douglas.

"Signal General McLaws that he is to join us by moving his men across the river as soon as he is able, and that his men should be ready to march at the first possible moment."

Jackson turned, looked toward the rocky bluffs across the river, wondered what McClellan would be thinking. *He'll hesitate,* thought Jackson, *at least for a time. A day. Perhaps two.* If General Lee meant to give battle north of the Potomac, in Maryland, then a general engagement would be fought near Sharpsburg. It was Jackson's duty to join Lee and Longstreet.

The bulk of the day would pass while his men cooked rations and made ready to move. He would march them through the night if he had to, but by tomorrow morning they must be reunited with Lee north of the Potomac or face ruin the second time in as many days.

Jackson turned, saw Douglas waiting for instruction. "Find Powell Hill," said Jackson. "Advise him that he must see to the surrender of these men as quickly as possible, then move to Sharpsburg via Boteler's Ford." Jackson again lapsed into silence, deep in thought. After some moments he became aware that Douglas was waiting for further orders. "Attend to your duties, sir," he said. Douglas saluted quickly, then rode off to find the brigade commanders.

CHAPTER 8

THE VILLAGE OF SHARPSBURG RISES OVER A ROCKY PLATEAU BE-tween Antietam Creek and the Potomac River, surrounded by small farms that crowd against the limits of the village and trace the path of the roads away toward the north and east. Farmer's fields are marked by rough, irregular outcroppings of limestone that rise from beneath the grass, run in broken lines through fields of corn and hay, breaking the surface to glow whitely, bonelike, in the summer sun.

The midday heat made the white houses appear to dance and shim-mer, the dark roofs steady, floating on the shifting walls as the South-ern army approached. Weary soldiers in the ranks had the impression of a town deserted, abandoned by its inhabitants, given over to their presence. Everywhere shutters were drawn as against a late-summer storm, animals herded into the great shadowy barns, the air heavy with heat and dust from the approaching army that crowded the roads, pushed into the town, flowed through its streets in long, hot columns.

From a hill nearby Robert E. Lee watched the marching soldiers, long, broken lines of men tramping through the heat, heads down, salt stained. He stroked the neck of his horse, feeling the animal's damp warmth, breathing deeply, the scent of the big stallion remind-ing him of home. A breeze moved through the oaks overhead, the leaves moving slightly, rustling with the dry sound of ancient paper, a fragile sound, high among the branches. Lee glanced at the sky, searched for some sign of rain, saw only pale blue, a white heat that promised no relief from the sun.

Men passing by saw him, tipped their hats, smiled shyly. Shining red faces, slick with sweat, openmouthed, moving past him in the stifling air, staring. He returned the salute, touched the brim of his own hat.

A group of soldiers broke ranks and approached him, thin boys with weary faces, deep-set eyes, doe eyes, watching him, waiting, won-dering. He looked on as they were stopped by his calvary escort, waved to the trooper. "Let them pass," he said slowly.

They came toward him slowly, cautiously, timid. "Good day, sir," said one of the soldiers, a boy with dark hair and a black rifle. A velvety voice, smooth and low, a lovely accent, that made Lee think of the mountains and home and warm summer evenings. He looked down upon the lean face, into dark eyes that gave nothing away, looked back evenly into his own. Other men were nodding, urging this boy to speak. There had been a hasty discussion; no doubt, he had been appointed a matter of importance.

Lee smiled. "Good afternoon," he said. The soldier smiled, a nervous smile. "You are a Virginian, sir, are you not?" Lee asked politely.

The boy nodded. "That I am, General Lee," said the soldier, turning to glance at his fellows, seeking assurance.

Lee smiled, stroked the great warhorse again. He had acquired the animal years before the war in Rockbridge County, an extraordinary animal. "Are you from Lexington, by chance?" he asked.

"Hard by there, General," said the man. "My house is nearer to Goshen, a mite to the northwest of Lexington."

In the boy's words there was the peculiar accent of the Blue Ridge. Lee thought of blue-green mountains, cool breezes, mossy creeks, silver-green fish rising in dark waters to dappled sunshine. "I see," he said absently. "It is handsome country there. Not unlike the country we have just passed through."

"Yes, sir," said the soldier proudly. "It is fine country. Fine country."

"They breed excellent horses in those mountains," said Lee. He patted Traveller's neck affectionately, felt the great strength abiding in the patient animal. "I found this good fellow there," he said proudly.

"Yes, sir," said the soldier, "it's horse-breedin' country, that's for certain."

Behind the soldier an officer cleared his throat. Walter Taylor. There would be dispatches, work to be done. The boy glanced rearward, saw Taylor waiting, impatient, jealous of his time. "Ah, this is all very well," Lee said, trying to put the soldier at ease, "but I believe you have in mind some business in which I might be of assistance?"

The soldier gripped his hat with both hands, twisting it into a tight bundle. "General," he began, "if it wouldn't be too much trouble, sir. Me and some of the boys was wonderin' if we was going to have a fight soon, sir. You see, the thing is, we are most played out from the marchin' and all. We'd just rather sit still a bit and let the Yankees come on to us."

"I see," said Lee. He paused, searching for the right words, aware that the men before him were waiting. Odd army, volunteers, and yet they march and fight like true soldiers. But they were not, and you could not lead them the way you led a professional army. These men did not fight for pay, or seek advancement, they answered a higher calling; and so he must remember that, make allowances, speak to them the way you spoke to a neighbor, or a son.

A word came to him from his school days: *yeoman*. An old word, an older concept. English, very old. Must have been something like this then. Free men, who served no king, who fought for freedom and their rights, and who would answer no master.

"We have endured much," he began, "but we have more before us." He looked again at the thin boys, saw the worn faces, the tired eyes. "We are fighting for the right to build our own nation, for our rights as Virginians." He paused, realizing that the soldiers standing before him simply wanted to know when the grueling marches would end, when they might rest, return home.

Lee turned, looked past the village, saw the ridge just beyond it, a shadowy wood, a promise of cooler air. The Potomac River would be beyond those trees, and beyond that, Virginia. He felt suddenly tired, weary of it all. He told himself: *Soon. We might all be home soon.*

He faced the small group again, smiled down at them as a father might, had a fleeting thought of his own boys somewhere in the marching ranks. Word had come that one of his sons was wounded. Mary's son. He would have to explain that, tell her of it, make her understand that they were not just her sons, they were Virginia's sons. "We shall make our stand on those hills."

The boy nodded, a wispy smile. "Yes, sir," he said evenly.

"Well, then," said Lee, "you must return to your commands. It would not do for you to fall behind."

"Yes, sir." The soldier nodded. "Thank you, General," he said.

Lee watched, saw the soldier and his fellows walk slowly back, rejoin the marching column. He turned his gaze to the east, looked again at the dust-covered columns. In the distance he noted a familiar figure on horseback, massive shoulders, a firmness in the saddle, the hint of great strength, even at this distance. He waited patiently, glad that Longstreet was here, anxious to speak with him.

Longstreet dismounted, handed his reins to an aide. He smiled. "Good day, General," Lee said warmly.

Longstreet grinned, nodded, slapped dust from his trousers noisily. "Hello, General Lee," he said.

There was an exchange of pleasantries, Longstreet guarded, anxious to speak, searching for the words. Lee waited, knew Longstreet would come to it in his own time, his own way. A breeze moved the branches and Longstreet was bathed in bright light; Lee noting with alarm the fatigue on his face, an unhealthy pallor, and then Longstreet shaded his eyes and shadow fell across his face and he was the same indominitable Longstreet.

Lee felt a sudden chill, a cold, eviscerating shadow passing through him, thought: *I cannot afford to lose him. Not Longstreet.* "You must take care to get your rest, General," he said. "I need you to be at your best."

Longstreet smiled up at him, oblivious, full of the vitality of youth, said, "Been hard pressed the last few days." There was a pause; on the road the army rattled by. "Not like McClellan to come on this fast," he remarked.

"No," Lee agreed, "he is moving more rapidly than we might normally expect."

"He gave our cavalry a run for their money this morning, near Boonsboro."

Lee raised an eyebrow, glanced at Longstreet. Not like General McClellan to move that fast. A new factor, something to think about, remain wary. "A pursuit is not unexpected, even from General McClellan. We have enough infantry available to handle any affair with his cavalry."

Longstreet nodded. "We do," he said slowly, running a hand through his hair, "but we need to concentrate." Another pause, then, "How far along are Jackson's people?"

"Harpers Ferry fell this morning. I expect General Jackson's divisions to begin arriving this evening, perhaps tomorrow morning."

Longstreet grunted, chewed his cigar, said nothing. Lee turned away, knew that Longstreet was thinking they should move back across the Potomac River, use it as a barrier between themselves and the Federal army.

"You prefer a movement across the Potomac?" Lee asked.

Longstreet stared straight ahead, said nothing for a long moment, then, "Makes sense. We're strung out, Jackson's people will be tired when they get here. If McClellan hits us first, we don't have enough infantry to hold him off while Jackson moves up."

"General McClellan will not attack today," said Lee.

" 'Spect not," said Longstreet evenly.

"I do not think he will believe himself ready to attack tomorrow either."

Longstreet smiled, slowly, a patient smile, a look of amusement on his face. He turned to Lee, the brown eyes bright, shining, "Nope. Not like ole George to be in a hurry."

Lee felt instantly better, said quietly, "No."

"Still, we move back across the Potomac today, leave a few guns at the ford to slow 'em down, and we could be back with Jackson by nightfall, concentrate the army on the south shore somewhere, make 'em come to us."

"General McClellan would not pursue us into Virginia. He will consider that he has done all he can if we retreat back across the Potomac River."

"Suppose so," said Longstreet. "But the boys could use a rest. Harvey Hill got pretty cut up yesterday on South Mountain."

Another pause, more men moving past. A band playing, an unrecognizable melody, strained, wafting through the hot air. Lee thought: *His mind is set. He thinks we should move south, abandon Maryland, put the Potomac River between ourselves and General McClellan's army.*

He took a deep breath. He knew that Longstreet was right, that the army was footsore, that men were leaving the ranks from exhaustion, falling behind, that animals and men alike were succumbing to the heat, and that his decision had been made and that they would not leave Maryland without a fight.

He had moved the army into Maryland for a purpose, issued a proclamation to the people of that state in the name of the Army of Northern Virginia. From that there could be no falling back, no retreat. He turned toward Longstreet, sure of his answer, knowing what must happen. "This army will not retreat from the field without giving battle," he said calmly. "I have come into Maryland for that purpose, and I am resolved to it."

Longstreet nodded. "Figured as much," he said. A pause. "Here, then?" he asked.

Lee looked at Longstreet, steady eyes, massive strength, an officer of great skill. "Here," he said quietly.

"Have you looked the ground over, sir?" asked Longstreet.

"Yes," answered Lee. "Those hills," he said, pointing to indicate a low ridge beyond the western limits of the small village, "will offer our artillery an elevated position from which to take the Federals under fire." Lee found a small branch, drew a semicircle in the dust, "This will be our main line of resistance," he said. "To the north, we will anchor our position on the Potomac, our infantry posted along the reverse slope of those hills and ridges, out of sight of the Federal gunners."

Longstreet nodded. "And to the south?"

Lee drew another line on the ground. "The Antietam is crossed by three bridges in the vicinity of Sharpsburg," he said, drawing lines to indicate the approximate positions of the places where the stream could be crossed. "The creek itself is not a formidable obstacle to an attacking army, but the position of the bridges will create natural choke points for the Union forces. The Federal commanders will attempt to utilize them if they are not destroyed by our own forces." Lee paused, met the younger man's eyes. "We will not contest all the bridges."

Longstreet raised an eyebrow, a questioning glance.

Lee smiled, a sudden thrill running through him, the feeling of lightening in a black summer sky. "Two of the bridges can be easily defended by our men." Lee pointed again at his drawing, indicated the southernmost bridge. "You must take care to post a strong force of rifleman there. The position is a naturally strong one for the defense. The western bank of the Antietam here is hilly, the eastern approaches are lower, affording little cover for an attacking force."

Longstreet grunted, patiently, turning it over in his mind, asked, "Fords?"

"We must post a screen of cavalry, with some infantry support farther south to guard our flank; but I believe that General McClellan will confine himself to the area in front of us. The banks of the Antietam here are wooded; in some places our scouts report that the country is so thick as to be nearly impassable."

Longstreet exhaled, swept his eyes over the ground Lee was proposing to defend. After a long moment he asked, "The ground in our center doesn't offer much in the way of defense, General." Longstreet narrowed his eyes, squinted into the bright sunlight, asked, "How do you mean to defend it?"

Lee turned, again pointed past the town. "Beyond the village the ground falls away in a large depression. When you reconnoiter the field, you will see that a farm lane bisects the center of our lines. The lane has been worn over time and is depressed to the height of a man's waist in some places, as deep as the shoulders in others. It will form a natural strong point on which to form our center. The ground behind it will support our batteries."

Longstreet gazed westward, saying nothing for some moments. Lee waited patiently, knowing that Longstreet was thinking of the ground, visualizing the placement of troops, batteries of artillery. "You have questions, General Longstreet?"

"Some," said Longstreet slowly. "I don't care for standing with the Potomac at our back."

"We shall have the advantage of interior lines, sir," said Lee. Then, "Our men will not be broken by the Federal army."

Longstreet hesitated, started to say something, then shook his head.

"You must speak freely, General," said Lee. He waited, knew that Longstreet would not favor a stand here. Better the river should be at their front, force General McClellan to maneuver around it. They could easily destroy the remaining bridges, contest the fords with only minimal losses. They could hold the Northern army north of the Potomac River if they desired until the weather made the roads impassable. It would be spring before another general engagement. Nothing would be decided.

"Our position lacks depth, sir," said Longstreet quickly, the words spilling out. "Even if Jackson and A. P. Hill can move up in time, and we get all our men into position, the Potomac River is at our back."

"Yes," said Lee, "General McClellan would not offer battle in a position such as this."

"Probably not," said Longstreet. "George McClellan would never do anything they advised against at West Point."

"Yes," agreed Lee, "General McClellan is cautious. And he is methodical. He will expect us to fall back across the Potomac, as you suggest. When his cavalry finds us here," Lee pointed again at the long, rocky ridgeline to the west of the small village, "he will become wary, unsure of our intentions." Another pause. Lee swept the stick through the muggy air, said, "That ridge will conceal our infantry from his cavalry; our cannon will force him to deploy. General McClellan will hesitate, call upon Washington for their reserves. By the time he is prepared to make his assault, General Jackson and the others will have arrived."

Longstreet let out a long breath, squinted toward the woods beyond the village. "We'll have precious little here if he decides to attack as soon as even a part of his army is on the field."

"General McClellan will make no such attack," answered Lee.

"If the worst were to happen, General," said Longstreet, "we've got no place to go,"

Lee held up a hand. "General McClellan will not expect us to stand here."

"No," said Longstreet, "but he'll bring up every gun between here and Washington before he fires a shot." Longstreet glanced down, shifted uncomfortably, said, "Even if we've got a slight advantage in ground, the Yankees will have long-range cannon with them, if I know McClellan."

"Yes," said Lee, "General McClellan will not be so incautious as to offer battle before he has all his batteries in place, as well as his reserves." Lee held Longstreet's gaze, knew Longstreet was thinking it over, wondering how McClellan could fail to see the opportunity. "It will take some time for him to place his batteries. We will use this time to our advantage. General Jackson understands the need for a rapid march from Harpers Ferry to join us here. He will not delay."

"Even with Jackson and A. P. Hill, the numbers favor the Yankees," offered Longstreet. "He has a sizable army, sir."

"Yes," agreed Lee. He paused. "General McClellan has only recently assumed command of his army. They have been defeated within the past month and abandoned the field in disorder. He is in the process of arranging his command structure. He will have difficulty organizing his units, coordinating the movements of his troops."

Longstreet smiled, a genuine smile, and Lee felt instantly better. "I would gladly accept the burdens of commanding so large an army, General," Longstreet said slowly.

Lee turned, laughed, enjoyed the humor. "We will have the advantage of operating on interior lines. To reinforce one section of our lines our men will have to move but a short distance, while the Federals will have to march a much longer distance. We must take full advantage of that as the day develops."

Longstreet swiped a hand across his face, loosened a button, looked at the sky. "Hot one," he said. Another long pause, then, "I've seen better ground, sir. We could get across the Potomac, force the Yankees to come at us, make them cross the river instead of having it at our back."

Lee shook his head slightly. "We shall make our stand here, north of the Potomac."

"In Maryland?" asked Longstreet.

"In Maryland," said Lee.

CHAPTER 9

THE BIG HORSE PRANCED AND SNORTED, ARCHED HIS NECK, strutted for the cheering soldiers. Townspeople lined the streets, children waving colored ribbons as he cantered past, women smiling from the shadowed porches of redbrick houses. George McClellan felt exultant. His men were marching, and fighting, as they had never done before.

The Rebel army was in full retreat. Lee would be driven back into Virginia before nightfall. The campaign had been an unqualified success.

He touched the big animal's flanks with a heel, smiled broadly at a pretty girl with hair the color of summer straw, felt the charger sidestep, touched the brim of his hat as the girl floated by.

Reports put the Rebel army in retreat. Washington had been relieved; Northern cities were no longer threatened.

Amid the cheering, soldiers, he and his escort of cavalry passed through the town of Boonsboro. He continued to hold his horse in, prancing him to the delight of the people lining the road, the animal straining against the reins, wanting to be let out. Ahead were columns of marching men, infantry, a steady blue stream of men that filled the road, stretched beyond his sight, surged toward the horizon. Beyond that would be the cavalry, riding ahead, harrying the Rebels as they made for the Potomac fords. It had all gone almost too well.

A group of prisoners moved past, lean, ragged men in homespun uniforms, pinched faces, defiant eyes. He watched them for a moment, had the thought that they were an insolent lot, surly.

The South had always been a bit of a mystery to him. Graceful cities, elegant women, duels fought under ancient oaks. Odd mix, not something one could easily understand. Courtly officers, very refined, true gentlemen. Lee, and most of the others, aristocrats. But these men, the common soldiers, were little more than uneducated frontiersman.

Ahead he saw a group of officers, a bit of high ground; someone had found a likely spot from which to observe the enemy. There had been reports of Rebel infantry deployed across the turnpike, drawn into a line of battle. He rode toward the group, confident that the

Rebels they were observing were no more than a rear guard detailed to protect the main body as it crossed the Potomac back into Virginia.

He rode into the party of men, dust rising around him, the air stifling, smothering in the midday heat, past a brick house, the farmer standing in the yard, watching. He glanced at the house, red bricks, white trim, an air of order, symmetry. Officers were saluting, offering their congratulations. Someone brought out a flask, cigars were passed around, there was laughter. McClellan thought of a lawn party, Philadelphia, long ago.

An aide appeared, waited, expectant, an anxious look on his face. He turned, nodded to the man. "General, we have established contact with the Rebel main body, sir," began the officer.

McClellan nodded, smiled, knew the man was a volunteer, no previous military experience. A college man before the war, someplace North, Boston, maybe. "Go on," he said, good-naturedly, doubting that the man had seen any more than a small rear guard of infantry supported by a few cannon.

"Yes, sir," said the man. "Well, General," began the officer, "the Rebs have drawn up on the other side of Antietam Creek, just to the west of us here." The man pointed, indicating almost due west. "You can see 'em, sir, if you like. All that's needed is to walk to the top of this hill here and they are in full view."

McClellan smiled. The man was in earnest, he realized. He actually believed that the entire Rebel army had drawn up in line of battle between Antietam Creek and the Potomac River, with only one ford at their back. Robert Lee was not the type of general to make such an obvious blunder. "I see," began McClellan. He glanced about, saw the number of officers waiting for him to speak. Now would be the time to give them a lesson in the art of war, make them realize the power of deductive reasoning. He dismounted, called for a map. The sheet was spread on the ground before him. "Major," he asked, "where would you put our present position?"

The man pointed, indicating a spot just east of Antietam Creek. "The road there, General," said the officer, "is the Boonsboro-Sharpsburg Road, and we are just a bit north of it. When you top the rise, you will see Sharpsburg before you, and between us and the village is the valley of the Antietam," said the man confidently.

"And where do you place the Rebels, sir?" asked McClellan.

The man drew a long, sweeping curve, encompassing the small village of Sharpsburg, beginning at the Potomac on the north and ending at a spot on the Antietam on the southern end. "Just about here, sir."

McClellan nodded. He looked at his officers, saw that they were waiting for him to speak. "Have you sent cavalry forward, Major?" he asked.

"Yes, sir," nodded the officer. "Rebel infantry took them under fire."

"Skirmishers?" asked McClellan.

"Some," began the officer, "but the men tell me the Rebels are here in force. A few batteries have already opened on us when we were probing their lines, General."

There was a stirring on the road, riders moving along the column, a dark mass of lathered horses, billowing yellow dust, blue uniforms. McClellan recognized the dark horse with the bobtail, knew that Burnside was at hand. He nodded to the officer. "Thank you, Major," he said. "If you would be so kind as to wait while I speak with these other officers, I may want to ask you a few more questions."

Burnside dismounted, waved. McClellan smiled, waited for his friend. Noticed Fitz John Porter pacing, hands clasped behind his back. He looked again at the map at his feet. Porter's men were nearby; just behind, in column of march, were Burnside's divisions. Other units were posted farther south, guarding their rear, holding Jackson at bay somewhere in the vicinity of Harpers Ferry.

He walked toward Burnside and Porter, smiling, wondering that it had all gone so well. He smiled, nodding to the other men. "General Burnside, what a day we are having," he said expansively. "Reports are that the Rebels are in full retreat, heading for the fords at Sharpsburg."

Burnside smiled through his thick whiskers. "We have had a fine time of it," he agreed. "The men are in good spirits."

McClellan looked at the group around him, saw a few whom he recognized from before the war, many new faces. Volunteer soldiers, men from every walk of life, answering the call. He must remember to speak to them, make them feel a part of it all. "Ah, yes," began McClellan, "all our days should be as good as today."

The group of officers smiled, laughed appreciatively. McClellan shook hands with men introduced to him by Burnside, a sea of unfamiliar faces. Not like before, when they had all been Academy men, when all the officers had been regular army, familiar. This was different, less fraternal. Something was missing, something intangible, the

sense of belonging that was present everywhere in the old army, before all this had come about.

He glanced again at Burnside, caught his eye, smiled. He felt a
pang of conscience at the sight of that honest face, an undeniable stab
of guilt. Burnside should have been in the vanguard; his men had
earned it. He had failed to mention him in his dispatches to Washington. Burnside had handled the affair on the mountain well; he was
deserving of praise. It had been a foolish oversight. He would have
to talk with Burnside later, in private. Explain the situation to him.
They had been friends a long time; *Burn would understand*. He knew
how the politicians in Washington were plotting to remove him, Mc-
Clellan.

Politics. It was the bane of every officer and every gentleman. And
yet he was forced to deal with the realities of political maneuvering
by those who did not favor him, as though it was another enormous
Rebel army as deadly and dangerous as the one now in front of him.
"Well," he said, "this is very pleasant, gentlemen, but we have work
before us yet today."

A ripple of laughter from the group. "Perhaps we should climb to
the top of this hill, see what the Rebels are about," he said. From
somewhere in the group a voice encouraged him to give the Rebels
hell. McClellan turned. "I only hope there are a few left on our side
of the Potomac," he said easily, smiling at the unfamiliar faces. Another ripple of laughter as they climbed the hill.

He slowed his gait, motioned for Fitz John Porter to join him. "Ah,
General Porter," he said jovially, "it would appear that you are not
enjoying our outing as much as some of your fellows."

Porter smiled tightly, "I wish that I might, General."

McClellan noted Porter's concerned tone. "We are driving them,
sir. This is no more than a rear guard in our front."

Porter shook his head, breathing heavily as they climbed the grassy
hill. "I think that the main body of the Rebel army may be offering
battle, General."

McClellan looked at Porter, remembered suddenly the reports of a
huge Rebel army. In the back of his mind an alarm sounded, softly,
insistently. "How can that be? Offering battle with a river at their
backs? They would have no line of retreat. It is unthinkable," he said,
shaking his head. "General Lee would not risk such a battle."

Porter remained silent for a moment, thinking. "I believe the portion of the Confederate army commanded by Longstreet and Harvey

Hill is before us. It is too early to determine accurately in what numbers they are present."

McClellan felt his pulse quicken; the alarm was sounding again, far away. "What has led you to this conclusion?" he asked.

They crested the hill. Porter pointed across a hazy valley, grassy fields, rows of corn, shadowy trees following the sweep of a creek. "Our cavalry reports that they are there, on that ridge beyond the village, in line of battle."

He turned, caught the gaze of the aide, asked, "What creek is that?

"The Antietam, sir," the man answered.

McClellan stared toward the west, soft, rolling hills, the earth folding and falling away, rising slowly toward a long plateau, a rocky brow, rising again toward the Potomac, the river beyond his sight. In the distance he could make out a road, a line of white against the darker background of oak and chestnut and hickory that shimmered in the heat, framed the neat farms, concealed the river beyond.

The village of Sharpsburg sat squarely on the southern edge of the plateau, houses and churches perched atop a series of small hills, the crossroads meeting in the center of the small town.

The Antietam wound through the small valley, slipped past the town beneath a stone bridge, disappeared out of sight, faded into another wood. Beyond the Antietam, the ground rose, steadily, a gradual rise, a long, low ridge that paralleled the far road, dominated the ground between him and the wood.

He took a pair of binoculars from his saddle, brought them slowly to his eyes, peered through the glass at the shadowy wood. Long moments passed before he saw them, gray-and-brown figures moving in the half-light, just visible, a wisp of smoke rising between the trunks. A hidden army, waiting, coiled.

Lee had turned, was inviting battle. Jackson must still be miles south, near Harpers Ferry. And yet here they were, waiting, challenging him.

He turned, looked at his officers, saw them watching, smiled easily at Burnside, said, "Well."

"They have a slight advantage in ground," said Burnside.

"Yes," said McClellan, "but in what strength are they present? Have we any information as to that?"

Burnside shook his head, "From all reports we judge this to be the commands of Longstreet and Harvey Hill. General Hooker estimates no more than twenty thousand men, perhaps as few as fifteen thousand." Burnside cleared his throat, continued, "These are the brigades we engaged yesterday on South Mountain. They have been fairly well cut up by that engagement, in poor shape to handle an advance by us."

McClellan adjusted the binoculars, wiped the lenses with his pocket cloth, brought them to his eyes. He peered through the hazy glass, moving them slowly along the ridge, south to north. The muzzles of cannon were visible, half hidden in the trees.

From behind him he heard someone say, "They've seen us," followed by laughter. The report of the cannon echoed across the valley; smoke rolled from the wood. A shell tore the air, glanced along the hill, sputtered and hissed to a stop in a geyser of black earth. There was more laugher, officers joking behind him, nervous glances toward the gun line across the valley.

From his right he heard commands being shouted, one of his batteries going into action, horses being driven to the rear. In moments the gun fired, followed by the remainder of the battery. The concussion rolled across the field; smoke swirled in the still air, drifted heavily over the brow of the hill, settled lazily among the wispy summer grass.

"This is no mere rear-guard action," said Porter sullenly.

He turned, nodded to Porter. "No, it would appear the Rebels are present in some force." Another shell tore the ground nearby, failed to detonate. Dirt thrown up by the impact of the shell spattered the group of officers waiting nearby; men were laughing, slapping the soil from their sleeves.

"The Southern batteries suffer from poor ammunition," said Burnside, "but not from poor gunnery."

A number of officers laughed, nodded; someone clapped Burnside on the back. McClellan smiled. He turned to Burnside. "We are giving them a rather tempting target," he said.

Burnside glanced at him, dark-eyed, good humored. *No fear there*, thought McClellan. *Good old Burn, steady as ever.* Another shell cut the air, exploded behind them, nearer the farmhouse. Geese were squawking, flapping noisily near the barn, the farmer shepherding his family into the cellar.

He turned to Burnside. "Perhaps you could ask these officers to wait for me at the farmhouse while I make my reconnaissance," he said.

Burnside informed the group to move down the hill, out of sight of the Confederate gunners.

McClellan glanced again toward the village, saw movement in the streets, a thin line of soldiers, a single horse. "General Porter," he said, "if you wouldn't mind, I should like you to accompany me while I survey the Southern positions."

"Of course," answered Porter.

For some moments he studied the Rebel positions in silence, tried to peer into the dark wood, see beyond the shadows. Their lines were formed, as near as he could see, in a semicircle encompassing the small village of Sharpsburg. In the north they appeared to have anchored their lines on the Potomac; in the south, they swept up to a series of small hills lining the Antietam. Cannon bristled just below the crest of the ridge.

After some minutes he asked, "What do you make of this turn of events?"

Porter hesitated, then said, "That's their main body, George." A long pause, then, "Lee means to give battle."

"Mmm," said McClellan, "it would appear so. But why here? This ground does not favor him. Why not withdraw across the Potomac?"

Porter crossed his arms across his chest, said slowly, "Perhaps he means to lure us into an attack for which we are ill prepared."

McClellan turned, looked sharply at Porter. "You mean bring Jackson up from Harpers Ferry via Pleasant Valley, fall on our rear and flanks when we have committed to an assault on Lee here?"

"Perhaps," said Porter. "Harpers Ferry fell this morning. That means Jackson and the others with him are free to maneuver for an attack. By acting in concert with Longstreet and the others"—Porter pointed at the low ridge across the Antietam—"he may be able to envelop us."

McClellan thought for a moment, said, "Yes, I see what you are suggesting."

Porter shrugged. "It's possible," he said evenly.

McClellan nodded, said, "General Lee commands a large army. If he is offering battle here, he must believe he has enough infantry on hand to repel any assault we can mount against his front."

"Umm," said Porter. "It would appear he has turned." Porter pointed, said, "If that's his main body."

McClellan peered across the valley, said, "The number of batteries he has on that ridge make me believe it is his main body." He paused, knew that Porter was correct, that Jackson had disengaged, was loose, possibly swinging around behind him, that Lee had turned for a reason. "If Jackson gets behind us . . . ," he said, letting the thought trail off.

Porter turned, "We'll be cut off from Washington," he offered.

"Yes," said McClellan. "John, I have to be careful here. I can't afford to have Jackson running around behind me while I've got Lee and Longstreet on my front."

"No," said Porter softly.

"Have we anything reliable from the cavalry?"

Porter shook his head. "No."

"Damned tricky," he said. "One mistake here and they could be between us and Washington." There was a long silence. A single cannon fired, the report echoing through the muggy air.

"We're a long way from Washington," offered Porter.

"Right," he said. He turned, saw Porter was watching him. "I'm on my own up here."

"The thought had occurred to me," answered Porter.

"Well," said McClellan, wondering how many men waited beyond the Antietam, lying in the silent wood, watching. "If we are defeated here," he said, "then all is lost. Everything. Washington will be left uncovered, Baltimore and Philadelphia. All of it. It will mean the end of the war."

Porter cocked an eyebrow, said nothing.

"We shall have to bring up the entire army," he said.

"Yes," said Porter, "I had thought as much."

McClellan turned, studied Porter for a moment. "Do you suppose they will attack?"

Porter shrugged. "General Lee is an aggressive officer. He has a history of offensive operations against us. It is not out of the question that he is contemplating an attack."

McClellan glanced at the sun; the day was getting late. Perhaps four, five hours of sunlight left. Even General Lee would not be so bold as to attack at night. "Have we any heavy batteries available to us?" he asked. "Here?"

Porter turned to him. "Not yet. The heavy guns have not yet arrived."

"I can't move farther without those guns, John." He turned, glanced toward the turnpike, saw them moving out on the dusty road, a great swelling mass of men, marching toward him, spilling over the road. The army was gathering, its strength building with every hour. "I will order the Sixth Corps to hold the roads in Pleasant Valley, prevent a movement there by Jackson." What he needed now was time. A day, maybe two, gather his army, bring those guns up.

"Yes," said Porter, "that should hold them if they come that way."

"I will need those batteries, John."

"It will take some time. Get them sorted out, move 'em out of the columns, find emplacements for all of 'em." Another pause, Porter staring across the valley. "A day, maybe more."

"I can't go in without those batteries. It would be foolhardy." He shook his head. "I won't do it, John. You know I can't risk the army."

"True enough," said Porter.

McClellan noted his hesitation. "There is some other matter that concerns you?" he asked.

"Yes," began Porter slowly,

"Go on," said McClellan, continuing to observe the Rebel positions.

"Some of our men are new." He turned, faced McClellan. "In fact, they have not been trained properly; some have almost no training."

"You feel these troops should be held in reserve?" asked McClellan, "that we should allow your regulars to do the fighting?"

Porter shook his head, "That might be wise. But I believe we must also consider holding our best men in reserve. In the event the volunteers break under fire, we can shore up any gaps in the line with units we can be certain of."

"Ah." McClellan smiled. "A reserve force of seasoned regulars." He clapped a hand on Porter's back, said, "Splendid. I am reminded of Napoleon's Old Guard, John."

Porter smiled, wistfully, a hint of embarrassment. McClellan saw an odd expression cross the handsome face, knew that Porter was thinking of Washington and the charges against him, that he had been slow to come to the aid of General Pope on the Manassas plain. He smiled at Porter, said, "You shall do great service here, John. Great service, and the nation shall know of it."

Porter stiffened, said, "One hopes so."

"Your regulars, John. I know I can depend on them; the entire country will depend on them in the coming battle."

"I shall do my best, sir. You have my word on it," said Porter formally.

"Of course," said McClellan. "No one who knows you would think otherwise." McClellan looked again at the small valley, was reminded of an exquisite painting he had seen, years back, a museum, Belgium, perhaps, or France. A small painting, the name of the artist escaped him, a landscape, muted hues, a delicate hand. Exquisite. A building filled with beautiful paintings; nothing like that here, not yet.

He smiled at Porter, searched for the right words, but what do you

say to an officer whose honor has been questioned? He inhaled, dry
hot air, the fuzzy smell of straw, said, "The fate of the nation, John."
He pointed, swept his hand in a long arc across the valley before
them, one arm around Porter's shoulder. "The fate of the nation will
be decided here, by what happens on those fields in the next day or
two."

"Yes," said Porter, "I suppose you are right."

"I'll need your help, John. We'll have to bring up every division,
put every gun into the line. We can afford to spare nothing; not a
single cannon must be left out of the action."

Porter turned toward him, subdued, said, "Of course, George. I'll
see to it, if you like."

He smiled, knew that things would be better now, that Porter
would busy himself with bringing the army up, forget the other matter
for the time being. "We must move quickly, John. Every moment will
count now; all could be lost if General Lee moves against us before
we can concentrate the army, get everybody here, in place."

"We'll be ready, George. A day is all we need."

"Fine," he said, relieved. "We have a splendid view of the field
from here." He looked again out over the valley of the Antietam.
Destiny had brought him to this field. The Rebels were at bay, their
backs to the Potomac. God had delivered them to him. Now the task
was his. He turned, looked toward the comfortable brick farmhouse
where Burnside waited with the others. "I shall make my headquarters here then. See that the word is passed to the corps commanders."

CHAPTER 10

LEE HAD BEEN DOZING, DREAMING OF MUSIC, A CHOIR, A FAMIL-
iar hymn, the voices veiled, hovering just beyond consciousness, and
then he had discovered that he was praying, quietly, alone, the prayer
little more than a thought, noiseless. He blinked, came slowly awake,
his mind foggy, heavy, still half asleep deep inside a chair in the warm
interior of the house. On the other side of the door his officers were
waiting; there was a comforting murmur of voices. He closed his eyes
again, rested, listened to the familiar tone, thought: *Jackson, a solitary
fiery light, soul of a martyr. I must trust the Almighty,* he thought, *and these
men. He has sent to me.*

He rose slowly, coming awake leisurely, relishing the feeling of rest,
his mind blurry after having slept during the heat of the day, the feel
of soft chairs, a real bed. Someone had left a basin, there was a pitcher
and cool water; he washed his face, wiped the sleep away, was reminded of the small pleasures of home.

Through the window he saw rolling fields, ripening corn, the
ground rising toward the east, a hazy valley, lovely soft hills, a sprinkling of trees, dark against the late-summer grass, a distant image of
spreading branches, antiquity.

Just beyond his window, in the yard, someone had taken chairs
from the house, arranged them in the shade beneath the spreading
branches of a chestnut, and now his officers were sitting there, and
he could hear their voices and the sound of their laughter. Lee
glanced at the sky, knew that the afternoon was nearly spent, the
light would begin to fade in another hour, perhaps two. There would
be no movement by the Federal army today. The hour was too late,
the light already beginning to fade.

He thanked Providence for their hesitation. The Union army had
begun to assemble late yesterday, the infantry marching in over the
rolling hills, coming along the same roads his men had passed over,
spreading across the hills and ridges to the east, silent, waiting.

He closed his eyes, thought: *General McClellan has hesitated a full
day. He will attack tomorrow or he will not attack at all, and then I must
move.*

Another voice came from beyond the door, familiar, heavy, com-

forting, the voice of James Longstreet. They had spoken earlier, the
army moving toward Sharpsburg, concentrating, the Potomac River
between them. Longstreet had protested, wanted to move toward
Jackson and the others at Harpers Ferry, force the Federals to cross
the Potomac, move back into Virginia.

But there was a deeper issue that he had not spoken of with Longstreet. He had made a promise to the people of Maryland, and, in
the end, his word meant more than tactics, and so he had ordered the
army here to Sharpsburg.

He sighed, felt suddenly tired, wished for a moment that he could
be at home, with no army to command and no battle to be fought.
Alone, in the quiet room, with only the sound of his own breathing,
Lee thought: *You are an old man and you have given your word to these
people, and your soldiers are worn and so we must fight here. If not here then
it will be some other place, and so it may as well be here, before General
McClellan has an even larger army that he can bring into Virginia.*

He opened the door, stepped across creaking floors that reminded
him of a house he had rented in Saint Louis, when he had been an
engineer and the Mississippi River and the heat and humidity of summer had been the opponent. He waved away an anxious Walter Taylor
with a cup of coffee, smiled at Longstreet and Jackson and the others.
"Gentleman," he said.

Longstreet rose from the map table, smiled awkwardly, nodded,
waited for him to speak. He took Jackson by the arm, said, "Perhaps
you could show me where your divisions are, General. I am most
anxious to have them join us."

Jackson bent over the map, pointed to a spot, said, "Somewhere
between here and Harpers Ferry."

He nodded, said, "They are still some distance away."

"Yes," said Jackson.

"I had hoped that we might all be assembled by this afternoon,
this evening at the latest."

Jackson returned his stare, said, "McLaws won't be up before tomorrow sometime. Powell Hill is probably still seeing to the prisoners
and stores we took at Harpers Ferry." A pause, Jackson calculating
distance, time, then, "He won't be here before this time tomorrow."

"I see," said Lee. Half the army was still en route to the field.
They would arrive tired from the march, footsore, drained by the heat.
He looked through a window, across the valley, toward the dark trees
that hid the Federal army. Over there they'll be tired, too, but there

will be more of them, and they will bring more cannon than we can
ever hope to have, and more can be called from Washington and Ohio
and Pennsylvania, and so it must be here. And it must be soon.

Lee looked at Jackson, said, "General Longstreet favors a move
back into Virginia. Force them to pursue us; then we can take up a
position on better ground."

"Yes," said Jackson, "I'd thought the same." For a moment there
was silence, Jackson glancing at the map, then, "The Potomac is a
problem, no question of that. Difficult to get across, to get everybody
here, and more difficult to get back across in a hurry if we need to."

"Yes," said Lee, "I am aware of that. But we shall have the advantage of operating on interior lines, while General McClellan shall be
forced to move on exterior lines. It will be difficult for him to coordinate his attacks over such a large area."

"You think he's going to attack us?" said Longstreet unexpectedly.

There was an awkward moment, Lee thinking that Longstreet had
expected him to order an attack. But he could not. His cavalry was
exhausted, the infantry in worse condition. He must wait for General
McClellan to attack. It was only necessary for him to offer battle by
standing here, that must force an attack by the Federals. "General
McClellan will attack, I believe," he said.

"Maybe," said Longstreet. "But it ain't like ole' George to go on
the offensive."

"No," said Lee, "but we have forced his hand by invading the
United States. Washington will not allow him to wait while our army
occupies a portion of their country." The words hung in the air, somber, lifeless: *invasion, United States*. The thought was there, insistent,
hot-blooded, pulsing through him. *Foreign soil; you are on foreign soil,
an invader.*

The thought burned its way into his brain, settled in his chest like
a sickness, the revulsion searing its way into him. How had it come
to this?

Lee met Longstreet's eyes, knew he felt it too, forced his mind
away from it. Later, he told himself, you will think on it later, but
now you must attend to the matters at hand; you are here and there
is a purpose for you and you must serve.

"He sure came after Harvey Hill up on South Mountain," offered
Longstreet.

"Yes," said Lee. "But he was in possession of our operational orders
then." Jackson's head came up suddenly, a brief glimmer of something

unreadable in his eyes. "We have moved beyond that now. He will be unsure of how to proceed against us; our stand here will not be what he anticipated."

"Are we to stay on the defensive then?" asked Jackson.

"General McClellan will attempt to probe our lines, conduct a reconnaissance by fire, determine where we are weak. His attack will be slow to develop, difficult to coordinate." Lee walked to the map table, traced a finger along the arc that someone had traced onto the paper marking their lines. "You will be on the northern end of our lines," he said to Jackson. "General Longstreet shall have the center and the southern extremes of our position." He traced the Antietam with a finger. "The creek will be an obstacle for them; they will have to cross it to begin any attack. We should be able to observe their movements in several places, and it will slow their advance, force them to move across the creek in column, then deploy in line of battle. As they develop their attack, we will move our arriving infantry to answer it, send batteries to threatened areas as they are needed."

He glanced up, saw a worried glance exchanged between the two younger men. *They doubt that we can do it. Perhaps you are risking too much, asking too much. To offer battle here was to hazard everything. Destruction of the army, the loss of the war, the end of the Confederacy.*

He remembered the soldier he had spoken with yesterday. Something he had seen in the man's eyes. Weariness, but more than that, more than exhaustion even. Resignation. The boy had simply wanted to put an end to all the marching.

Jackson nodded, said, "I believe I understand."

Lee looked into the pale blue eyes, wondered again at the fierceness within the man, the indomitable spirit. A hint of madness, of great suffering. A biblical warrior. "General McClellan will hesitate to commit his reserves; he will wait, expose advancing units to enfilading fire from our batteries, flanking maneuvers by our infantry." He looked at Jackson, said, "We must exploit these opportunities as they arise."

Longstreet and Jackson nodded in unison. Longstreet asked, "Any indication where he'll hit us first? Any word from the cavalry?"

"None. He has not made any move beyond a few shots from his batteries."

"Well," said Longstreet, "tomorrow will tell the tale. Guess we'll find out what the Young Napoleon is made of."

Lee smiled, felt instantly better, knew that Longstreet was a pessimist by nature. Now that the task had been set out, things would be better, preparations could be made, order issued.

Longstreet picked up his hat, smiled at Lee, shook hands with Jackson, gripped Lee's hand with ironlike fingers. "Guess I'll go get my boys set up then."

"Yes," said Lee, "my tents will be south of the village."

Longstreet nodded. "I'll see you this evenin' sometime, General."

When Longstreet had gone, Lee turned to Jackson, said, "General Longstreet would prefer a movement south of the Potomac."

Jackson hesitated, glanced again at the map, said slowly, "He's right about the ford. The one behind us is rocky, not the best for our purposes if we have to move in a hurry."

Lee crossed the room, stood before the window, light pouring in from a late-afternoon sun, a clear white light that illuminated everything. There was a garden in the yard, summer squash and beans, heads of lettuce, all in neat rows. "Do you recall how timid General McCellan was on the Peninsula?"

"He was slow to move," said Jackson calmly, his voice even.

"He will not believe himself ready to give battle tomorrow. He will be cautious, unsure of himself, his movements will lack authority." Lee turned toward Jackson, looked into the pale eyes, felt the fierceness of the younger man. "We must exploit that; move aggressively when the time comes."

Jackson cocked an eyebrow. "You believe we will be able to take the offensive then?"

"We shall have opportunities; we must exploit them as they present themselves."

"His artillery is going to be a problem."

"Yes," said Lee. "He will place every gun he has available."

Jackson said nothing, waited. After a moment Lee added, "It will not be better for us in a week or a month. They grow stronger over there every day," nodding east, toward the hills where the Federal army waited. "While we do not," he added.

"You mean to end it here?"

"If possible, if we could defeat them, decisively, in their own country, we might end the war."

Jackson rose, his face unreadable, thoughtful. "Well," he said slowly, "I should be off. I'd like to see the field before the light fades, get an idea of what sort of position we'll have tomorrow."

"Yes," answered Lee. "Once the fighting begins you must not hesitate. Should an opening present itself, you must send your men forward, keep the Federals off balance."

"Yes," said Jackson, "I understand."

Lee smiled, sensed that Jackson wanted to leave, to make his reconnaissance, see to the details of placing his divisions. "Ah, General, I am keeping you, and you have a great deal to accomplish. I know you will not disappoint me tomorrow."

Jackson smiled, a wan smile that belied his nature. "Tomorrow then," he said, and left the room. Lee returned to the window, watched Jackson walk through the yard, his officers drawing back, clearing a path for him, bidding respectful farewells.

Jackson mounted, rode away, a silent gray figure on horseback. He will know what to do tomorrow. Some officers had to be told, in detail, what was expected, what had to be done. Not Jackson. He was an instinctive fighter, a brilliant tactician. Tomorrow he would sense the flow of the battle, like a sailor reads the tides or senses a storm with only the barest shift of the winds. Jackson would know the right moment, throw his brigades against them at just the right instant, catch them off balance, in the middle of a movement, unaware of his presence.

He drew in a deep breath, felt the familiar calm settle over him, the feeling that comes when you have done all that might be done, when events have been taken as far as mortal man can take them. Now it is in the hands of the Almighty. You have done what you can, and now you must trust in your officers and in these men who have followed you to this place and who will give battle on these fields, and in God, for all things rest in His hands and no others. *For thine is the kingdom, the power, and the glory.*

The words came to him as if from a mist that rises over silent water, soft, clear, distant. Trust in Him, for there is no other, and you are only a man, and what is a man in the end but dust?

CHAPTER 11

A LATE-AFTERNOON SKY HELD THE PROMISE OF RAIN, HIGH THIN clouds, a slight breeze out of the west drifting lazily through the tops of trees. Joe Hooker could smell rain, a distant, far-off smell of dampness and something else that he could never put words to, but it was there; and so he knew there would be rain tonight.

He shaded his eyes with his hands, knew that rain would settle the dust, cool the animals down. So long as there was not too much rain that would swell the creek between his men and the damned Rebels.

He swiped a hand across his forehead, cursed under his breath at a thousand flying things that buzzed and swirled around him. He was in a foul mood and he knew it and there was damn little that would improve it but getting under way and driving in on the Rebel army.

He had ridden to army headquarters earlier and been briefed on McClellan's plan. They would attack in the morning, he driving in from the north, down the Hagerstown Pike, his divisions anchoring on the road, moving south, their objective the village of Sharpsburg. Burnside and his divisions would attack on the southern end of the field, move across Antietam Creek on Lee's right, roll him back toward the Potomac, swing north toward the village. If it went well, they would meet somewhere near Sharpsburg. If they got stalled, McClellan could reinforce where it was needed or open a third assault on the Rebel center.

Lee's army was trapped, pinned between their own army and the Potomac River and any fool could see it, all that was needed was to ride forward and look; but instead the idiots at headquarters had talked only of bringing up more cannon and reserves of infantry and a thousand other things that had nothing to do with fighting a battle.

McClellan had held them back for an entire day; a full day of good weather and sunlight that should have been used to attack the Rebel army head-on had been wasted. McClellan had made a great show of riding around on his horse, parading for the troops, seeing to the finer points of placing brigades and cannon and wagon trains. Things that could have been handled by a competent colonel were personally supervised by the commanding general of the army.

George McClellan, commanding general. Just the thought was

enough to irritate him, pull at him like briars, a thousand tiny cuts
that annoy but never do any real harm. He felt the anger rising, burning, clenched his jaw, said nothing to the aides and orderlies who
waited, just out of hearing.

Hooker spat, squinted toward the west, tried to see beyond the
trees lining Antietam Creek, reminded himself that at least half of
being a general in this army meant being a politician.

He had never really learned that, not in the old army, and not in
this one. He had criticized old Winfield Scott, long ago, before the
Rebellion, and his career had been cut off at the knees. They had
conspired to limit his rank, the old fools who sat in Washington behind
mahogany desks and made such decisions.

And now he found himself subordinate to a peacock like George
McClellan. He turned in the saddle, saw that his regiments were on
the road, men shuffling forward, cursed his luck.

There had been other problems. It was no secret in the army that
he liked to have a drink now and then. It had never affected his ability
to command, but it was there; and he had been passed over for pro-
motions because of it.

From ahead there was a popping of rifle fire, a few shots, echoing
back through the forest. Nothing serious. Maybe a nervous private
shooting at the wind, a shadow, or maybe they had run into the Rebel
skirmish line.

Lee and Jackson and the others were out there, beyond the trees
and the creek, waiting. He eased the horse forward, wondered for the
thousandth time how many men they had. Reports were all over the
place; no way to tell what they had, or where they were. Just drive
ahead, blindly, try to make contact; sooner or later you had to run
into them.

He felt a sudden thrill, the sensation slicing up through him, his
heart racing, and he knew that it was close, sensed that the Rebels
were near, just beyond the trees. Soon they would engage, tomorrow
morning at the latest. The Rebels were worn, falling back. Lee's army
was hollow, a great gaping vacuum. One good push, a breakthrough,
get in among them with the infantry.

Lee had overplayed his hand, pushed his men too hard, too far.
And now they were here, with a river at their back and impossible
lines of supply, and all that was needed was to drive in among them
with all they had and keep pushing till you found the weak spot.

From ahead a battery opened, a sudden sharp crashing that brought
his head up in alarm. So. They had found them, run up against their

guns. That meant they were just ahead, beyond the Antietam, on the other side of the wood.

His men were marching, long columns, dipping down into the little valley that the creek passed through, a steady line of infantrymen climbing the far side, moving toward the west and the turnpike that led into Sharpsburg, disappearing around a bend in the road.

Once they got to the road they would have the Rebels pinned in the town. No way out for them then; they would have to fight. His staff told him that the ground beyond the road was broken all the way to the Potomac, too rough for easy movement of men and guns.

That meant the trap had been sprung. Even if they sensed it now, it was too late. No way to get past them, and far too late in the day to organize an attack on his men as they took up their positions. Lee had gambled. And he had lost.

From the rear of the column he heard the approach of horsemen, turned, saw the neat figure astride the great black horse, a superb figure in the saddle, held a hand up in greeting. McClellan reined in amid a great cloud of dust, smiling broadly, a cigar clenched in his teeth.

Hooker saluted, said, "General."

McClellan was smiling, a broad, toothy smile as if the battle had already been won. "General Hooker." He beamed. "How are you?"

"Fine," said Hooker tightly, pointing to the west. "We've had some contact. Sounds like they've got a battery beyond those woods."

McClellan nodded. "Their main body?"

Hooker shrugged. "Possibly. I won't know for a while. But I suspect it's their main body."

"Splendid!" said McClellan. There was a general nodding among the crowd of officers who trailed him, a murmur of consent. Someone passed a flask around. "Have you any idea who is in front of you?"

"Not yet," said Hooker, "we've only just made contact."

"We've got to get on their flank, General, if we are to move them off this field."

"Yes," said Hooker, "I believe my lead elements may already be beyond their flank."

McClellan clapped a fist into his open palm, his dark eyes glowing, said, "Splendid, Joe! That's the spirit we need. Once we get around their flank, we'll be in a good position to roll them up, drive them back into the Potomac."

"I'd like to know how many men they've got over there." Hooker paused, glanced ahead at the silent wood, wondered what waited beyond. "Could be the whole damned Rebel army up ahead for all I know," he said gloomily.

"Not to worry," said McClellan cheerily. "I've ordered up another corps to follow yours across the creek. You'll have all the men you need."

"Will they be under my command then?" asked Hooker.

"Yes, yes," said McCellan hurriedly. "You just step off at dawn and drive right into them, Joe. Push them back toward the town and the river. I'll see to the rest."

"How will I coordinate my attack with General Burnside?" asked Hooker.

McClellan flashed him another smile, said, "You will both attack at dawn. You should be able to hear his guns from your position on the field, but don't wait for him. I want you to move forward as soon as you are ready in the morning."

From the west there was more rifle fire, sustained fire that Hooker knew meant they had run into something more than a cavalry screen or a skirmish line. Someone had thrown a regiment out as flankers, was pushing the Rebels away from the road, clearing the way for his columns.

McClellan saluted, drew in the reins, wheeled off with his staff. Hooker sat for a moment, listening to the firing, wondered how many of them were waiting beyond the wood.

No matter, he thought, *in the morning we will attack, and if McClellan is good to his word and moves up another corps or two, and if Burnside will only push them on the other end, it could all be over by noon.*

IT HAD RAINED DURING THE NIGHT, A SOFT RAIN WITHOUT WIND or thunder, the kind of rain that farmers long for in the spring when the earth has been turned and crops are in the ground. The air held the smell of it, heavy, musty, a faint hint of the sea. Joe Hooker looked east, saw the first uncertain streaks of light that signal the dawn.

He had spent the night in a barn close behind his soldiers, his staff finding what rest they could among the animals and stalls and the movement of the army outside the rough walls. He could hear the regiments forming beyond the barnyard. In the darkness, men were assembling, shuffling into formation.

An hour, less even, and they would step off into the dim light, begin the day. And the fighting.

The hours before a battle are always the hardest. Less tolerable, even, than the fighting. A battle consumes a soldier, fills his mind and his body with purpose. The waiting before a fight is insufferable, a void, when a man's mind wanders, fills him with memories of home and longings for a life past, saps him of his fighting spirit.

He strode into the barnyard, found his horse, a fine white stallion that stamped and blew impatiently at his approach, the animal sensing the atmosphere, knowing something was about to happen. He stroked the powerful neck, swung into the saddle.

No campfires marked the bivouacs. His soldiers had slept in the rain without fires, eaten a cold breakfast. From somewhere in the dark beyond the barnyard a bugle sounded, a dry, clear sound, a missed note. He recognized the "assembly," felt his pulse quicken.

Hooker rode out onto the road, his eyes adjusting to the dark, became aware of massed shapes, lines of men standing in the growing light. Long columns of infantry, shoulder to shoulder, stretching away, beyond the farm, as far as he could see, disappearing into darkness.

Men were watching him pass, rows of silent faces, dark eyes. Hooker realized that they were waiting for him to give the command that would send them forward, anxious to begin the fighting, settle the issue.

The road loomed up out of the dark, glowing in the faint light, a high fence, wooden rails on either side of a muddy track, leading south, pointing like an accusing finger at Sharpsburg. He wheeled his horse about, cantered down the line, the sky lightening, streaked with gray and white in the east, the sun still hovering below the horizon.

He peered toward the east, straining to catch some glimpse of movement, the arrival of reinforcements, remembered what McClellan had said. Another corps, possibly two. *I'll need them*, he thought, *and whatever else he can send, before this is over*.

A battery opened up, from the plateau near the town, the shell screaming across the field, a long, fiery arc that disappeared into shadow, trailing death and fire like a comet. Another cannon fired, then a third, and Hooker felt the peculiar sensation one feels just before a big fight, when you know something terrible and tremendous is about to happen and you are powerless to stop it, be it good or bad.

The smell of burnt powder drifted over him, an acrid, stinging, bitter cloud that fouled the air, a warning of the danger that sped past unseen. He inhaled deeply, thought: *This is the best of it, when the issue has not been decided and it is only my army and theirs and nothing, absolutely nothing, has been decided*.

This is what we live for, all of us, this moment, when it is about to begin and men are standing to their arms, the battle flags have been uncased, and you feel more alive than you could ever feel anyplace else.

Men sometimes told themselves, and others, that they served a greater good: the nation, or the army. But he knew this was only a thing to be said aloud, that deep down, where a man really lived, in his heart, or maybe in his soul, if he were lucky enough to have one, that all of them lived for the thrill that came with battle, and with command.

A phrase came to him, something he had heard long ago, in Mexico, or maybe at the Academy, he couldn't be sure now: *Advance under fire.* The words had burned themeslves into him, like a tune that you hear once but know instantly. The music staying with you, coursing through your brain, finding its way into the tips of your fingers, drumming, insistent, always there, just out of reach.

Hooker had heard this music his entire life, but only rarely had he heard it played aloud. It could only be played on a battlefield, and only by cannon and rifle and men with grim, determined faces.

He had heard it in Mexico, when Lee and Longstreet and the others had all been there. They had heard it too, known its effect on a man's soul, felt its power. And afterward, when the fighting had stopped and the music had come to an end and they had known that they would survive, life had been the sweeter because of it. He had felt more alive, everything had been better somehow because of the fighting.

And when they had left Mexico, when the fighting had ended, and the music had receded, he had felt its absence, maybe more than he had felt even its presence. He had searched for it, but there was no substitute. Not army life, not the companionship of his brother officers, not the whiskey, although he had thought for a time that perhaps it was.

And now he was here again, and the music was playing louder than he had ever heard it, and soon they would all be together again. Only this time it would not be like before. They would all hear the music again, but in a way that none of them could have imagined all those years ago in Mexico or at West Point.

It occurred to Hooker that the calling to be a soldier was something akin to the addiction he had witnessed in men who were overcome by drink or opium, or even love for a beautiful woman. And that once it took hold of you, body and soul, it never loosened its grip on you, and you could never be free of the terrible longing for it. The awful irony of the day was not lost on him, and yet he longed for these moments, lived for them if the truth be known, was powerless to end his desire to hear, if only once more, the strange, terrible music that had ruled his life.

The soldiers in his lead division were standing in rank, long lines, facing south, toward the small village. The light was coming, slowly, the sky turning the color of flint, gray and indistinct, the light creeping in with the fog, softening the night slowly, steadily, peeling away the edges of darkness that hover along the horizon. He took a deep breath, the air heavy with last night's rain and the smell of ripening hay, and the moist, dank smell of earth from the farmer's fields.

In the gathering light he could make out the fields now, lovely round hills, rolling away toward the town, just visible in the half-light that was not quite dawn. The hint of a breeze, a fine mist of rain, stinging his face with wet nettles. Not yet, he told himself, wait for the light. And for McClellan and Burnside.

A drum was beating, insistent, a long steady roll that signaled men to find their colors. The front regiments were neatly formed, ready to step off, and then the drumming stopped and there was silence for only a moment and he heard someone shout an order that was picked up by other officers and echoed down the line, disappearing in the pale light and the mist.

Hooker trotted the big stallion between two regiments, swept his hat off his head, saluted the men standing in ranks, headed for the center of the line. Soldiers saw the great warhorse, cheered, knew that their time was at hand.

To the south, beyond the hills, the Rebel lines were draped in a fine mist, a soft, blowing mantle of gray. He could see the roofs of the town in the half-light, fog shifting and moving in the hollows between the hills. An officer approached him on horseback, saluted smartly, said, "The divisions are formed and ready to advance, sir."

Hooker saluted automatically, tried to remember the officer's name. A Pennsylvania man, from somewhere out west, Pittsburgh maybe. "Major," he said, "I want you to make it clear to the follow-up brigades that they are to maintain a distance of no less than two hundred yards between your lines and theirs."

The man stared back at him with glassy, feverish eyes, said, "Yes, sir," automatically.

Hooker glared at him, tried to determine if the man had understood what he was trying to tell him. Sometimes it was like that with an inexperienced officer. They looked you in the eye, heard what you were saying, even told you they understood, but in fact they were so lost in the excitement that they understood nothing, or forgot what you had said in the next instant. And then orders weren't conveyed to the next command, or got bungled up, and all of a sudden ten thousand men were marching off in the wrong direction.

There was no telling what was waiting for them up ahead, and these damn volunteers were hard enough to manage even under the best of conditions. If the brigades stepped off too close together they would not be able to manuever without running into one another, or the rear rank would crowd in on the front rank and the enemy artillery would rake the packed formations with canister. It would be over before it had begun. Better to spend the time now, be certain that they maintained the proper interval.

He hadn't heard any firing from beyond the town; Burnside hadn't begun his assault yet. There was still time to get it right, avoid a disaster.

He grabbed the major's sleeve, said, "I want you to tell the follow-up brigades that they will not move forward until the front ranks are well beyond this farm. Am I understood?" he asked.

The man nodded, said, "Yes, General. Two hundred yards between brigades, enough room to maneuver, sir."

"Good boy!" said Hooker. "Now make sure they understand it back there," he said, pointing to the rear where another line of infantry waited.

The man smiled, white teeth, a handsome sunburned face. Hooker noticed the stubble of a beard, thought him impossibly young to be a major. And then the man was saying, above the roar of cannon, "Yes, sir!"

Hooker clapped him on the back, saluted as he rode away. The regimental color bearers had advanced, each man standing a few paces in front of his regiment, waiting for the signal to hoist their flags, begin the attack. He trotted into a group of officers, said, "Gentlemen."

There were smiles, nervous glances toward the enemy. Hooker pointed, beyond the delicate hills and the fields of corn and summer hay. They were watching him, paying attention now. "Your objective today will be that bit of high ground, a mile or so to the south of us."

The officers nodded, seemed to understand. "Our right will be loosely anchored on the Hagerstown Turnpike." He pointed, "That rail fence runs along the turnpike, gentlemen, right into Sharpsburg. Use it as your guide if you become confused. It will mark the right flank of our advance."

More nodding, someone lit a cigar, asked, "When will our batteries begin firing, sir?"

"When you step off, and they have enough light. There'll be enough fire to keep them hot over there," he said confidently.

There was laughter, men shaking their heads, smiling in the first pale light of morning. He pointed toward the Rebel lines, said, "A mile or so to our front where the Hagerstown Pike meets the Smoketown Road, you should meet them head-on."

Officers were peering into the darkness, staring ahead. Someone asked, "How will we know when we've gotten there, General?"

Hooker smiled, said easily, "You'll know, son. There will be plenty of Rebels there to greet you." There was more laughter. A shell hissed past, tearing the air; a few of them ducked their heads reflexively, sheepish looks on their faces afterward.

"Well, sir," continued the officer, "it's just that my boys got here late, sir. And we're lined up in the first rank, and I've not had a chance to see the field in daylight, and so I'm not as clear as I might be on just where I'm supposed to be going."

"Fair enough," said Hooker. "Now all of you look." He pointed, said, "Just beyond those hills, the ground falls away. Do you see it?"

More nodding. He searched their faces, saw that each man was looking, understood. "Fine. Beyond the hills and the cornfields, the ground rises. The Rebels have batteries on that high ground. When you get close, you will be below their guns, in the hollow between the hills. Your men will move through those cornfields, angle toward the high ground and those batteries."

"It will be damn difficult to see where we're going, General. Once we get into the corn and the low ground."

Hooker felt his temper flare, resisted the impulse to scream at the man. This wouldn't be necessary if McClellan had moved them up earlier, or he had more professional officers in the ranks, or there had been time and daylight enough to reconoiter the field the day before. But there was no time for that now, no time for anything other than to point them in the right direction, get them going. Burnside would be going in soon, might already be moving toward Lee's right. So he said slowly, with as much patience as he could, "Take a good look at the ground in front of you. Memorize its contours. Your perspective will change as you advance, so you must know where you are going. It will be for nothing, gentlemen, if we don't all go in together."

"Fog is going to make it tricky, sir. The fog and the hills and those cornfields."

"Yes," he said. He pointed again, the light better now, the sky turning from gray to a fine summer blue in the east, the fog hovering low over the ground, as deep as a man's waist, pooling in the low spots, shifting. A wood had emerged from the darkness, and a small white schoolhouse in front of it, close to the Rebel lines. Mist moved over the field, drifted among the shadows and branches. "There," he said, "all of you can see that school, can't you?"

There was a chorus of replies, mumbles, officers searching the distance, straining to see the enemy lines.

"Good." From just in front of the school a battery opened, six bright flashes stabbing the murky fog. "That battery and that schoolhouse, gentlemen. If you become disoriented on the field, you shall advance upon that schoolhouse. You should be able to see it from even the lowest spot on the field."

He saw that each of them understood, felt a wave of relief wash over him. Too many damn volunteers; you had to lead them by the hand, explain everything to them. But they didn't lack for enthusiasm; you couldn't fault them on that score. It was all a matter of pointing them in the right direction, showing them how it was to be done. Maybe an engineer officer or two, lead them out on the field, be certain they got it right. But there had been no time. They had arrived too late, and now they would have to go in on their own, do their best.

"It's a church," he heard someone say.

Hooker turned, looked at the officers, caught the eye of the man who had spoken, asked, "Sir?"

The man cleared his throat, looked about nervously, said, "Ah, General, I only said that the building is a church." Another nervous glance, then, "I meant no disrespect, of course, but it's a church, sir, not a school."

Hooker almost laughed, realized he didn't know the man. A smooth-cheeked boy who was staring back at him nervously, shifting in the saddle, waiting for God knows what. "Your name, sir?"

"George Smalley, General. From the *New York Tribune.*"

Hooker stared at the boy for a long moment, an ill-fitting army uniform that made him appear foolish, younger than he was. He resisted the impulse to laugh, asked, "And how did you come to be with my officers today, Mr. Smalley? And in an army uniform at that?"

"Well," began Smalley, "I was told that your command was the one to follow, General, if I wanted to see the most action, get the best story."

Hooker chuckled, said, "And I am assured a flattering story in your paper, Mr. Smalley, if you stay with my command?"

Smalley smiled, answered, "I'm sure the general will be well received by my readers."

There was laughter from the other officers, a nodding of heads. "And how do you know that that building is a church and not a school?"

"I took the liberty of talking to some of the local people. They told me that a Baptist sect has services there, General. It's just that simple."

Hooker turned away from Smalley, winked at a colonel nearby, said, "You shall stay close with me today, Mr. Smalley. I wouldn't want the *Tribune* to miss out on a good story."

There was laughter, Smalley smiling, grateful. "Of course, General."

Hooker returned to his officers, said, "All right, gentlemen. Mr. Smalley's church is your objective. Don't lose sight of it, and hold on to each other's flanks as you advance. Remember, parallel to the Hagerstown Turnpike and we should have a fine day of it."

Around him men saluted, mounted their horses, trotted off to find their commands. He peered south, wondered if Burnside had stepped off yet. Best to go in together, keep them busy on both flanks. That would make it easier on everybody, keep Lee guessing where the main thrust would come from.

Orders were shouted, men's voices disappearing into the fog and thick air, flags raised, a bugle sounded, clear and crisp. Officers were dismounting, slapping the rumps of their horses, the ranks opening as the animals trotted toward the rear. One animal had gotten it wrong, was trotting down the line of soldiers, wild-eyed, looking for its fellows.

Hooker stood in the stirrups, raised his sword above his head, flashed the long blade down toward his boot and ten thousand men stepped toward the rolling hills and silent woods and the enemy beyond as though with one mind and one purpose.

To the rear a battery fired, a sudden sharp explosion of sound that broke the air over them with unexpected violence; then all the guns were firing in a quick, rolling barrage that was louder than any thunderstorm he had ever witnessed. From the right and left other batteries joined in, the shells cutting long arcs over the men, slashing into the dark wood, disappearing among the trees where the Southern soldiers waited.

From the cornfields ahead there was flash, then another, followed by a dozen more, bright orange stalks of flame, disappearing in an instant. Skirmishers firing on his men, the Rebels unseen, hidden among the head-high stalks of corn, bullets whizzing past.

He raised his eyes, searched the thick fields for signs of the Rebels, saw movement, men running along the neat rows, dark shapes, long rifles carried high, ducking in and out of his sight. More flashes, more bullets coming past, here and there men going down in the tall grass, clutching an arm or a leg.

From his own ranks a fife was playing, the notes high and clear above the crashing of cannon, coming in snatches between the reports of the big guns. Hooker felt the old thrill, the excitement, his heart pounding, a tingling in his limbs. He glanced back, saw the regiments in line, stepping confidently through summer grass and fresh mown hay, men shoulder to shoulder, rank upon rank. In a moment he knew it was true, that this was the best of it, the moment you waited for all your life. The thought struck him that nothing, absolutely nothing, can be finer than bringing an army into combat.

A shell tore past him, buried itself into the ground nearby, throwing a sudden geyser of black dirt over him with a sound like rope snapping. He laughed, gripped the big horse with his knees as it reared in fright, pulled the reins in, forced the animal down, stroked its neck. He smiled, saw that Smalley, the reporter, was nearby, wide-eyed, taking it all in. He waved the boy over, nothing more he could do now; he had done what he could, set them in motion. Now he had to wait, keep them moving forward, see that the others didn't bungle it, come up too close behind them, stack up right in front of the Rebel cannon.

Smalley rode alongside, bright feverish eyes, half wild with excitement, said, "General, I wanted to thank you for allowing me to stay with your corps, sir."

Smalley's voice was high, excited, and Hooker could not help but think again that Smalley looked ridiculous in the uniform. He smiled, decided he liked the boy, said, "You may not want to thank me, Mr. Smalley, if the Rebel batteries continue firing our way."

Smiley laughed, said, "I've never actually been this close to the fighting, sir. It's very . . ."

Hooker held up a hand, noted that his men were moving well, keeping their alignment, the infantry marching steadily, the lines of soldiers rolling over the uneven ground, rifles at shoulder arms. Companies of skirmishers had been advanced in front of each regiment, and he could see them wading through the tall grass, advancing in hesitant, cautious movements. The hills beyond were silhouetted against the sky, pale and fine, and promising heat. But for the moment there was no heat, only a thin rain that might be no more than fog, and the dark shapes of soldiers moving out ahead, beyond the grass, and the farmer's fields, and the Rebels in the distance.

"The real fighting hasn't begun yet," he said, and suddenly it streaked through his mind, naked and ugly and all the more alarming for the simple truth of it. Burnside should be moving, closing with the Rebels beyond those hills.

But he had heard nothing from that direction, no firing, not a single cannon, and somewhere in him he knew the truth of it, that there would be no attack from that direction. That his men would fight on their own, and that maybe, if his luck improved, McClellan would remember and order another corps to give him a hand before it was too late.

He took the binoculars from their case, tried to see beyond the town, where the ground dipped down toward the Antietam, hiding what lay beyond from sight. He could make out a line of trees, just the tops, green and dark, rising above the brow of a hill beyond the town. More Rebel batteries, dark figures standing by the guns, waiting. Hooker steadied the binoculars, watched the solitary figures silhoutted against the morning sky, waited and hoped that they would move into action, fire those cannon against Burnside's men as they began their assault.

He silently cursed Burnside and McClellan and all the other bumbling fools at army headquarters who couldn't coordinate an attack, who couldn't move men or regiments or armies. It could all go terribly wrong. If they waited much longer, his boys would be in and the Rebels would throw their reserves at them, and it would be more than he could handle even if McClellan did send him another corps.

A battle was a terrible, delicate thing. A matter of timing and balance that forgave no general his mistakes. A matter of acting with confidence, precision. And there, in the gathering light of dawn, with ten thousand men marching toward the enemy at his command, he knew that George McClellan would fail him.

He swore under his breath, fought the growing realization that Burnside had not gone in like he was supposed to, that his divisions were fighting alone. He glanced toward the southeast, wondered what McClellan was up to, why he had given no signal.

Out along the turnpike his formations were coming under heavy artillery fire. Flashes from the muzzles of Rebel cannon were visible from beyond the turnpike, bright specks of orange and white in front of the wood, an enfilading fire that his men were marching into, every step farther into the Rebel trap, the long lines of infantry exposing themselves at right angles to the fire. An artillerist's dream, an infantryman's nightmare.

Someone had told him the ground west of the turnpike was empty. Impassable was how they had described it. But the woods there were alive with enemy soldiers, the fire from that direction becoming unbearable. A brigade at least, maybe something bigger, was concealed behind the rolling ground and timber. They had failed him again, the damn cavalry or McClellan's staff officers with their superior attitudes and smug expressions.

"Damn!" he said aloud, saw Smalley and others turn toward him. "Goddamn them all!" he said, the shells falling among his men, tearing great smoking holes in the formations out along the turnpike. The space between his lines were alive with wounded men, crawling to the rear, some lying on their back, arms waving in desperation, begging for help.

Hooker felt the revulsion well up in him, tasted bile in his throat, swore under his breath that someone would pay for this if he lived beyond the day. To waste their lives because the area had not been properly scouted, or because Burnside or one of the others hesitated when he should have been moving forward to the attack.

The sun rose over the ridge to the east, broke through the clouds, and brilliant light flooded the field, illuminating everything. Hooker saw it then, a twinkling, a glimmer of light on metal, beyond his front rank, among the shadows and the rows of corn. He brought the binoculars to his eyes, but he knew already what must have happened.

He could see them clearly, now that the sun was out and the light was more certain. Soldiers, standing to their arms among the tall, green stalks, waiting. With the binoculars he could see their faces, fuzzy, hovering in the yellow glass, bathed in shadow.

He looked around, saw only Smalley. "Mr. Smalley," he said, "take these binoculars and examine that cornfield in front of our men."

Smalley did as he was told; Hooker watching, seeing the boy's expression change with the discovery. "I see them, sir."

"Good," said Hooker. "Take a good look, be certain that you know that cornfield from anywhere on the field."

Smalley handed the binoculars back after a long moment, said, "I can find it again, sir."

"Right," said Hooker. "I want you to ride and find our batteries." Hooker pointed, to the rear. "Tell every battery officer you can find that I have personally ordered that they fire on that cornfield. And that they do it now."

Smalley nodded, said, "I'll do it, General."

Hooker waited, saw Smalley ride hard toward the rear, head for a line of guns. The second rank was well beyond him now, marching steadily toward the high ground farther south. A shell fluttered in nearby, struck a rock, whined off behind him.

The only way out of this mess was to drive in among them. Break the Rebel lines to his front, push them off that bit of high ground to his front. If he failed, his formations would be cut to ribbons by the Southern guns from at least two directions, but he had committed to the advance and now there was nothing left but to go forward.

The sun was well up now, burning in over the ridge and the trees, the fog fading away, lying only in the low spots, the air clearing. There would be heat today, real heat, but it was an hour or more before that would became a worry and anyway it was too late now in any event.

He saw a shell strike the white side of the church, great chunks of brick and mortar falling away, an ugly dark hole in the wall appearing when the smoke drifted off. From the wood the Rebels were firing steadily, a constant rain of small arms and heavier shells ripping into his formations. On the pike a hole had been torn in his ranks, the column appearing clumsy and unbalanced where an entire company or more was missing from the formation. Soldiers were stopping to fire, shooting in the direction of the wood, unable to continue marching without hitting back.

Dark figures appeared in the clover west of the wood, Southern soldiers, breaking cover to shoot down the length of his infantry, rifle fire raking his men from the front and side. The attack was developing well, rolling down on the small village just as he had planned, but the Rebels beyond the turnpike worried him, stuck in the back of his mind, and he was unable to resist searching the trees there for an indication of their size. No way to move around them; he was beyond that now. Just have to continue moving south, push them out of those woods, maybe throw a brigade or two out west of the pike, cut off the Rebels there from the rest.

If there was to be an attack from Burnside, it must come soon if it was to do any good at all. Otherwise . . . he allowed the thought to trail off, refused to think of it now. Later, if it came to that.

A battery erupted to his rear, from near a dark wood, out of sight, the shells arcing overhead, trailing smoke, smashed into the cornfield. A steady stream of fire, the shot exploding in neat orange spheres of flame over the corn, splinters of smoke rocketing in every direction.

Another battery advanced, unlimbered their guns, wheeled the heavy cannon into line. The gunners began firing into the cornfield, double-shotted loads of canister, bouncing the deadly lead balls off the ground in great clouds of dust, the shot careening through the corn, scything it away, killing everything before it. Plumes of smoke and torn corn were thrown skyward, only to be ripped in half by another shell burst. Before his very eyes the Southern soldiers disappeared in a deadly storm of explosions and shell fragments and torn earth.

Hooker stared into the field, saw that the Rebel soldiers were being swept away by the fire of the cannon, their formations disintegrating where moments before living, breathing men had stood. The soldiers were consumed in great heaving clouds of dust and rock and earth. Each explosion sent a new plume of shattered earth skyward, tore another gap in the Southern lines.

Gunners from each of his batteries now focused their fire on the cornfield. Shells poured into the small meadow like a heavy summer rain, driving themselves into the earth, or skittering along the ground in furious streaking blasts. The explosions merged into one continuous sound, an unearthly trumpeting of death that made Hooker turn his head for an instant.

Before his eyes the cornfield disappeared, yard by yard, beneath an angry barrage from his guns. Long arcs traced the trajectory of shells low over the field, the balls exploding among the corn and the soldiers standing in ranks. The field disappeared under the furious bombardment, smoke obscured everything but the next explosion, and the very earth appeared to open and steam in a seething venting of smoke and gas and disentigrating bodies.

In ten minutes it was over, the neat rows of corn before him had been cut away. What remained was a fuming ruin of torn earth and dying soldiers. They lay among the smashed stalks, their bodies in odd, impossible poses, or crawled toward their own lines in slow, tortured movements.

He shook his head, wondered what it might all come to, all the fighting and killing. The men in the cornfield were dying because someone had foolishily ordered them forward, a handful of men to stop thousands. For a moment he felt pity for them, then he remembered all the good Northern boys who had died in the past months and the pity was swept away and replaced with something hard and unforgiving.

His own infantry was moving steadily now, men appearing from the low ground between his position and the Rebel lines, seeming to wade through the smoke. He could see segments of his lines, dark blue ranks of men calmly marching toward the Rebels. They were in good order, moving steadily, officers out front, file closers a few paces behind to bring up any stragglers. And then Hooker saw the flag, a lone soldier carrying it and a breeze caught it at that moment, just as his men were nearing the broken cornfield, and lifted the colors for all of them to see.

And just as suddenly men were cheering, a great roar of maddened voices, cheering the sight of the old flag, and he felt as though they would carry the plateau and the church and the day. Somehow it didn't matter just then that McClellan had bungled it because his formations were holding and his men would be on them in a few minutes, and it all seemed to be working for once.

And then his infantry engaged, a thousand rifles fired with a single command, and then another thousand, the smoke and flame rolling down the front rank with a noise so loud and so strong that it deafened a man, until all you saw were the billowing white clouds and another rank moving up to fire and you knew they had forgotten everything but the need to load and shoot and hurt the enemy as badly as he might be hurt by one man and one rifle.

Above the inferno of cannon he heard the snap of bullets slicing the air, and the voices of men cheering or screaming or cursing. The moans of the wounded blended with the sounds of battle, echoed along the length of his lines, rose above the ravaged earth and the tight ranks of soldiers, merged with a hundred other sounds until he heard nothing distinctly, and then his mind was overwhelmed and it seemed for long moments he could hear nothing at all.

They had advanced well beyond the bleeding earth of the cornfield; they were standing in long lines, shoulder to shoulder, firing in great heaving volleys that slammed into the Southern soldiers and the woods beyond with a horrible sound.

His infantry rolled over the field, long lines of dark soldiers dipping down into the low ground, rising again with the gentle swelling of the earth, flags and guidons spiked above the solid lines of soldiers. Officers were trying to keep them on line, slow down fast-moving brigades, prevent gaps in the line, push ahead toward that bit of high ground and the cannon and the church beyond.

Hooker watched as a long rank of Southern soldiers rose from a concealed position, leveled their weapons in one silent, graceful gesture, saw the black rifles explode in a cloud of smoke and flame. Men fell as if blown over by a hot wind. Great holes were left in his line where soldiers had gone down, and above it all he heard distinctly the sickening *ca-thunk* of bullets striking bodies even from this great distance.

For long moments the two lines faced each other, feet planted, firing at each other over what seemed only yards of ground. Soldiers on both sides seemed to disappear into the smoke and flame, falling to the grass in silent mounds, or staggering back with the impact of unseen missiles.

Without warning he detected the Southern line breaking, not breaking really, just wavering. Nothing dramatic, just a man here and there leaving their line, turning away from the fighting. Lean men in gray-and-brown uniforms, single soldiers, then small groups of two and three, breaking ranks, moving back toward the church and the dark trees, and safety, turning to fire back at his own men as they went.

Groups of them were stacked against the high fence that bordered the turnpike, like so many leaves caught against a branch that has fallen into

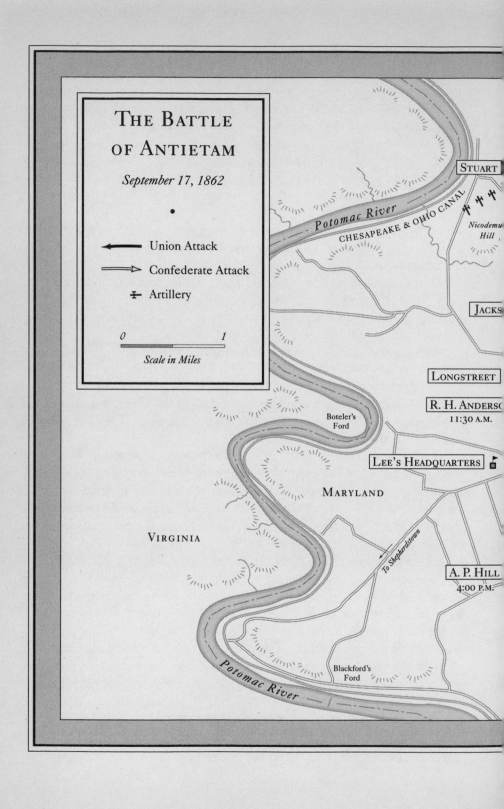

THE BATTLE OF ANTIETAM

September 17, 1862

•

⬅ Union Attack

⇢ Confederate Attack

⊩ Artillery

0 —————————— 1

Scale in Miles

Potomac River

CHESAPEAKE & OHIO CANAL

STUART

Nicodemus Hill

JACKS

LONGSTREET

R. H. ANDERSO
11:30 A.M.

Boteler's Ford

LEE'S HEADQUARTERS

MARYLAND

VIRGINIA

To Shepherdstown

A. P. HILL
4:00 P.M.

Blackford's Ford

Potomac River

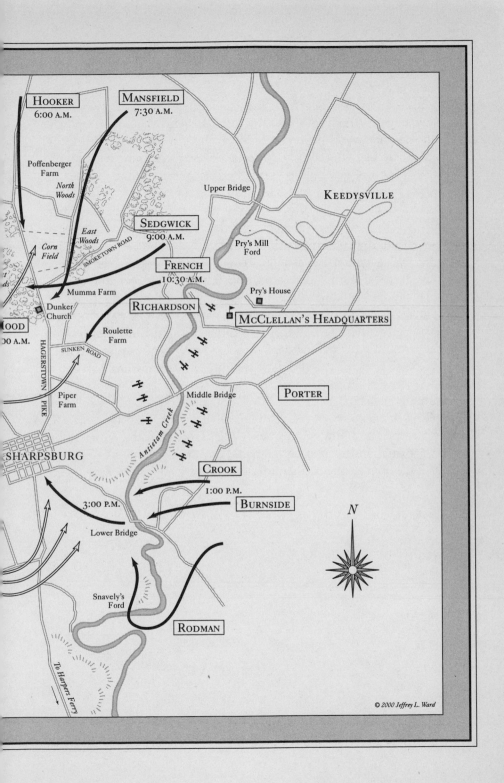

HOOKER
6:00 A.M.

MANSFIELD
7:30 A.M.

Poffenberger
Farm

*North
Woods*

*East
Woods*

SEDGWICK
9:00 A.M.

*Corn
Field*

SMOKETOWN ROAD

Mumma Farm

FRENCH
10:30 A.M.

Dunker
Church

RICHARDSON

Upper Bridge

KEEDYSVILLE

Pry's Mill
Ford

Pry's House

McCLELLAN'S HEADQUARTERS

OOD

00 A.M.

Roulette
Farm

SUNKEN ROAD

HAGERSTOWN PIKE

Piper
Farm

Middle Bridge

PORTER

Antietam Creek

SHARPSBURG

CROOK

3:00 P.M.

1:00 P.M.

BURNSIDE

Lower Bridge

N

Snavely's
Ford

RODMAN

To Harpers Ferry

© 2000 *Jeffrey L. Ward*

a stream. His men saw their chance, poured a murderous fire into the retreating Confederates, and men fell down by the fence like summer grass before a rake.

Hooker gazed on for long moments, unable to look away, wondered how much longer it could last, what waited beyond the fence, and the road, and the dark wood beyond. He swept his eyes over the field, saw the ruin that had been his corps, the wounded men streaming back toward the rear, the infantry beyond now merged into one long line of riflemen that was not nearly as long as it had been an hour past.

From the right, beyond the turnpike, he could see Rebel soldiers breaking the cover of the wood, firing into the rear of his brigades. A sudden sickening thought swept through him, that Burnside had bungled it, that he hadn't gotten his assault off and that no attack was coming, and that he had walked his men into a trap. That beyond the little church, out of sight in the shadowy wood, waited Jackson, or Longstreet, or God knows who, and with more Rebel infantry waiting for the right moment to come up against his exposed flank. And that without Burnside to worry about they would rout his shattered divisions, sweep him from the field, drive him back beyond the jump-off point, and scatter what was left of his corps.

He turned, glanced again toward the southeast and the silent hills and wondered if any help at all was coming. Or if it had been more of Mc-Clellan's strutting and now he was being left alone, with the entire Rebel army on his front and maybe on his flank, and he had either to fight his way out or die trying, but no damn help would be here from army head-quarters or anyplace else.

CHAPTER 12

THE BIG FEDERAL CANNON ACROSS THE ANTIETAM HAD BEEN throwing shells into the wood where his brigades had been resting since before dawn. Soldiers had found whatever shelter they could among the rocks and trees, but in truth there was little real cover to be found and the big shells hurtled in with deadly regularity, exploding high overhead, or bouncing off branches and the trunks of trees before crashing to the earth and detonating in a cloud of smoke and bits of dirt and rock.

Stonewall Jackson knew that the Union gunners were firing blindly, shooting at nothing in particular, just guessing where his brigades might be and firing at that spot, hoping to hit his infantry, or an ammunition wagon, or anything of value. The air around him smelled of burnt powder and shattered iron and the heavy, sweet smell of cut wood and roasting meat from the breakfast fires, and Jackson wondered for a moment that the Yankee gunners never seemed to run short of ammunition.

A shell burst nearby, without warning, and for a second he was blinded by the flash, stunned by the sudden violence of it, the great crashing noise that slams into you and reminds you that all men are mortal, and frail, and given only a short while on this earth. He brushed bits of leaves and splintered wood from his sleeves, saw Kyd Douglas nearby, a worried look on his face, waved him off.

Not today, he thought. *Soon, perhaps, but not today.* All men die, it is the way of things, and in time death and the Almighty come for every man; but today he had work, and the Creator had sent him to this place for that purpose, and so it would not be today.

Another shell crashed through the limbs overhead, a shower of leaves descending in its wake, drifting slowly to the floor of the forest in neat arcs. There was laughter nearby, a regiment assembling, shifting its position, edging closer to the front of the wood and the fighting beyond.

Douglas drew alongside, said happily, "It would seem the Federals gunners have their heavy weapons in position, General."

Jackson nodded, slapped at a mosquito that hovered annoyingly close. From the fields beyond the wood there was renewed firing, a steady drumming of massed rifles. The roar of the battle seemed never to fade, the noise droning on seamlessly, a constant fountain of sound that numbed the senses, shocked men into silence, enveloped their very being by its presence.

Sometimes the firing would fall off. For a minute or two it would lessen; then it would resume and for all the world it seemed as though every man in both armies had chosen to fire his rifle at the same instant. And in those moments the world would become senseless with the din of battle, as though the sounds had transformed themselves into a brilliant white light that blinded men and animals alike and held them transfixed, unable to move, or speak, or think.

Jackson steeled himself against it, rode forward, saw for himself that his entire front was being assaulted, a great line of blue infantry sweeping over the fields and valleys, walking down on him in steady, deliberate steps. A great serpentine wall of soldiers who moved with the certainty of death in measured cadence.

The Federals were making a determined push, a corps, maybe more. Coming on in long lines of infantry, running their cannon up close behind the brigades, hurling men and metal at him without restraint, a flood of men rushing across the plain before him.

He had held his reserves back; a few brigades waited now, close to the edge of the wood, among the shadows, out of sight of the advancing Yankees. Men lay in slight depressions and folds in the ground, huddled beneath stone ledges, prayed that they would not be hit by a ball or a splinter from a shell, waited for the order to advance.

It was almost time. A few more minutes. Let the Federals develop their attack, overextend themselves. Then he would send his brigades in after them, take them in the flank, fire on them with massed infantry from two fronts, relieve the pressure on his lines, force the Union soldiers to fight on two axes or retreat.

He nudged the horse forward, motioned for Douglas to follow. Lee had been right. They were opening on the northern end of the field, searching for a weak spot, moving their assault down his line in echelon, searching, probing, trying to force a breakthrough, push him back toward the river.

A counterattack now would catch them off balance. Most of their brigades were beyond the range of their light guns; their advance would now be covered only by their long-range artillery.

"Come along, Mr. Douglas," he said, nudging the horse toward the limit of the woods. The sun shone brightly beyond the trees, the light white, harsh, forcing him to squint as he gazed toward the field.

A wagon rumbled by, the mules straining against the weight, the teamster cursing, flicking the whip over the rumps of the animals. A file of men rose, shuffled toward the wagon, waited with silent, wary faces while a sergeant passed out ammunition.

The air had lost the chill and damp of the night, the day was becoming hot, and a thousand flying things rose in small clouds that made men slap and swat at thin air and curse as though they had never been in a church in their lives. Jackson glanced up, through the covering of branches, tried to guess the time by the angle of the sun, but could see little beyond the mantle of leaves and thick branches and a dirty layer of smoke that drifted by in foul, gray streaks.

From near the edge of the wood a drummer began to beat the "long roll," calling units to their colors. Men rose wearily, slowly, found their place in ranks, and stood waiting for orders. He walked the horse forward, saw the hard, narrowed eyes, the brittleness that a man's features take on when he knows the fighting is near and there is nothing that can be done but to go forward and fight, and maybe die, but that is all there is and nothing else, and so he goes.

At this moment, when the fighting is upon him, and every man turns within himself and thinks not of home, or country, or even family, but only of his fellow soldiers, and wonders if he will live up to the expectations of others, or even his own bragging, the cold reality of it settles into his very soul with the grimness and finality of death; and then an order is shouted and his feet betray him and he is moving forward with the others, come what may.

The steady rhythm of the drum filled the small glade and Jackson's eyes were drawn toward the sound, the drumsticks a shadow against the head of the drum, the sound of it masculine and strong and somehow comforting, and he understood suddenly why soldiers obeyed its call when spoken orders had no effect. He stared down at the drummer, the boy's features a mask of concentration, the skin drawn tight over the fine bones of his face, eyes closed, a shock of dark hair over a face determined not to show fear.

Jackson turned away, moved suddenly by the youth of the drummer and what was about to take place and the tragedy of it all, and he glanced toward the brilliant sunlight beyond the woods where the soldiers waited and saw the small church. Gleaming white through the trees, shimmering in the morning sun, and for an instant he felt the presence of the Almighty, and wondered why He allowed men to bring such tragedy upon themselves.

He felt a profound rush of emotion, understood the tragic beauty of soldiers and drummers and bravery in that one instant. And then he remembered what he must do, and he waited for the emotions to pass, and then the familiar, unforgiving bindings around his heart returned and bore down on him with the weight of mountains, and in a moment the wave of emotion had passed with no more gravity or being than the shadow of a bird that glides by on a sunny day.

Jackson glanced again at the drummer, saw the boy standing in ranks, just inside the shadow of the wood. A soldier standing next to the boy ran his hand along the drummer's shoulders, touched the boy's face with a dirty hand. The drummer shook his head, faced forward, shrugged off the comforting embrace of the older man. From the corner of his eye, he saw that Douglas was following his gaze, staring in the direction of the boy.

"Mr. Douglas," began Jackson, "have we enough headquarters runners today?"

Douglas turned toward him, the dark features brightening, said, "We always need couriers, General."

"See to it then," said Jackson, nodding in the direction of the drummer. Douglas trotted his horse forward, Jackson watching as he pointed the boy toward the headquarters' guidons in the rear. There was an exchange of words between them, the drummer edging away from Douglas, backing toward the protection of the soldiers. A man broke ranks and with a swift motion placed the boy in the saddle behind Douglas, his drum bouncing lightly as Douglas wheeled his horse and moved off. Men in the ranks turned, looked in his direction. The soldier who had been standing next to the boy took his hat off, bowed his head slightly. Jackson touched the brim of his kepi, nodded to the man.

A battery beyond the wood let loose in the next instant, the salvo violent and unexpected, smoke rolling away from the guns, sliding down the slope of the hill, drifting toward them on the slightest breeze. The reports of the big guns echoed through the trees, shook leaves and dirt from the branches overhead, a fine layer of grit descending with each new shot.

Douglas returned, minus the boy, said, "The fighting has been heavy already, sir. General Stuart sends his compliments. He's calling for more ammunition for his guns and is concerned about an advance by the Federals against his position in force."

Jackson stared for long minutes out beyond the pike, wondered what the Union commander must be thinking, what he might know of their position. Their assault was meant to break his line, push them back into the Potomac by sheer weight of numbers.

His left was not well anchored, just a few calvarymen and some light artillery. Beyond that nothing all the way to the river. A great emptiness, a void, beyond the rocks and trees and a few of Stuart's horsemen there was . . . nothing. He squinted into the sunlight that fought its way down to the floor of the forest, remembered that men often confine themselves to what they can see, limit their vision and their efforts to what is before them. It was a failing of many officers, and the officer directing this attack against him now was guilty of it.

The weight of the Federal assault had been thrown against his center, the attacking brigades converging just in front of the small church, striking at his artillery and massed infantry. They had come straight into him, sent no cavalry to probe his lines, feel their way along his front, seek out the vulnerable spots, push into the gaps.

Once they had committed they had not tried to shift their attack, turn his flank, drive a brigade or two between his men and the Potomac.

Jackson turned to Douglas. "Those men," he began, looking in the direction of the infantry waiting just inside the tree line, "whose are they?"

Douglas followed his gaze. "The boy told me they are from Louisiana, sir."

Jackson nodded, "General Hays's Louisiana Brigade," he said quietly.

"Yes, sir," said Douglas. "They are somewhat odd in their habitats, General, but they have a reputation as fighters."

"Yes," said Jackson slowly, "their reputation is for more than fighting."

Douglas grinned. "They have some renown in the army for being inventive foragers."

"Foreigners," mumbled Jackson, remembering the complaints brought to him by the townspeople near the last bivouac of the Louisianians in Virginia. There had been problems, items missing from farms; fence rails and livestock, for the most part. Hungry soldiers were willing to risk any punishment for a good meal. The Louisianians, however, seemed to take a particular delight in it that the others lacked.

Douglas grinned. "A fair number of them, General."

"Let us hope the Federals have heard of their reputation as fighters," said Jackson. To his front there was a sudden rumble of musketry, the sound rising, spilling over them, rolling off toward the river, gliding through the wood.

From the east there was movement, the fluid motion of troops, massed infantry, long lines of huddled men materializing from the shadows. A brigade, emerging from the shelter of a wood. A silky movement, an impression of men gliding through knee-high grass, swinging around in a slow, steady arc, pink faces visible above dark uniforms.

Across the fields the Union regiments slowly formed, the infantry uncoiling in an ever-growing line that shook itself out, spread across the hills, descended into the hollows out of sight, reemerged on the slope of the next hill. The first ranks formed, lurched forward unsteadily, paused while another line assembled behind the first, flags and guidons and regimental colors dotting the great formation at regular intervals.

A silent order was given, too far away to be heard above the din of battle, and the entire line stepped forward in a single movement as though a breeze had sprung up suddenly behind them and pushed them into motion. The marching men moved steadily toward him, an inexorable movement, slow, calm, unwavering.

The Federal infantry slipped down the face of a hill, disappeared from sight, only their flags and the occasional gleam of a bayonet visible above the corn and the rolling ground. Slowly they emerged from the narrow valley, purposeful, determined, closing the distance, growing larger with every step.

When the lines were perhaps three hundred yards apart, the Federal soldiers halted, an order was shouted, and the front rank knelt. In unison the front and rear ranks brought their weapons to their shoulders and fired, a sheet of flame bursting from the lines as though a single finger had pulled the thousand-odd rifles.

For a moment it was all obscured by smoke and dust, and the Union soldiers seemed to float in a cloud that had strayed too close to the earth and been pulled down to glide just above the grass. And then the smoke drifted away and he could see that his regiments were disintegrating, men having been knocked out of ranks, great holes torn in his lines by the sudden force of the volley.

While he stared the Union men cheered, a deep, resonant sound that seemed not to come from human beings, but to well up out of the very earth and hurtle toward him, as though a single great beast had chosen that moment to announce its presence on the field.

Everywhere along his shattered lines men lay crumpled in soft mounds. Long rows of soldiers had fallen precisely where they had stood only moments before. Those who were able were walking back toward the shelter of the wood. Small groups of men simply left their colors, stumbled across the meadows, sought shelter beyond the rifles of the Federal infantry.

With a start he realized that his defenses were close to being broken, his lines breached. McClellan, if he pushed another corps in behind this one, would break their lines, and there was little that could be done about it.

"Order General Hays's Brigade in, Mr. Douglas. Let's see what type of mettle these men have today."

Without a word Douglas rode off to find the commander of the Louisiana Brigade. Within minutes a mounted officer galloped down the line, waving his hat, exhorting the men to do their duty, give honor to their state. Jackson narrowed his eyes, saw that the soldiers were capping their rifles, speaking to one another in hushed tones.

The officer on horseback rose in the stirrups, his sword catching a shaft of sunlight that had found it way through the branches overhead, and then an order was shouted and Louisianians raised their rifles over their heads as though moved by a single hand. And suddenly they were screaming the peculiar high-pitched battle cry that he had heard often, the sound of it unnatural, primal, a thing to be feared. A beacon of blood lust, a reminder of ancient battles fought on dark moors and shifting bogs before the time when men were Christian.

The entire brigade stepped off, and the Louisianians emerged from the wood into bright sunlight, crossed the clover field in a single long line, and swarmed over the fence near the turnpike. The grass beyond the wood was burnt and smoking from the fighting, the blades bent and blackened, an ugly dark scar.

A big Union regiment appeared at the edge of the cornfield, the soldiers unsure, hesitant, looking about, waiting for their officers to dress their lines. The Louisianians knelt, delivered a volley that tore and ripped and slashed into the soldiers and the corn.

From near the church a cannon boomed, the battery firing blindly into the corn and smoke, the ground shuddering and trembling with each explosion. Shells clawed great swaths through the massed infantry as men in both armies began firing as rapidly as possible.

The Union soldiers fought where they stood among the stalks of corn, sheltering behind whatever was available, some lying between rows of broken stalks or among rocks and folds in the ground. Units disappeared into the smoking ground around the turnpike, drawn into the maelstrom of close combat, the fighting reduced to clusters of men firing at one another across the road or a bit of open ground.

A group of Southern soldiers broke from their lines, ran across a grassy swale, and plunged into the Federal ranks. Other men imitated them, and the fighting swirled around a small hillock that rose from the middle of the cornfield. Soldiers lunged toward the rise in the ground, groups of ten or twenty men charging toward it, melting into the smoke and flame, lost from sight in seconds.

In moments it was impossible to tell where the lines of one army began and the other ended, the fighting raged everywhere, and men fought singly or in small groups against whatever was in front of them. Batteries from both armies were pouring fire into the small field and the earth there appeared to heave and shake with each new blast.

Jackson lifted his gaze, saw that the Federal troops were slowly retreating beyond the corn, withdrawing back toward the woods to the east. Clusters of men were streaming back out of the field, seeking the cover of the trees beyond the fields, turning to fire as they went, a last defiant gesture.

In the seething ground of the cornfield he was not able to see just where the Louisiana Brigade stood. Men moved everywhere, but without any apparent aim. An officer on horseback was riding back and forth, attempting to establish a line. From his position he could see that the Louisiana Brigade had simply dissolved, the soldiers consumed by the fighting, the brigade spread before him in a great bloody swath that littered the field.

Pockets of men fought on, but by and large the brigade had ceased to exist. Another advance by the Federals and he would not be able to hold his line. A good push in division strength and the Federals would sweep what remained of the Louisiana Brigade out of the corn, cross the turnpike, and roll him back toward Sharpsburg, crowd him back on his own supply trains.

He glanced east, saw that the sun had risen white and pale above the mountains, knew that the day was only begun, that across the fields the Union commanders would be deciding their next move, hurrying units toward the front, sending them against what was left of his division.

He removed his hat, ran a hand through his hair, fanned himself slowly, the muggy air in the wood bitter with the smell of burnt powder and the heavy, dank odor of torn earth.

Jackson looked for Douglas, saw him conversing with another officer, waved him over. "General Hood, Mr. Douglas. I want you to find him. Tell him that I shall require him shortly. He is to advance beyond the church to our front, cross the Hagerstown Road and the other road that intersects it, and engage the Federals."

"Yes, sir," Douglas answered again. "Will there be anything more specific for General Hood, sir?" asked Douglas.

Jackson turned away, stared in the direction of the smoking fields, saw the carnage that the day had already brought. He shook his head slowly, said, "General Hood will understand what has to be done."

CHAPTER 13

SMOKE FROM THE CAMPFIRES DRIFTED LAZILY SKYWARD UNTIL it caught in the branches of the oaks, where it hung suspended like a vaporous gray ceiling. A barrel of flour had been broken open and someone had found a bit of lard and the soldiers of the Texas Brigade stood in small circles around their fires and fashioned hoecakes on blackened ramrods. Bits of fat dripped from the iron rods, hissing and sizzling among the coals, the aroma of the lard mixing with the smoke and smelling fragrantly of hickory and bacon and home and adding to the hunger of the men.

John Bell Hood turned and saw Judah McBain standing nearby, watching, waiting for Hood to notice him, as silent as an ox and nearly as strong. Judah McBain had been a blacksmith before joining the army, and his trade had shaped him over the course of a lifetime. Where God had made him a big man, weeks and years spent in his shop hammering hot iron had furnished him with cords of muscles that appeared ready to burst from beneath the skin of his shoulders and neck. When McBain walked, the great muscles of his shoulders shortened the swing of his arms and made him appear, if not comical, then at the very least distinct.

Hood stepped away from his staff officers, nodded to the big man. "Mornin', Jude."

"Gen'ril," said McBain, "I was hopin' we might have a word."

Hood smiled, knew that McBain was not a man given to idle chatter. Words to Judah McBain were like precious coins, each one special, to be used carefully, thoughtfully, never to be wasted. Each sentence spoken by McBain had been thought out well in advance, mulled over, turned and twisted and played in his mind until he knew exactly what it was he wanted to say and just how he would say it. And now he was here, his mind at ease, his features a study in sincerity; and he was looking intently at Hood, the dark eyes concentrated, ready to speak his mind.

Hood nodded, knowing what was to come, what the big blacksmith had sought him for, knowing that he could not really refuse the man again.

"Reckon I would like to go with the fellers this mornin'," said McBain, a slight nod of his head, eyes steady, holding Hood's.

Hood met the gaze, said, "I can't really spare you, Jude. Blacksmiths are hard to come by in this army."

The big sergeant pulled at his beard, an interminable moment passed when it was so quiet that you could hear the rustle of birds in the branches above, and then McBain came to the point, almost reluctantly, as if by asking he would give offense to Hood and wished with all his heart that the entire matter could somehow be avoided. But at last his features tightened and he said, "I might've stayed to home if being a smithy was all I was after. Seems to me I've come a long way, Gen'ril, and done an awful lot of walkin', just to sit back and watch the fightin'."

"Yes," said Hood. He paused, dreading his own words, gazing into the honest face, knowing what he must do, understanding that it was unfair to keep him back, that a man's pride meant more than most things did in this life. That you could ruin a man like Judah by refusing him, holding him back from taking his place in the lines, place a stain upon his honor, his good will, make it impossible for him to hold his head up among lesser men who had stood in ranks during the fighting. And it wouldn't matter, in the end, that he was valuable at his trade and that you couldn't afford to be without him.

"Well," said Hood quietly, somberly, "you go along with the boys this morning, Jude."

McBain nodded as though he had received a benediction, touched the brim of his hat in silent thanks, and Hood wondered what he might have just done and how it could be explained to a woman back in Texas or children who might never know their father. Hood watched as the blacksmith joined his fellows, shook his head, and then an aide was at his elbow, an impatient look on his face, and he asked, "Yes, what is it?"

"General Jackson, sir. He's requesting that we form the brigade and go in, sir."

Hood nodded, saw that the boy was grinning as if a pretty girl had just asked him to go for a buggy ride after dark. "Fine, have the assembly sounded."

The boy turned, ran off toward the nearest knot of soldiers, slapping men on the back as he went, disappeared among the dark trunks of trees and fluttering leaves.

Someone handed him his reins and he ran his hand over the worn brass and dark leather on the horn, swung into the saddle with a practiced motion, the leather creaking as it took his weight, the big horse snorting, sidestepping as Hood found the stirrups. Hood saw soldiers turning toward him, anxious faces, men gulping down the steaming hoecakes, sensing the moment, knowing what must happen.

He nudged the horse with his knees, rode out to take his place in front of the brigade. He would have to say something, he knew. Men expected a few words, some small encouragement before a battle.

He trotted his horse down the line, looking for the center of his division, feeling them gather around him, the collective tensing of a thousand souls.

Not all of the men would hear him. Few, in fact, would be within earshot. A few dozen at most would hear his words. A hundred or so more would learn what he had said from others while they advanced to meet the enemy.

He had ridden to the front earlier, watched the fighting in the first light of day, seen the rolling, smoking ground beyond the forest where they had bivouacked. The meadows and fields rising and falling in softly rounded mounds of earth, as if it were not land at all but a green sea that swelled and rolled before the wind, undulating in gentle waves that swept toward the hills and the rising sun.

Hood wheeled his horse, looked into the pinched faces, the dirty uniforms of the men standing in the long line that snaked through the shady woods. In a glance he saw them all, remembered the difficulties they had shared, the other battles, in Virginia. The long, dusty marches through Maryland to this place at this hour. He knew he could not deceive these men, could not lie to them. No matter how terrible the circumstances, they deserved better from him than deception. They had taken him as one of their own, and it was not in him to deceive them.

"Men of the Texas Brigade!" he shouted and was surprised to hear his own voice ringing through the morning air. Men turned toward him, expectantly, hushed in the shadows cast by the trees, the sunlight washing over them in unexpected rivulets of light. They were watching him now, crowding forward, pressing in on him, straining to hear. A lean boy watched him with somber dark eyes, stroked the flanks of his great horse as he passed, a reverent, gentle touch.

In those few moments Hood saw them all. Steady, calm, waiting for him. He felt a sudden tightness in his throat, the pride and affection welling up in him. He wondered if he could trust his voice. Before he was ready Hood was speaking to them, the earnest, worn faces staring silently back. "General Jackson has called upon us for our support. I have given him my word that the Texas Brigade will not fail him."

He noticed a few of them nodding, knew that they were ready. Saw the peculiar light in their eyes, the same thing he had seen before other battles. Men lost their fear of death, or maybe suborned it to some other deeper, unspoken emotion. It enabled them to walk calmly toward the enemy in even the most pitched battle.

These men knew battle well, held no illusions of easy victory or glory, or a thousand other lies that boys believe when their uniforms are new and their courage untested. And yet the men who stood before him now were willing to go into that hell again, face whatever lay ahead.

No textbook could teach it, or even put a name to it. It wasn't courage, exactly, that sends a man forward into battle. As certainly as he knew that few officers could inspire it, Hood knew these men possessed that unspoken quality in abundance. He had heard men, articulate, veteran officers, attempt to describe it. Usually around a campfire, after a bottle had been passed, but no one ever really found the right words.

Hood felt a familiar lightness, knew that he was ready to lead them into whatever waited beyond the woods and the shadows. Knew that, on this morning, in this place, he too had no fear of cannon or massed infantry or anything else that waited beyond the trees. Hood felt a terrible, bittersweet sensation overtake him. It was pride and joy and a thousand other emotions, and he knew that he was ready to die with these men today on this field.

"Will you honor that pledge?" he asked, his voice booming through the shadows, glancing off the trunks of trees.

There was a moment of silence, and then they were shouting, holding their rifles aloft, yelling for him to give the command that would start them toward the enemy. Hood stood in the stirrups looking at them, knowing that he loved them in a way he could never speak of. Knowing that death waited for them in the bright Maryland sunshine. Knowing that they fought not for the Confederacy, not for Robert Lee, not even for honor, but that they fought for one another. He removed his hat, tipped it toward the lean boys standing in ranks, realized that these men were the best the South would ever send into battle. He wheeled his horse about, nodded toward an officer standing in front of his regiment, pointed silently in the direction of the enemy.

The division moved through the dark woods accompanied only by the sounds of their own footsteps and the crashing of shells overhead, emerging into the bright sunshine in a steady line that eddied and swirled around trees and reformed silently in the deep meadow grass at the edge of the wood. Hood narrowed his eyes against the light, squinted into the distance, searching for the Federal battle lines. Just beyond the woods was the turnpike, on either side a chest-high rail fence, the wood gray and worn except where it had been ripped by the fighting and the splintered new wood shown through in ragged white gashes. Soldiers were sent forward and the rails were thrown to the ground and gaps in the fence appeared where the brigades might pass.

Along the edge of the forest regiments appeared, the lines growing steadily, a rippling wave of men that rolled along the limits of the wood, past the small church, disappeared into a bit of low ground.

The rolling pastures to his front were covered with soldiers, broken muskets, the refuse of war, entire brigades and divisions having come apart in the fighting, their remains scattered across the fields as though by a great wind. Officers and men alike were streaming back toward the safety of the woods and their own lines. Men were down everywhere, lying in the grass, crawling in agonized movements toward the wood behind them, the smoke drifting in great ragged clouds along the ground, a skulking, foul-smelling reminder of war.

He collared a man with long white hair, an old man, heron thin with shocking blue eyes. Hood looked into the glittering eyes and asked, "Where are the Yankees?"

"Up ahead," drawled the soldier, staring at Hood, searching his features. The ancient soldier leered up at him. "In that cornfield yonder," he said, nodding toward the north, spitting a long stream of tobacco juice into the dust. "But you best come loaded for bear, Genr'l. I expect most of the damned Yankee army is up there, and they're waitin' for you and them fellers you got with you."

Hood nodded, noted the man's grimy face, powder-stained uniform. "Are you wounded?" he asked.

"Don't expect I am," said the man evenly.

Hood glared at the soldier. Felt his anger rising. The man had left his colors, abandoned his fellows. "Where is your regiment, sir?" he asked sharply.

The old man shrugged, noncommittal. "Don't reckon I could tell you. Got kinda turned around up there," he said, indicating the cornfield. "Used up all my cartridges too," he said, the voice high-pitched, a sound like flint scraping steel. "And what I could scrounge off'n the dead fellers."

The man continued to stare at him, eyes steady, expressionless. Hood felt his face flush with anger, realized the man was being insolent, reprimanding him. He tightened his grip on the reins, knew that he should move off, abandon this straggler. He touched his horse's flanks with a heel, felt the animal gather himself, the muscle taut beneath the saddle.

The soldier reached out in a lightning movement, raw hands grabbed the bridle, viselike; the stallion snorted, bared his teeth. "Ain't like down in Virginny, Genr'l," he said quickly. "They've learned a thing or two. Got some grit to 'em today."

Hood glared down at the old soldier, nodded. "They'll break," he said confidently. "Always do."

The soldier grinned, a toothless grin that mocked Hood's confidence. "Mebbe," he said. "Your boys got their work cut out fer 'em."

Hood nodded, felt suddenly uneasy, a feeling like a gust of wind that springs up cold and damp on a sunny day. "Find your colors," he said. "We'll need every man before the day is over."

The soldier released the bridle, nodded. "Good luck, to you, Genr'l," he said.

Hood glanced back at the division behind him, men marching solemnly, heads up, bayonets gleaming in the sunlight. A great streaming mass of soldiers that flowed across the meadow, sweeping everything before it, and his heart swelled again with pride and joy and happiness at being a part of it, of them, and this day.

A battery beyond the hill in front roared and canister ripped by overhead, raw, hardened iron, moving just out of reach, unseen, a harbinger of death. The balls gave voice to the air above them, a fluttering noise like quail that rise suddenly from the ground, coming up from nowhere, passing so close you can hear the wind rushing over feathers. In the small hollow his soldiers laughed, grinned encouragement to one another.

Men were beginning to sense the enemy, moving quicker through the open field, leaning toward the hills and the cornfield and the Union men beyond. The ground was torn and smoking from the fighting, wounded soldiers huddled in small groups or lying serenely in the grass waiting for the fighting to pass. Hands reached out to his men as they passed by, grabbing whomever was near, begging for help. His ranks opened around the supplicants, swirled past, men turning their heads, perhaps tossing a canteen to an outstretched hand, shaking their heads in pity, hardening their hearts with each step.

At the edge of the corn, a Union line was trying to form, officers running over the uneven ground, pressing men into ranks. His soldiers stopped as with one mind, leveled their rifles, fired. Smoke blossomed along the length of the line, slammed into the corn and the Federal soldiers with a terrible meaty sound that left him weak. When it cleared the Union line had dissolved; the corn where they had stood was blasted and ripped for some distance, men writhing on the ground in agony or lying in odd, twisted heaps.

His soldiers yelled, the odd high-pitched wail that sent chills down his spine and made grown men quake with fear. And then they were running, the entire line sweeping forward, rifles leveled and the great gleaming bayonets out in front. Plunging in among the stalks of corn, screaming and shooting, chasing what remained of the Federal soldiers through the clinging leaves.

Hood saw a Union gun crew attempt to swing their cannon around to meet the assault. Lean soldiers in gray and brown flashed from the corn, raced toward the shining cannon, swarmed over it just as a gunner pulled the lanyard. There was a violent blast from the muzzle, men went down, disappeared in a gale of shot and dust. And then his men were on the gun, and there was a wild moment of swinging rifles and in another instant Union boys were raising their hands, trying to surrender before it was too late.

Ahead someone was waving the flag back and forth, the cloth brilliant against the green of the corn and the meadow beyond, and there was more confusion as men ran toward it, and another brief furious struggle that could only be seen in glimpses and then they had swept beyond that too.

Firing erupted in unexpected bursts from all directions as men encountered the enemy among the head-high corn. Brief vicious exchanges of gunfire were followed by a surge of men in that direction, the fight over as suddenly as it had begun. Officers were shouting orders, trying to reestablish a line, move men in a single direction, push the Federals out of the field, beyond the corn and the small rise to the east.

An officer reached him, galloped up wild-eyed and eager, a member of Jackson's staff. "General Jackson sends his compliments, sir, and requests that you advise him of the situation on the field."

Hood stared at the man blankly for a second or two, knew that Jackson was waiting on him to move the Yankees out of the corn, beyond the turnpike, relieve the pressure on this end of the field. He glanced briefly in the direction of the Union lines, knew somehow that they were waiting for him behind those hills, great huddled masses of men with cannon and rifles and endless baggage trains. "Tell General Jackson," he said slowly, "that I am going on while I can, but that I must have reinforcements."

The man saluted, a flashing smile of white teeth below a wispy moustache, wheeled off on his horse without a word. Hood watched him go, wondered silently if Jackson would send him help, if there was any help.

Artillery erupted on his left, near the turnpike, a blast of hot air and iron, his men absorbing it, coming apart with each step. The Yankees had gotten a battery in place and case shot and canister thundered into his lines like molten hail. He rode over broken ground, his mount dodging, sidling in nervous, wild-eyed leaps over shattered soldiers lying in the long grass. Hood pointed men toward the cannon with his sword, shouted for them to storm the guns, shoot the gunners and the horses and whatever else they could see through the blinding, choking smoke.

Ahead the fighting swirled around the cannon and then someone pulled a lanyard and the shot boiled out of the barrel, and men disappeared in great billowing clouds of blood and smoke. Hood almost turned his head, and then the anger overcame him and he screamed for them to take the damn guns, and suddenly they were running for them in long strides, men clawing over the fence, desperate, angry, closing suddenly with the cannon. Union boys went down before the sudden fury of the assault, and then there was a brief, frenzied moment when his men began shooting the battery horses and suddenly the big animals were everywhere, clawing and kicking savagely, wild with fright as they tried to break free.

Hood rallied the men, put them back into line. And then Jude McBain was there, smiling up at him with that great, slow smile, his face sweat-streaked and blackened from the fighting. McBain put a hand out, stroked the neck of his horse, said, "You'd best leave the horse behind, Genr'l."

Hood stared at him blankly, uncomprehending, deafened by the roar of cannon and the savagery of the fighting, unable to think.

"Them Yanks see you on this horse and . . ." There was a long pause, the big blacksmith searching for the words, not quite certain of himself. At last he said, "Well, it wouldn't do for you to ride any farther."

Hood swung out of the saddle, slapped the horse on the rump, hoped that it would make its way back to their lines. He patted Jude's shoulder, began to shout for men to fall in, rally around their colors.

A few men were trying to tip over one of the heavy cannon, rocking it back and forth, straining under the enormous weight of it, heaving against the brass and wood of the carriage.

Hood ordered them back into line. A thin line, fewer men than before. Not enough. Jackson had said that they must drive the Yankees back. No choice then; they would have to go on, press forward, come what may.

Shells began to fall into the small depression where his officers were trying to reform the division. A Federal battery had gotten the range, was putting fire on them in earnest, fusing the shells to explode overhead.

A salvo exploded just above them, white hot splinters rocketing down, killing men as they stood waiting for orders, knocking them to the earth in heaps.

He waved the men back, walked toward a small rise, tried to peer beyond the corn, see what the Yankees were about. In the distance a big Union regiment was forming, spreading out in a growing pool of blue that covered the hillside beyond the range of their guns. He watched for long moments, knew that beyond what he had already done it was simply madness. He could ask no more of these men.

With a growing sense of dread he watched as the Union infantry maneuvered, took shape under the cover of their own guns. Prepared to renew the struggle for this one piece of ground.

An officer approached, a young lieutenant whom Hood had seen often, a handsome boy who danced well and was a favorite among the ladies. The lieutenant saluted, said, "The colonel is down, sir. So are most of the company officers, sir." The boy turned, glanced back toward a knot of soldiers standing beneath their colors in the meadow. "What I mean, sir, is . . ." There was a long pause, the boy struggling to compose himself, his face red, straining with the effort.

Hood reached out, put a hand on the boy's shoulder. "I know."

The young lieutenant wiped his face with his sleeve, studied the ground at his feet. "Never been like this before, General. The damn Yankee artillery is everywhere."

Officers were sending to him, requesting orders, instructions for their regiments. Casualties were high, ammunition exhausted. Someone had thought to send a regiment or two to them from the right; beyond his sight, he could hear them going in. A sudden violent explosion of rifle fire. Put some pressure on them, give him a minute or two to make his mind up. Harvey Hill, maybe. He had been over on the right the evening before.

Hood signaled to an officer, waved the man over. "Order the men back," he said.

They walked back through the green stalks in silence. Men stopped to help the wounded, carry them back toward the small church that loomed out of the smoke ahead. Everywhere men were down, groaning terribly, calling for water.

Hood saw the big bay standing near the road, cropping grass. The animal lifted its head nervously as he approached, flattened its ears as he grabbed the reins. He mounted, looked about, felt a terrible sadness overcome him.

His division was ruined. The bravest among them would be left here, in this field, buried in unmarked graves by strangers. A soldier walked past him, moving slowly, gingerly holding a hand over a bloody wound in his arm. They were drifting back, small groups of soldiers, a tide of men moving back toward the chapel and the dark wood.

Hood looked into each face, searched every expression, waited for some recrimination, some expression of bitterness. None came. Just a steady trickle of men breaking from the corn, walking through the ruined meadow.

In a daze Hood looked about, knew that they could never really recover from these few minutes in Maryland. That, somehow, they had lost more on this field than lives.

Someone was speaking, the words a murmur, behind him. He turned, stared woodenly at a boy of eighteen or twenty wearing the uniform jacket of a captain, a round, tanned face beneath a shock of blond hair. "Yes?" said Hood.

"General Jackson requests to know the position of your division, General Hood," repeated the boy.

Hood looked away from the boy, wondered briefly how old he might be, his gaze sweeping over the field where they had fought. He closed his eyes, remembering the sight of them in ranks this morning, the sound of some anonymous soldier's laughter coming to him through the night in a darkened bivouac. *A soldier's life*, he thought, his mind trailing off into blankness.

"Sir?" said the officer.

Hood turned, stared vacantly at the boy for a long moment, fought against the grief that swelled in him, knew that this boy would never understand until it was too late. That none of them understood the terrible tragedy of it, the futility.

Hood looked into the placid eyes, thought: *He should be home some-*

place, courting a girl, holding hands and stealing kisses when her father wasn't about. A feeling of grief swept over him, a slow, steady tide that he sensed would never leave.

"Your division, General Hood?" insisted the boy. "Its position?"

Long moments passed, Hood feeling hollow, vacant. Inside something was breaking, slowly, gingerly, like fine glass on stone. He turned, knew that the boy-soldier was waiting for his answer. The army would go on. There would be other fields, other battles.

He turned, slowly, looked into the boy's eyes, stared for long moments without recognition. "Dead upon the field, son," said Hood slowly. "Dead upon the field."

JOE HOOKER NARROWED HIS EYES, PEERED ACROSS THE EXPANSE of grass and rolling ground to the smoky wood where the Rebels waited. He drew in a deep breath, glanced behind him at the sun, saw that it had risen just over the rocky ridges to the east.

An hour, maybe two, since the fighting had started. Soldiers wandered about the field, sullen men with hard eyes who had seen their fill of fighting on this day. Two of his three divisions were wrecked, the regiments having been shot away to nothing in the fighting since sunrise.

Meade's division was up north, beyond the big barn where he had spent the night. They had not engaged, and now they were waiting, out of sight, holding the flank of the entire army. One division, a single division to take whatever Lee could throw at them.

He ran a practiced eye along the length of the Confederate line, searched for some sign of movement that they were coming again, forming, ready to lunge out of the wood and hit him again. He turned, rose in the stirrups, listened for some sign of battle from the south, beyond the town and the line of dark trees that marked the course of the creek. Silence.

"Damn him!" he said to no one in particular, wondering what excuse Burnside or McClellan or the both of them would give for not having gone in when they were supposed to. He was being cut to ribbons, throwing everything he had at the Rebels, and so far not so much as a shot from Burnside's end of the field.

For long moments he stood heavily in the stirrups, the field strangely quiet, the fog and the smoke settling lazily into the small valleys where the fighting had been heaviest.

The field was hushed, silent, not even a breeze moving through the tall meadow grass.

Eye of the storm. They'll be back. And soon.

Hooker gazed toward the small town. There was movement there. Men and wagons, artillery rumbling between the buildings. A plume of dark smoke smudged the sky. A house had caught fire from the shelling.

A hill rose above the town, round shouldered, a sprinkling of trees. He could see cannon there, a few guns, dark silhouettes of men moving about. If Burnside had engaged, those guns would be firing. He stared at the hill for long moments, waited. Nothing.

Odd place for them to stand. River at their back, nothing much between our army and theirs in the way of terrain.

The realization hit him like summer lightning on a moonless night, rushed up at him from the recesses of his mind, white and blinding, and in an instant he knew the truth of it. Their last charge had been an act of desperation, a bluff. There was nothing more behind it.

The Rebels were fought out. Spent. The morning's fighting had exhausted them, consumed them as his own divisions had been consumed.

He searched again for some sign of movement from the wood beyond the small church. Nothing. Lee and Jackson were exhausted, their men licking their wounds in the trees beyond the church.

If they had anything left they would have followed up their last charge. Sent heavy infantry against his scattered formations, tried to turn his flank. Instead there was . . . nothing. A great gaping void beyond the wood and the church. A hollow army. The thought struck him like a blow.

Now was the time to press his attack home, drive them back off that bit of high ground, force them off the long ridge. With another division or two he could roll up Lee's flank, drive them into the Potomac, force them to abandon their guns and baggage trains.

He swung into the saddle, saw that the sun was well up over the ridge to the east. Plenty of time left to force the issue, bring them to terms. No excuses now about a lack of daylight. The army was here, all of it. The men were in a fine mood, no matter that a division or two was out of the fight. He glanced again toward the town. The roads were empty, silent, shining white in the bright light.

They were hurting over there too. Licking their wounds, out of sight.

He slapped the reins against the neck of the horse, glanced toward the east, wondering where the Twelfth Corps was, how far back?

They should be close by, just beyond the Antietam. A mile to the rear at most. An hour's march. If McClellan would give him another corps or two, it could all be over by noon.

It was clear now, they had hit the Rebels from the north at dawn, forced them back toward Sharpsburg. Lee had counterattacked. Keep him off balance, make him think they were stronger over there than they really were. Lee was relying on his army's reputation, his past victories, trying to forestall another attack.

It had almost worked.

Now he must hit them again, regain the ground lost in the last charge, keep pushing them back in on their own lines, toward the Potomac, always herding them toward the river.

The Twelfth Corps would be moving onto the field in almost perfect position. Bit of luck there, but that was just what they needed. They would come onto the field in column; there would be some confusion, nothing that couldn't be sorted out. An hour to deploy them, swing them in a long line facing the Hagerstown Road. Simple. Align them on the road, advance straight toward it. Even the volunteers couldn't confuse that.

Superb. Lee and Jackson, caught in a vise between his men and the river.

Shots popped from the wood beyond the cornfield. Scattered firing, the Rebels shooting slowly, carefully. Hooker smiled, realized the men firing were single soldiers, aimed fire, not massed volleys. They were running low, advanced beyond their supply wagons, unable to get support because there wasn't any available. All that beautiful open ground between them and the Rebels beyond the Hagerstown Road.

The Twelfth Corps men would push them out of the woods. Weight of numbers they had called it at the Academy. Jackson should have known better. Lee, too.

Now he would make them pay the price for their mistakes. More firing now, the sharp report of cannon. A battery was swinging into position, raking the cornfield in angry salvos.

He could feel the tempo of battle resuming, the big Parrott rifles firing from beyond the Antietam, suppressing the Southern artillery, forcing them off the high ground. Shells exploded in dirty geysers on the ridge near the church; the air heaving and tearing with each explosion. The Rebels had no cannon large enough to challenge the long-range Parrotts, the Northern guns were firing easily, forcing the Southern battery off the ridge.

Now was the time. If only McClellan or Burnside or someone would have the sense to hit them on the other end of the field. A division-size assault would suffice. Anything to distract them, give him an hour to bring the Twelfth Corps up, get them on line, prevent Lee from shifting men toward this end of the field.

From behind a regiment emerged from the wood, a big regiment, new uniforms, gleaming buttons. Volunteers. He could see the hesitation, the unsure movements.

He slapped the reins against the neck of the horse, galloped toward them, saw with relief that they were from the Twelfth Corps.

An officer broke from the head of the column, rode toward him, saluted, reined in, his horse skidding to a stop in the wet earth. "General Williams, sir."

"Yes," said Hooker, "Where is he?"

"He's down, General," the man explained. "Not ten minutes past. They're moving him to the rear now."

An alarm sounded in him, far away. An insistent drumming, a warning. They had panicked at Manassas with much less severe fighting. The Twelfth Corps was coming onto the field without direction. Big new regiments, inexperienced officers, volunteer soldiers. It could all go wrong in an instant. One more Rebel charge like the last one and they would break before they had gotten into the fight. The entire corps might go, take to their heels without firing so much as a shot.

No time for any complicated maneuvering. Just line them up and send them across those fields toward the road and the Rebels beyond it.

Just let McClellan and the others stay out of it long enough for me to see them off. Another hour.

He stared again at the hill, the waiting Southern artillerymen.

Damn McClellan and his never-ending caution. Good men will die because he is too timid to commit the army.

Hooker spotted an officer, a colonel, kneeling behind a fence, staring off toward the west and the woods where the Rebels waited. "Colonel," he shouted, "prepare your men to advance."

The officer turned toward him. He was lean and dark eyed, with a narrow, hatchet face that Hooker mistrusted. He spotted Hooker's rank, made a half-hearted effort at a salute, seemed reluctant to leave the fence. "Advance, General?" he asked.

Hooker jerked a thumb toward the Rebel position. "Who is in front of you, Colonel?" he asked.

The man shook his head, "Just the Rebs, sir," he replied.

Hooker nodded. It was very clear now. They had withdrawn their artillery; their cannon would be headed for a secondary gun line. Their infantry, what was left of them, would be in those woods, or just on the other side of them. Lee and Jackson were trying to save their gun line, pushing their weakened infantry out in front, counting on the woods and the earlier charge to intimidate him.

He peered at the shadows and trees, cursed McClellan again. The damn cavalry had been held in reserve. No way to know what was beyond the church and the wood without cavalry. He would have to go in blind. It was no damn way to fight a battle.

And there was no time to wait, even if McClellan would release the cavalry to him. Every minute that passed gave Lee time to reinforce, reorganize his lines. Time was of the essence. Better to drive in on them now, not give them time enough to straighten things out over there.

He signaled to the colonel. "A word with you, sir."

The man stood, walked over as Hooker nudged his horse forward. He stopped on the rise, facing west, looking again at the small white church that had been his objective for most of the day. He pointed. "Send your men forward, toward that church, and into the woods beyond." Hooker looked at the officer, saw him nod, knew that he understood. "Your men will find Rebel skirmishers in those woods, maybe a company-sized unit or two, but you must not fall back. Am I understood?"

"Yes, General," said the colonel. His voice was hesitant, unsure.

"They are giving ground; our attacks of the morning have weakened them."

The colonel smiled, a grim smile full of tobacco-stained teeth. "Whole damn Rebel army is likely to be in those woods, General."

Hooker shook his head, saw where the colonel was going, knew that his officers were listening. "Not very likely, Colonel."

The colonel turned, looked around, searched for some sign of support. "I would like to wait on the Twelfth Corps to move up, sir. Support my boys."

Hooker felt his temper rising. The man was a colonel, in charge of a regiment, and yet he seemed to lack confidence. The whole damn army was infected with McClellan's caution, his fear of losing. None of them could see it, understand that you have to take the offensive to win battles. "See here, Colonel," he began, pointing toward the woods, "they have withdrawn their guns from that plateau. The fire your men are suffering now is coming from beyond the woods to our front. If you advance, their gunners will lose contact with your position; the accuracy and rate of their fire will diminish." Hooker looked at the man. "Do you understand?" he asked again.

The man looked up at him, his face a mask, his eyes sullen. "Yes, sir, I do. It's just that those woods are likely to be full of Rebels, and we are only one regiment. I've got no one on either flank to support my advance, General."

"You won't be in those woods by yourself very long, Colonel," explained Hooker. "The Twelfth Corps is moving onto the field now. They will move up to support you within the hour."

The man nodded. A grim, uncertain look on his features. "I'll get my men moving," he said.

"You'll do fine, Colonel. The Twelfth Corps will be on the field within the hour." Hooker felt his horse shimmy, a sudden nervous movement. The big animal shied, sidestepped. He tightened his grip on the reins, heard the unmistakable sound of a minie ball striking the big stallion, saw the trail of blood down the white flanks. Damned Rebels had seen him, were shooting at his horse.

"Best get off this hill, General," said the colonel. "Rebs have got our range."

Hooker nodded. A ball snapped past. "Get them moving, Colonel," he said.

He felt the sudden jolt in his right foot, a hot, stinging fist, knew he had been hit by a ball. His horse reared, its eyes white with fear. "Those woods," he said fighting to control the big animal, "don't allow the damned Rebels to push you from them." He glanced down at his foot, saw the neat hole in the heel of his boot, a trickle of shiny blood on the black leather.

The man saluted. He wheeled the horse, saw that his orderly corporal was behind him. Only a little longer now, move those other two corps up, get them on line. Into the fight.

Simple matter really, show them the ground, communicate to their staff officers where the line of advance would be formed, where to post their batteries. Bring up their brigades. Once everybody was on line, step off.

He felt a sudden dizziness, realized the wound in his foot was bleeding. The horse slowed to a walk. The big animal was suffering from his own wounds. Fine mount, be a shame to lose him. *Maybe he won't have to be put down,* thought Hooker. They had been shooting at him from very long range.

Foolish thing to do, expose himself on that crest. Still a general had to lead from the front. No other way to lead soldiers. They sensed weakness, wouldn't follow a man who lacked courage.

A courier approached, saluted. Pointed to a formation of Union soldiers nearby. The man was going on, speaking to him about a battery, placement of the guns. Hooker nodded, told the man to order the guns forward on his authority.

He motioned to his corporal, waved the boy forward toward the woods where the advance elements of the Second Corps were emerging, a steady procession of men standing to their arms in the morning light. He moved his foot, carefully, waited for the pain. It came quick enough, a burning sensation that left him nauseous. He struggled to maintain his seat in the saddle, waited for the dizziness to pass.

The orderly was watching him, keeping his distance, undecided as to what to do. Hooker waved him over. "Corporal," he began—Hooker felt himself sliding into unconsciousness, threw a hand over the orderly's shoulder—"help me down, son."

The corporal brought his mount close, grabbed Hooker's uniform coat with a rough hand. The two animals walked toward the wood, slowly, his leg jarring roughly against that of the orderly. Hooker tried to force himself to think clearly, remain alert. He knew he was losing blood, that he would pass out soon.

He moved the foot again, another burning jolt of pain that brought him up sharp, focused his senses. They were among the trees now, soldiers standing about, some looking at him, mouths open. A few men recognized him, attempted a cheer. He lifted his hat, waved it toward them.

Somewhere a drum was beating, men were shouting, slapping each other on the back. A snatch of conversation came to him, men congratulating one another on the day's fighting.

Victory. Someone said it. He could hear happy voices, lots of handshaking.

He felt a sudden stab of apprehension. It was too soon; they had won nothing yet. The only thing the morning's fighting had won for them was an opportunity. And an opportunity had to be exploited. They must not lose their momentum, give the Rebels a chance to recover, establish a line.

Men were grabbing him, lifting him out of the saddle, laying him on the ground. A surgeon appeared above him, asked if he wanted brandy. He shook his head, tried to speak, knew he was slurring his words. The orderly kneeled by him, removed the spur from his boot, nodded to the surgeon. Hooker winced in pain and the boy stopped.

He had to get word to Sumner, Mansfield. Move their corps forward, drive into the Rebels right at the woods, near the small church. Mind the flanks, those guns beyond the woods. Can't leave their right unprotected. Damn Rebel artillery would cut them to pieces. Bound to be infantry nearby, the Rebel commanders wouldn't post those batteries without infantry support.

"Corporal," he said. The boy turned, looked at him with great dark eyes. Hooker realized that the orderly thought he was going to die. From a wound in the foot of all places. "Find General Meade," Hooker paused, fought to stay alert. "Tell him that he is now in command of the First Corps, that I have been taken from the field." Hooker grabbed the boy's sleeve, held him. "Tell General Meade he must communicate the situation to General Sumner when he comes up with the Second Corps."

He looked into the orderly's eyes. "General Meade will understand, but tell him all they need is one more good push. Concentrate the Twelfth and Second Corps, everyone to attack toward the little church and drive them into the Potomac."

Hooker paused, felt the pain coming in small, bright waves, closed his eyes. "Go, son. Now," he said. The orderly ran off, Hooker watched with satisfaction as the orderly swung into the saddle, rode off.

When he woke he was in an ambulance, the surgeon leaning over him. "You lost consciousness, General."

Hooker nodded, "How long?"

The surgeon shrugged. "Five minutes, sir. No more."

Hooker nodded. "Have you seen General Sumner or General Mansfield?"

An odd look passed over the surgeon's face. Hooker wasn't quite sure what it meant. "Well?" he asked expectantly.

The surgeon swallowed. "You were speaking with General Sumner a minute ago, sir. I was just there"—the man pointed—"while the two of you spoke. Maybe you don't remember due to your wound, General."

Hooker blinked, realized Sumner had probably looked in on him, then left when he saw that he couldn't tell him anything. Hooker felt a sinking feeling in his chest. "Take me to General McClellan's headquarters, Doctor. And when we get there wake me in order that I may speak with General McClellan or you'll spend the rest of the war wishing you had."

The surgeon swallowed. "Yes, sir," he said.

Hooker waved the man away, felt the ambulance jolt forward. McClellan would be a mile or two to the rear. He would give him his appraisal when he arrived. General Meade had been on the field with his division since daylight; he would understand what was needed. *One more good push*, thought Hooker, the ambulance jarring along toward army headquarters.

CHAPTER 14

THE SOUND OF FIRING HAD BROUGHT HIM SHARPLY AWAKE WELL before dawn. The first scattered firing of skirmishers groping toward one another in the dark, then the heavy rumbling of massed cannon that grew with each minute until it merged into one continuous roar, the sound steady and powerful and constant, like water rushing down a rocky gorge.

It had been as he expected. General McClellan had moved against the left, a heavy attack, massed infantry supported by long-range artillery. An attack meant to break his flank, roll his army back on itself, force them into the town and the river beyond.

"General Lee?"

He turned, saw Walter Taylor, his hands full of dispatches. "Yes, Mr. Taylor?" he asked, resisting a smile.

"General Walker sends word that he is moving to reinforce the left with two brigades. General McLaws's men are on the field and will be in position shortly."

He nodded, thought: *General McClellan is reluctant to commit his army. He is attacking with less than his full strength.*

Lee listened, heard only sporadic firing. From the right, beyond the town, there was nothing. A great, vacuous silence. *They have disengaged. General Jackson has turned them back, and now they will reorganize, perhaps shift their attacks, move down our lines obliquely, search for a weak spot.*

McLaws was up, Walker nearly in position.

Trust. I must trust these officers. They will know what must be done.

The road beyond his tent was crowded with the slow-moving wounded from the morning's fighting. Men shuffled past, heads down, hushed.

He turned, saw that Taylor was waiting, asked, "Have we any word from A. P. Hill?"

Taylor dropped his eyes, appeared to search the ground for an answer. "None, General. I am told that his division was moving at first light this morning."

Lee nodded. "Yes," he said.

Major Venable appeared from out of the mist, a stricken look on his face. Venable was a valuable officer, a trusted aide.

Lee waved him forward. "You have news from General Jackson?"

"General Hood, sir. He reports that his division has suffered greatly. He does not expect to be able to return to the fighting today in any great force."

An alarm shot through Lee, a warning. A sudden unexpected caution. Hood.

"Is General Hood hurt?" he asked.

Venable shook his head. "No, sir. Not that I know of anyway." Venable looked away, said, "He was quite firm that his division is out of the fight, General."

For a moment he stared at Venable, the thin face, the soft eyes, wondered if the man could have gotten it wrong. Hood.

I cannot spare General Hood's division.

There was a long moment when no one spoke. From beyond the town, the firing was picking up, the deep bass of heavy cannon rolling toward them from the direction of the Antietam.

A bombardment. General McClellan is renewing his attack. Another half hour, perhaps less, and he will send his infantry.

One of his batteries answered, from beyond the wood to the northeast. He looked at Taylor, asked, "Well?" There was a pause, a long moment when he considered not riding forward, leaving Jackson and Hood and the others to their work. At last he said, "I should have a look at things then."

The news of Hood lingered, tugged at the back of his mind, refused to go away. Hood could not be spared, not today.

Lee mounted, guided the big horse past slender oaks, out toward the road where the wounded streamed past in unsteady confusion. The orderly sergeant was out in front, moving through the traffic in the road, making a path, shunting men and wagons aside.

Soldiers stared as he passed; great dark eyes followed him as the little procession wound slowly through the town. The odor of camphor drifted by, a sweet, sickly smell, and then he saw the wounded lying in someone's yard, and the surgeon's tent just beyond the house. Taylor began to speak, but he held up a hand, hushed him, removed his hat.

A cannon clattered by, the gun and carriage moving slowly, heavily, two horses straining against the weight of the gun, the crew gazing at him, staring as they made their way back toward the supply trains.

Behind the big gun another of the battery horses limped along, trying to stay with its fellows. Lee saw that the animal had been cut from its traces, the leather harness dragging behind over the bricks of the street. The horse moved slowly, unsteadily, intent on not being separated from the others.

A small buzzing cloud shadowed the mare, a long, dark swath of blood stained her flanks. Lee watched as the horse drew even, saw that he was the only person aware of it. "Orderly," he said, "stop that animal. Now, sir."

The orderly turned, unaware of the wounded horse. "Sir?" he asked.

"That horse," said Lee, pointing, "I want it stopped." He felt the anger grow inside him. He looked toward the artillerymen as they continued down the street, apparently oblivious to the plight of this animal. Lee felt the anger rise, fought back the urge to yell at the cannoneers.

The orderly stepped in front of the big animal, said, "Whoa, now, girl."

The horse shuddered, stopped, dropped its head with an air of resignation. The big sergeant stroked the great muscles of the neck, spoke to it soothingly. Lee watched as the orderly turned, said to him, "Reckon she's done in, General."

Lee glared down at the man. Soldiers in the road had stopped, men elbowed their companions. "Give that animal some water, Sergeant," he said, his voice brittle with anger.

"Sir?" asked the orderly.

"I want you to take that animal to water, Sergeant," he repeated. He stared at the man, wondered for a moment how mortal men could become so callous, indifferent to the suffering of another being.

The sergeant looked around, a puzzled expression on his face. "Now, General? You want me to take her now, sir?"

Lee nodded. "Yes. Mr. Taylor and I will wait here for you."

The sergeant bobbed his head, said slowly, "I'll do it, General." He pulled on the bridle, the mare stepping forward painfully.

"Sergeant," said Lee.

The man turned, looked up at him. "Yes, sir?"

"After you have allowed her to drink her fill, you will find a suitable place and put her down."

The sergeant nodded. "Yes, sir. I figured as much."

Men continued to move past, Lee and Taylor waiting in the road, looking straight ahead. A few moments, then a single shot rang out from behind a nearby barn. "Well," he said to no one in particular. The orderly returned; Taylor motioned to the soldier.

They moved at a trot through town, men stepping aside for them, women staring from porches. He swung the great horse northward, passing more houses, and then the village slipped away, and they were riding between fields of corn and summer wheat, and ahead a column of infantry was raising a haze of dust with their passage.

McLaws. Ahead of him, beyond the dust, would be Walker's division.

And Hood. Somewhere ahead, among the trees, Hood would be waiting. The thought struck him again that Venable's report was exaggerated.

It was like that sometimes, when the fighting was particularly heavy, and men were down in great impossible numbers and entire regiments came apart in the face of superior fire from the enemy. He had seen officers so stricken by the carnage of war that they lost their nerve, were shocked, numbed, unable to carry on.

Only this is General Hood, and that officer will not lose his nerve.

The terrible certainty of it sunk in then, the truth of it hit him, clear and blinding, a white-hot revelation that struck so hard that his breath caught in his throat for an instant. Hood's division was out of the fighting, lost, and there was no one who could replace them.

I have gambled everything on General McClellan's reluctance to aggressively engage his army, and now I have lost General Hood's division and there is only Walker and McLaws to answer their next attack.

He swung off the road, through a meadow of clover that had not yet been cut, and the sweet smell of it wafted up to him through the muggy air.

Ahead he saw a lone horseman, recognized the solitary figure of Jackson.

General Jackson will know the situation.

Lee rode up, reined in alongside Jackson, smiled. "General, are you well this morning?"

"Fine," said Jackson.

Lee sensed the other man's calm, looked into distant blue eyes. There was great resolve there, profound determination. A feeling of quiet strength. "How are we faring, General? I have had reports that the fighting has been very heavy."

Jackson nodded. "There's been heavy fighting." He pointed, indicated a spot beyond the wood. "Around the little church. They came after us. I posted some of our batteries there, and they made a fight of it. Looks to be Joe Hooker's corps."

Lee peered through the wood. The chapel gleamed white between the trunks of trees. "I am sending you the divisions of McLaws and Walker."

Jackson nodded. "I expect they'll be back. Another half hour, maybe a bit more."

"Yes," said Lee. "Walker's people should be in place by then. General McLaws's division is no more than a half-hour march from you now."

"Good," said Jackson.

"General Hood's division," he began. Jackson was shaking his head, staring straight ahead.

So it's true then. General Hood's division is out of the fighting.

Jackson turned toward him, bright-eyed, steady. "General Hood's men have done all that I can ask of them today," he said simply.

Lee nodded, accepted it without comment. "Can we hold?" he asked.

There was a long pause. Jackson shifted in the saddle, the leather creaking noisily. "Hooker will be back, but with Walker up and McLaws on the way, we shouldn't have a problem."

"I can send you another battery," offered Lee.

Jackson shrugged. "Shouldn't need them. I've established a secondary gun line out of sight of the Union's long-range weapons." Jackson turned, looked toward a group of artillerymen moving their cannon into position. "So long as they don't send too much our way at once, we should be fine."

From the wood there was a soft popping of rifle fire. Lee pointed, asked, "Can you hold that wood?"

Jackson hesitated for a moment, considering the question. After a long minute he said, "If McLaws gets into position in the next few minutes, he'll be on their flank as they move across the open ground beyond the little church. Walker and what's left of Hood's men can hold them until then."

Lee stared at the silent woods. Artillery rumbled from the east, long-range guns. To the south there was silence.

If General McClellan coordinates his attacks on both ends of the field, the situation will become impossible to maintain.

"You must hold this line at all costs, General," Lee said at last.

Jackson smiled. A rare, bright smile, the blue eyes shining, almost gleeful.

"I have no one else to send to you. Powell Hill has not arrived, and I do not expect him until afternoon at the earliest."

"I'll hold," said Jackson quietly.

Lee tightened the slack in the reins, prepared to move off. "See that your flank to the north is well anchored. They must not get behind us."

Jackson brought his hand up in salute. Lee looked again at the bright eyes, the broad face. "If they expose their flank to General McLaws, we shall have an opportunity to punish them."

Jackson nodded. "I'll see McLaws understands." There was a long pause, Jackson silent, pensive. "It would take General McClellan out of the fight," he said slowly.

"You believe that it can be done, given our present situation?"

Moments passed, the firing from beyond the wood growing, spreading along the front, rolling down the lines. Jackson shrugged. "Maybe," he said at last.

"Well," said Lee.

"We'll need another division to do it, leave Stuart's cavalry to hold the flank, counter any move they make."

"Yes," said Lee.

"It won't come easy, General," Jackson said, after a moment. "They've fought well this morning."

"No," said Lee. "We will have to wait, see how the morning develops. I may require you to attack in order to relieve pressure on our lines in other areas."

Jackson nodded, silent, brooding. "Maybe a brigade or two, swing around to the north, cross the turnpike, come in behind them, get in among their rear areas."

Lee watched the younger man, sensed the inner fierceness, thought: *He will know what must be done.*

Lee pulled the horse around, raised a hand, moved off toward the village glowing in the morning sunlight. He rode to a small rise in the ground, gazed toward the north, peered into the haze and smoke, thought: *They have not used their cavalry to scout our position. General McClellan does not know our disposition. He is attacking blindly, reconnoitering our lines by his own attacks. And he believes himself outnumbered.*

He turned, glanced back toward the lone figure on horseback, saw Jackson dismount, lead his horse toward a cluster of aides. He sensed again the unapproachable solitude, the repressed fury. A sudden wave of relief washed over him, a feeling that if Jackson could hold, then the entire line would be held, and no army of men would break it.

A breeze rattled the leaves in the trees, brought with it the sweet, heavy scent of ripening hay, and Lee felt again the indomitable will of the younger man, the unyielding resolve.

A shell rattled by, hissed out of sight, disappeared over the crest of the hill.

Taylor was waiting, a respectful distance away, a reproachful look on his face.

Through the trees he could see the road, a single track leading north, a barn, another wood. Beyond that there was only the Federal army.

If they come that way, through that wood, there is nothing behind this line but the river, and you will have lost everything.

He closed his eyes for a moment, saw a vision of a windy plain, the old army out West, the second cavalry, full of young faces that were a bit older now, most of them here. Some of them beyond those trees, making ready to move this way.

Good men, all of them.

A dry, hot day, the chaplain droning on beneath a Texas sun, his mind drifting, wandering. He had sat among those men, head bowed, quietly read the from the Old Testament. A story of Roman conquest, of Jewish sects hiding in the mountains of Galilee.

The Jewish commander had ordered a lieutenant to handpick a few men for an impossible mission. They had marched through the desert, a day of heat and sun, and at the end of the day the men had been allowed to drink from a stream. The lieutenant had picked only twelve men, though he might have chosen twice that number. When asked why he had chosen so few, he replied that he selected only the men who cupped their hands and lifted the water to their mouths, their eyes never leaving the horizon, careful, waiting, watching for the Romans.

Their name came to him, from long ago, through the heat and the years and the misty curtain of memory: Zealots.

Jackson was his zealot, his eyes always on the horizon, waiting, watching. A single purpose, a refined fury that knew no limits, had no bounds.

And so they will come again, those men who are not Romans, and Jackson will be waiting, and men will die, and the line will hold because Jackson has said it will hold.

And God will judge us all.

CHAPTER 15

A CHURCH BELL RANG, A SINGLE PEAL THAT BOUNCED AND ECH-
oed along the rock walls of the canyon, piercing the quiet, then slipping away, fading into the distance. Powell Hill slipped the gold watch
from his pocket, saw that it was midmorning, squinted into the blinding light that flared off the surface of the flat water near the middle
of the river.

He had been up since well before the dawn, watching the light
build steadily behind the green mountains until at last the sun had
crested the ridge and flooded the valley below with gleaming light.

He had fought the urge to order them on the road even before
daylight, to start them marching north toward Lee and Jackson and
Longstreet and the Yankee army that waited somewhere ahead, out
of sight, beyond the mountains and the river. He had waited while
men and animals were fed, the columns assembled, and the teamsters
whipped their animals onto the road; and when he could stand it no
longer, he left word for them to step off as soon as possible and then
he had ridden out ahead of the infantry to a spot where the road was
clear and there was a bit of high ground that he hoped would give
him a view of things.

Hill wiped his face with the cloth from his pocket and stared in
silence at the valley stretching away before him. The Potomac wound
past rocks and brush-covered islands that rose haphazardly in midstream, the clear water pooling and eddying close to the muddy
banks, swirling and foaming around obstructions, falling away toward
Harpers Ferry.

In the distance there was a low rumble, a long, steady sound that
moved slowly down the valley, hovered over the quiet water, merging
at last with the murmur of the river far below.

He felt a tightening in his chest, an urge to ride ahead, see for
himself what was happening.

They had engaged. Somewhere near Sharpsburg, Lee had turned,
invited an attack, and McClellan had gone for the bait. And here he
was, miles back, out of the fight, with little chance of arriving in time
to see real action.

From the north came another rumble, the sound like that of a thunderstorm that hovers just over the horizon, then rolls in on black clouds. He stared at the empty road that stretched along the river, a dusty track leading nowhere, disappearing beyond a curve, a bright ribbon through the forest that seemed to mock him.

By the time they got there, it might all be over. That was the hell of it. Come all this way, march the men until they were just about played out, get to within a few miles of the big fight, and then miss the whole damn show because Jackson had left him behind to guard a few prisoners and some captured cannon.

Hill cursed, glanced at the sun for the hundredth time that morning, wondered how hard he could push them in this heat.

No way to tell what kind of shape they were in up north either. He had sent couriers forward, but by the time they covered the distance and made their way back to him, it could all be said and done.

And no way to push his brigades any harder either. Jackson be damned; his men were close to done in. The endless heat and the bad food were more than a match for any man.

He turned, saw the head of the column sweeping around a curve in the road, a great sweating mass of men who bounced along through the shimmering heat, heads down, leaning into their stride.

A dark knot of men broke from the line of march, headed for a tree near the side of the road, and lay down, arms over their faces. He moved toward them, wondering what to say to soldiers exhausted by weeks of marching and fighting on scant rations.

An officer saw him, veered from the column, and moved toward the men. Hill waved him off. "Never mind them," he said.

He stopped his horse near the group of soldiers, the men so tired they did not even look to see who had approached. Hill dismounted, walked toward the group. When his shadow fell across their faces one of them moved his hand away, peered at him through the sunlight.

"We'll git movin' agin directly," he said. "Just need a minute or two to git our wind," said the man.

Hill nodded, offered his canteen. The man took it, swallowed the water greedily. He held it toward one of his companions. "You mind?" he asked.

"No," said Hill, watching as the others drank from the canteen.

"You from the cavalry?" one asked.

Hill smiled, knew they did not recognize him.

"Yep," he answered.

The soldier chuckled. "Sent to round us up, keep us on the move then?"

Hill nodded. "Orders are we are to get to Sharpsburg. Assist General Lee."

A second man moved his hand away from his face, squinted up at him in the bright light. The soldier studied him through narrowed eyes, then looked at his companions. "Talks mighty fancy for a cavalryman," he said to no one in particular. He continued to stare at Hill.

After a moment the soldier added, "Assist General Lee and all." He elbowed the other boy. "Ain't like you and General Lee are goin' to be havin' coffee and biscuits together this evenin'. Now is it?"

Hill smiled. "No, probably not," he said casually. "Still, I'm ordered to keep you moving."

"Suppose the army can spare us a few minutes then, friend?" asked the man, winking at his companion. "That is, if you and General Lee don't mind so much."

Hill nodded. "Suppose so," he said. "But we'll all have to get up with the rest of the army as fast as possible."

"Well then," said the first soldier, "whyn't you loan us that horse of yours? Reckon that would get us to Sharpsburg a mite faster than these tired ole' feet of mine."

The men grinned, exchanged glances, laughing at the joke. Hill smiled, shook his head. "You boys had anything to eat today?" he asked.

"Ate like kings up to Harpers Ferry yisterdy," answered one. "Them Yanks appear to be a bit better fed than us, that's fer sure."

"Why you know, they had oysters in tin cans," said another. "What do you make of that? Oysters." The man shook his head, apparently unable to comprehend an army that dined on seafood in the midst of the mountains.

"Oysters," repeated Hill. "You don't say, now."

The soldier nodded, slapped his haversack. "Got a bag full of them tins here to prove it too."

Hill grinned. "Well," he began, "you boys get back on the road once you've got your wind."

"We'll do it, Colonel," said the first soldier, grinning broadly. "Wouldn't want to disappoint Genr'l Lee or our friends in the cavalry."

Hill nodded, touched the brim of his hat. "I'll have that canteen back too, if it's all the same to you gentleman."

The soldiers laughed, chided their companion. "Thought we was goin' to skin you for that canteen, trooper."

Hill smiled, caught the canteen as it was thrown to him. "Sharpsburg," he said, moving off.

There was another rumble, low and distant, and Hill felt the tension return, bear down on him.

He raised his eyes to the horizon, saw only white sky, a dirty cloud of dust blowing over the road. At least if they were still firing, the battle wasn't over. There might still be time.

Be a shame to miss this one. There was speculation that this might be the last battle of the war. Beat the Union army one good time on their own ground; it would almost certainly force them to call it quits. Plenty of people up North were tired of the fighting.

The thought struck him that his would be the only major command of the army to miss out on the action if it ended before he got there. All of them were up there: Lee, Longstreet, Jackson.

And the others. Good-natured old Burnside, who could never quite seem to get things right. George McClellan, who could never do anything wrong.

He had known George McClellan and Ambrose Burnside since West Point. They had been more than classmates. They had been friends. He and Burnside had spent long nights together, breaking curfew, drinking into the small hours of the morning. Enjoying the forbidden pleasures of cadet life.

He and George McClellan had fallen in love with the same girl.

Ellen Marcy. A sudden unexpected pang of emotion welled up inside him, an almost forgotten bittersweet memory that made him pause in the bright sunshine, if only for a moment.

It was all so long ago that now it seemed almost to be someone else's life. He rarely thought about her, or the times before the fighting when they had all been so different, or maybe just younger, and there had been endless parties and dancing, and groups of pretty girls smiling at you as the music played.

There had been an engagement too. So long ago it seemed, sometimes, as if it had never taken place at all. She had worn his ring on one slender finger, whispered of love and children and a thousand other things that a young man and a pretty girl talk about on soft summer evenings.

He had danced through a magical summer with Ellen, a summer of music, long walks in the moonlight, stolen moments in her mother's garden, and summer skies full of stars.

A summer when every moment away from her was an eternity, when every waking thought seemed to be only of her. Even now he could remember the perfume she wore, the warmth of her touch, the delicate curve of her neck.

There had been many pretty girls that enchanted summer, but only one Ellen Marcy.

He had loved her the way a young man loves for the first time. Recklessly, carelessly, without reservation. He had abandoned all reason, consumed by thoughts of her during the day, dreams of her by night. He had awakened with the dawn and his first thoughts had been of her, dreamed of her through long nights.

For Ellen he had been willing to give away everything he had worked for at West Point. The army, his commission, his career; their meaning had faded when he was with her.

When he closed his eyes he could still remember her scent, the sound of her laughter.

The return of her father from the frontier had spelled the end of his engagement to Ellen. There had been angry letters from the West. Ellen's father, himself an army officer, knew too well the privations of army life. He had no desire to visit the harsh realities of a life spent in remote army forts on his favorite child.

It had ended, all too soon, amid her tears and a great deal of bitterness on his part. He had never forgotten her, and he had never forgiven old Colonel Marcy.

In the end, when it all seemed inevitable, he had chosen to be a gentleman about the whole thing. There had been a few letters, not much more. The pain had faded with time. Eventually he had learned that George McClellan was courting Ellen.

From mutual friends he learned that she had turned Mac down also. It seemed almost ironic. They had been friends at the Academy, shared things that young men away from home experience for the first time.

There had never been any animosity. He had understood how much hurt her rejection would have caused his friend.

Mac, the golden boy. A good family in Philadelphia, always at the top of the class at the Point. The best postings the army had to offer, even a tour of Europe, observing foreign armies. Everyone expected her to accept his proposal. Instead, Ellen had refused.

Old Colonel Marcy. Mac was from a good family, but he was still an army officer, and no army officer would do for the daughter of Colonel Marcy.

Mac had left the army. Gone into railroading, somewhere in the West. Eventually he had wound up in Chicago. Burnside had joined him, down on his luck, out of the army, his patent on repeating rifles rejected by the army. He had asked Mac for a job. Mac had found a place for him. A good spot, some responsibility, prospects for advancement, able to see to his family. The two of them, together, just like at the Point.

Eventually he learned that Mac and Ellen had become reacquainted. There was talk of marriage. Apparently the railroad suited Colonel Marcy's plans for his daughter better than soldiering.

They had been married. He sent his congratulations. He had been happy for them. Mac was fine man; he would do right by her. No hard feelings.

Hill had married too. Old friends, all of them.

From ahead another deep rumble. Sharper now, the sound reverberating through the valley, echoing deep inside his chest. He glanced again toward the head of the column.

So we'll be together again, this last time maybe, he thought. And then perhaps this will be over and things can go back to like they were before.

Maybe not just like before, but something very similar. Their friendship would withstand the fighting. A man didn't turn his back on a friend over a difference of opinion. Mac and Burn would understand; they would all talk about it someday, over a bottle if it came to that, smooth out any hard feelings.

Maybe it would end today. He would be glad to be done with it. No shame in that. He had done his share. They had made their point, and we've made ours. Now it's time to call it quits, end all of this, let us go on our way.

Hill glanced ahead, past the sweating men, beyond the gleaming water, thought: *Mac and Burn are up there somewhere waiting for me.*

A cannon and its crew rolled past, horses sweating, the gun tube gleaming. Old friends, all of them. Beneath the shadow of his hat brim, Powell Hill smiled at the memories, was struck by the terrible irony of what might take place. A sudden chill passed over him, as lightly as a shadow, and in that instant his only thought was: *Be careful, Mac.*

JOE HOOKER AWOKE TO STIFLING AIR THAT SWIRLED AND buzzed with flies, and cool plaster walls, and a throbbing in his foot that drummed at every nerve and made him grit his teeth against the pain. The surgeon, a lean, humorless man with round spectacles and a bagful of long, shiny instruments, hovered over him, occasionally prodding the wound until he winced with pain and cursed, and the man drew back as though he had discovered a snake beneath the torn flesh and Hooker waved him away in disgust.

He pushed himself up on one elbow, thinking that it was damned silly to be here, lying in a stranger's bed, while outside he could hear them fighting. A wave of nausea swept over him, then the hot pain, forcing him to shut his eyes while it swept through his foot in raw, stabbing needles that radiated up his leg and forced him to groan as he settled back into the bed.

The worried face of the surgeon appeared from beyond the open doorway and Hooker looked at him in disgust and said, "Go," once, very loudly, and the man withdrew. From the hallway he could hear voices, men talking, discussing the fighting. He braced himself for the pain, rose on one elbow, said, "Send my officers in, Doctor."

From beyond the hallway a chair scraped the floor, and then one of his staff officers appeared, a major. Hooker's foot thrummed steadily in rippling waves of pain. He set his face, asked, "What news, Major?"

"Heavy fighting on the north end of the field, sir. The Rebels are counterattacking from the wood beyond the Hagerstown Road."

"Counterattacking? In what strength?"

The major shrugged. "A division, General, at least. Maybe two, hard to say at this point, sir."

Hooker nodded, sank back onto the bed, swatted at a fly that buzzed annoyingly close. There was another shocking spasm of pain. "I will need to speak to General McClellan, Major. As soon as possible."

The major nodded, asked, "Shall I go then, sir?"

Hooker nodded, not trusting his voice. He felt suddenly light-headed, waited long moments for the sensation to pass, then said, "Yes. See that General McClellan understands the urgency of my speaking with him."

He lay back on the bed, stared through the window at a lovely rectangle of blue sky. From the yard below he could hear men talking, loud laughter. In the distance a battery fired, a steady, strong thunder that bounced and rolled through the window while he stared at the white ceiling.

Sixteen shots. An entire gun line. The army was heavily engaged. The firing shook the walls of the house, rattled the glass panes of the windows.

Hooker sighed, knew those were the army's heavy guns thumping away at the Rebels. They would have nothing on the other side that could answer those guns. Lee would be holding on, trying to counter his advance of the morning, spare his infantry from their batteries.

Now was the moment. Keep the pressure up on Lee. He stared at the ceiling, wondered if McClellan were up to it.

McClellan would get the shakes. It was almost inevitable. He was no good at this part of it, when the fighting was heaviest and men were streaming back from the front and shaking their heads as if there was no hope and swearing that the damned Rebels weren't flesh-and-blood men but some sort of demon that could never be beaten in a stand-up fight.

He would never stand up to it. With his constant worrying that he was outnumbered, his supposed inferior number of artillery pieces, or any other one of his pet excuses.

The man lacked . . . maturity. He had been told all along what a wonderful general he would make. As though flawless reports and shiny buttons and good grades at West Point were all it took.

The army had groomed McClellan to be a general since the day he had left the Academy. And now here he was, with the largest army any officer had ever seen at his disposal, and he was too timid to fight it the way it was meant to be fought. He had all the trappings of a general except one. He lacked the instinct to drive into the enemy with everything you had and destroy him.

George McClellan would never understand that. Nor would he ever understand that winning battles involved fighting, sometimes to the very last of your strength.

Fighting, not when you had all the advantages, or even some advantages, the kind of fighting where victory comes not with a great, gleaming cavalry charge, but merely belongs to the man left standing at the end of the day.

In the end, when the reports were written, it would all sound very logical. *The army could not advance due to the local superiority of the enemy forces and the strength of his artillery batteries.*

He would have a dozen good reasons why he could not advance, could not support an attack, risk the reserves of the army. And there would be a small drove of neatly uniformed officers who would nod in agreement and convince the politicians and the newspaper editors that only the Young Napoleon could save the army, and the Union, from the Rebels.

Hooker sighed. A boy-soldier.

Lee would understand all of it. He already had taken the measure of McClellan. That was plain enough to the professionals in the army.

He swore, tried to sit up, the pain rocketing through his foot and leg in burning spasms. "Goddamn it, why now?" he asked aloud.

From the doorway someone cleared his throat, there was the sound of a boot being scuffed along the floor. Hooker turned his head, saw that Smalley, the reporter, was standing outside the door.

"Yes, Mr. Smalley?" he asked.

"I, ah, well, sir, I've been asked to tell you that General McClellan is conferring with General Porter at present and is not available." Smalley stood with his hands folded over his belt, looking miserable and boyish in the uniform somebody had loaned him.

"Conferring?" snorted Hooker. "Good God, what next?" he asked under his breath. Hooker glared at Smalley, who looked ridiculous in the uniform. At last he settled back onto the bed and waved Smalley into the room.

"What business brings you to army headquarters, Mr. Smalley?" he asked.

Smalley shrugged, said quietly, "I thought I might speak to you about the fighting, General."

"Your story, Mr. Smalley?"

The boy nodded. "Yes, they'll be waiting for me to send something to New York."

Hooker grunted, said, "Uh-huh, I suppose they will."

"It would be interesting, General, if you could provide me with a few of your thoughts on the battle."

Hooker cocked an eyebrow, said, "It's hardly done with, Mr. Smalley."

Smalley took a tentative step into the room, bobbed his head. "Yes, of course. Still, my readers will want to know what has taken place. What we can expect."

"Too early to say. There's been heavy fighting. You've seen that for yourself."

"Yes," said Smalley. "But the opinion of one of the army's top generals is always of interest. Perhaps a quote or two about the progress of the battle, sir." Smalley paused, looked anxiously at him, added, "If that isn't asking too much."

From the window the sounds of fighting drifted in. Hooker could hear noises in the yard below, a cavalry detachment rattling by. He looked at the boy, thought of the morning, the endless waiting for Burnside to begin his attack, for McClellan to send him another corps.

He clenched his teeth, rose in the bed, said, "We've attacked them very aggressively; the First Corps has been heavily engaged since day-light."

Smalley had a small pad out, was scratching furiously in it. Hooker smiled, tightly, continued, "The Second and Twelfth Corps have moved up to continue the assault on the enemy. I expect that casualties will be heavy in those units."

"Is the fighting along the entire front?"

Hooker felt the bile rise in his throat, wondered what Smalley might be getting at, if he had a purpose in asking that question. He shook his head. "No, so far the army is attacking on a rather narrow front." He held up a hand, "But I would ask that you not print that, Mr. Smalley. Only a few of our officers know the plan devised by General McClellan. It wouldn't do for that to be printed in your paper."

Smalley glanced up, held his gaze for an instant, resumed his writing in the notebook. "Of course, sir. I will respect your wishes."

"Has General Burnside's corps attacked, General?"

Hooker stared at the boy for a long moment. Smalley quickly glanced away, refused to meet his gaze. Hooker couldn't read the expression on the younger man's face. With a start he realized that the question had been deliberate, that Smalley had been watching, waiting for his reaction.

Smalley had been at his headquarters that morning. He would have been in position to overhear his officers talking, maybe some of the things he had said to his senior staff. He had criticized Burnside for his slowness, McClellan for his timid nature, his reluctance to engage the army.

He studied Smalley for a moment. Perhaps it was just talk, something he had heard around headquarters that morning.

An alarm sounded, somewhere far away, indistinct, but insistent. There was trouble here. Smalley was looking apprehensive. Joe Hooker had been in the army long enough to know when something was afoot.

He glared at Smalley, waited for him to drop his eyes, said sharply, "Perhaps you had better tell me what is on your mind, Mr. Smalley. And with whom you have been talking this morning."

Smalley glanced up quickly and Hooker saw something in his eyes that was not quite fear but something very like it, and then Smalley looked away and it was gone.

"Come now, Mr. Smalley. I have been in this army a long while, and I know a thing or two about army gossip and the type of men who spread it." He paused, gave the boy time to think, said at last, "Let's have out with it, son."

Smalley paused, nodded once, very slightly. "There's been talk, sir. Among some officers."

Hooker raised an eyebrow. "What sort of talk?"

Smalley dropped his eyes to the floor, mumbled something that Hooker could not hear. "What?" he asked.

Smalley glanced nervously around, rose quickly, shut the door to the room. "Ah, some of the officers, sir. In the First Corps, that is . . ."

Smalley paused. Hooker looking at him intently. "Some of my officers what, Mr. Smalley?"

"Ah, well, General," said Smalley, "this is rather awkward, sir. But some of your officers asked if I would speak to you about taking the field again, sir."

Hooker shook his head. "I cannot, sir. The army will drive them without me on the field."

"Perhaps," continued Smalley, "you might consider it. Even if it's in an ambulance?"

Hooker shook his head. "If only I could, sir," he said. "But I would be of no service to the men in this condition."

"If the men could only see your headquarters' flags again, General." Smalley paused, appeared nervous. "Some of the officers feel that the fighting will . . . stall"—another pause—"without your presence."

Hooker watched the young man carefully, wondering who had asked him to come on this mission at this time. "Are there other issues here, Mr. Smalley."

Smalley looked up, a furtive glance, his eyes showing something Hooker had not seen before. "Yes, General."

Hooker grew impatient, began to sense where all of this was going. "Well, then, man, let's have it. Ask what it is you've come to find out."

Smalley looked at Hooker. A long, quiet moment passed when nothing seemed to move in the stifling air that filled the room. At last Smalley said, "Some of the officers fear that the fighting on the field will not continue in an aggressive manner without your presence, General." Smalley cast a glance over his shoulder, searched the hallway as if to see who might be listening. "There has been talk among the officers suggesting that the army might be better served if you were to take command."

Hooker stared at this mere boy for a long moment in disbelief. Then the anger came on in a rush at the mere suggestion that Smalley was making. It was audacious, unthinkable, that any officer, or any group of officers, might suggest to this man that he wrest command away from George McClellan.

Mutiny. That was being suggested to him by this man who was neither regular army nor volunteer soldier. They had sent a correspondent to him, a man not subject to the governance of military law, to ask him to relieve George McClellan from command of the army in the field in the midst of a battle.

He had feared, privately, that McClellan would not be as willing to engage the army as he should have been, but this had never occurred to him. No doubt, now, that he had made an incautious remark or two to his officers on the subject. But a mutiny had never been in his thoughts. And now officers, his officers, were scheming to relieve General McClellan, and they had sent this man to find out if he were amenable to the suggestion.

He fought to control his anger, compose himself. He looked at Smalley, wondered at the man's brazenness. Strange war, strange army.

Volunteers. Not accustomed to life in the military, its peculiarities. The insistence on chain of command, the relinquishing of personal freedoms for the good of the whole. An army of men raised in a society that stressed personal freedoms, unable to comprehend that military service is not another exercise in democracy.

Hooker raised a hand, stopped Smalley from speaking further. "We shall speak no more on this subject, Mr. Smalley," he said firmly. "I shall not take the field again today. My wound prevents me, and my officers must know this." Hooker paused, saw the man appeared chastised, continued. "You will find my officers and advise them that they are to execute the orders of my second in command."

Smalley nodded. "Yes, of course, General. It is just that, well . . . I was asked to come to you."

"Yes, Mr. Smalley, I believe I understand." He paused, his mind trying to take it in. At last he said, "We live in strange times, sir. The country in turmoil, a Rebellion." Hooker sighed. "A generation ago this would have been unthinkable, to see the United States torn apart in this manner. Now men think of nothing else." Hooker lay back on his bed, felt suddenly very tired. "We cannot afford further divisions, Mr. Smalley. This army must not question its commander. General McClellan is a fine officer, and he is privy to more information than either you or I. He will conduct the battle as he sees fit, and we shall prevail." Hooker glanced at the younger man. "Am I making myself clear?" he asked.

"Quite clear, General."

"I want no more talk such as this. Am I understood, Mr. Smalley?"

"Of course, General," said Smalley, looking relieved.

Hooker nodded. "Very good, sir. Now if you would excuse me, I think it best if I rest for a few minutes."

Smalley smiled. "Certainly, General."

"You did fine service on the field this morning, Mr. Smalley." Hooker fixed Smalley with a firm stare, said, "You should be proud of yourself." He cleared his throat, cautioned himself to speak carefully. No telling who might be about, listening in the hallway. "Well," said Hooker, "you should certainly have enough facts for a story for your paper."

"Yes, General. And thank you, sir, for the kind words," answered Smalley. "It was my pleasure, and my duty to the country." Smalley grinned, turned, walked across the room toward the hallway.

"Mr. Smalley," Hooker called after him.

The younger man turned, a questioning look on his face. "Yes, General?"

Hooker fixed him with a firm stare, said, "Your service this morning," he said, searching for the right words. "Well," began Hooker, "I would be disappointed to read of this in one of your newspapers."

Smalley looked at him, an expression that Hooker took to be relief crossed his face. "No, sir. Of course not."

Hooker nodded. "Very well, Mr. Smalley. Now if you will excuse me, I believe I should rest. I expect some of General McClellan's staff along shortly."

Smalley smiled. "I will close the door behind me then, General."

CHAPTER 16

JACKSON STARED THROUGH YELLOW GLASS AT THE WOOD AND the small chapel beyond, saw movement among the trees, a blurry image of blue soldiers and horses. A single line of infantry, standing to arms, waiting in the shadows.

He returned the binoculars to their case, rubbed his eyes with a dirty hand. From the wood there was more movement, a restless shifting.

From the south, beyond the wood, where the land rolled and fell away toward the town, there was a flurry of firing. Scattered rifle fire, smoke rising from a depression beyond the wood and the road, drifting slowly over the grass. A skirmish line being driven in.

Beyond the turnpike more infantry appeared, a dark line of men walking steadily through the knee-high grass, flags spiked above the closed ranks. A brigade, maybe more.

A rider approached and Jackson turned, saw the solid figure of Lafayette McLaws. He waited, saluted as the big man reined in, nodded in greeting.

"Mornin', General," offered McLaws. There was a moment when neither man spoke, McLaws staring at him through the great brown eyes; and then, as if on cue, McLaws cleared his throat, pointed west toward a column of men. "My boys are moving into position now, sir. We should be goin' in directly."

Jackson nodded. "We must drive the Yankees from these woods."

McLaws removed his hat, ran a hand through the wet hair plastered to his forehead. His face was red and flushed, and where the brim of his hat fell and blocked the sun, the skin was white and pallid. Jackson recalled that Lee had once described him as dependable. A good soldier, a man you could count on in a fight.

McLaws glanced at the sky, squinted into the blinding light. "I spoke with some officers from one of Hood's brigades."

Jackson waited, a single moment passed when nothing on the field moved, when no guns fired, and it was just him and McLaws, and the silence. And the memory of Hood's men sweeping forward into the smoke and the corn and the fury of battle.

Jackson knew that McLaws understood that Hood's division was wrecked, strewn across the grass like so many trees fallen in the forest after a great windstorm. That somewhere beyond the wood waited a great army, with rifles and cannon and more men than they could ever hope to bring to the fight, and that his job was to go forward and find that army and destroy it.

Jackson stared straight ahead, said at last, "Hood's division is out of the fighting."

McLaws turned, caught his eye, and there was a brief moment when Jackson saw apprehension cross his features, but the old steady McLaws returned in the next instant and he said, "I'm told the fighting has been heavy."

"Yes," said Jackson, "somewhat."

A shot whistled overhead, skidded into the earth nearby with a dull thud, and the acrid smell of burnt powder drifted past. McLaws turned, looked in the direction of the shell, smiled crookedly. "Any word on what's behind those Yankees in the wood to my front?" he asked.

Jackson shook his head. "No," he said. "They have moved up another division in the past half hour. I anticipate that they have supporting divisions in trail."

Jackson shrugged, knew that it made no sense to gloss over it, stared for a moment at McLaws, said at last, "Perhaps another fifteen minutes behind this division. I would expect that they would be close by."

McLaws glanced toward the wood, said nothing for long moments. The sounds of his brigades moving up could be heard. A horse whinnied excitedly from somewhere, its rider cursing, trying to bring the frightened animal under control. There was laughter among the soldiers watching the struggle between horse and rider, and Jackson thought silently: *A good sign, when men can laugh just before a battle.*

With some men it was all tension and fear before a big fight. They figured the odds, guessed what they were up against, resigned themselves to it.

All that was left was for him to give the command, send McLaws forward. But he must come to it too. McLaws would reason it out, turn the thing over in his mind until all the options had been played out and there was nothing left but the fighting, and then he would go in. It was better that way; there was time left yet. Not much . . . but some time.

"Can you spare me any batteries?" asked McLaws suddenly. "Be nice if we could have a few big guns to help us out if we get into a fix up there." McLaws cast a worried glance behind, toward the spot where his men would be forming. "Wouldn't hurt us to have a battery or two near that ridge. Throw a few shots toward those woods."

Jackson put both hands on the horn of his saddle. "You'll have all the guns I can spare, but you'll have to go in with what's here now. I've got nothing else to give you.

McLaws frowned, cleared his throat. Jackson sensed the reluctance, knew that the other man didn't like the odds. At last McLaws said, "Huh. Gonna' take some doin' if I'm all you're sending."

"General Walker will be going in with you."

"Am I supposed to wait for a signal gun?"

Jackson shook his head. "Form your division, go in when you are ready, but it has to be soon. The wood and the ground around the chapel have to be cleared of Federals."

McLaws sat his horse heavily, swiped at a bug that buzzed by.

He knew what McLaws was thinking. What they must all be thinking. *Too many of them, too few of us.*

"Suppose I'll be off then." A long moment passed, McLaws gazing at him, waiting for something more, staring at him the way an animal stares at you when some familiar routine is being altered, when it senses the change, is wary of it. McLaws was waiting, hoping for something more.

Only there was nothing more. There was only the wood between them and the Federals, and more Union troops moving up; and so McLaws would have to go in alone, and Walker would come up or he wouldn't, but it would have to be done soon no matter the odds.

"Drive them north, General McLaws, into those fields beyond the wood and the church. Our batteries will do what they can for you, but the Federals must not be allowed to control those woods."

McLaws tightened the reins. "Yep," he said. "Do you want me to wait for General Walker to come up? His division was just behind me."

Another shell rattled past, struck a bit of gray rock, whined off into the pasture behind them. "Go in now. With everything you have. I'll move Walker into position when he arrives on the field."

McLaws smiled, white teeth showing through the thick, brown beard. To Jackson he appeared strangely boyish in spite of the beard. "My boys will drive them, General," he said. "Always do."

Jackson stared into the brown eyes of the other man, said nothing because there was little that could be said. And in any event he was no good at this sort of thing. This part of it was always awkward at

best, when you have done all that you can and you order a man
forward, knowing in your heart and in your mind that you may never
see him again, and he hands you some piece of himself like a Bible
or a bit of colored ribbon given to him long ago and asks you to deliver
it to his mother or his wife if the worst were to happen.

A bit of smoke drifted by, there was another thunderous volley from
a battery beyond the trees, and the very ground seemed to vibrate.

"Well," said McLaws, "best get my boys movin'."

"Yes," said Jackson.

McLaws saluted. Jackson pointed toward the gloomy wood. "Those
woods, around the little church, they're the key to our position."

McLaws nodded, smiled from beneath the brim of his hat, rode off
in a cloud of dust.

In the village there was constant movement now. A line of gray-
and-brown soldiers that snaked through the town, disappeared behind
houses, emerged again moving north along the turnpike.

He could feel it all coming together, the hand of Providence at
work. McLaws was almost ready; Walker was moving into position.
They would catch the Union commanders unaware, an enfilading fire,
a pincer movement that would force the Federals to face two fronts
or retreat.

He closed his eyes, wondered what Providence had in store for
them on this day, felt the infinite smallness of man, the futility of
men's actions. For in the end, what are men but so much dust?

It all comes to mean very little in the end, the things that men
have done, or might have done if the day had gone differently, or if
any of a thousand other choices had been made.

Jackson closed his eyes, inhaled deeply, knew that the Almighty
would rule this day as He ruled all days. That neither he, nor Mc-
Laws, nor Lee would decide what happened here; that men are small,
fragile creatures; that what men do counts for little when measured
against the heavens.

A battery began firing, broke his reverie, the shells passing over
the wood in fiery arcs of smoke and death. He could hear the shouting
of the Union soldiers, sense their confusion. One of Stuart's batteries
opened from his left, found the range, dropped shells steadily into
the massed blue ranks.

He heard it then, the ghostly sound of a thousand different voices,
a single long note that rang and echoed from beyond the wood. He
turned, searched the horizon for them, saw nothing. Walker's men

were going in, raising the peculiar high-pitched Rebel yell. It floated to him over the fields, above the sound of cannon, clear, spectral, unearthly.

There was the sudden violent sound of volleyed musket fire, and he could see smoke rising from the low ground beyond the turnpike. In the next moment a line of infantry appeared, swept forward toward the chapel in a long, graceful arc that belied the death and misery all around.

Shells from his batteries were falling steadily among the blue ranks near the little chapel, plunging down into the trees, bouncing wildly off the great dark trunks. He raised the glasses again, studied them for long moments, sensed the confusion in their ranks.

From the north a new line of Rebel infantry came swinging out of the woods, the men made small by the distance, a rippling line of flags and dark rifles and gray-and-brown soldiers that quickly grew and stretched before the silent trees shimmering in the heat. An officer was riding before the men, standing in the stirrups, and Jackson could see the light glinting off the sword, the horse plunging, wheeling, tossing its head in excitement.

From a long way off he heard the disembodied voices again, eerie, haunting. It floated toward him, passed by overhead, drifted toward the waiting ranks of blue soldiers.

The men near the chapel were turning now, sensing the trap, beginning to understand that they were cut off. That to stand among the trees, to hold their ground, meant to be isolated from the rest of their army.

A few of the Union soldiers had already turned, were forming a line to face the new threat. He could see their officers trying to get a brigade on line, the frantic gestures, heard a faint command or two shouted over the distance.

A courier broke from the wood, galloped for the rear. There was a flurry of shots from Walker's men, white blossoms of smoke appeared along the line, the rider leaning low over the neck of the horse, moving with each stride, his arm reaching back, whipping the animal into a gallop.

Union sergeants near the chapel were pointing, urging the men to run, hurrying them into rank, shuffling soldiers into a thin line.

Jackson watched as the gray-and-brown formations drew close, fired into the Federal ranks in a long, billowing sheet of flame that tore and ripped into the boys hurrying into formation. For an instant it was all obscured by smoke and distance, then the wind shifted and the smoke cleared and he could see plainly where the firing had shattered the Union ranks.

Another line of somber gray soldiers advanced, stepped neatly through the first rank, fired again in a single burst that shook and thundered across the grass between the two lines. The Union formations simply dissolved, melted into the grass and the stones and the leaves as though a thousand men had not been there only a moment before, as if nothing had been there. As though flesh-and-blood men had not stood there with all their desires and dreams and thoughts of home and children and all the other myriad things that men forget when they put on a uniform and take up a weapon and march off to war.

Union boys were running back toward the chapel, toward the safety of the wood, trying to escape the advancing soldiers and the rifles they carried and the small, unseen harbingers of death that tore the air and splintered trees.

A group of soldiers had gathered in the lee of the chapel like so many boats running with the wind before a storm, were pressing in on one another, seeking the shelter of the building.

In that instant one of Walker's brigades emerged from a bit of low ground. They crested the small rise, the infantry uncoiling in a long, shimmering wave that bristled with rifles and grim, determined faces.

Heads turned slowly in the Union ranks, saw the danger, understood what was about to take place. Even at this great distance Jackson could sense the confusion, knew the fear that was sweeping through the ranks of good Union boys like a cold wind that springs up suddenly and chills a man's soul on even a warm day.

From across the meadows and fields he heard their collective moan, a sound of resignation and regret and grief. And then he saw the raised sword held aloft in front of the gray infantry, and in the next instant the blade flashed down, and the rifles exploded, and there came a blinding fury that spared no man.

In that instant, when the enemy has taken you by surprise, and that first terrible volley has been fired, and the missiles of death have not yet struck, no man thinks of glory, or duty, or even home. He thinks only of the death that waits for him in the bright sunshine, of the awful finality of it all, of the terrible frailty of his own life.

Every man hopes, and prays, and longs for his own survival in that one instant; knows the savage fear that comes with the realization that death is speeding toward him; and that it is blind, and unjust, and uncaring.

And then the terrible missiles sweep in, and men die, or scream, or simply fall to the ground in impossible motionless shapes that have neither life, nor light, nor the spirit that separates men from beasts.

And in that moment, Jackson knew, there is no such thing as glory. There is only fear, raw and unbridled, and capable of making even the strongest man lose his nerve.

JACKSON WATCHED CALMLY AS THE FEAR SWEPT OVER THE BOYS in the Federal ranks. Saw the first few break from the group, hesitantly, then a trickle of men began running for the turnpike, moving east, toward safety. Away from the gray soldiers and their rifles and the death that came for them in the bright light of day, without hesitation or reason.

He watched them, dark figures sprinkled against a backdrop of wheat and trampled corn, some running, others simply walking east, heads down, moving toward the safety of the woods beyond Antietam Creek.

Another volley smashed into the Union men still standing to their colors in the wood. And in the next instant their officers had lost control of them, and men began to break ranks in groups and run back toward their lines.

The Union formations around the chapel simply dissolved as he watched. Men threw down their rifles and ran, left the wounded behind to face certain capture.

The fields beyond the turnpike slowly came to life with the Union soldiers fleeing the small church and the gray infantry and the rifles. Men were running, throwing down weapons and gear, sprinting through the long grass and the broken corn, never looking back.

In the wood someone was waving a flag, the flag of the old Union, just visible through the trees, half obscured by smoke and shadow. And then there was a wild explosion of rifle fire and men seemed to rise from the ground and swirl around the old flag; and in the next instant it was down, and the firing fell away and he could hear them cheering.

He turned then, knew that it was over, that McClellan had been pushed back, that he would not come this way again, not on this day, not on this field. He brought the horse around, saw Douglas and the others waiting for him, the bright, expectant looks on their faces, thought suddenly of the Union boys lying among the trees and the old flag spinning slowly down among the shadows.

He walked the horse slowly past the small pool of aides, who smiled and slapped one another on the back. There was a sudden movement; one of the them shoved a bottle into a saddlebag. He stared straight ahead, felt the steady movement of the horse beneath him, wondered what you said to men when they have done what you have asked, when it has all gone well, when other men have died at your hand.

"Send to General Lee," he said quietly to no one in particular. "Advise him that we have turned back their attack, that our left is relieved, and that I do not expect another attack here today."

CHAPTER 17

GEORGE MCCLELLAN DESCENDED THE STEPS OF THE COMFORT-able brick farmhouse where he had spent the previous night and said an absent-minded good morning to his staff officers. His mind was heavy with sleep, foggy with lack of rest and the oppressive heat and the weight of moving the army north and bringing it to battle with Lee.

He had slept fitfully, uneasy that beyond the rolling meadows and tree-covered hills the entire Confederate army waited in silent ambush. A vast army, well equipped, poised, tested. A veteran army. A determined army, ready to destroy his own.

The rooms on the first floor of the big house were crowded with men, the air heavy with cigar smoke, the smell of leather, and cooking food. He smiled to himself, felt the army was poised, ready. Soon, very soon, it could all be decided.

A host of couriers and sweat-stained horses waited in the yard, anxious to give their reports, return to their commands. McClellan nodded to a boy with a sunburned face and a shock of red hair and wearing the shoulder insignia of a captain and asked, "Have we news from the front?"

"Yes, sir," said the man, a nervous expression stealing across his features. "Heavy fighting on the northern end of our lines. General Hooker's First Corps reports large numbers of casualties."

McClellan nodded, patted the boy on the sleeve, mumbled, "Fine, then," absently. That was always the way of things. First reports always made mention of heavy fighting, great numbers of casualties, an enemy host just beyond the firing. Then the smoke cleared and calmer heads prevailed, and you found out that it wasn't as bad as all that.

Someone offered him a plate of food, a steaming platter of eggs and ham and fragrant bread, but he had no appetite and so he waved it away. In the house everywhere there was activity. Officers were hurrying from room to room, bending over maps, directing subordinates and couriers to every point on the compass.

The atmosphere inside the small rooms was stifling, the smell of warm bodies and woolen uniforms and smoke from the previous night's fires overpowering, and so he walked out onto the porch of the house, down a flight of steps, and into the muggy sunshine.

A rumble of artillery rolled in, a dark, ominous sound that tumbled toward him, slipped away to the east. He glanced toward Sharpsburg, gleaming white in the light, saw that the small valleys stretching away toward the village were filled with smoke and movement. A smudge of black smoke rose from the fields between him and the village, a single dark plume rising into a windless sky.

Heavy fighting.

The words rang in his head, a distant alarm. But it was always heavy fighting. Nothing to worry about, not yet, the day was still too early.

On the western side of the house they had thrown up a small fence to guard against errant shells, a low barricade of earth and fence rails. Officers sat behind the fence, watching the fighting through telescopes or binoculars. He removed a cigar from his pocket, gazed across rolling hills, saw light glinting off the Potomac River. He wondered again why Lee had chosen to stand here. Poor position to assume, very poor.

"Splendid view," someone said.

McClellan turned, saw Fitz John Porter, looked into the great dark eyes, sensed the tension there. His reputation called into question, a stain on his honor.

He smiled. "Good morning," he said easily. "I am told General Hooker is driving them."

Porter nodded. "If you would like we can see the field better through our glasses. Here." Porter extended a hand, indicated an upholstered chair that had been brought from the house.

McClellan sat, gazing through the lens toward the smoky field. In front of him the hills stretched away toward the valley of the Antietam. "What do you make of this, John?" he asked.

"What's that?" asked Porter.

McClellan shook his head. "I am not sure of this entire endeavor." He paused, wondered what the best way to approach the subject might be, said at last, "Why would General Lee give battle here? Nothing here favors his standing, John." He shook his head. "He should have withdrawn across the Potomac, offered battle from there, south of the river."

Porter shrugged. "Doesn't make much sense when you put it in those terms."

McClellan turned quickly. "You think we have been duped then?"

"Hard to say. They're haughty people, George, but I'm not certain how much trickery they've got in them."

There was a long pause; in the valley below a drum rolled, the sound softened by distance and the humid air.

"You ever been South much?" Porter asked at last. "Before the Rebellion?"

McClellan shook his head, stared out into the valley and the smoke. "No. Not really."

"They're different from us, you know."

There was a pause, McClellan staring into the silence and the smoke, wondering what the day would bring, and then Porter said softly, "They're funny people, George. They talk about God and the Bible one minute, and in the next they're ready to fight a duel." Porter shook his head, scraped the toe of a boot through the dust. "I heard once of a duel between two brothers."

McClellan cocked an eyebrow, said, "Really?"

"As the story went, one brother was killed, the other untouched."

"Matter of honor, I suppose," said McClellan, wondering where the story was going. "Does make you wonder what became of the second brother though."

"Spent the rest of his life repenting," answered Porter, shaking his head as if in disbelief at his own story. "If I remember correctly, the brother that won the duel became a minister, traveled on the circuit preaching against the evils of violence and the vanity of man and other such things."

"Remarkable," said McClellan.

Porter stared silently ahead, at last offered, "Funny people, no way around that." After a moment he shrugged, added cheerily, "That's what was told to me in any event."

"A woman, probably," McClellan said.

Porter laughed. "No doubt, George, no doubt."

A battery fired below them, heavy cannon, the reports echoing along the hillside. Plumes of white smoke turned dirty gray, drifted into the small hollows between the hills.

Porter sighed, began, "We're one country, but we're not one people. Never have been."

"Mmmm," said McClellan. "Suppose you're right after a fashion." He paused, thought of the Southern boys he had known at West Point. An odd mix of civility and religion and violence. There had been lots of talk of honor and feuds and blood oaths.

"Strange people," said Porter. He turned suddenly toward Mc-Clellan. "Beautiful women though."

Porter was smiling, the dark eyes shining. McClellan felt suddenly relieved, smiled back. "Maybe when all of this is over we'll go back down South, John. Take a trip, maybe New Orleans. What do you think?"

Porter looked at the ground, ran the toe of a boot through the dust. "Take a few years before that could happen. My sense of them is that they're not a forgiving people."

"No," said McClellan. "You're probably right. It will take a while."

He paused, lit the cigar, drew in the fragrant smoke. Porter might be right. About many things. "I have wondered about giving battle here." He turned, looked into Porter's dark eyes. "It has come quickly, John. Very quickly."

"Yes," answered Porter. "Still, we have them at bay. Now is as good as time as any."

"Of course," said McClellan automatically. "General Hooker reports heavy casualties; his formations are ruined on the northern end of the field."

Porter raised an eyebrow, said nothing.

"I have ordered the Twelfth Corps to relieve him. The Second Corps is going in also."

"Best to stay on the attack, keep them moving over there." Porter nodded, indicated a spot on the horizon.

"Of course." For a long moment McClellan said nothing, his mind racing, trying to divine Lee's purpose, his reasoning. Always he returned to a single thought, a single fact: *Lee has chosen this ground: he is giving battle with the Potomac River at his back. This is his ground. Beware.*

"Better to keep them on the defensive, carry the fight to them."

"Yes," said McClellan. "I've ordered Burnside to open on our left. He's going to have to get across the Antietam, and I expect them to put up a bit of a fight at the crossing point, but once he's across we'll be pushing them on both flanks."

Porter turned, raised an eyebrow. "They'll have trouble dealing with that," he said.

McClellan smiled. "My plan is to press them on each end of the field until we find a weak spot." He paused, waited to see that Porter was listening. "Once we've determined where we're able to move them, I'll commit the reserves, exploit any breakthrough we make."

"Splendid, George," said Porter easily.

McClellan thought he detected genuine approval in Porter's voice, a sense that at last the army was acting in concert, moving with decision against the Rebels.

Firing welled up from the hills, a sharp sound that ran along the grassy hills, moved beyond them. Smoke rose lazily above the screen of trees that followed the course of the Antietam, drifted among the branches in the heavy air. McClellan strained to see what was happening, could make out only the vague shapes of men through breaks in the dirty haze. "Can't see much," he said gloomily.

"Yes," said Porter. "Tough to know what's going on exactly."

"Hooker's down," he said aloud, somberly. "That's a bit of bad luck."

"General Mansfield too," said Porter. "I'm told it's mortal."

A sudden alarm shot through McClellan. Hooker and Mansfield down, out of the fighting. That left only old Bull Sumner to take charge on the right.

Porter turned to him, asked, "You hadn't heard? About Mansfield?"

McClellan shook his head. "No."

Bull Sumner. An old Indian fighter, grown old in the army, back when things were different, when they were all Academy men. An old man. No place for him here, not really. Maybe before the war, in the old army. But not here, not now.

Warfare was different now. Faster. They had all learned a lot, out West, from the Europeans. No place for an old man like Bull Sumner, old ideas of how things were done.

The thought shot through his head that a single mistake, one bad decision, coming at the worst possible moment, could lose the entire day for him.

He shook his head, said absently, "I'll have to keep an eye on Bull Sumner then."

Porter chuckled, said, "Might be a good idea, George. God knows what old Bull will think to do."

McClellan faced Porter, said suddenly, "This is our ultimate test, John. It will all be decided today. I can't afford a single mistake."

"Yes," said Porter slowly. "I think we all know that."

"The politicians in Washington have forced me into this fight, you know that. The army isn't ready to fight today, I'm not ready to fight today, but I've been given no choice."

"Well," said Porter, "at least we've had a day to bring up as much of the army as we can."

McClellan sighed, said, "I would have preferred more time. Another day at least. I've got entire divisions far in the rear, the army has practically no reserves except your corps."

Porter nodded. "My men are ready, George. And they're regular army. If the worst were to happen, they'll get between Lee and the rest of the army, or Washington, if it comes to that."

He turned suddenly, faced Porter, the sounds of battle faded, his mind raced, focused on that single thought. The army beaten, disorganized, streaming back toward the fortifications around Washington as it had just three weeks ago.

It could all happen again if he weren't careful. God only knew what Lee had hiding behind those hills, what might be waiting for him in those damn woods beyond the village.

He would attack, but he would do so with caution. Best to force Lee back on his heels slowly, probe until he knew what he was up against. The politicians in Washington be damned; he would do things his way. He could not afford to throw caution to the wind and make a grand general assault.

"Well," he said at last, "I shall hold your corps in general reserve, John."

Porter nodded, waited.

"I can't afford to gamble with the fate of the army, John. We're all that stands between the Rebels and Washington if the day should go against us."

"Of course," said Porter easily. "You're right to hold a substantial reserve back, George. Keep them out of the fighting but ready to move in if we need them."

McClellan shook his head, stared into the distance, saw only grassy hills and green cornfields, a white sky that promised more heat. "I'm fighting blind here, John. I've not had the proper time to scout Lee; I can't possibly know his dispositions."

"Yes," answered Porter, his face unreadable. "A general must always know the limits, George. What his men can accomplish, what the other man is thinking, what the enemy can accomplish."

McClellan smiled, slapped Porter on the back. "Precisely," he said. He turned, waved an aide over. "Have my mount brought up," he said, feeling the pressure melt away, if only for a moment. "Splendid march the men made, getting up here in just a few days," he said.

"Yes," said Porter. "It's been an impressive campaign."

He turned, looked back toward the green mountains to the east. The road was clogged with infantry, a long, winding track filled with soldiers and cannon and mounted officers. "I'm proud of them, John."

Porter nodded. "You should be; they're your army."

McClellan laughed, pleased at the compliment, said, "Let's take a ride, see how they're doing out along the lines." He inhaled a deep breath of muggy air. "Always good for the troops to see their general is about, facing the danger with them."

Porter smiled, said, "Fine idea, George."

CHAPTER 18

LONGSTREET FELT THE HEAT RISING, BURNING OFF THE MOIS-
ture from the previous night's rain, his clothing moist with his own
sweat. He lifted his eyes to the sky, saw only a blazing white sun that
hovered overhead, seemed not to move. He unfastened first one, then
another, of his uniform buttons. The day was early yet, but already
the heat had saturated his clothing.

From his pocket he took a cigar, rolled it between his fingers, inhaled the rich smell of the tobacco. He swung into the saddle, glanced
east, tried to peer into the haze and trees, wondered what the Federals were up to beyond the Antietam.

Harvey Hill had moved his division forward. The men were waiting
now, resting on their rifles or stacking fence rails along the sides of
the lane where the brigades had taken up their positions.

He moved across the grassy slope, saw only the crest of the next
hill, knew that the Yankees were just over that rise, making ready to
come this way. Someone's farm, well kept, the fences gone now, taken
for firewood or stacked as a parapet, a swath of tall grass marking the
lines where the rails had stood.

Harvey Hill appeared, nervous, full of energy. "Mornin', Pete."

"Mornin'," said Longstreet easily.

Hill pointed an accusing finger, said, "My boys are going to be in
a tough spot if they come this way in any force."

"Yep," he answered.

Hill shook his head reproachfully. "This is a bad spot, Pete. Be
hard to defend this ground with twice the men I've got. And my boys
are out in front of the whole army."

"No choice, Harvey." He narrowed his eyes, squinted into the
bright light and the heat, wondered how a man could keep from melting in weather like this. "The Old Man ordered us to hold here, and
this ground is as good as any."

Hill turned, glanced toward the village shining white in the sun.
"How about if we pull back a bit, say the crest of that hill in front of
Sharpsburg. That would straighten out our lines." Hill paused, stared
at Longstreet with silent, dark eyes. After another moment he added,
"At least that would get us out of this damn ditch we're in."

Longstreet turned, looked past the orchard toward the houses. "Can't do it, Harvey." He pointed. "Yankees will take your boys under fire with their long guns the minute you start moving back up that hill. And they'll keep 'em under fire until you move back into the town or you come back down here where they can't see you."

Hill scratched his chin, appeared to think for a long moment. At last he said, "This is going to be a tough spot to hold, Pete." He pointed toward the east where the ground rolled and swelled and the lane disappeared around a small hill. "They send any of their people around that way and my boys will never get out of here. It will be over before it gets started."

"You'll have to watch for that, Harvey." Longstreet nodded, indicated a spot over the hill where the Federal army waited. "There're some boys over there know their business." Longstreet pointed a finger at the other man's chest, said, "You're going to have to make them pay for coming at you headlong, if that's what they do. Your men can fire on them as soon as they crest that hill in front of your lines."

"Can't do that forever, you know. Somebody over there will wise up to it eventually."

Longstreet shrugged. "Maybe. Maybe not. If George McClellan doesn't get in their way, then they'll sniff us out and they'll make short work of it."

Hill sighed, said mournfully, "That's what I'm afraid of, Pete."

"Well," said Longstreet, "I'll send you what help I can if it comes to that. And I'll see that a battery or two keeps an eye out for you. In the meantime you'll just have to hold your ground here."

Hill ran a hand over the back of his neck, swiped at a fly with his hat. "Bad ground, Pete. Once they've seen it they'll know." Hill shook his head. "No way around that. We'll hold the first attack off, but then they'll have gotten a look at our position and they'll know to move around to the right there and come after us that way."

"Yep," answered Longstreet. "No other way for it though. You'll have to do the best you can; you've got the center of our line and that means you've got to hold."

Hill glanced down the muddy track that was filled with his infantry. Someone had started a fire and a wisp of smoke rose lazily from among the clutter of men and weapons. "Do the best I can, Pete."

Longstreet nodded, touched the brim of his hat. "Be seein' you, Harvey."

He moved off, across a grassy field that bordered an orchard, the trees heavy with fruit, branches bowed and bent at odd angles. A

house was burning and he paused for a moment to stare at it, watched
the roof slowly collapse and fall into the flames.

Longstreet had a brief thought of the family that had lived there,
worked the land, wondered what their name might be, where they
were now. Then he warned himself to dismiss such thoughts, better
not to dwell on those things too long.

He turned, saw that Lee was nearby, watching, waiting for him. He
dismounted, handed the reins to an orderly sergeant, and walked toward the spot where Lee waited.

"Mornin'," he said to Lee.

Lee smiled, a slow, genuine smile that made Longstreet feel somehow grateful. "Good morning, Peter," said Lee.

"General," said Longstreet, feeling suddenly awkward, aware of
the loose buttons on his uniform coat.

Lee turned toward him, the dark eyes shining, confident. "General
Jackson has turned back their assault on our left."

"Yep," said Longstreet. "Figured that's what all the noise was this
mornin'."

Lee smiled, a smile that spread slowly across his features, and
Longstreet thought for a moment that he might laugh. Instead Lee
reached out, touched his sleeve slightly, said, "The fighting has been
very heavy. We have lost the use of General Hood's fine division."

The words hit him like a blow; Hood's entire division, out of the
fighting. For a moment he felt the terrible sense of dread a man feels
when he realizes that no matter how hard he tries, the other man will
win; that he has been outclassed, and there is no power on earth that
can help him. Then Longstreet lifted his gaze to the gray horizon,
tried to see beyond the rolling hills, but there was only smoke and
sky and hazy trees shimmering in the heat and the cold feeling in
the pit of his stomach passed as suddenly as it had come.

"What happened?" he asked slowly.

"The assaults this morning were very heavy. General Hood's men
were up against one Union corps, possibly two."

Longstreet nodded, ran a hand through his beard. McClellan and
the others were stacking units up, sending them in one behind the
other. A Napoleonic battle, designed to wear down an opponent by
attacking in force on a narrow front. A textbook plan, one you learned
at West Point.

"That would do it," he said slowly, wondering what might be left
of Hood's division, how many of them were down. "Sam Hood make
it through?" he asked.

"Yes," said Lee.

"That's something, then, at least."

"We must be grateful," said Lee, his voice suddenly soft, hushed. Longstreet was reminded of a preacher, a man he had listened to long ago. A gentle man with soft hands and a rich voice who had visited the small country church where he had worshiped as a boy.

"I expect another assault," said Lee.

Longstreet nodded, waited, wondered where Lee might be going with his remark. But in the end that was all there was, a simple statement; and so he said, at last, "How are we doing on the right? You brought Walker over, didn't you? To give Jackson a hand?"

"Yes," said Lee.

"That means we're thin on the right, down by the bridge."

"Yes," said Lee slowly. "But the ground there favors a defense. I believe we have sufficient men to hold there, if they should come that way."

Longstreet turned it over in his mind, wondered what they were waiting for over there, past the grassy hills and the dark trees.

The thought blew through his brain in hot, searing gusts that his lines couldn't possibly hold, that they were trying to do the impossible. He looked away, thought to say something, but couldn't, forced the thought back down into his mind.

One good push, he thought, *and they'll be through someplace, and then they'll get in behind us and it will be a mad dash for the river and whoever is left will try to make a stand on the other side. But there won't be anything left, not really, just stragglers, and the cannon and the ammunition trains will all be gone.*

After a moment he asked, "Can Stuart give Walker any help down by the creek?"

Lee shook his head. "I have asked General Stuart to hold our flank on the left. His men are posted between General Jackson's men and the river."

"Be nice to get some of his cavalry around behind McClellan. Give 'em something to think about over there."

He waited, Lee blinked in shadowless light, said nothing. "Well, just a thought. Stuart's probably got all he can handle up north."

"If there is an opportunity," Lee began, "we must not fail to exploit it. I have sent word to General Stuart that he should be prepared to move against them if such an occasion arises."

Longstreet cocked an eyebrow, waited for Lee, wondered again where it might be going. "You think we can hit back at them hard enough to force the issue?" he asked.

"General McClellan doubts the ability of his army to give battle. He will not maneuver with confidence today." There was another pause, the silence punctuated by single rifle shots; a bullet snapped by overhead, unseen.

Longstreet turned, stared at the calm face, the steady eyes. "There're other men over there who don't lack the stomach for a fight," he said slowly. "Joe Hooker is one of them, among others."

"Yes," said Lee calmly.

They were walking now, passing behind one of Harvey Hill's brigades, the men at rest, rifles propped against fence rails, soldiers lounging in the grass. And then they saw Lee, the simple gray coat, the single row of stars on the collar, and suddenly men were getting to their feet, slapping the dust out of their trousers, removing their hats, staring as they passed.

It was like that with Lee, no loud cheering, no grand gestures. Someone called, shouted a pledge to stand here or die, and Lee turned, touched the brim of his hat in a graceful gesture that made Longstreet feel suddenly very clumsy.

Lee turned toward him suddenly and Longstreet saw the resolve in his face, the determination. "We shall prevail on this field, General," Lee said slowly.

For a long moment Lee said nothing, just stared blankly out over the hills, hands clasped behind his back. At last he turned toward Longstreet, said quietly, "When armies give battle it is never so simple as a matter of numbers, or cannon, or even the terrain."

Lee smiled, a wistful turning up of the corners of his mouth. "When I was younger, your age even, I believed more in the mathematical aspects of warfare. So many cannon, so many regiments, so many rounds of ammunition for each man and each piece of artillery."

Longstreet waited, knew that Lee was thinking of the huge Federal army beyond the hills and the trees to the east. He could feel their strength gathering, building like water behind a dam, a great tide of blue soldiers that waited just over the brow of the next hill.

"And now?" asked Longstreet.

"Well," said Lee, the dark eyes shining, "it is more complicated than that." He turned away, indicated the soldiers nearby, said, "Now I know that much of it rests in their hands, in how strongly they believe in themselves."

Longstreet sighed, knew that the other man was revealing something he had thought about a great deal, things he had come to after a lifetime in the army, of living among soldiers and lonely army barracks and endless windswept horizons out West.

"Suppose you're right," said Longstreet.

"They must have a sense of themselves, of being a part of something greater than any individual, of something that they can believe in. An army that they can be proud of; in the end that means more than the uniforms or the parades or the other things they thought were glorious when they ran off to war."

"Yep," he said awkwardly, "nothing glorious about fighting in somebody's cornfield in Maryland."

"We shall prevail," Lee said again simply.

Longstreet nodded, knew that when Lee spoke like this there was no argument to be had, that his mind was set. That Lee would fight here, on this field, until the matter had been settled, come what may.

"Could be a close thing," he said.

"Yes," said Lee, "but this army will hold the field at the end of the day, come what might. I am convinced of it."

"I expect they're going to come after us. If not here," he said, nodding to indicate the soldiers strewn across the ground, "then down toward the stone bridge, or maybe they'll reorganize and give Jackson another push."

"Yes," said Lee quietly. "We will be ready. I do not believe that they have the resolve to break our lines."

Longstreet paused, wondered for a moment at the other man's confidence, doubted for the briefest instant that any army could hold back what waited beyond the meadows and hills to the east.

Lee sensed his hesitation, said, "You must believe in them, Peter," nodding to indicate the soldiers in the narrow lane.

Longstreet turned, followed Lee's gaze, began to say something; and then Lee reached out, grasped his arm with a touch as light and fine as summer rain, and said, "I trust that you will know what must be done, General."

There was an awkward pause, Longstreet looking into the steady dark eyes, groping for the words that never seemed to come when he needed them most, and then Lee removed his hand and signaled for his mount and was gone.

LONGSTREET HAD FOUND A SPOT IN THE ORCHARD WITH A VIEW of Harvey Hill's lines and settled down to wait. He had sent his staff off to tend to the hundred-odd things that had to be done before a battle and never seemed to matter in the end because nothing ever happened like you thought it might.

He settled back against the trunk of a peach tree, pulled the brim of his hat down over his eyes, felt suddenly drowsy in the heat. The sun was up now, beating down on the men in the ranks, and there was a steady stream of soldiers bearing canteens and moving between the infantry waiting in the hollow between the hills and the wells that had not yet been worked dry.

From the corner of his eye he saw men pointing toward him, glimpsed the figure of Harvey Hill moving his way. He pulled a cigar from his vest pocket, chewed on it, waited for Hill to make his way over.

Hill walked toward him with an impatient stride. "Pete," Hill said, when he was still some distance away.

Longstreet lifted the brim of his hat with a finger. "Harvey, how's it going?" he asked.

"Well," said Hill, "I've seen better ground. I can tell you that."

Longstreet smiled. "No doubt, Harvey. Seen better myself."

"They'll be comin' this way pretty soon, Pete. Some of the boys can hear 'em making ready." Hill turned, pointed toward the big round hill just beyond his lines. "You can stand down there in that damned ditch I'm supposed to hold and hear 'em plain as day."

Longstreet glanced at Hill, chuckled. "Suppose they got to do something to get ready."

"I could use some guns, Pete," Hill continued, pointing, "up there, in that orchard."

Longstreet turned, eyed the spot where Hill had pointed. "Good place for a battery," he said slowly.

"They across the creek yet?" he asked.

Longstreet shrugged noncommittally. "Probably," he said. "Even George McClellan could get a brigade or two on the road by this time of the morning."

Hill removed his hat, wiped a hand across his forehead. "Pete, it's gonna be a mighty long morning for my boys unless you bring in some guns." Hill turned, looked again at the ragged line of infantry. "I'm pretty thin too. Sent over three brigades to help Jackson out earlier."

Longstreet turned toward him, said slowly, "Get any of 'em back yet?"

Hill shook his head, smiled sheepishly. "Not much. A regiment or two at the most. They were cut up pretty bad. Went in to support Hood's attack. Ran into some big Yankee brigades up there in those woods," he said, pointing toward the northern end of the field.

"Yep," agreed Longstreet, "plenty of 'em about. That's for sure."

"Sent over most of my batteries too," said Hill, feeling suddenly foolish. "Haven't seen them since either."

Longstreet was smiling, white teeth showing through the thick beard. "Harvey, it would appear you are in a fix," he said.

Hill smiled. "Suppose so," he said.

"Old Man said he would move Dick Anderson's division up to give you a hand," offered Longstreet.

"Yes," said Hill, "that'll help." Hill looked about nervously, added, "Don't suppose you would go and hurry him along now, would you, Pete?"

"He'll be here in time," Longstreet answered. He paused for a long moment, then said absently, "Anderson is a good man."

"I'll need him before this is over."

"He'll be here," said Longstreet.

"Wouldn't mind a battery or two."

Longstreet smiled. "Harvey, I'll see what I can do about those cannon." He touched the brim of his hat, smiled again, said, "Should be a gun or two up toward the town."

"You may run into some of my boys up there," said Hill, motioning toward Sharpsburg. Longstreet raised an eyebrow. Hill said, "Sent 'em back earlier. Told 'em to send along whatever guns they could find."

Longstreet smiled again, laughed, shook his head. "Harvey, you are not one to miss an opportunity."

Hill smiled in spite of himself. "I try, Pete," he said. "I do try."

There was a smattering of rifle fire, the reports echoing back over the hills. Longstreet turned. "Your boys, you think?" he asked.

"Yep," said Hill, pulling his hat down onto his head. "Suppose that's my skirmish line."

Longstreet nodded. "Best get movin' then, Harvey."

"Suppose so, Pete."

"Well," said Longstreet slowly, "you keep that pretty head of yours out of harm's way and I'll see about those guns."

Hill touched the brim of his hat with one hand. "I'd appreciate it, Pete. I'm gonna need some help."

"I'll see to it, Harvey," said Longstreet. He watched Hill stride down the hillside, disappear among a sea of men and rifles, turned and waved a staff officer over.

"Go back to Sharpsburg," he said, "and order any cannon you can find to move forward and put fire on that hill." Longstreet pointed, indicated the round hill beyond the line of men in the sunken lane.

The aide saluted, said, "Yes, sir," with a questioning look.

"Something else, Captain?" asked Longstreet.

"No, sir, not exactly. But I don't see what they're supposed to fire at."

Longstreet turned, looked again at the grassy hilltop. "You will," he said.

CHAPTER 19

HE HAD BEEN AWAKENED BY BRILLIANT LIGHT FLOODING THE tent and the bawling of the brigade sergeant major, and all the small sounds of an army as it comes suddenly awake, forces itself up off the ground and into ranks.

And heat.

He had slept on the ground, and a single army blanket, and the rough wool pulled and scratched at his skin, and even the night had been so hot that he had lain awake for long hours and thought about home, and his orchards, and winter snows, and fall breezes that came off the lake and lifted the curtains away from the windowsills and swirl through the house in the dead of night.

He had forgotten the Southern heat. Summer heat that builds all day long, saps a man's strength, soaks his clothing with his own perspiration until all he wants to do is find a bit of shade and try and sleep through the day.

Maryland had that kind of heat, even this time of year, and he was not accustomed to it and it had spoiled his mood and made all the marching seem insufferable even to an old soldier like him.

He would have to remember the heat. The sun would take more than a few of them today if he wasn't mindful of it. His boys were good soldiers, but they were all New Yorkers, for the most part, good Irish boys with fair complexions and quick tempers, who would not do well in the Maryland summer. Boys who had never been beyond New York City before the Rebellion.

No experience with heat either, at least not this kind of heat. He raised a hand, shielded his eyes against the sun, peered into a cloudless sky and overpowering white light.

Israel Richardson held the steaming cup of coffee in one hand, swallowed a mouthful of the bitter fluid, grimaced as the hot liquid burned its way down. Army coffee always had that faint taste of tin and something else that was bitter and indecipherable.

He was in command of a division, ten thousand souls who would do his bidding, follow his orders. He had trained for it his entire life, and now that it was here he had no orders, no real idea of who, or what, waited beyond those trees and the hills to the west.

He resisted the impulse to curse, to wonder aloud what McClellan and the others had been doing for the past day.

An entire day, wasted. The army had concentrated yesterday, brought the Rebels to bay, then sat on its haunches like a great fat beast that doesn't know what to do with its prey.

Out on the road the wounded were moving past in a steady procession. Men with vacant eyes limped past the small sycamore grove where he had established his headquarters. They shuffled along, ambled slowly out of sight, searching for the hospital tents, or simply looking for a place to sit down.

The battle had raged for most of the morning, the roar of gunfire beyond the small valley where his division waited, the noise of battle moving slowly south, toward his men sitting along the banks of the Antietam.

Richardson raised the tin cup to his lips, stared at the road over the rim, swallowed another mouthful, thought: *We'll be going in blind. No one has told us what's out there, beyond those trees.*

Out in the road there was a stir, men cursing, shuffling to the side of the lane. A rider was weaving his horse through the confusion, spotted the headquarters flags, brought the animal over hard, swung out of the saddle in a fluid motion. Someone pointed in his direction and the boy trotted toward him.

The soldiers saluted, asked, "General Richardson?"

He nodded, suddenly tired of it all. *Boy-soldiers*, he thought, looking at the courier, *playing at war.*

"Dispatch from General French, sir. He's requesting that you move your division up and engage the enemy."

Richardson resisted the impulse to smile, asked, "He say where we're supposed to move up to, Corporal?"

The soldier turned, pointed back down the road, past a small grove of trees. "The Rebs are in a bit of low ground just over that hill there, General. That's where they want your division to come up."

Richardson squinted into the bright light, stared in the direction indicated by the rider. "Fine, then. You get back to General French, tell him I'm on the way."

The boy ran back to his horse, swung into the saddle, spurred off in a cloud of dust. A new wave of firing rose from beyond the hill, heavy firing, a steady impossible sound.

He tossed the last of the coffee onto the fire, stood transfixed while it hissed and sputtered in the coals, waved the sergeant major over. "Get 'em up, Sergeant Major. We're moving."

The sergeant major was a great, hulking man, with flaming red hair and a brogue, and he drank to excess, and was quick with his fists when he was drinking; but he was dependable in a fight and Richardson liked him inordinately in spite of himself.

The man saluted, said, "Aye, sahr."

Richardson said, "Column of files."

"Aye, sahr." There was a slight pause, then, "And who would the general be after havin' out front, sahr?"

"Well," he said, "what kind of fight does the Irish Brigade have in them this mornin', Sergeant Major?"

The sergeant major straightened, brushed the ends of his moustache with a hand, glanced over one shoulder toward the men waiting out by the road, then back toward Richardson. "They're after havin' a bit of a row this fine mornin', sahr, if I'm not mistaken," he said conspiratorially.

"They'll do then, Sergeant Major."

"Aye, sahr."

"See to it," he said, and watched as the Irishman turned and moved out toward the road. Men were already standing at his approach, brushing the dust off their trousers, reaching for their weapons, moving into ranks.

He felt a sudden surge of pride at the sight of it, knew that it wouldn't be long now. Another half hour, get them on the road; then the fight would be on.

He silently prayed that this one wouldn't be like the others, that this battle would mean something, would define something.

If they win this one, then we'll just have to let them go. Nothing more to be done. We're about played out.

He wiped the sweat from the back of his neck, wondered what McClellan and the others were up to at headquarters. Too late for that now, nothing left but the doing, and that was his end of it.

Out on the road the men were standing, looking toward him with anxious faces, waiting for him to give the order. He caught the eye of the sergeant major, raised one hand very slightly, and then someone bawled an order and a thousand men straightened and stepped off in a single instant, and he felt the peculiar thrill you feel just before a big engagement.

He glanced out over the marching men, wondered what it would all come to today. No way to tell, not yet. Nothing had been decided yet. That was the beauty of it, and maybe the tragedy, but ultimately that was why they were all here, to decide the matter and to hell with this endless marching through heat and dust and fighting for a bit of ground that no one wanted the day after the battle was over.

The column swung down into the small valley, beneath graceful sycamores and pin oaks, splashed across the Antietam, the stream waist high, the men cursing and laughing at the chill water. And then they were across and moving uphill, toward the sound of firing, and the smell of smoke was thick in the air among the trees and his horse was tossing its head, the mare's eyes wide with excitement.

The wounded who had been unable to make it across the creek stared with helpless eyes as they moved past. Among the shadows men were everywhere, some with wounds, others wild-eyed and frightened, out of the fight, cowering like animals. Richardson could see by their faces that the fighting had been heavy ahead.

The oaks thinned suddenly, the forest stabbed by great gleaming rays of sunlight, and they emerged into startling white light, and for a moment he could see nothing, his eyes accustomed to shadow, closing against the cloying light; and then slowly his eyes adjusted and the field emerged.

French's men were ahead of them, standing on the crest of a long ridge, firing down into the low ground toward the west, and Richardson turned and signaled for the sergeant major.

The Irishman appeared at his elbow, said, "Sahr?"

"Let's get 'em out of the woods at quick time, Sergeant Major. Get them on brigade front." He pointed toward the line of infantry standing just in front of them. "We'll be moving up in support of those men."

The sergeant major saluted, said, "I'll see to it, General, sahr."

Richardson nodded, said, "We'll have to be quick. God knows what the Rebs are up to over there."

"And if I may, sahr, and beggin' the general's pardon, sahr."

He stared down at the man, said, "What's on your mind, Sergeant Major?"

"Well, sahr, its just you've a habit of moving a bit forward in the heat of the moment, sahr. And the damn Rebels have a love of shootin' officers, you know."

Richardson smiled. "I'm aware, Sergeant Major."

"Aye, lad. And as a general rule, an old soldier like meself sees a certain amount of justice in the shootin' of officers."

Richardson cocked an eyebrow.

The sergeant major raised a hand, said quickly, "It would be a

damn shame, it would, sahr, it you was to come to harm. Be hard on
the boys, sahr; they've grown accustomed to you."

"Right," he said. "Well, you stay close, and I'll do my best."

"Right, General," said the Irishman.

The brigades were well out of the wood now, men moving quickly
to form ranks, spreading out, shoulder to shoulder, a rolling tide of
blue uniforms.

A bullet whizzed past overhead, slapped into a tree somewhere
behind him and he turned, looked after it, half expecting to see something. A leaf floated lazily to the ground in its wake. Richardson
smiled, hoped that no one had noticed.

An order was shouted and men dropped their rifles off their shoulders, a thousand weapons *thunked* heavily into the dry ground and
regiments dressed their lines. More orders were shouted, sergeants
and officers screaming above the din ahead.

Knapsacks and haversacks hit the ground and then they stepped
forward. Five paces, the line of black knapsacks marking the spot
where the regiment had stood a moment before.

Ahead someone was waving a small flag, an officer, signaling, asking
for them to come up. A colonel caught his eye, he motioned to the
man.

Forward.

More shouting, more orders, and then suddenly they had stepped
off, entire regiments moving at a steady pace through the high grass,
closing in on the back of French's brigades.

Brigade front.

The formation was holding, a wavering line of men and rifles that
pushed through the grass. The ground sloped upward slightly, there
was knee-high brown grass and Richardson absently picked at it, ran
a single stalk through his fingers, bent it double with his thumb,
thought oddly: *Time to hay this field.*

A cannonball struck ahead, bounded wildly toward them, bounced
once, very high, passed cleanly over the heads of the marching men.
There was laughter, men smiling, turning to follow the dark ball back
toward the rear.

Richardson turned too, saw the file closers walking behind the
ranks, pistols in hand. He had ordered them to shoot stragglers; now
he wondered if they would.

Between the lines there was an explosion, earth and grass cart-
wheeling skyward amid dirty black smoke. The Rebel artillery was

seeking them, probing, looking for targets, finding the range. He peered over the line of men, tried to see through the smoke to the guns. Nothing.

The fire from French's brigades was slackening, dissolving into individual shots now, not the steady roar of massed troops. They were trying to break off and suddenly the thought struck him: *They're out of ammunition. French went in with sixty rounds to a man, and now they're out and they've only been at it for a half hour.*

Brigades on the crest of the hill were filing off the firing line, moving to the right, making room for his regiments to come up, assume their position. He could see them plainly. Officers were turning toward him, smiling, waving them forward.

He felt a sudden spasm of relief; maybe this time it would be all right. French's brigades were moving off in good order, no hurry, no breaking of ranks. A parade ground movement.

Now was the time to move his boys into the fight, prevent the Rebels from catching their breath. Keep them off balance. They had to be low on ammunition over there too.

"Sergeant Major!"

The Irishman turned, cupped a hand to his ear.

"Quick time!" he screamed.

The big man nodded, raised his hand, yelled, "Quick time... *Haaarch!*"

Officers and sergeants up and down the line picked up the command, repeated it. The line lurched forward, a hesitant, uncertain movement that rippled down the ranks. And then they were all moving forward, trotting through the long grass, closing in on the Rebels and the cannon that he couldn't see and whatever else waited over the brow of the hill.

An explosion rocked him, covered him in fine black dirt, made it impossible for him to hear for long moments. The smell of burnt powder stung his nostrils, and he knew that the ball had been close. He glanced about, saw that men were sprawled in the grass in odd, impossible shapes. He recognized a boy from one of the New York regiments, saw him holding a great bloody wound in his stomach, pulling at his shirt, covering the gash with blood-stained hands, eyes wild with fear.

He moved past the boy, thought: *At least he'll go quick with a wound like that.*

More shells poured in. Every few seconds there was a new explosion, men crumbling to the ground, vanishing among the tall grass.

Men put their heads down, bent as though a fierce wind was blowing, only there was no wind, just the shells and the smoke and somewhere ahead the Rebels.

Near the crest of the hill the grass was on fire; he could see the flames clearly, feel the heat. But there was no wind and so the fire wasn't spreading; there was only an ugly black slash where the flames had been and wispy smoke rising from the scorched ground.

Without a command his men slowed, lowered their rifles as they came to the crest of the hill. Wounded were everywhere, lying among the grass, touching his soldiers as they passed, asking for water. They reached the spot where French's division had stood, and he could see a line of men who had fallen as they stood, a neat row of bodies sprawled in the grass, silent, unmoving, his men stepping carefully over them.

And then suddenly they were there, a long, snaking line of men in gray-and-brown uniforms in a bit of low ground a couple of hundred yards down the hillside. He stared for an incredible moment, saw the dark rifles come up to their shoulders, and then all along the line white smoke rolled out and in the next instant the bullets slammed into his ranks with great meaty *thunks*, and men were down everywhere.

Richardson raised an arm, covered his face against the unseen bullets, felt a stab of wild fear scythe through him. It passed as quickly as it had come, and he lowered his arm and peered through the smoke and stared again at the men below him in the hollow of the hill.

They had piled fence rails and branches along the side of the road to form a breastwork and were standing four deep in the lane. Rifles were passed from hand to hand, those in the back loading, those up front firing.

He watched, the long rifles moving through the enemy ranks with deadly urgency, passing over men's heads, the smoke billowing out, the balls whistling up at them.

Another volley rushed past, more men fell, dropped to the ground. Below, the Rebels continued to load and fire, individual shots now, no prepared volleys.

A command was given and rifles came up in a long, rippling wave all along the front. In an instant his men fired, and the entire line disappeared in a great rolling cloud of white smoke. For long moments he could see nothing through the smoke that hung in the air, slowly slid down the hillside toward the Rebels.

The Rebel line emerged from the smoke in bits and pieces. Lean,

dirty men were furiously loading and firing, an officer was walking
behind their lines, shouting to his men, pointing at the Federal lines
with a gleaming sword.

From his lines there was another volley, a tremendous, deafening
explosion of a thousand rifles, and he wondered how his men could
hear the command to fire above all the noise. Richardson walked the
line, screamed at men to aim low, knew that they wouldn't, that soldiers load and fire like demons in the heat of battle, give little thought
to aiming.

He turned, saw that another regiment was emerging from the wood,
the men marching sedately, glancing with worried faces toward the
firing. A shell ripped by overhead, exploded in a dirty cloud between
the two lines of men.

The Irish Brigade had the bit between its teeth now; men were
firing steadily, some lying in the grass, kneeling, shooting into the
hollow where the Rebels waited behind their barricade. The noise
from the firing was terrific. He screamed orders but no one heard, not
a man responded.

Richardson saw a two-gun section emerge from the dark wood and
wheel onto the field. He ran over uneven ground toward them, waved
for them to fire over the Rebel infantry, take the Southern cannon
under fire, watched in horror as one man ran the elevation screw all
the way up, pulled the lanyard. The charge roared out of the gun, cut
a long, ugly swath through the grass and dirt.

He cursed, ran toward the man, screaming for them to fire at the
Southern guns on the next crest. A boy pulled the lanyard on the second gun. It jumped rearward, belched smoke and flame. He turned,
watched the shell pass harmlessly over the Southern troops below, slam
into the side of the hill.

He reached the first crew, spun a big sergeant around roughly by
the sleeve of his uniform jacket. The man stared angrily at him with
black fishy eyes, saw the rank on his collar, said nothing. Richardson
pointed toward the Southern battery, said, "That's your target, Sergeant, not their infantry."

The man turned slowly, stupidly, stared in the direction of the
Southern artillery. Richardson saw an officer, a lieutenant, left the
sergeant, stumbled over the rough ground. The lieutenant stared at
him with wide eyes, attempted a salute. Richardson brushed off the
salute, screamed into the lieutenant's ear, "Have your men elevate
their guns, Lieutenant."

He grabbed the boy's sleeve, pointed in the direction of the South-

ern artillery. "You can't hit their infantry from here, boy. They're below your line of fire."

He waited, saw that the boy understood. "Good. Now what I want
from you is for you to fire on their guns across the way there. Do you
understand?"

The boy nodded, said, "Yes, sir," but Richardson could barely hear
him over the noise. He slapped the young lieutenant on the back,
pointed again at the Southern cannon on the opposing hill, screamed
into the boy's ear, "Their artillery, son. Shoot their damn guns!"

The lieutenant nodded.

Richardson saw that he understood, said, "Good man."

He crossed the open ground back to where the Irish brigade was
making its stand. Men were standing in the bright sunshine, loading,
firing steadily down into the lane where the Rebel line held.

He walked behind the regiments, caught glimpses of the Confederates through the smoke. Their line was alive with movement, a dark
knot of men behind thin, gray fence rails. Lots of casualties there too.
Men sprawled on the ground where they had been knocked out of
the lines. He stood for a moment, stared toward the village, the orchard behind the Southern infantry. Nothing behind them but a few
batteries scattered among the trees.

He had a searing thought that if his men could break through here
they could push them all the way through the town, beyond it, get
in among the Confederate rear area. He glanced east, back toward
the gloomy wood and the valley of the Antietam.

What I need, he thought, *is another division. Someone to come up and
lend a hand. A few batteries, move their cannon out of that orchard.*

From down the line there was a sudden burst of firing, men screaming. A soldier had run forward with the colors of the Irish Brigade,
was waving them, exhorting the men to give it their all. He watched
as a few brave soldiers advanced beyond their own lines, fired at the
Confederates behind their parapet.

From beyond the Irish left, he saw movement, Union troops moving around the Confederate right. He ran toward them, found an officer, ordered the man to bring them over the hill, swing down on the
flank of the Rebel lines, form a line that could fire down the length
of the enemy position.

The officer ran off and in minutes the regiment appeared over the
crest of a small knoll. The men wheeled out perfectly, brought their
weapons up, and delivered a volley that swept through the Southerners below. Richardson thought for a moment that he could hear a

single moan rise from the Rebel lines; then the tempo of the firing resumed and he was deafened by the sounds of battle again.

Men began to slip from the Southern line. Small groups of two or three scrambled out of the lane, ran through the corn, disappeared among the stalks. Richardson watched their officers try to stop them, saw them running along the length of the line, grabbing men leaving ranks, shoving them roughly back toward the firing line.

He stood transfixed, watched as the Southern line melted away, disappeared among the corn and the orchard; and the smoke that hung over the road drifted down the slope toward the parapet.

Along the length of his lines men were firing wildly, screaming, yelling at the fleeing Rebels. An officer on horseback was behind the line, exhorting the men to fire at the backs of the Rebels.

Richardson stared in disbelief for long moments, wondered how it could have ended so suddenly. Soldiers began slapping one another on the back, grateful to be alive, to have driven the Southerners from the field.

He turned, peered east, wondered if they could see what had taken place from army headquarters, if they understood the Southern center was broken, open to an advance.

Below him, down the grassy slope of the hill, there was only silence. The Southern dead lay where they had fallen, sprawled across the small lane in every manner. Here and there the wounded moved, waved a hand, called for water. He stared for long minutes, unable to comprehend it.

It had ended all too quickly. Men were still firing, but the Southern line had melted away, drawn back into the corn and the trees like so much smoke blown along on unseen wind.

He turned, began walking down the line, thinking that he must get word back to headquarters, tell them to send whatever they had to him here. They could funnel men into this break, force a wedge between the two halves of Lee's army. By midafternoon it could be over, all that was needed was a concentrated effort. They could be made to understand at headquarters. McClellan was a good man, just a bit slow at times. But he would see this; they would all see this.

A line of prisoners was moving slowly up the side of the hill, shepherded by his men, rifles held at the ready, bayonets fixed. The prisoners climbed steadily up the slope, heads down, eyes fixed on the ground.

His soldiers stared openmouthed as the dirty Rebels passed by in silence. Someone called out to them, a taunt. A Southern boy looked up, a dark face, grim features, stared at the line of dead lying in the grass, moved on without saying anything. A sergeant cursed, told his men to keep quiet.

Soldiers were crowding in, staring at the passing line of prisoners in openmouthed awe.

"Them Johnnies look about played out."

Richardson turned, saw the sergeant major. "Umm," he said, glanced down into the remnants of the Confederate position, almost turned away at the sight of it.

"Scrappers," said the sergeant major.

Richardson turned. "What's that?" he asked.

The big Irishman nodded in the direction of the prisoners. "Those lads are scrappers, sahr," he said confidently.

Richardson chuckled. "You changin' flags on me, Sergeant Major."

The other man pushed his hat back on his head, took the cork from his canteen. "Not likely, sahr. I've no desire to live down South." He nodded, indicated the line of prisoners. "But the lads there put up a bit of a fight, sahr, and we had the upper hand from the start of things."

He turned, looked at the sergeant major in surprise. "You believe we've had the upper hand?"

"Aye, General."

Richardson shrugged. "Can't see how you figure it."

"Easy enough," said the sergeant major.

"You want to explain that?"

The Irishman nodded. "They've come farther, and they've done it in a shorter space of time."

Richardson shook his head, smiled. "I'll be damned," he said at last. "Never figured you to believe the newspapers about them being green-eyed monsters and all that other rot they print every time we have a battle."

"Ah, General, you're not thinkin' with your head, lad. You're just proud of the boys, and it's cloudin' your ability to see things clearly."

He laughed, said, "Nothing is going to spoil this moment, so why don't you just go ahead and explain your theory to me, Sergeant Major."

The sergeant major rubbed his chin with a dirty hand. "Easy enough, if you just give it a little thought. The newspapers couldn't be more wrong, and anyone with half a mind can see it."

Richardson turned, cocked an eyebrow. "You think so?"

"Aye, lad, I do." The other man nodded in the direction of the dead men lying in the hollow of the hill. "They started with less than us. Fewer states joined the Rebellion. They had no army, other than a militia unit or two, and there're fewer people livin' in the states that rebelled than those that stayed with the old Union."

Richardson knew by the tone that the other man had given this some thought, that this wasn't just idle talk. "Go on," he said.

"Well, it's just this, General. I've been soldierin' a long while. And I've seen all manner of men that came to the army and made soldiers of themselves. Men from here and men from the old country."

"We all have," he said slowly.

"Aye, we have. And the boys lyin' there"—the sergeant major nodded, indicated the Southern dead—"have learned quicker than most. And they've made fine soldiers."

"And?" said Richardson.

"And they're almost played out over there, sahr. And beggin' your pardon, General, but any damned fool can see it."

"Maybe," he said.

"Just you take at look at them prisoners. Lean as a winter wolf and not a good set of boots among 'em."

The sergeant major fell silent, stared out over the hill, pointed toward the town, glowing white in the sun. "They're runnin' a bluff, lad. Sure as Irish love whiskey, they're runnin' a bluff."

Richardson turned, stared at the sergeant major for a long moment, knew that he had been thinking the same thing, that other officers in the army had been talking of it for days. "I've thought that myself," he said.

The sergeant major nodded. "Today's as good a day as any the Lord has given us to find out, lad."

Richardson smiled. "See that ammunition is brought up for the men and water. We'll be moving out before too long."

"Aye," said the sergeant major. "I thought you might come to it, sahr, in the end."

"Remember the water, Sergeant Major," but he had already turned, was walking off toward the rear, shouting for someone to bring the wagons up closer.

Richardson stared out over grassy hills, wondered what it would all come to today. They had held against French, almost against his men. And then they had come unraveled, their lines crumbled, faded into the dirt and the corn, and the orchard beyond. He shook his head, knew suddenly that the sergeant major was right.

They *were* played out over there, and here he was in the center of their lines, with a great blowing hole staring him in the face. All he had to do was form the division, waltz right up to the town, shove them out of the way, and it could all be over in a few hours.

An enormous breach, a great, gaping swath of open ground, lovely round hills and apple orchards and not one Confederate regiment between him and the Potomac. A man could walk all the way to Sharpsburg now, not run across a Southern soldier.

He smiled, thought: *We've done it. We'll finish today, and then we've got to set it right somehow. But we've done it today.*

The sky turned into brilliant orange light. He felt the concussion roll over him like a great orange fist, saw the waves of light and shadows in his eyes. The ground came up, hit him in the back with a solid *whump!* that sent the air rushing out of his lungs.

He stared into the cloudless blue sky, his mind foggy, waves of searing pain rolling through his brain like some inner tide. He blinked, felt the most exquisite pain, closed his eyes again, held his breath against the next rush, was surprised to hear someone moan close by, then realized it was his own voice that had betrayed him.

He lay on his back, tried to move, felt only the white-hot pain rush up at him, blind him, force the air from his lungs. Richardson waited for it to pass, long agonizing moments, he stared at the sky, stalks of grass that waved softly over him as he lay on his back in the hayfield.

"Over here, lads. I've found him."

The voice of the sergeant major drifted down to him. The round face appeared above him, blocked the light, the shadow of the man passing over him, forcing him to blink. "Ah, lad, look what you've gone and done to yerself," he heard the sergeant major say as if from a long way off.

Richardson tried to answer, but couldn't make a sound. He grinned, tried to raise himself, felt only exquisite pain. There was a pat on his shoulder. "Lay still, lad. And don't mind that wee wound you've got. I've sent for the surgeon."

Someone had fashioned a stretcher from two rifles and a heavy army blanket and Richardson could feel hands grabbing his uniform, lifting him free of the clinging grass, sliding him onto the rough wool.

An image from his boyhood came to him, of rocky mountains white with snow, and icy black rivers, and forests of maple and birch and great soaring stands of hemlock. There had been a hunt, and blood flecked the snow where the big buck had passed; and he had followed the animal down to a stream, watched in silence as it plunged into the swirling black water, climbed the slope on the opposite side, disappeared over a crest.

He tried to lift a hand, to stop them, tell them to send to army headquarters, have them bring up more men, more cannon, push ahead. Voices above him were talking, the words indistinct, a murmur, and the heat had come back with a vengeance; and he felt suddenly that he had done all that he could, and the others must see to the army because he could not.

And then he remembered the great dark eyes of the deer, and the sound of winter wind very high in the trees, and he felt a great gaping sadness that he knew would never end.

CHAPTER 20

BEYOND THE PLOWED FIELDS AND STANDING CORN, AMBROSE Burnside could see the western bank of Antietam Creek. The ground on the far side rose steeply away from the water in a series of parallel ridges that dominated the fields and pastures on the east side of the Antietam and a screen of heavy smoke drifted among the branches of the oaks and sycamores rising from the rocky slope.

The banks were heavily wooded for as far as he could see, and a single tree rose from the rampart near the edge of the small stone bridge. Among the large trees on the far side he could see the dark shapes of Rebel soldiers, the shadow movements of men dodging among the trunks and rifle pits.

He had already made two attacks on the Rebel positions and neither column had managed to get as far as the bridge. The defenders had shot the columns to pieces while they struggled across nearly a half mile of open ground. Rebel cannon posted on the high ground south of the village had added to the difficulty, taking the columns under fire the moment they broke cover and started toward the bridge.

Burnside looked about him, took in the expectant faces, officers waiting for him to issue orders, renew the assault. He opened his hand, unfolded the small piece of paper sent to him by McClellan. The commander of the army was impatient for him to carry the bridge, threaten the Confederate right. He glanced at McClellan's aide, standing among his officers, waiting for him to respond to the communiqué.

He felt the frustration growing, slowly, deep inside him. He and his staff had not been properly briefed; there had been no real chance to question McClellan about his plan for the day. No written orders had been issued. Now, apparently, the plan was changing. No longer was he expected merely to demonstrate against the Southern forces in front of him; he was expected to assault the bridge, drive the Rebels from the western bank. Threaten Lee's entire right, cut off his line of retreat.

He had made the normal requests for reconnaissance, for reinforcements to support his attack. There had been little word from Mc-

Clellan or army headquarters. Just this smirking officer with the terse message to carry the bridge as soon as possible and the implication that he was not following orders.

He looked again at the crumpled piece of paper, drew his fist closed around it. Ahead the bridge glowed white in the midafternoon sun, disappeared in a graceful arch toward the far bank.

A single bird sang from somewhere, a lovely clear whistle. Behind him someone cleared his throat. Burnside turned, saw McClellan's courier looking at him, waiting.

He lifted his eyes beyond the bluff, saw only a cloudless sky through the trees, thought: *God knows how many men Lee has over there.*

"Cavalry," he said under his breath.

"Sir?"

Burnside turned, saw that it was McClellan's staff officer looking at him. "I said we should have cavalry here. To develop the enemy's flank, determine where the fords are, what lies beyond those bluffs," he said crossly.

"Yes, sir."

Burnside turned, glared at the man. "Did the commanding general's staff think about that? Perhaps our cavalry could have scouted the Confederate position; then maybe I would know what to expect beyond the Antietam, or where the fords lie."

"I'm sure it was taken into consideration," began the man.

Burnside wheeled on the officer, the anger welling up in him. "I wouldn't be so certain if I were you, Colonel."

"No, sir," offered the colonel. Officers standing nearby shuffled their feet, looked away.

"Well," said Burnside angrily, "why is it you have been sent here, Colonel?"

The man cleared his throat, glanced about him nervously at the other officers, said, "General McClellan sends his compliments, sir. And asks that you take the bridge as soon as possible by whatever force necessary."

Burnside felt his face cloud with anger. It welled up in him like a swarm of angry wasps, and his face flushed and he started to curse the man, then stopped himself.

It was just like McClellan. Expect others to do the fighting, see to the details of it while he spent his time at headquarters planning grand strategies and delivering charming monologues to a host of visitors and reporters.

He felt suddenly betrayed by McClellan. A lifetime together, their days as cadets at the Academy, service in the old army, then the years in business. Mac had always been there, gracious, ready to lend a hand.

And yet . . . there was something lacking. MacClellan had been the rising star. There had been a certain expectation on his part of, if not admiration, then an unspoken acknowledgment of his future greatness. A willingness to brush you aside if something else drew his attention.

Burnside suddenly resented it, saw it all coming apart, a great unstoppable tide of disappointment washed over him and the anger faded, hardened into something else that he could not put a name to.

Beyond the plowed ground, shimmering in the heat, the bridge waited in silence. The field was strewn with dead horses and the bodies of his soldiers, and the sweet, sickening smell of blood and death drifted toward him on a warm breeze. A single cannon fired, far away, not threatening. *Ca-thump*.

Burnside felt the anger subside, die away. "McClellan seems to think that I am not trying my best to carry this bridge."

The colonel returned his gaze evenly, answered, "The commanding general wishes the Confederate right to be developed, sir. It would support our efforts on the northern end of the field. I am sure that you appreciate his concern."

"And the reinforcements I was promised?" he asked. "Are they en route?"

The colonel looked away, eyes darting, evasive.

"I see," he said. There would be no reinforcements. Soldiers, entire divisions, would sit idle while his men died in droves assaulting the damn bridge. "Well," he said to no one in particular.

Mac had promised to support his attack, send him whatever reinforcements he needed. An empty promise.

There had been other promises. In Virginia, reinforcements that never came, apologies and excuses afterward. In a week or two there would be glasses of good whiskey and talk of old times and, in the end, when you needed him most, there were only empty promises and vague reasons why he couldn't have been there.

And orders. For the moment there were orders, and orders move armies and force battles, and the stone bridge was waiting to be carried and he had orders to do it with whatever force he could bring to bear and no matter the cost.

And no matter that Mac had always been a bit lacking when it came to getting behind you in a fight.

Ca-thump. The cannon fired again, the sound rolled toward him through the muggy air.

He listened, waited for the counterbattery fire, heard only silence. He put the binoculars away, closed the leather case, listened for more artillery.

Nothing. A great empty vacuum.

He waited, long moments, he wondered why the firing had died away. A wagon clattered by, the mules straining against the harness, and he suddenly knew that the army's attacks had been stalled.

It was an enormous front, miles long. There would be difficulty in coordinating assaulting columns. There had been little time to plan the offensive, bring them all together for one final briefing where you could lay it all out, make everyone understand what had to be done.

He removed his hat, wiped his forehead with a handkerchief. His hair was wet with sweat, beads of it dripping along his forehead, the sun beating down relentlessly.

Before the invasion they had offered him command of the army, asked him to replace stodgy old Pope. They had meant to bypass McClellan.

He had refused. No choice really. He wasn't meant to command armies, and he couldn't pull the rug out from under Mac like that. So he had refused, ridden through the night to tell Mac of their offer, had a whiskey with his old friend. They had talked.

In the end Mac had been returned to command of the army. He was the logical choice; they had no one else who could bring it all together, put the army back on its feet.

He had returned to his corps. Mac had promoted him, given him command of his corps and Hooker's First Corps. They had moved north, pursued Lee through the mountains, Mac struggling to reorganize the army. Only a couple of short weeks since the last general engagement, and now here, another one hard on its heels.

He lifted his gaze, saw the bridge glowing gold and brown in the sunlight, leafy heights beyond.

No choice now. No time to be petty. Do your duty, be a good soldier. Everything else could wait for another day. The hurt feelings, the small insults, all of it had to wait.

Mac was the golden boy, no harm in that. Every man has a destiny. Maybe the bridge was his.

Remember the good times, the nights drinking at West Point, Mac laughing, a girl on each arm, all of them together. It wasn't so long ago.

Mac should never have taken Hooker's corps from him, but what of it, in the end? Would men remember that? Speak of that years from now?

Something hard and unyielding in him insisted it was wrong, knew it was wrong. An affront. You should expect better treatment from a friend, had a right to expect it. He would have done better by Mac, remembered that they were friends.

And yet, what would you have done? The same? Maybe. No easy choices to make when armies meet and men die.

Faith. Not just duty, but faith. All those years ago, when he had been down on his luck, Mac had shown faith in him. Now it was time to return the favor. Mac needed the bridge, and the reasons why weren't as important as the fact itself; and Mac's future riding on the outcome of the day. And maybe the fate of the army, even the nation.

He felt suddenly petty, regretted his angry words to the colonel moments before. He turned toward the man, said, "These are trying times, Colonel."

"Yes, sir," the officer answered.

Burnside smiled, the corners of his mouth turning upward slightly beneath the heavy whiskers. "Tell General McClellan that he shall have his bridge."

The colonel saluted, smiled knowingly. "Yes, sir," then spun on one heel and strode away.

Burnside turned toward his own staff, saw the expectant looks on their faces. "Order another assault upon the bridge. I want it carried, gentlemen, if it takes us all day."

Within minutes two regiments had formed under the brow of the hill a few hundred yards east of the bridge. Men were struggling up the long slope in the muggy air, neat blue columns, rows of rifles, gleaming bayonets. Orders were given and men began to shrug off their haversacks and other equipment. Canteens, tin cups, and blankets all hit the ground as the soldiers cast off any item that wasn't necessary for the attack.

An officer flourished his sword and the column gave a spasm of forward movement, the men slogging toward the crest of the hill. The first soldiers topped the rise and were met by a sudden storm of artillery, the shot arcing in among the running men. Bursts of canister and fused shells plowed into the long columns and white smoke blossomed from the heights beyond the bridge. Men lowered their heads, held their caps with one hand, ran forward into the fire as though they were running into a summer shower that would pass as quickly as it had sprung up.

Burnside watched as the colors moved forward steadily over the broken ground. For what seemed an interminable period the columns moved slowly toward the valley of the Antietam. Men were dropping away at every step, the front ranks of the two columns appeared to melt in the bright afternoon light.

From the right, near a copse of trees, a cannon was firing at the Rebels. Its shot bursting in steady rhythm among the trees on the far bank. Burnside sensed that the fire from the Confederates was slackening, falling off ever so slightly. He took a step toward the top of the hill, anxious to see if the assault force would make it to the bridge.

When the head of the column was a mere fifty yards from the bridge, he saw the colors swing off to one side, the soldiers following, taking shelter on the east side of the creek. Men were hugging the ground, trying to find shelter from the killing rifle fire. Orange flame leapt from the dark hillside, stabbed the shadows, disappeared instantly in white smoke.

Soldiers crouched next to the fence rails lining the road by the bridge, hands over their heads, trying to find any shelter from the galling fire from the heights on the other side of the water. Even from his position Burnside could see the small plumes of dust raised in the road by stray bullets.

He had an overwhelming urge to call them back, to move them out of the deadly fire. For an instant Burnside fought the urge to order a retreat, bring them out of the withering fire of the rifles on the far bank. Save as many of them as he could, while there was still time.

All that would be necessary was for him to order a bugler to sound the retreat. Men would die as they attempted to retrace their steps, but perhaps they could find the ford, cross farther downstream, flank the Rebels. Move away from this damn bridge and the hill beyond.

The field in front of him was strewn with wounded, alive with men crawling or limping back toward the rear. A battery behind him somewhere fired, four quick shots that caused the air to vibrate, made the ground underfoot tremble and shake.

By the stream someone had raised the colors, Burnside saw the flag being waved back and forth, felt a momentary hope, then the soldier went down and the colors plunged to the earth in eerie silence. He felt his hopes fall, a feeling passed over him of sudden despair, like water rushing over a dam, an unstoppable sadness.

Near the bridge a shell exploded, there was a sudden black plume of smoke, and the sound of green wood breaking, and Burnside watched as a tree slowly crashed to the ground. He stood transfixed, saw the trunk fall, tumble down the hillside toward the stream.

The battery fired again, close by, four great explosions that deafened him, made his ears ring. And then suddenly men were on their feet, cheering, and he glanced toward the left and saw the reason.

A column of men had staggered to their feet, were rushing the bridge. A cluster of blue uniforms gained the ramp, wavered, seemed to pulse and shake at the very foot of the stone arch. The hillside blossomed in orange flame, the column lurched toward the wooden deck of the bridge, unsteady, faltering. Men stood on the bridge deck, reeled momentarily, lurched ahead in uncertain movements.

A soldier stood near the stone wall of the bridge, waved the national colors, others streamed past, a swift blue tide that pushed onto the bridge, disappeared over the arch into the trees beyond.

From the right more men were running, another column, streaming onto the bridge, pushing across in a steady line. Soldiers stopped to fire, lunged ahead in small groups, vanished among the brush on the far bank.

On the hillside, among the trees and undergrowth, Burnside detected the first signs of movement. Dark figures emerging, clawing their way up the slope, darting among the trees. Dark silhouettes appeared on the crest of the ridge, slipped over the horizon in rapid movements.

Nearby the battery let loose another salvo, the ground shuddered. He waved an aide over, said above the inferno, "Order another brigade forward. We're across. Let's not lose our momentum."

A sergeant bawled orders, men rose quickly, formed ranks. A column jerked spasmodically, shook itself out, moved off at the double-quick. A cannon ball waffled in, exploded overhead, men ducked, there was laughter.

Burnside turned, smiled at the officers nearby. Men were shaking hands, slapping one another on the back. A bottle was being passed around, men were drinking in quick, hurried movements.

Jacob Cox approached, a small man, natty appearance, had the look of a soldier about him but had been a lawyer before the war. After Reno's death he had taken over command of the Ninth Corps. Burnside smiled, nodded.

"General," said Cox smiling, "I believe we've got that bridge."

Burnside beamed, felt the relief flood over him. "Yes." He grinned at Cox. "Splendid," he said.

Cox was smiling, a wide, almost foolish grin. All around men were laughing, pointing to the bridge. The firing had died away; in the distance the sounds of men cheering could be heard. "Well," said Burnside, "I suppose we've done it then."

"Yes," said Cox.

"Let's ride up there, Cox. See what the situation is on the far side. Have a look at things."

Cox smiled, an aide appeared, handed them their reins. Burnside mounted, rode over the broken ground toward the bridge gleaming in the sunlight. He rode past wagons already filled with wounded and scores of shapeless mounds that had been living, breathing men when the sun rose this morning.

Close to the bridge men were smiling, taking off their hats as he and Cox passed, staring. He could feel their excitement, their joy at having taken the bridge, beaten the enemy. A rare thing in this army, very rare.

"Don't see them run very often," said Cox.

Burnside smiled, laughed. "No, not often," he said.

"Twice now," said Cox.

Burnside glanced at him, raised an eyebrow.

"Here," said Cox, indicating the bridge. "And at South Mountain a few days back."

"Yes," said Burnside. "The men have performed better than anyone has a right to expect."

A group of prisoners was sitting beneath the shade of a large sycamore, and Burnside stared at them for long moments. Small men with dirty clothing of every description, heads down, staring sullenly at the grass. The ground nearby was littered with the bits of cartridge paper, the earth torn in great gashes of black, the soil ripped and splattered. Someone had found a Confederate flag, was showing it to his fellows. There were black stares from the prisoners.

He pushed the horse to the top of the rise, saw the village beyond squatting serenely on a bit of high ground above the creek. White clapboard, the spire of a church, a single dirty plume of smoke.

He had a sudden premonition that Lee's army was beaten, that the way to the river was clear. The thought came to him clear and bright, like a summer sky charged with lightning.

He turned to Cox, said suddenly, "Order everything forward. I want every man and gun we have across this bridge as fast as possible."

Cox blinked, wheezed, stared stupidly for a moment, said automatically, "Yes, sir."

"We'll have to act quickly. They've fallen back for now, but they'll reorganize soon and throw up a line."

"I'll see to it," said Cox. Cox paused, waited, blinked.

"Yes?" asked Burnside.

"Well," said Cox, "it's just that we're gonna have this creek at our back, and we've only got the one bridge to move the men across, General." Cox paused, rubbed his chin with one hand, glanced back in the direction of the Antietam. "Gonna take some time."

Burnside waved a hand at him, said evenly, "See to it. Be as quick as you can. Have the men wade the stream and use the bridge just for the ammunition wagons if you have to; but for the love of God, move them up as fast as you can, Cox."

Burnside saw a smile of understanding pass over Cox's features, knew that the man understood that an opportunity existed, that it would last for only a little while. That soon more gray soldiers would file into position between them and the village; but for now, at this moment, the way was clear and he meant to drive on the town, force the issue.

"I'll get it done, General," said Cox. He wheeled on the big horse, rode off amid clouds of dust.

Burnside turned, stared out over rolling hills and fields of summer wheat and apple orchards. He sensed a great emptiness, a silent, brooding vacuum that stretched away, across the hills, beyond the town, all the way to the great wide river beyond. He inhaled; the air was thick with the smell of burnt powder and summer heat and the faint odor of camphor.

Behind him he could feel the army gathering, drawing itself up, coiling, ready to spring like a great beast that has stalked its prey, found its moment. All that was needed now was a little time. A few hours, form them up under the brow of the hill, stack units behind them, then push on toward the village and the river beyond.

It was close, so very close. A little time. Burnside pulled the gold watch from his pocket, noted the hour, looked up into a white sky, the sun high overhead, thought silently: *There's time yet.*

CHAPTER 21

POWELL HILL HAD THOUGHT IT WOULD BE COOLER DOWN BY the river, where the road followed the Potomac and was shaded in places by ancient oaks and chestnuts, and a breeze was likely even on the hottest days. But in fact the heat had pursued them even there. It seemed to rise off the surface of the water, float toward them silently, smother them in a never-ending-embrace.

The faces of his soldiers had gone white and clammy beneath their hats and men marched openmouthed, their breathing audible, their pace uncertain in the humid air. It reminded Hill of the hospitals back in Richmond; rows of men sweating on makeshift cots, laboring with each breath, and for a moment he glimpsed an unspeakable vision that his entire division would die before they ever saw the battlefield ahead.

Word came back that the column had found a ford; there was yelling, the excitement rippling down the column like a fireball, washing over it, spreading the relief that comes with any change, any sign of a landmark, to men who have marched hard and have no idea when the end might come. He spurred ahead, splashed across a rocky ford, pushed the sweating horse up the far bank.

Lee was there, sitting on the great gray horse, dark-eyed, waiting for him. Hill nudged the animal through the press of traffic on the road, saluted. "General," he said.

In the village he could see that all was confusion, wounded men and broken artillery trying to move to the rear, his men already crowding in, cluttering the road, pushing past lines of men who stood at the wells and waited for water with hard, glittering eyes.

Lee smiled, said, "I am glad that you have found us, General."

Hill smiled back, saw the worry behind the courtly features. There was something in Lee's face he had never seen before; he stared for a brief moment, glanced away. *Never knew the Old Man to look worried before.*

"My boys are moving up now, sir."

"Yes," said Lee. "General McClellan has moved more aggressively today than I have expected. You must get your men onto the field as quickly as possible."

Powell Hill absorbed the news in silence, thought: *Wonder what kind of burr's gotten under Mac's saddle.*

He grinned, felt suddenly foolish in the presence of the Old Man. Lee had a way of doing that to you, making you feel that whatever it was you were about to say, he had already considered, anticipated your every thought, was just waiting patiently for you to come to the same realization, put it into words. Hill said at last, "Not like Mc-Clellan to come on that fast."

"No," said Lee solemnly. "They have pressed us along our entire front. I believe they will renew their attacks south of the village."

"That where you want my men, then?" asked Hill.

"Yes," answered Lee. "My officers will direct you.

"Fighting been heavy?" he asked.

Hill saw something in Lee's features, a pale shadow that passed over his face, was instantly gone, covered up by the old Lee. In an instant he was the professional soldier again, the commander who never worried. Lee turned to him, said, "The fighting has been very heavy. I will not be able to support your attack. You command the reserve of this army, General."

A bugle sounded from beyond the houses in the village, the notes faint. *Recall.* He recognized the notes even at this great distance.

Hill saw Lee turn in that direction, stared for long moments. Lee pointed, toward the southeast. "Beyond those orchards is Antietam Creek. They are across, probably in corps strength. You will have to prevent their advance with your men, General."

Hill nodded solemnly, watched the Old Man carefully from the corner of his eye. There was something there, something new, uncertain. "I'll have the division up directly, sir," he began.

Lee shook his head. Hill looked into the dark eyes, wondered.

"No," said Lee. "We cannot wait for your entire division to come up. You must go in at once, with whomever you have available."

He turned, stared back toward the ford, saw a ribbon of water, light glinting off the surface through the trees, men climbing the long slope, heads down, like so many silent ants. "Be a while before most of my boys are up." He continued to stare toward the Potomac. At last he turned toward Lee, said, "I can get a brigade or two into the mix in the next hour."

Lee shook his head again. Hill saw that Taylor and Marshall and the others were nearby now. He glanced in that direction; men were avoiding his gaze, refusing to meet his eyes.

Lee turned to him. He looked into the dark eyes, waited for him to speak in the heat and the bright light. A chill passed over him, cut through him with an icy blast, and suddenly Powell Hill was aware of the mortality of men, of all men. In that instant he sensed something of his own death, knew that eventually it comes for all men, silent, unforgiving, remorseless.

In that moment he knew the situation, knew what Lee was telling him. That he had to go forward, with whatever he had, no matter that it was not enough, that it could never be enough. That if he hesitated, if he failed, then all of them, their collective self, would fail this day, here, on this field, in Maryland. That there could be no reprieve, that the die had been cast and that he was all that was left among them. That only he could change their destiny, but he must act, and it must be now.

Lee gripped his arm, a sense of urgency to his touch. Hill looked into the dark eyes, was grateful that there was no fear there, only a certain urgency. Lee said, "You must go forward, General. If you are able, push them back across the Antietam, but you must attack with whatever men you have on the field."

Hill nodded, smiled, wondered if Jackson and Longstreet and the others knew how badly it had gone. He pulled the reins up, the horse snorted, tossed his head, blew air past the bit. He saw Lee's staff watching him, handsome Marshall, young Walter Taylor. The other men averted their eyes, refused to meet his own.

They know what I'm being asked to do. Sacrifice my men, my division, he thought. *They know.*

He rode through the town, past the sallow faces of the wounded, past houses filled with men who could no longer walk. He turned a corner, glimpsed a row of dead men lying in the sun behind someone's carriage house, stared for long seconds, turned away at last.

Near the center of the village the column had turned, was moving south, past a church that had been struck by artillery fire. The mortar had been jarred loose from the lath underneath and lay in smoky piles near the foundation, the wooden framing stood bare and naked and obscene in the bright light of day.

Hill automatically searched the graveyard next to the church, saw rows of gleaming granite and marble, more dead in silent mounds. He spurred the horse, anxious to get out of town, away from the dead and the dying. Better to find the fighting, clear his head, banish thoughts of dead soldiers.

A chill moved down his spine and he turned, glanced back toward the cemetery, saw the shadow of the spire had fallen across the

graves, that it lay across the dead soldiers like a shroud. It occurred
to him that they were lying in darkness, even amid the brilliant light,
and that soon they would be covered by earth and grass and darkness
of a different sort, and that the hand of the Almighty moved in terrible
and desperate ways that men were not meant to understand.

The road was filled with marching men, not a solid mass of infantry
as it should have been, just small groups of men who had managed
to hold on, continue moving through the heat. Dark knots of soldiers
were standing in the road, a line beginning to form, officers hurrying
men into a formation.

He pushed the horse toward the men standing in the road, heard
the first scattered shots from somewhere east of the town. He topped
a rise, paused, scanned the rolling ground that lay between the
road and the creek, failed to see a single Northern soldier. Smoke
covered much of the field, uneven ground that undulated in long
ridges, was planted in corn; farmer's fences bisected the lots, disappeared into narrow hollows. Lots of open ground, small hills, deep
hollows and rocky ravines. Good ground to conceal troop formations.

A battery opened up from near the village. He turned, saw that the
guns had been run forward, were on a long ridge just south of the town,
no infantry visible anywhere. His eyes followed the arc of the shot until
it disappeared into the valley that marked the course of the creek. The
shells dipped below the ridge. There were muffled explosions from below, near where the creek must be. He searched again for infantry
near the guns, saw only cornfields, an orchard.

*That's where they'll come from then, that low ground, near the creek. They'll
be forming up now, under the lee of that ridge. Mac will think to drive on
the town, get between the two wings of our army.*

There was more firing now, from near the village. The sharp popping of rifles, a Union regiment appeared, marching steadily, a neat
formation. Hill could see other men, running among the orchard,
pausing to shoot, moving again. No massed formations, nothing that
would hold for long. A delaying action, a rear guard. Only this was
not the rear. This was the main line, and it would have to be held.

He spurred ahead, found an officer standing in the road, waving
his men into a line with his sword. He pointed toward the orchard,
said, "Get them on line and let's hit them as hard as we can."

The officer turned toward him, glanced at him with angry eyes,
said, "We'll step off directly, sir." He looked around, added, "I've got
less than half of my regiment here, General."

"No matter," said Hill, "get them into the fight. Do what you can to slow down the Union advance."

Hill left the man standing openmouthed in the road, scanned the horizon again for signs of Union formations. The fighting near the town had intensified. Solid formations of Union infantry were advancing steadily toward the heights near the town.

He watched as one battery began to pull back, was struck by a shell from beyond the creek, the gun and crew disappearing in a black geyser of flame and smoke and dirt. A line of blue infantry emerged from a bit of low ground, swept toward the ridge abandoned by the battery. On the brow of the hill there was hurried movement, confusion, the crews dragging the guns away by their tongues, not waiting for the battery horses to be brought up.

The blue line was energized at the site; men began to run; he could see the flags bouncing over the field, bobbing among the small knolls and valleys, rushing toward the village. The line hesitated at a low wall, blue uniforms poured over, reformed, moved again toward the ridge guarding the town.

Powell Hill felt as though it had all been for nothing. The long march into Maryland, the fighting at Harpers Ferry, the hot march toward this place today. In another ten minutes they would be in the town, among the baggage trains of the army. And then there would be . . . disaster.

The blue brigades dipped into a bit of low ground, emerged again moments later, bayonets gleaming. From beyond the town a battery was firing, the shot falling among the marching infantry. Gaps appeared in the Union line. Men were blown apart, vanished in smoky geysers. But it was not enough; they were coming on, in good order. Another few minutes.

A line of gray-and-brown infantry rose, unseen, from behind a stone wall, defied the Union advance, dark rifles pointed at the blue soldiers, white smoke rolling out all along the line. The Union brigade staggered, stumbled, men fell out of ranks, were swallowed by the deep grass and corn.

Another volley, more smoke, the sound of battle moving toward him; the two lines appeared almost to touch. Smoke lay between the lines in great dirty clouds, covered the men, hid both armies from sight. Men's voices and the sound of rifle fire floated to him over the fields, was diminished with distance. Through the smoke he saw the blue line charge, heard the two groups of men collide, watched in

silent horror as the gray-and-brown soldiers gave way, fell back toward
the village.

To the east, near the creek, other infantry was appearing, solid walls
of blue, long, gleaming rows of bayonets held aloft. A battery appeared, close to the village, the cannon dark and ominous on the
ridge, silhouetted against the sky. They had seen the Federal infantry,
understood the threat. Shot was pouring into their ranks, exploding
in vicious bursts over the heads of their formations. Blue soldiers went
down with each explosion; he could hear men shrieking even at this
distance.

The advance around the village had slowed. Soldiers near the town
were shooting from behind houses and barns, pouring rifle fire into
the advancing Federals. Union soldiers were a few hundred yards
from the outskirts of the village, fighting their way toward the cluster
of houses, moving in slow, deliberate rushes. No careless charges now;
the firing was too intense. Men were more careful, wanted to gain the
town, get in among the buildings, find cover from the bullets that
sought them out with every step.

The Union brigades filing up out of the valley of the Antietam
began to step off in orderly rows, dipping among the low ground,
reemerging moments later as they topped a rise. Powell Hill could
see that they were angling toward the village; moving on the oblique,
sweeping in long, graceful lines toward Sharpsburg and the ridge
where the artillery had been placed.

A second line of infantry emerged from the hollow near the creek,
swarmed out of the low ground, a slow-moving mass of men that
paused at the crest of the ridge, shook themselves out, swelled and
rolled and expanded at every breath. A rippling wave of blue infantry
that appeared from the valley of the Antietam, the patient blue line
growing until it disappeared beyond a bit of high ground crowded
with oaks and chestnut.

A bugle sounded, the notes carrying over the field, clear and distinct above all the firing, the music familiar. Suddenly they were moving, the blue soldiers lurching forward in instant obedience, moving
toward the village.

He could hear more bugles, shouted orders drifting over rolling
ground, and the blue lines began to separate, angle toward the village,
and the white houses, and the long ridge spiked with cannon. The
line of Southern infantry had evaporated, disappeared into the smoke.
Here and there men were shooting at the advancing Yankees, knocking them down with careful, aimed fire, sheltering behind trees and

houses. Small groups of a half-dozen men refusing to give ground without a fight. But there was no line, just individual soldiers refusing to give up the fight. Nothing that would hold back even so much as a regiment.

On the road another of his brigades had formed, a few hundred men, to face thousands. They were standing in the dusty lane, waiting, looking at him, wondering. He rode past, asked a sweating soldier, "Whose brigade is this?"

The boy stared back with hollow eyes, said, "Branch's brigade."

He galloped past the soldier, searched the ranks for O'Bryan Branch. Hill saw him, just off the road, sword in hand, shoving men into line. He swung down off the horse, caught Branch's look of surprise.

The other man sneezed, wiped his face with a dirty cloth, said, "Damn this dust." Branch looked up at Hill, smiled brightly. "Afternoon, Powell."

Hill took the hand extended by the other man, the thought crossing his mind that it was an odd gesture on a battlefield. Soldiers saluted, and Branch was an old soldier. In the Seminole Wars, in Florida, years before, he had served with distinction. Gone on to enter politics, had even been a member of Congress.

They had all learned to despise Congress in the years before the war. Too much meddling. Washington had gotten too big for its britches. And now here was Branch, a congressman, commanding one of his brigades. Good Carolina boys, superb soldiers, only the best of them here now.

Boys from the Blue Ridge, lean boys raised among towering pines and gray rocks, smoky blue mountains. There had been some trouble with them; they were difficult men to command. Never easy to reason with a man accustomed to doing everything for himself, seeing things his own way.

Branch had smoothed all that out, seemed to get along with them. Difficult thing, to lead independent-minded men. He nodded toward the line of soldiers, said curtly, "Get 'em into the fight, O.B."

Branch turned, glanced at the soldiers, said, "I've got less than half my boys, Powell."

"Yep," said Hill. "You'll have to go in with whatever you've got here." He pointed, past the smoking ground, toward the village, white clapboards, gleaming cannon on the ridge. "They're going for the town," he said. "They'll try and cut us in half, get between us and Jackson's command up north. You've got to get across this field, move your brigade across lots, hit 'em from behind with everything you've got."

"They're after those batteries up by the ridge there."

"The hell with the cannon," he said. "Try and get in behind them, take them from the rear. Our boys in the town will see you movin' after 'em from the high ground. They'll know what to do. Once you get close enough, open up on 'em with everything you've got. I'll try and get a battery or two around to give you a hand."

Branch squinted into the sun, stared across the open ground toward the town. "Not going to be easy; they've got a few regiments moving already. My boys will have to move fast just to get into the fight."

"Yep," said Hill. "But you're all I've got, and the Yankees have already driven one line back into the town. Least we can do is give 'em something else to think about."

Branch smiled, said, "Going to be a pretty good scrap from the looks of it, Powell. You comin' along?"

Hill smiled. "I'll be along directly. Soon as I see that all our boys are up and into the fight."

Branch touched the brim of his cap. "See you out there, then."

"Be seein' you, O.B," said Hill, and in the next instant Branch was gone. A line of men stepped off, almost into silence. There were no drums, no bugle sounded to signal the advance. Branch raised his sword and they vanished into the broken corn and the rolling ground and the never-ending heat. The earth appeared to swallow them whole, an entire brigade disappeared into the hollows and gullies, vanished among the standing corn.

Hill watched for long moments, saw a regimental flag appear above the stalks, float over green leaves, rise and fall with the unseen ground beneath the corn.

They were moving quickly, closing in on the unsuspecting Federals. No contact, not yet. No artillery fire chasing them across the field, stalking their every movement, following them with iron and fire and death.

From the ridge there was increased artillery firing. He could see a gun line had formed, massed cannon banging away at the advancing blue soldiers. Smoke rolled off the ridge, slid down the slopes, pooled and eddied in the low ground beneath the guns. He searched, looked for some sign of infantry, another line, something to keep the Union soldiers from those guns.

Among the orchards there was movement, steady firing. A reinforced skirmish line, stragglers who had been herded into a makeshift line. Nothing that would hold the Federals back.

Branch's men were invisible, hidden among the rolling hills, out of sight. From near the town there was a flurry of firing. He turned, saw the reason, felt his heart sink in his chest. A blue line was running, sweeping toward a few cannon on a knoll near the town. In an instant the blue soldiers swarmed over the guns; men were sitting astride the gleaming brass tubes. Someone was waving the national flag back and forth, more Union infantry was sweeping up the hill, crowding in on the town.

On the road the tatters of another regiment had managed to assemble. A thin line, men standing in sweat-stained clothing, leaning on their rifles, breathing hard. They had come too far; the heat and the pace of the march and the lack of rest had bled men out of the ranks at every step and this was the reward.

There're not going to be enough of them to make a difference. But I've got to go, send in what I've got, no matter it won't be enough.

Maxcy Gregg appeared, red faced, swiped at his forehead with a pocket cloth, spat. "It's damn hot, Powell," he said. "Reminds me of summers back home."

From the north there was firing, artillery, a battery, no more. Gregg lifted an arm, pointed toward the line of men waiting in the road. "That's all I've got here, Powell. Rest of my brigade is strung out between here and Harpers Ferry."

Gregg glanced at the men standing in the road, looked at them the way a father admires a favorite child. He shook his head slowly. "That's all I've got left. It's not enough, but what's here is the best."

Hill nodded, wondered how many men were lying by the side of the road, out of the fight. "Damn," he said under his breath.

"This damn heat forced 'em out of the march. I lost half of 'em in the last five miles."

There was another long pause, Gregg wiping his nose, wheezing, trying to rid himself of the cloying dust. "You want me to go in with 'em like this?"

Hill glanced at the soldiers, saw how pitifully few waited for the order, cursed silently, knew that this was all there was, all that there could be. That beyond the fields, and the woods, on the far bank of the Potomac the road was lined with stragglers, men who had given up, fallen away as the sweating columns left them behind. He turned, looked hopefully toward the ford, saw only an empty road.

Lee's words rang in his ears, haunted him as he stared at the boys standing in the road in the glaring sunlight. He would have to send them in. Branch had gone in, was out there alone, waiting for him to send help.

There were not enough of them. There would never be enough. Too many of them. Too few of us. It had been that way from the beginning. Would be that way until it was finished. Until someone said, "Enough," and the fighting ended.

He lifted his eyes, saw that they were still fighting near the town, men shifting among the orchards and the standing corn, firing on the Yankees. Branch was out of sight among the hollows and ravines. In a few minutes he would come up behind them, take them from the rear if all went well.

There was a chance. A small chance, no more. They would have the element of surprise. Maybe catch them unprepared. If the artillery and whoever was left in Sharpsburg could hold for a few minutes, they might just turn the Union assault.

He caught Maxcy Gregg's eyes. Gregg was watching him, waiting, like a patient dog; and Hill knew he had been lost in his own thoughts, that the other man was waiting, wondering what the orders would be. Gregg didn't even know the situation, had just arrived on the field, and now he was being ordered forward without so much as a by-your-leave.

"Let's go," he said. "I'll go in with you. Maybe we'll catch 'em by surprise."

Gregg ran along his lines, waving the strange foreign sword that he carried into battle, pointing toward the corn, and the hills, and the town beyond. He was shouting something, but Hill couldn't hear him above the firing, and then all of them shouldered their weapons and began moving through the grass and the corn, walking over the rough ground, stumbling toward the firing ahead.

Among the stalks he lost sight of the town, could see only cornfields and broken ground, another round hill rising ahead. They descended a slope, waded through more stalks, struggled up the far side. From the low ground he could just see the roofs of the village, and then they topped a small rise and the village loomed ahead, and somewhere between them and the village must be Branch's brigade and then the Federals; but for now he could see damn little.

An order was shouted, sergeants echoed the command, and they were moving off at the oblique. The pace quickened. Without an order being issued, men were moving at the double-quick, and suddenly they emerged from the corn into a stubble field. A quarter mile ahead a low wall slanted across the field, stones piled without mortar, and the men were running for it, taking their rifles off their shoulders, fumbling for the small firing caps.

A ragged line reached the stone wall, knelt behind, leveled rifles over the top of the wall. Ahead there were blue uniforms, a regiment moving up a slope, another regiment on line in front. He began to count regimental colors, realized that at least a brigade was in front of them.

There was the singular sound of several hundred hammers being locked to the rear, a rippling metallic clicking that ended with the wall exploding with rifle fire. The report of the regiments' rifles was followed by men standing, the whirring of ramrods leaving rifle stocks, paper cartridges being torn, bullets being run home. Another line of infantry rushed up, knelt behind the wall. There was a second tremendous explosion. Hundreds of rifles were fired simultaneously. Men were yelling, cursing, loading, and firing now without commands or discipline or rhythm.

The hollow below them filled with smoke, a heavy, sulfurous cloud drifted into the low ground, lay in the windless air. The Federal line reeled from the initial volley. Hill saw men turning, pointing back at them, disappearing under the storm of fire and lead.

Behind the wall his men were firing at anything that moved. The ground was littered with paper from torn cartridges, and men screamed or cursed or laughed as they fired. Soldiers who had marched through the heat, had willed themselves to march beyond their own limits, through pain and hunger and thirst, now fired into the Union infantry with abandon.

In minutes the Federal line began to break. Soldiers ran in confusion, collided with the regiment ahead of their own, ignited panic and fear in those men. Single soldiers, then small groups broke from the ranks, dropped their rifles, ran in any direction, desperate to escape the killing fire from behind the stone wall.

In moments it was over. His men were standing, holding their rifles over their heads, screaming like demons released from hell itself. Officers began to walk the line, trying to reassemble the men, form the regiment for another advance.

He had the thought that they should push a skirmish line ahead of the main body. There could be another Union line beyond the next rise, turning this way. A thousand rifles, cocked, ready, waiting for them to crest the next hill.

But there was no time. They would have to push on, take the chance, keep moving the Yankees. Too many of them; too few of us. Have to keep them on the move, exploit every gain, hope to keep the momentum, not let them have time to form a line, organize a defense.

Maxcy Gregg appeared, grinning broadly, triumphant. He bent close, yelled into his ear, "What's next, A.P.? Are we going to hold this line?"

Hill shook his head, yelled back, "There isn't any line. We've got to keep moving, Maxcy. We're on their flank, and I don't think they know we're here yet." Hill pointed toward the town. "Branch is up there somewhere; we've got to try and make contact with him and turn their attack away from the town."

Gregg smiled, a brilliant smile that defied the situation. "Goddamn, Powell, did you see them run?" he asked.

Hill smiled back in spite of himself, nodded. "Yep, I saw it, Maxcy."

"I don't think they knew we were here before the boys fired that second volley."

He laughed. "Don't let it go to your head, Maxcy. The next bunch we come across won't make it so easy.

Gregg laughed, flashed another smile. "I'll get the boys movin'," he said.

More fire erupted from the town, heavy explosions, a long, rumbling thunder of cannon. Gregg stopped, pointed back toward the town, screamed, "We're in good shape now, Powell; they got the artillery on line to give us a hand."

Hill waved, watched as the wounded began walking back toward the road, wondered how they would find their way through the confusion. In another minute they were on line again, men stepping over the stone wall, advancing on brigade front. There had been only a few casualties; the soldiers were smiling, unaware of what lay ahead, of how bad the odds were.

They walked through the Union line, past wounded lying among the stalks and misshapen mounds of dead. Here and there a soldier broke from the line, helped himself to a cast-off knapsack.

Another few steps and they were past what had been the Federal line, the corn crushed and broken where men had fled. He was grateful when they had left the Union dead behind, pushed the thoughts of them out of his mind. Good boys. Shame it had come to this.

All of it an accident of birth. Maybe you were born up North, maybe down South. Your fate decided, even before you knew. Maybe it had always been that way, men's lives decided at birth, shaped by an unseen hand.

In the end it all came down to chance, simple plain dumb luck. Every soldier trusted it, believed in it. No one ever thought he was going to be killed; it would always be the other man, the soldier standing next to you. Never you.

A bullet whirred by overhead in the warm air, slapped the stalks behind him, shook him from his thoughts. He smiled, stupidly, laughed to himself.

Another bullet slid past, closer; he ducked reflexively.

Movement ahead, blue figures darting among the corn. A skirmish line, falling back, getting off a few shots, warning the others that they were here, that death was coming for them and you had best be prepared. Soldiers near him shifted their rifles to the ready, capped the heavy guns. An officer nearby said, "Steady, boys."

Hill felt the tension increase, knew that it would all break loose again in a moment. There would be another tempest, more fighting, another line of blue infantry posted on another hill, and that this time they would be ready and men on both sides would die.

The line was moving up a hill, another round slope, more corn and broken ground that had been plowed in the spring and left all summer to grow in the Maryland sun. The corn was as high as a man's head, taller in places, the leaves clinging, grabbing at your arms as you walked past, crowned with sticky tassels.

Ahead he saw them, blue uniforms, standing among the stalks, pink faces beneath the blue hats. From the ranks near him there was a collective sigh; men held their breath, waited for the volley for an impossible length of time.

An order was shouted, echoed down the line, the advance stopped. Rifles came off shoulders, sergeants ran behind the line, prepared them to volley, and still the blue line held, immobile, staring, watching. Around him men were capping the heavy rifles, hammers were locked to the rear. A few seconds now.

Another order, a rippling wave of rising rifles, all along the front rank, coming up to meet men's shoulders.

In the blue ranks now they knew men were stirring, looking up and down the line. Hill could feel the tension, knew that the Union soldiers had seen the awful truth, that somehow their officers were still uncertain. Soldiers were turning, a few called out, unsure voices, pleading for an order to fire.

Hill understood that over that few yards of ground they were stand-ing in place, waiting for the terrible missiles, held there by honor and duty and courage and even fear, and a thousand other things that men rarely speak about.

In those few empty seconds Powell Hill understood the terrible drama of war, of all wars, that men die not because of what they believe, or who is right, but because of chance—simple, frivolous, vain chance.

And in those moments Powell Hill knew that what happened here today mattered very little. That a hundred years from this moment, or a thousand, it wouldn't matter that men had fought here, that one man had been heroic and another cowardly. That all men, and all that men do, passes from memory, fades like so many autumn leaves. That memory, like all things, dies with those who remember, and that in the end it would all have no more substance than a shadow.

In the next instant the soldiers beside him fired, a single over-whelming explosion that sent a thousand deadly missiles hurtling to-ward the Union line. Hill watched in fascinated horror as the blue soldiers reeled, swayed, were pushed back by the invisible missiles.

Their line seemed to falter, to bend before the hot invisible wind, and then it steadied. Rifles came up, there was an uncertain volley, ragged firing. Bullets whined by, overhead. Here and there men fell, pushed back out of the line by the heavy bullets. A boy nearby went down, screamed, pushed a hand into a bloody gash in his thigh.

Another order, men stepped aside, opened ranks. The second line advanced, leveled their weapons. Another tremendous single crash. Smoke boiled out, obscured everything, stung his eyes.

Men were screaming now, loud vulgar shouting, shaking their fists at the soldiers across the field. He could see that the blue line was breaking, men were running, dropping their rifles, disappearing into the stalks of green corn.

Near the center of the Union line an officer on horseback was waving his sword, trying to rally his men. A color sergeant ran toward him, a few men stood, rallied around the mounted officer and the flag, tried to form a line, stop others from breaking.

Soldiers beside him began shooting at the officer, screaming at oth-ers to do the same. There was a flurry of firing.

One soldier calmly broke ranks, took a single step forward, primed his rifle, glared at the Union officer. Other soldiers on the line ap-peared to pause, seemed to wait for this one man with glittering black eyes to fire.

Hill gazed at the rifleman, saw the determined look about him, the calm eyes that never left the Union officer, never broke the silent faith of the battlefield. In that instant he knew what would happen, what must happen. He felt a sudden unspeakable sadness, an unmistakable flutter, a wave of pity and admiration, an overwhelming sense of loss at the futility of it all.

He watched as the soldier cocked his rifle, saw the hammer sweeping down, moving through its cold mechanical arc, metal glinting in the sunlight, an inexorable movement of grace and beauty and death. He watched it all, saw the soldier shuddering with the recoil, tried to follow the deadly missile in its flight.

Above it all Hill heard the single shot, knew that it could end only one way, that there could be only a single result. That all men die, that something greater than mortal men decides the fate of each man, that on this day fate, or destiny, or simply death was coming to claim the life of the brave Federal who had risen to rally his men.

In another instant it was over. The officer reeled, slid down out of the saddle, melted into soft earth. With that single death a sudden wave of fear passed through the Union ranks; soldiers began to desert their line, run back into the tall corn. In a few moments the top of the hill was silent, the flags and soldiers gone.

He wondered if, in the end, this was all there ever was. If any one man, any one army could really be enough. If any of them understood why they were here, what it all meant.

Around him sergeants hustled the soldiers back into line, there were more shouted orders, Maxcy Gregg out in front, waving the odd sword, smiling at him, jubilant. He glanced down the line, saw the wounded lying among the corn. No flags to be waved here, not now. Now it was real.

This is what it is really all about, what war really is. Impossibly hot days, empty bellies, and death and agony and bloody wounds in some stranger's field.

The line advanced slowly, warily, topped the slope. A shell screamed in, men were ducking, there was shower of blasted earth and hot air. Around him men laughed, grateful to be alive.

They crested the round slope of the hill and he felt suddenly naked, exposed. Federal cannon had them, were firing at them steadily, the shells coming at them in low, graceful arcs, trailed by white smoke. There was a flurry of explosions, a terrible white rain of metal, great swaths of smoking ground where the shells struck. Men went down, vanished among the explosions, lay in unspeakable bloody heaps of clothing and flesh. Other men turned away so as not to see, bent their heads, kept moving.

The brigade descended the hill, moved into a small hollow, started up another slope. Shells arced by overhead, exploded with dull thuds in the soft earth. More shells rained in. The Union artillery had lost sight of them, was firing blindly, probing for them, throwing shells into the folds of earth between hills.

Hill called a halt, the line shuddered, stopped, men knelt or lay on the ground in exhaustion. He found Maxcy Gregg, striding the line, full of nervous energy. "Let's go have a look, Maxcy."

"Right," said Gregg. "I'm thinking they've got another line not too far off, Powell. Maybe we can use this low ground to move around toward our right, flank them again."

"Maybe," said Hill. "We've got to find Branch; he's probably engaged somewhere ahead of us, closer to the town."

Gregg pointed the way, began walking up the hillside.

They climbed the slope, the backs of Hill's legs aching with the exertion. Too much time in the saddle, but his boys had walked it all, in this heat. They topped the hill, moved through the green stalks.

He brushed corn aside, strained to see, walked again toward the light, hoped that ahead there was a clearing and that no one over there had thought to throw out a skirmish line and that even now someone wasn't pointing a rifle at them. But ahead there was only a breathless dry wind that moved slowly through the heavy stalks, rattling the leaves, shifting the muggy air.

They came into a clearing. There was startling sunlight, row upon row of cut corn. A bullet whiffed by, slapped into the stalks behind them. Hill peered into the distance, but there was no movement, just the silent trail of the bullet.

Sniper maybe, farther back, hidden among the trees.

He lifted his eyes, scanned the tree line close to the creek. No movement, nothing. Just a line of dark trees shimmering in the heat.

"Best move back a bit, Powell; they've probably got a line out up there someplace."

He smiled, said, "Yes, probably." In front of them there was only a great rolling field of brown earth. A lovely empty field that was devoid of movement, a farmer's field, without cannon or infantry. He turned toward Gregg, wondered at it, felt the tension ease just a bit. "You see anything?" he asked.

Gregg nodded his head, pointed. "There."

Hill followed his gesture, saw the Union infantry, began counting flags, six brigades, maybe more. Better part of two divisions. They were withdrawing, moving back toward the valley of the Antietam, the soldiers marching beneath the old flag, moving steadily, slowly.

Gregg gave a low whistle. "They got some infantry over there, no doubt about it," he said.

"Yes," answered Hill, wondering if they were Burnside's men, if McClellan was over there, wondering why they had fallen back. He shook his head, sensed that beyond the creek more men were gathering, building their strength. Be just like Mac to build up his strength, come at you when he was all ready, not a moment before. He glanced at the sky, shielded his eyes with a hand against the light.

Hours of daylight left. They'll be back, and I'll be here with a couple of brigades that nobody else would ever think to call brigades. And no artillery to speak of, and it'll be Burnside or McClellan and there'll be hell to pay.

To Gregg he asked, "What do you think?"

The other man shrugged. "Hard to say. You?"

He shook his head. "Don't know. We hit 'em pretty hard, but I can't believe they're gonna call it quits just like that."

From the ridge there was more firing, a long, thunderous roll of artillery. They stood in the silent corn, watched the shells descend into the blue ranks. Hill shook his head, said, "Damn if I can feature it, Maxcy." He turned, looked at the other man. "You'd think with that kind of infantry they'd just walk right over us." He shook his head. "Never seen anything like it."

"No," said Gregg. "They'll be back, I suppose."

"Well," said Hill after long moments—the blue infantry was reforming, disappearing beneath the ridge, moving out of sight of the guns near the town—he glanced at Gregg, said, "I'll be damned."

Gregg laughed, clapped a hand across his back. "You and me both, A.P., but they damn sure picked up and left things to us."

Hill smiled, hoped that Gregg was right, knew in his heart that it was impossible, that Burnside and Mac were just pulling back, reforming.

There was a cluster of officers nearby, men laughing, passing a bottle around, grinning at one another, grateful that it had gone so well. Someone handed him a dispatch. He read it, blinked, stared at the paper for long moments, read it a second time. Branch was down, somewhere on the left. One of his colonels had signed the dispatch, was requesting that they move left, close the gap in their lines.

He turned, handed the paper to Maxcy Gregg, stared out over the smoking ground toward the valley of the Antietam.

Gregg folded the paper, handed it to an aide. "Damn shame," he said.

Hill nodded, didn't quite trust himself to speak. It was the way of things; men died. You expected it, lived with it, remembered them sometimes, spoke of them around a campfire or in an odd moment when something reminded you of them and the memory rose up through your mind like the memory of a dream.

Hill signaled an orderly for his horse, said to Gregg, "Maxcy, let's move to our left, tie in with Branch's brigade."

Gregg nodded. "I figured as much. I sent a couple of my officers off to find Branch's flank."

Hill slapped dust from his hat, swung into the saddle, said, "They'll be back."

Gregg smiled, chuckled. "Yes, I suppose they will, with infantry like that."

"I'll be over on the left then. See if I can give 'em a hand over there."

Gregg touched the brim of his hat. "Powell, you be careful over there; the ladies in Richmond would be awful disappointed if something happened to you."

He chuckled. "I'll do my best, Maxcy. You mind things here and send for me if you need help."

"I will, Powell, I will." Gregg turned, back toward the Antietam, nodded toward the ridge where the Union infantry waited. "They come back and you can bet I'll send for you."

A memory flashed across his mind of himself and Burnside and McClellan, singing some foolish song at the tops of their voices, arms on each others' shoulders. They were younger then, just cadets, and there had been a forbidden tavern close to the barracks at West Point.

Long nights spent drinking bad beer, lots of laughter and talk of days to come and where they might all be in ten years. The sort of thing young boys do when they are not quite men and not quite boys and have to find their way between those two worlds. The sort of nights that memories are made of, the hours that bind men's hearts together, beyond wives and wars and the failings that come all too quickly to a boy when he leaves his father's house and makes his way in the world.

There had been a lot of years between then and now. Life takes hold of a man, forces him to make choices, shapes him. None of them had escaped it. There had been lost loves, failed businesses, marriages, children, and a thousand other things that a man considers and weighs and then makes the best decision he can. And then you are off in that direction and life changes again.

They had grown, matured, married, failed at some things, succeeded at others. And yet, beyond it all, each of them had remained those same boys. Always able to share a laugh, or the memory of some hardship at the Academy, or some small detail of their lives spent in the army.

And now they were here, in some nameless field in Maryland, and Burnside and Mac were just across the way, and there were hours of daylight left and he didn't have enough infantry to hold off even another small assault. And Mac would know it, and so would Burnside, and they would come again with their soldiers all in neat rows, marching in the bright light, through plowed fields, the national flag fluttering above them all.

"They'll be back," he said flatly, and he felt a sudden strange pride. At least it would be Mac, or Burnside, or one of the others he had known so long ago. When the end came, if they got driven back into the town and the river beyond, at least it would be friends who did it and not some stranger.

The thought struck him that maybe Branch was better off, just to melt into the soft clay, to let go, move beyond this field and this day and what was coming as soon as they reformed and came again in steady lines of infantry. He took a deep breath, shook the thought from his mind, tightened his reins, said, "Be seein' you, Maxcy."

CHAPTER 22

GEORGE MCCLELLAN WALKED PAST A TABLE LADEN WITH FRESH bread, summer sausage, and pitchers of milk so cold he could see drops of water condensing on the crocks. A fire had been built on the lawn and fat sausages sizzled and hissed over the coals. Tables and chairs had been removed from the farmhouse and placed on the lawn. A small crowd of headquarters officers sat in chairs taken from the dining room or stood near the cook fires and ate plates of steaming food.

He caught the eye of Fitz John Porter, nodded. Porter rose from the table, wiped his mouth with a white cloth, smiled at the others as he left. They walked in silence toward the knoll where he had watched most of the battle.

The sun was a red orb hovering just over the horizon, casting the clouds in great mantles of silver and orange, the horizon full of light, the ridges dark and ominous, silhouetted against the brilliant sky. McClellan lifted a hand, tried to shield his eyes from the blinding light, saw only murky shadow and glinting sunlight. From the south he could hear the occasional report of a rifle, but the field had fallen silent.

He turned toward Fitz John Porter, and said, "Damn fine show."

Porter agreed, smiled tightly. "Only a few more minutes, George. Then it'll have to end."

"Yes," said McClellan. "Burnside seems to have held them on his end of the field."

Porter grunted something unintelligible, knit his brow, was moody and silent for long moments. At last he said, "Lee will be back in the morning, in strength."

"You think they'll attack then? In the morning?"

"Yes," answered Porter slowly, thoughtfully. "They are well aware that our right is shattered from the morning's fighting. And now they have strengthened their commands facing General Burnside's men on the southern end of the field."

"Burnside sent word, John. He's asking that we send him the reserves. He thinks he can break through in the morning, drive them out of Sharpsburg if he's given enough men."

Porter coughed, cleared his throat, turned away, then back suddenly. "Reinforcements?" He shook his head, furrowed his brow. "From where does he propose we draw these men?"

"Perhaps you could lend him a division?" McClellan asked.

"Perhaps," said Porter. "But that would mean committing the reserve of the army."

"You would keep your other two divisions, of course. And your artillery."

Porter paused, glared off into the distance. "I can't do it, George. Not in good conscience." His face clouded over, became instantly dark, gloomy. Porter said darkly, "Hooker's men are disorganized on the right and in need of reinforcement. If Lee advances against us there in the morning and my corps is committed with Burnside on the left, it could be a very long day for all of us."

"You are that certain that Lee will attack?"

Porter shrugged. "General Lee likes to fight on the offensive." Porter nodded, gazed out over the hills and valleys, said, "I believe we must be prepared for a general assault in the morning."

"Perhaps," said McClellan, remembering his earlier promise to support Burnside's attack.

Porter shrugged, said suddenly, "I have already advanced some of my men near the village; they've engaged the Rebels on the eastern end of the town."

"Can't you send him something, John? A brigade? Stiffen his lines near the bridge?"

Porter carefully removed a gold watch from his pocket, noted the time, closed the lid with a practiced motion. He faced McClellan, dark eyes shining, shook his head slowly. "George, what would happen if you needed me in the morning and my brigades are off with Burnside? The army would be without its reserve. I'd be out of position, and my men wouldn't be able to shore up a gap in the line if you needed them." Porter shook his head again, appeared to search the horizon for some moments. At last he said, "I just don't think it's a good idea to release the general reserves of the army to Burnside right now."

He glanced again at the horizon, wondered how the army had managed to come this far in so short a time. Tomorrow there would be more fighting, more decisions, brigades and divisions would have to be moved to meet the new threat.

McClellan felt the weight of it suddenly, what some men called the burden of command. It descended on him without warning, suddenly, swiftly, like a deep rumbling that had not been there only a moment before in snow-covered peaks. But you heard it, far off, felt the warning, knew its power.

He closed his eyes for the briefest instant, inhaled. The evening air was bitter with smoke and burnt powder and held the blasted smell of battle. A horse whinnied from somewhere near the house. It was over for today, all of them exhausted, played out. "They expect the impossible, John."

"Washington?"

"Yes."

"Most of the time you have been able to deliver it."

"We are outnumbered here, John. You understand that, don't you?"

"I had thought as much."

From behind them there was laughter; someone was telling a story, men were smiling. He turned, saw a tall blond-headed captain standing in a circle of men, waving his arms, punctuating his tale with gestures and exaggerated facial expressions.

He turned back to Porter, felt suddenly tired, old. He could feel his strength leaving him, flowing out of him in a long, liquid gasp that would leave his body tired, his mind empty. He wished suddenly to be at home, with Ellen, and no army to command, no politicians to please.

He sighed, a deep sigh of fatigue, of exhaustion. "I believe that General Lee may maneuver, try to give us the slip."

Porter raised an eyebrow. "You think he means to disengage?"

McClellan shrugged. "It's possible. He could break off, try to get between us and the capital."

Porter stared into the fading light, rested one muddy boot on a fence rail. "We've not seen any sign of them breaking off. Our signal stations don't report any movement toward the Potomac fords other than some wagons." Porter paused, "They're probably just moving their wounded back across the river."

"He may have left a portion of his army in the valley. Keep them behind us, prevent our movement back across South Mountain."

Porter said nothing for long minutes, stared first at the horizon, then at the ground. "You think he means to break off then?"

"I believe he means to take Washington, if possible." He pointed southeast, toward a looming rocky ridge. "What if he gets across the Potomac tonight, leaves a small rear guard on the opposite shore to slow us down, then marches hard for the capital? How would I counter?"

"Surely you don't think he will break off?" Porter shook his head slowly. "I don't believe General Lee will abandon the field, George."

"A battle here or any other place is not his goal, John. He has to raze a city in order to force the end of the war. Washington seems the likely choice."

Porter drew back, brooded, said nothing. Minutes passed. At last Porter offered, "Well, in any event, I believe you must hold my corps in reserve."

"Yes," he said. He turned toward Porter, smiled. "Tomorrow, John, if they attack, you must be ready. I will depend on you to shore up our lines."

"Of course."

"It might be a long day, John."

Porter smiled, gleaming white teeth visible in the dusky light. "Hell, George, today has been a long day."

McClellan laughed, clapped him on the back. "I suppose it has at that."

"Well," said Porter, "I'll be off then. See that everything is ready for tomorrow."

McClellan reached out, touched Porter's arm. "I'll depend on you tomorrow, John. We'll need every man, every gun we can put in action."

Porter smiled again, full of confidence. "Don't worry, George. We'll be ready for them, come what may."

"Good," he said, feeling relief wash over him like a prayer. "I knew I could count on you, John."

Porter smiled brightly into the fading light, reached toward him, touched his sleeve.

"There won't be any help from Washington, John. I'm on my own up here. You know that. You understand you are my only reserve."

"I know," answered Porter.

"Well," said McClellan quietly. "Tomorrow will be another grand day."

Porter smiled again, patted his arm, walked into the soft night in silence, left him alone on the hill, gazing west into the last streaks of light, wondering what tomorrow would bring.

CHAPTER 23

ROBERT E. LEE LEFT HIS TENT, WALKED INTO THE STARRY night under a silky black sky. Campfires dotted the hills to the east, a thousand cook fires glowed warmly, the air heavy with woodsmoke and the tangy smell of roasting beef.

He took a deep breath of warm night air, walked slowly toward a stand of oaks, anxious to be alone, gather his thoughts. Around him the headquarters tents glowed yellow with light from lanterns; from the road there were the ominous sounds of traffic. Wagons carrying the wounded trundled heavily past, headed for the fords and Virginia.

He came to a bit of fence; the rails were gone, stripped for firewood. Lee stopped, paused among the posts that jutted from the ground in silence, leaned heavily against the nearest one. For a moment he stood, silent, brooding. From the east there was a single rifle shot, a sentry, or a skirmish line perhaps; a sudden movement in the dark, someone shoots. But it faded and nothing followed and so he let it go, pushed it out of his mind. And then he remembered the day and the carnage and he began to pray for all who had been lost.

He wondered suddenly what the Almighty must think of men, what judgment He would pass on all of them. And yet, what choice has a man? To raise his sword against his own?

He shook the thought from his head, knew that he couldn't dwell on such things.

Not now. Perhaps later when this is over and there is no more war you can think on it. Put all of this in perspective, decide what has happened, understand it. Now is not the time. Later.

Behind him there was a flurry of activity, the thud of horses on the road, riders approaching through the dark. A sentry called, challenged the horsemen. There was laughter.

He turned, recognized the familiar silhouette of Longstreet among a group of horsemen. Men were pointing in his direction. Longstreet dismounted, walked toward him. In the dark Lee smiled, glad to see the younger man, suddenly anxious to talk with him.

Longstreet walked slowly toward him with the peculiar gait common to large men who have spent long hours in the saddle. He drawled into the darkness, "Evenin', General Lee."

Lee felt suddenly grateful for his presence, said warmly, "Peter, I am glad to see you well."

Longstreet smiled, radiated strength, confidence. "Been a long day."

"Yes." Lee smiled again. "It's been a long day for all of us."

Longstreet removed his riding gauntlets, slapped them together noisily. "It was a close thing today."

"Yes," said Lee, waiting.

Longstreet faced him, Lee met the brown eyes, saw caution there, something else. "You can speak, General. I depend on you for that."

Longstreet blew out another breath, gathered himself. "It was *too* close, sir. They're too heavy for us; they damn near bowled over us in half a dozen places."

Lee waited, uncertain if Longstreet would continue, knew that it must come out. That sometimes a commanding general loses sight of the details, is not able to discern the true condition of his army. "Go on," he said calmly.

Longstreet looked at the ground, couldn't meet his eyes in the velvety darkness. For a moment both of them looked away, Lee thinking: *Perhaps he has been right all along, that I have asked too much of them.*

"Well," began Longstreet. Lee sensed the hesitation in his voice, waited. There was another silence, an owl whispered by overhead. Longstreet caught the movement, followed the great bird as it glided among the dark trunks. "We're low on ammunition. There's not enough left, even for the batteries that are still serviceable."

Lee waited, wondering where this was going, knowing that it was not the ammunition that bothered Longstreet, that it was something else, something deeper. There had been other battles, other close calls. This was different.

Longstreet scraped a boot across the ground, looked up at him with dark eyes. Longstreet took a breath, gathered himself the way a horse gathers itself just before a race, the muscles bunched, tense with energy. "Hood's boys are done in. Harvey Hill is not much better off; he tells me he lost maybe half his men this afternoon during that last attack. He's drawn his men back to the eastern side of town."

Longstreet shook his head slowly, "I'm not sure what kind of shape Jackson's command is in, but they can't be much better off than the other two."

"I see," said Lee. He watched Longstreet, knew where the conversation was going, understood that Longstreet had seen the details, knew that entire divisions had been wrecked in the fighting. He waited for him to continue. Best to let him say his piece, get it all out now.

"I think we've got to get back across the Potomac. No other way for it. If they come at us again tomorrow like they did today, I'm not sure we can hold 'em off."

Lee nodded, smiled, grateful for the darkness, glad that Longstreet could not see him well in the dark, read his eyes. "You believe we should retreat?"

Longstreet shifted his weight from one foot to the other, slapped the heavy gloves together. "If we get back across the river, they won't come after us. We can hold the fords, force them to fight on our terms if it comes to that."

It was out now, the words coming faster, Longstreet warming to it, anxious to say it at last. Lee knew that he had thought about it, brooded on this conversation. "You know George McClellan won't pursue us through Virginia. He thinks his army can't march more than a few miles a day. If we get on the road tonight we can put enough distance between ourselves and them so that they'll have a two-day march just to catch up."

Lee held up a hand. Longstreet caught the movement, stopped in midsentence. "This army will hold the field tomorrow."

Longstreet stared at him, motionless, openmouthed, said nothing. It was so quiet that Lee could hear him breathing, feel the surprise through the darkness.

The younger man turned, glanced toward the tents glowing amber with lamplight, toward the others who were waiting for them there, waiting for him to issue an order, tell them what had to be done. "There will be no retreat."

Longstreet's mouth moved, he started to say something, but there was only silence. At last he swallowed, said only, "Yes, sir." There was a tone of disbelief in his voice, of resignation.

Lee watched Longstreet, waited for the anger, saw nothing.

He thinks I am wrong. He has seen their strength. He believes there will be a general assault in the morning because that is what he would do. But there will be no assault. They will hesitate, and we will be here to offer battle.

"General McClellan will believe his army unable to attack tomorrow. He will not withdraw, but there will be no attack from those people tomorrow."

Longstreet nodded, waited.

"You must hold your position. Draw your lines in as you see fit, but we must hold our present position." Lee watched the other man, knew that he did not agree, that there had been talk among his officers. Talk of numbers and position and a lack of ammunition and such things. But none of that mattered, not now. What mattered now was that they hold the field, that they not refuse battle to an enemy that waited within sight.

The world must see that they were prepared to give battle, that they did not retreat in the face of the enemy. That was what truly mattered. Numbers were insignificant. Longstreet and the others sometimes lost sight of that, relied too heavily on figures, troop strengths. He must make them see that a battle is won or lost by the will of men, the desire in a man's heart, his belief in himself or his cause.

"Yes, sir," said the younger man obediently. He straightened, began to move off.

Lee said, "This army cannot retreat in the face of the enemy, General. Not now. We are committed. We must hold this ground, offer them the chance to renew the battle." He paused, strained through the darkness to see if Longstreet understood. One day he might be gone, and then the army would be commanded by Longstreet, or maybe Jackson, or even one of the others. These lessons had to be brought home now, understood completely, without doubt.

Longstreet nodded. "I understand, sir."

"We must hold this field, even if it is only for a day."

"We'll hold, General. Boys'll do what has to be done, I suppose, but I sure would like to get across that river. Make 'em come after us on our own ground."

Lee shook his head, knew that Longstreet was right. That there was no real advantage by having the army hold a day. He stared into the dark, past the fires, knew that the river waited just below the rounded hills, that they could all be across in a matter of hours, that McClellan would not pursue, maybe not for days, a week even.

There was time yet tonight. Issue the order. He closed his eyes for a moment, inhaled fragrant night air, and for just an instant he was tempted to nod his head, begin the slow movement back into Virginia. Longstreet would do the rest, see that they all made it across, even the wounded.

But he could not, something in him railed against it. His army had not been beaten; they had held the field. To retreat now, to withdraw without offering battle . . . He could not. So they would remain, and

General McClellan would attack, or he would not, but they would be here. And if the attack came, they would be ready; and they would prevail the same way they had prevailed today, because there could be no other way.

"This army stands between those people and Virginia, General." Lee looked into the honest face of the younger man, knew that Longstreet was right. That he was asking too much of these men, that he was asking them to endure beyond what mortal men can endure. And yet . . . there was no other way.

"I cannot tolerate another invasion of Virginia," he said softly, slowly, letting the words hang in the night air. "Our people have suffered too much. It is for you and me to spare them further hardship."

Longstreet was staring at him, through the dark, looking at him, waiting for something. He held up a hand, prevented Longstreet from speaking. "There are other considerations. Political reasons why we must hold our ground."

"The Europeans, you mean?" asked Longstreet.

"Yes," said Lee.

Longstreet spat, scraped a boot across the ground. "They won't help us out until we don't need their help, and by then it won't matter."

Lee smiled, laughed very softly. "You are right, of course."

Longstreet smiled crookedly. "Lovely," he said.

Lee smiled again, took Longstreet's arm. "We should go and speak with the others, but my mind is made up. We will hold here, see what develops from over there." Lee nodded, indicated the darkness, the campfires dotting the hills beyond Sharpsburg.

Longstreet snorted. "Well, I do sort of doubt McClellan would bother us tomorrow. He'll be too busy bringin' up his siege guns."

Lee patted him on the back, walked with him toward the amber tents and the laughter and the horses that shifted and stamped on their lines. Longstreet mounted, swung into the saddle with a practiced motion, the leather creaking as it took his weight.

Out on the road an ambulance rolled past. He and Longstreet turned, watched in silence. He closed his eyes, tried not to think of the dying.

A soldier's life.

"Ah, Peter. Come back later, when we can talk."

Longstreet gazed down on him with calm eyes. "I'll be back in a while."

Lee patted the silky muzzle of the horse, stroked the muscular neck. "You will be careful tomorrow, General."

The horse stamped, impatient to be off, and Longstreet tightened the reins very slightly. Lee was reminded of home, and his stables and the musty smell of saddle leather and haylofts.

Only now he was a soldier, and there was a war, and duty, and men who depended on him to lead an army. "Well," he said awkwardly.

Longstreet smiled, white teeth glowing in the darkness. He raised a hand, touched the brim of his hat. "Suppose I'll be off then. See to my boys."

"Yes," said Lee, releasing the bridle. Longstreet pulled the horse's head around, touched his hat again ever so slightly, moved off into the night.

EPILOGUE

Madam, put away your animosities and make your son an American.
—ROBERT E. LEE,
WHILE PRESIDENT OF WASHINGTON COLLEGE AFTER THE CIVIL WAR, TO
THE MOTHER OF ONE OF HIS STUDENTS WHOSE OTHER SONS
HAD DIED IN SERVICE TO THE CONFEDERACY

From a report written by Robert E. Lee and sent to Gen. Samuel Cooper, CSA. Adjutant and Inspector General, Richmond, Virginia, shortly after the battle of Sharpsburg.

CAPTURE OF HARPERS FERRY AND OPERATIONS IN MARYLAND

... on the 18th we occupied the position of the preceding day, except in the center, where our line was drawn in about two hundred yards.

Our ranks were increased by the arrival of a number of troops who had not been engaged the day before, and though still too weak to assume the offensive, we awaited without apprehension the renewal of the attack.

The day passed without any demonstration on the part of the enemy, who from the reports received, was expecting the arrival of reinforcements. As we could not look for a materiel increase in strength, and the enemy's force could be largely and rapidly augmented, it was not thought prudent to wait until he should be ready again to offer battle.

During the night of the 18th the army was accordingly withdrawn to the south side of the Potomac crossing near Shepherdstown, without loss or molestation ...

I desire to call the attention of the Department to the names of those brave officers and men who are particularly mentioned for courage and good conduct by their commanders. The limits of this report will not permit me to more than renew the expression of my admiration for the valor that shrunk from no peril and the fortitude that endured every privation without a murmur.

Respectfully submitted
Robert E. Lee
General